TUNNEL

By Stanley Johnson

Fiction

Gold Drain
Panther Jones for President
The Urbane Guerilla
The Doomsday Deposit
The Marburg Virus
Tunnel

Nonfiction

Life Without Birth
The Green Revolution
The Politics of the Environment
The Population Problem (editor)
The Pollution Control Policy of the E.E.C.

TUNNEL

Stanley Johnson

HEINEMANN : LONDON

William Heinemann Ltd
10 Upper Grosvenor Street, London W1X 9PA

LONDON MELBOURNE TORONTO
JOHANNESBURG AUCKLAND

First published 1984

SBN 434 37705 8

Photoset by Rowland Phototypesetting Ltd
Bury St Edmunds, Suffolk
Printed in Great Britain by
Biddles Ltd, Guildford and King's Lynn

For My Parents

Grateful acknowledgements
to Sir David Nicholson,
Major-General Nigel St George Gribbon
and Eric Merrifield of the Robbins Company

I

There were more people than usual in the Strangers' Gallery of the House of Commons. In fact the place was very nearly full. The duty policeman whose task it was to shepherd members of the public into their seats had a hard time of it.

"Move along there," he urged. "Move right up in the rows."

The benches were not only packed; they were narrow and uncomfortable as well, rising one behind another as in a Roman amphitheatre.

There was more room at the other end of the chamber in the Press Gallery. But not much more. The gentlemen of Fleet Street had turned up in force for the occasion and were waiting with their pencils and notebooks ready. From where he sat, Oliver Grantham could see two or three journalists whom he recognized. There was Charlie Shawcross of *The Times* and George Wheldon of the *Telegraph* for example. Of course one would have expected the quality papers, the 'heavies', to have their men there on such an occasion. But even the popular press was fully represented. At the distance of thirty yards, he found himself catching the eye of Alex Lyons of the *Daily Mail*, a burly quick-witted man who perhaps more than any other had served to whip up popular interest and enthusiasm for the project whose fate was about to be announced.

Grantham wanted to wave his order paper but refrained. It was all very well for the gentlemen down below, in the arena as it were, to wave their order papers. But observers were only there on sufferance. He contented himself with a modest lifting of the wrist, a gesture which Lyons caught and acknowledged. The *Mail* man signalled in return and mouthed as though saying: "Which way do you think she's going to jump? On or off?"

Grantham was pretty sure he knew the answer to that one but he kept it to himself. Better to wait and see. It was always possible that something could have gone wrong between 12 noon and 3 p.m.

Down below the chamber was filling up as the elected representatives of the British people made their way in after lunch. If he'd not been sitting where he was, if for example he had been in the central lobby, Grantham would have been able to witness at about this moment the archaic sight of the Speaker of the House proceeding in company with mace-bearers and assorted policemen to open the afternoon sitting. Proceeding was in fact the accurate word. Some went before and others came after. And for those who could understand the peculiar intonations with which it was delivered, the cry of 'hats off, strangers!' could be heard in the hallowed portals of the Palace of Westminster.

The first half-hour of the session was taken up with departmental questions. The Minister for Health and Social Security was at the despatch box. He had the usual mixed bag of queries. What was he doing about this? Why hadn't he done something about that? The Minister, who was a youngish man on his first major political assignment, fielded most of them deftly. His reputation wasn't going to be made or broken that day. He was performing, and both he and his audience knew it, more as a warm-up artist, someone to raise the level of interest and tension before the big moment.

At five minutes to three, the Prime Minister herself appeared. She slipped into the chamber quietly from behind the Speaker's chair looking, Grantham observed, both confident and happy. Others might complain about the Conservatives' 'landslide' majority, in the last election. Not the PM. She knew she had earned her massive victory and she was determined to make the most of it. Members of the front bench moved quickly to make room for her. The Prime Minister smiled courteously, almost regally. You could afford to be polite when you ruled the roost.

With the Prime Minister's arrival, the heart had gone out of question time. The Minister for Health felt he had done his stuff and decided, rather than move down the order paper and fit in another question or two which he might have done, to give a particularly long-winded answer which enabled him to sit down on the front bench next to the Prime Minister at precisely the moment when the hands of the clock in the chamber moved to three o'clock.

"I call the Prime Minister," the Speaker announced in his thin reedy voice. The kind of voice, Grantham thought, which would scratch a gramophone record.

As the Prime Minister rose to speak, the screens which were placed throughout the Palace of Westminster in the bars and smoking rooms, in the committee and tea rooms, recorded the fact. They also recorded the subject of the Prime-Ministerial statement because that, of course, was known in advance. "Channel Tunnel" was the heading. MPs who had not yet reached the chamber were encouraged by the knowledge that the Prime Minister was "up" to hurry on their way there. By the time the Prime Minister had shuffled her papers at the despatch box the last remaining seats in the chamber were full. Late-comers crowded in at the doorways or behind the Speaker's chair. From the Strangers' Gallery it was a pretty sight. Democracy in action. So often the benches were half empty; the speeches inane or repetitive or both. This time Grantham knew it would be different. The Press men, down at the other end, knew it would be different. They would get a few column inches out of this one.

The Prime Minister's delivery matched her mood. She spoke with quiet self-assurance, marshalling her arguments with customary precision.

"Mr Speaker, I shall be rather brief this afternoon, notwithstanding the importance of the statement I'm about to make. I know that the Honourable and Right Honourable members on both sides of the House . . ." She corrected herself, remembering the tiny rump of Liberals and SDP which was all that survived of the once-proud Alliance, ". . . I suppose I should say on *all* sides of the House, have a good deal of business to be getting on with today and I do not wish to detain them. I do believe it is right however at this point that the House should hear a statement from me as Prime Minister about the Government's policy and the Government's decision on the subject of the Channel Tunnel."

The Prime Minister gazed at the benches opposite in an intent, direct way. She then swivelled so as to look at the benches behind her. Some called her dominating; others, domineering. Either way, the PM's searchlight personality somehow managed to force itself into the far corners of the house, behind the pillars and below the overhangs, where members had crowded in to hear her.

"Honourable and Right Honourable members will know," she said, "however much or however little they care about history – and I do not pretend that history has the same fascination for all of us – that a *fixed link*, I refer to it by this title because that is after all what it is – a fixed link between this country and the Continent of Europe has long been talked of. Napoleon dreamt about it. Wellington dreaded it and in the last century when people tried seriously to get this project off the ground or should I say into the ground . . ."

She paused for the laughter which was not long in coming. Politics had become a solemn affair and the House, especially in its post-prandial mood, was prepared to acknowledge attempts at wit or humour however poor these might be . . .

". . . the threat of invasion from France," continued the PM, "the possibility of French troops emerging at a run out of some hole near Dover, was enough to deter the Government of the day, and indeed succeeding Governments, from proceeding. It is perhaps only in recent years that a combination of engineering capability and the necessary volume of traffic has existed so as to make the project of a Channel Tunnel both feasible and economic.

"Her Majesty's Government, having given most careful consideration to all aspects of this complicated question, believes that a Channel Tunnel would accord with our national interest. It would be the cheapest and most satisfactory way in the long run of providing for the dramatic and continuing increase in cross-Channel traffic, and it would reduce the barrier the Channel presents to our trade."

Again the Prime Minister paused and looked round the House.

"I need hardly add," she said, "that as a dedicated European I believe that this link into Europe, which is what the Channel Tunnel will be, is probably the single most symbolic and practical statement of our commitment to the European ideal that we will ever have. I make no apology for this."

Her voice rose several tones as there was a rumble of dissent from the hard-core anti-Europeans on the benches of both Conservative and Labour supporters.

"I make no apology for this," the Prime Minister repeated. "Our future is in Europe. Our present is in Europe. The Channel Tunnel will prove, as nothing else can, that Britain is indeed and will remain a part of Europe."

There were shouts from some of the rowdier supporters of isolationism.

"Blow it up."

"Don't build it at all."

"Why don't you fly the Concorde through it?"

The Prime Minister knew when to take an interruption and when not to. This was one of the times to pay no attention to the hecklers. She pressed on. On the whole the House was with her. "As I say, it would not only reduce the barrier the Channel presents to our trade, not only be a magnificent statement of this country's commitment to Europe, it would also offer an important new opportunity to our railways – after all we still have a railway network although I know we occasionally seem to forget this – for the development of through services. This in turn," the Prime Minister continued, "would, by improving long-distance communications, be a positive benefit to the regions.

"The Government recognizes, however, that certain of these advantages can be gained only if the potential for the development of through rail services is fully exploited. They have therefore decided that a high quality rail-link between the Tunnel portal and London, with provision for through services to provincial centres, is essential to the success of the project and, subject to the approval of Parliament, that this should be provided. In other words we believe it should be possible to run *high-speed* trains through the Channel Tunnel . . ."

There was another interruption, from an indeterminate source:

"Not at the same time, I hope."

This time the Prime Minister decided to acknowledge the interruption. "I'm grateful to the Honourable gentleman, whoever he may be, for making that point. I can give the House the categorical assurance . . ."

Once again there was that searchlight look as the PM somehow managed to concentrate all her attention on one questioner and one question . . . ". . . that there will be no question of trains running simultaneously on a single track in this tunnel in opposite directions. The most highly developed communications technology will be brought to bear on the operation of the system. That kind of mistake, I can assure the House, will be *neither humanly nor technically possible*!" The laughter dwindled away as the Prime Minister came to the central and most significant part of her statement.

"The Government believes that it would be right for the tunnel to be constructed, together with the improvements in the rail services which may be necessary. The Government will ask Parliament to pass a short Bill to provide the necessary powers. Once this Bill is passed, the Government will sign a treaty with France and an agreement with the so-called Chunnel Consortium which will be responsible for the construction, operation and maintenance of the project. I need not now go into the details of that Consortium. Suffice it to say that the Government has the highest confidence in its ability and is convinced that the project will be brought to a successful conclusion."

The Prime Minister turned towards the Speaker.

"I would like to end, Mr Speaker, by saying that the Government regards a Channel Tunnel as an important and valuable link between the transport systems of the United Kingdom and of the continent of

Europe and commends this historic project to Parliament and the country."

Watching from the gallery, Oliver Grantham was in no doubt about the warmth of the applause which greeted the Prime Minister's statement. It was strange, he thought, how this Chunnel project had once again captured the imagination of the public. On again, off again. On again, off again. There was a time, he reflected, when he had considered the idea was well and truly dead. When Britain was busy recapturing the Falklands, it seemed that there would never be the time, or the money, to take the final crucial decisions about the tunnel project. But when the conservatives were returned to power in June 1983, they seemed to have got a second wind. For any number of reasons, the project appealed to the new Government – and particularly to the Prime Minister, provided that the thing was done the right way. Which, of course, meant *her* way. Thank God, he thought, for that momentous election. It had put a new complexion on the whole thing. It wasn't only members of Parliament who had been impressed by what they had just heard. The Press Gallery, he noticed, had emptied rapidly after the Prime Minister's statement. They obviously thought there was something worth reporting.

Grantham decided not to wait any longer. He had heard what he wanted to hear. As he stood up to go, he looked down onto the floor of the House for a last time. Some of the MPs were already slipping out, although the Prime Minister had indicated that she would take questions. One Tory MP, looking particularly glum, was moving rapidly to the exit. Grantham realized that it was Brian Staples, the member for Felixstowe.

Besides being an elected representative of the people, Staples, Grantham recalled, had been chairman of and principal shareholder in North Sea Ferries, a thriving enterprise based in his constituency which in a dawn raid a few months back had taken over the late Keith Wickenden's cross-channel ferry business while at the same time buying up Sealink under the "privatization" of British Rail. The new operation had become overnight one of the largest transport businesses in Europe. Renamed Channel Ferries, but retaining Brian Staples as its head, it had by both fair means and foul achieved a virtual monopoly of the sea-routes which linked Britain with the Continent.

"Not a good day for you, Staples," thought Grantham. And he mentally added the rider that unless Channel Ferries diversified into something else very quickly, they would be dead, commercially speaking, long before the second millennium arrived.

He eased out along the row, pushing past those who had arrived after him and who still sat to hear the Prime Minister reply to questions.

He picked up his umbrella from the cloakroom attendant at the top of the stairs outside the Strangers' Gallery. Out of habit he looked at the inscription on the gold band below the handle. It read: 'Major General Oliver Grantham – if found return to Army and Navy Club'. There was a time, he reflected, when gentlemen would make a point, if they took your umbrella by accident, of making sure it was returned. Did they still? he wondered.

Grantham tapped the ferrule of the umbrella on the stone steps as he came down to the central lobby. He was a precise, athletic man. A soldier in character; a soldier in bearing. The pin-striped suit bought at Gieves a decade earlier fitted him as well now as it did then. He had light sandy hair and pale blue eyes. High cheek bones; freckles – but not too obtrusive. He had just turned fifty and had been out of the army two years. At the height of the Falklands campaign he had been something of a legend. The men of the Parachute Regiment had reached Port Stanley twenty-four hours ahead of anybody else. Grantham had promised that they would be there first – and he had meant it.

He had left the army not long after the Falklands campaign was over. He had had a 'good war' and he didn't want to push his luck. He knew that the moment had come to turn the experience he had acquired in a lifetime of soldiering to some other wider purpose. That was the thing about the army, you could get out while the going was good. He had made full colonel before he was forty; general five years later. He could have gone on of course; could have taken a staff job in the Ministry of Defence, for example; could have stayed in till fifty-five or even sixty. But he didn't see the point of it. The last thing he wanted was to end up behind a desk in Whitehall. Good paratrooper that he was, he knew when to jump. He had jumped while, by his reckoning, he still had ten or fifteen years ahead of him to make a new life, a new career.

Years before, he had played for Eton in the Eton and Harrow match at Lords. He had gone in third wicket down. By tea, he had just made his half-century. Back in the pavilion David Blakely, Eton's captain and Grantham's closest friend, had asked,

"What's it going to be, Oliver? Your first century at Lords?"

Grantham had replied: "As far as I'm concerned, I'll settle for anything over fifty."

He walked briskly enough through the central lobby of the House of Commons, acknowledging the policeman by the desk as he went out. The usual crowds of constituents were there, sitting patiently on the benches, waiting for their MPs to answer the green card summons. Yes, he reflected, life was a bit like cricket. He'd be happy to settle for anything over fifty. The army had seen his first half-century. Now he was embarking upon the second, and how it would turn out was anyone's guess. As he remembered it, Blakely had declared, that green, sunny afternoon at Lords so many years ago, when Eton were three hundred for five and Grantham himself was an unbeaten seventy-one.

He strode down the long corridor towards Westminster Hall. He paused at the top of the steps, as he always did whenever he visited the House of Commons, to survey the magnificent room where King Charles I had been brought to trial. More than any other part of the Palace of Westminster, the great hall embodied the attributes of the British nation. Grantham was a clever man; he was also a patriot. The one did not necessarily preclude the other. In part, it was patriotism which had led him to make his career in the army.

Unlike David Blakely, Grantham had been a scholar at Eton. Whereas Blakely had gone on to Cambridge and a spectacularly successful business career, Grantham had gone straight to Sandhurst. But over the years the two men had never lost touch. Friendships formed at school were friendships that lasted for life. Contact was made easier by the fact that both men had sons of the same age and the sons had in turn followed their fathers to Eton. With the end of Empire and the post-Suez withdrawals, army life was less exotic – in the most literal sense – than it used to be. Grantham had found it possible to get back to England at least for the Fourth of June. Once both he and Blakely had played against the school on Agar's Plough. They had enjoyed having their sons in the opposing team.

So one way or another the two men had continued to see each other. Their children were friends as the fathers were friends. Twice indeed Grantham had taken his family to visit the Blakely villa in Tuscany. Like so many officers in the British army, Grantham had a house near Fleet in Hampshire. Some people argued that there was a natural progression in an officer's life. You went from Camberley to Fleet to Aldershot. Majors, it was said, lived in Camberley; colonels in Fleet and generals in Aldershot. Grantham had reached Fleet on schedule but then, when his promotion to general came through, he'd resisted moving to Aldershot. He and his wife, Lily, an attractive woman two years his junior, were quite happy where they were. They had made friends in Fleet. Their children had grown up there. Grantham could sit at his desk in his study looking out on the wide sweep of lawn rolling down to the rhododendrons at the bottom of the garden and think with satisfaction of how he had created order out of a wilderness. Trees had grown which he and Lily had planted. He saw no point in planting trees merely to leave them behind. The point of planting was to watch them grow and, once they had grown, to contemplate their fullness.

This was more or less what Grantham had been doing on his first morning as a civilian for thirty-two years when the telephone rang. The call surprised him. He had deliberately kept his resignation from the army quiet. He didn't want the news to get out, to be pressured from one quarter or another to take this or that job. He wanted to have time to make up his own mind, to be a free man – for a while at least. He wanted a small pause for reflection; a tea-interval before embarking on the next half-century.

But that was not the way things had turned out. Grantham had picked up the receiver with some reluctance.

"Is that you, Oliver?"

He had recognized the voice at once.

"David! how good to hear you. How did you know I was back in England?"

"Your resignation was gazetted this morning."

"Don't tell me you read the *London Gazette*."

"I do if I think it's going to carry the news of your resignation." Blakely had come to the point. "I'd like to meet and talk."

So they had met and talked. Blakely had explained that among his varied business interests, he was chairman of Chunnel Consortium.

"We're bidding for the one of the largest engineering contracts in the history of the world, Oliver, bigger than the pyramids. Certainly the most significant in political and geographical terms. We've got German partners, Dutch partners, French, Italians – this is a true multinational grouping. But I need a man to run the whole show. Someone who can bring the thing together and deliver the goods on time. I want *you* to do it. Provided, of course, that the Government decides to go ahead and provided, too, that we win the contract."

Grantham remembered that conversation vividly as he walked out of the Palace of Westminster through the St Stephen's entrance into the summer afternoon. The crowds were waiting behind the barricades; shirt-sleeved policemen on duty were letting visitors into the building two or three at a time. He hailed a taxi in the street.

Well, he thought as he settled back in his seat, the Government *had* at last taken a decision and Chunnel Consortium *had* won the contract. The eighteen months he had spent preparing for this moment – talking to engineers and politicians and businessmen, trying to move the project off dead centre – had borne fruit. There had been other offers besides Blakely's. But he had gambled on the big one, and the gamble had paid off.

The taxi took him up Whitehall round Trafalgar Square and on towards Regent's Park. Sir David Blakely – he'd been knighted for 'services to industry' – lived in an elegant Nash house in Cambridge Terrace. Two Rolls-Royces were parked outside. A uniformed butler had the door open for Grantham before he had even paid off the taxi.

"Sir David is waiting for you, sir."

The drawing room on the first floor looked out over Regent's Park. The two men stood by the window. The butler brought champagne.

"No hiccups then?" asked Blakely.

"No hiccups. The Prime Minister performed very well. Her heart really seems to be in it. I listened to the whole of the statement, though I didn't stay for questions."

Blakely patted him on the shoulder.

"Why wait for questions when the champagne is waiting for you?"

They laughed. They'd known each other for so many years. They trusted each other. And yet there was a great contrast between the two of them. Grantham: fit, fair, civilian life still sitting lightly on his shoulders. Blakely: heavy-set, dark-haired but greying at the temples; a man who had grown used to dealing successfully with the complexities of the business world.

"Let's drink to it, then." Blakely raised his glass. "We're going to work well together. This is the team which is going to change the face of Europe. They've given us the green light, Oliver. That's all we needed. You've a free hand. Hire and fire as you like. I just want the tunnel dug on time."

The butler refilled their glasses. Grantham elaborated on the events of the afternoon.

"I saw Brian Staples in the House this afternoon. I must say he didn't look very happy with the Prime Minister's statement."

Blakely laughed. "You'd hardly expect him to. Staples has been working twenty-four hours a day for the last year trying to get the Government to come out the other way, trying to kill the tunnel project. Well, he's failed. The Prime Minister fought a war and won it during her first period of office. During her second term, she's determined to leave her mark on history in some other way."

"Do you think Staples will take it lying down?"

Blakely gave his friend a long, appraising glance. In spite of the spectacular success he had made of his military career, Grantham still had something to learn about the real world.

"One way or another, Oliver, Channel Ferries has a ten billion pound investment down there – if you add the ships and the ports and all the terminal buildings – not just in England but in France and Belgium too. You ask me if I think Staples will take it lying down. Well, I'll tell you one thing. *I* wouldn't if I were him. Just think about that, Oliver, won't you? Getting the tunnel dug is one thing. Dealing with the opposition is another. And remember I've hired you for both jobs."

David Blakely stood up. "Are you going down for the Fourth of June?"

Grantham nodded. "I thought I would. I've missed it for the last couple of years."

"Good," said David Blakely. "Let's go down together if we can. We might try and make a party of it."

"That would be fine."

The two men talked for a further half-hour. Now that the project had reached the operational phase, Blakely insisted that Grantham's already generous salary should be increased and the terms and conditions of his employment reviewed.

"You ought to have a proper title, now that we're on our way," Blakely said. "How about managing director? I think I had better stay chairman for the time being."

Grantham laughed. "I'm not *that* ambitious."

Blakely laughed in turn. "Just wait! It grows on you, you know."

When they were through, Blakely said: "Don't bother to call a taxi. I'll have the chauffeur take you."

Grantham looked at his watch. "That's very kind of you. I can probably get the six o'clock train to Fleet in that case."

"Train!" Blakely expostulated. "My dear Oliver, the next train you ride in is going to be the Inaugural Train to France going through the Tunnel. Until then, I suggest you leave trains well and truly alone. Fiendish things – and unreliable to boot. James will take you back to Fleet tonight and every night if you really insist on living there! But if I were you, I'd move a little closer to town. We'll take care of that of course."

An hour and a quarter later, a gold Rolls-Royce belonging to Sir

David Blakely and now on what appeared to be permanent loan to the newly nominated managing director of Chunnel Consortium turned into the drive of Grantham's house in Fleet. Grantham realized, as he got out of the car to find his wife Lily regarding the manner of his arrival with evident surprise, that he was going to enjoy this new phase of his civilian existence.

2

Forty-eight hours after the Prime Minister's statement in the House of Commons, Brian Staples flew to Athens. He took a ten o'clock flight out of Heathrow. With the time difference, it was well into the afternoon before he arrived in Greece. A one-hundred-drachmas tip encouraged his taxi driver to make for the Piraeus with all possible speed.

"*Flying Dolphin*! Six o'clock!" Staples tapped the face of his Rolex Quartz to indicate a sense of urgency.

The driver shook his head. "No *Flyink Dolphink*. Too many cars. Much traffic. Very difficult."

"Do your best." Staples produced another one-hundred-drachmas note and handed it over. This time the driver took him seriously and began weaving in and out of the evening traffic in his attempt to bring Staples to the Piraeus in time to catch the last hydrofoil to the islands.

Staples wound up the rear windows of the cab to keep out the dust and pollution. For his money, Athens was one of the most polluted cities on earth and he had seen a great many polluted cities. Somehow the Greeks never got it together. They joined the Common Market and in theory at least accepted the rigorous air-pollution standards which had been laid down by the European Community. But in practice nothing had happened. The atmosphere of Athens was menacing and unhealthy. The best thing that ever happened to the Acropolis, thought Staples, was when Lord Elgin brought the marbles back to London. There at least they had some chance of survival. He caught a glimpse of the Parthenon, on his right, as they went through the city centre. Pheidias' masterpiece was covered in scaffolding. It had been like that the last time he came to Athens, Staples recalled. He supposed it would be that way the next time he came, too. The Greeks were losing the fight against air pollution. That was their problem, thank God. Not his.

Once they were through the city itself, the traffic eased. They made good time over the last few miles to the Piraeus.

"Marina Zia?" The driver enquired, as they reached the waterfront.

"*Nai.*"

The blue and gold hydrofoil was already preparing to leave as the taxi came alongside. Staples paid off the driver and jumped on board.

"Poros?" he asked.

The man at the head of the gangway nodded. The hydrofoil would go to Poros first, he intimated, and then it would go on to Hydra.

"Poros will do me."

Staples settled back into his seat as the revolutions of the hydrofoil's engines increased. He felt the boat rise. By the time they were outside the harbour, they were already travelling at forty knots and the hull was clear of the water. Staples walked to the stern and watched the city of Piraeus recede into the distance. The spray blew up around his face. Seconds later they were passing through the rows of giant tankers waiting to berth.

A line of Greek, ancient Greek, suddenly came into Staples' mind. It was the opening sentence of Plato's *Republic*:

'I went down yesterday with Glaukon to the Piraeus.' Nine words altogether. Plato, Staples recalled, was said to have written and rewritten them over and over again so as to get the right balance and meaning. Well, the Piraeus had changed beyond all recognition since Socrates went down there with Glaukon. The big ships had replaced the little ships. And the big men had replaced the little men. Half the tonnage in the bay, Staples knew, belonged to one of the biggest men of them all: Georgios Karapolitis. Karapolitis was not only the owner of the Karapolitis Lines, which covered both passenger and commercial cargo, including oil tankers; he was also the president of the Federation of Greek Ship-owners. You couldn't be a bigger man than that. Not in Greece anyway.

They were running down the shore of the Peloponnese. The gaunt coastline, marked with an occasional lighthouse, stretched ahead of the boat. Staples was surprised at how empty the landscape was. He would have expected the coast this close to Athens to have been developed to the limit. But then, he realized, that it was only close by boat or by hydrofoil. If you wished to reach it by car, you had to drive right round by the Gulf of Corinth and come back on the narrow dirt roads. The time and, in a literal sense, the motion involved was enough to discourage most weekenders.

The island of Aegina flashed by on the left. Twenty minutes later the engine note changed as the hydrofoil began to settle back down into the water. They pulled into the quay-side at Poros. Staples, carrying hand luggage and nothing else, stepped out with half a dozen other passengers. The rest were obviously heading on for Hydra or Spetsai.

He looked up and down the quay. There were two or three cafés along the waterfront, crowded with tourists; French, Germans, English, Swedes, even a Japanese or two, they would congregate in the late afternoon in the little port; they would buy whatever foreign newspapers happened to have arrived and sit drinking their *retsina* or *ouzo*, watching the boats come and go in the narrow passage which separated the island of Poros from the mainland.

Today their patience was richly rewarded. Apart from the arrival and departure of the *Flying Dolphin*, and the passage of an Italian cruise-ship, the residents and visitors who were in Poros that afternoon had the good fortune, if such it could be called, to witness the arrival of Georgios Karapolitis' personal launch, the *Queen of the Aegean*. Richly liveried in purple and gold, the boat stood out amongst the lesser craft along the waterfront. On board were three crew men, also dressed in the colours of the owner. One of them stepped off onto the quay-side. As Staples looked around wondering what his next move was to be, he heard a polite but firm greeting.

"Mr Staples? Mr Karapolitis has sent his boat for you. Will you come this way."

"How did you know I had caught the hydrofoil at the Piraeus? It was a close thing."

The man smiled. "Mr Karapolitis owns the Flying Dolphin Lines. These things are not difficult for him to know."

"No, I'll bet they're not." Brian Staples nodded thoughtfully and followed the man into the launch.

They set off in the direction of Hydra, following in the wake of the *Flying Dolphin*, which had continued its journey ahead of them. Fifteen minutes later the launch turned sharply out of the main channel and made for a headland which dominated that particular stretch of coastline. As they drew nearer, Staples could see a small sandy bay which faced the sea like a half moon. Steps ran up from the bay to a house which jutted out from the cliff about a hundred feet above sea level. The house was surrounded on three sides by a wide open terrace. Staples could see people on the terrace. He waved, as the launch came into the jetty, and one of the people – he supposed it was Karapolitis himself – waved back.

A few minutes later they were having drinks together outside.

Georgios Karapolitis was a genial expansive man. Around sixty years old, he was broad-shouldered and heavily built. His hair was dark with scarcely a touch of grey, slicked back from the forehead. Dazzling white teeth. The very model of a modern Greek shipowner, thought Staples.

"I'm so very glad you could come," said the Greek.

Staples couldn't help thinking that Karapolitis's greetings were somewhat insincere since it was he, Staples, who had requested the meeting in the first place.

"I'm so glad I found you at home this week. I know you travel a lot. Unlike us MPs." Staples laughed, signalling that the life of an MP was very much a boring deskbound affair compared with that of his host.

"Meet my daughter, Iona," Karapolitis said, as a smiling young woman with a classical profile came out to join them on the terrace.

"What a lovely name!"

"It's a lovely sea, the Ionian Sea. Do you know it?" The girl had a soft dark voice. As soft and dark as she was herself.

"Yes, I do know the Ionian Sea. I've been to Ithaca."

"Ah, like Ulysses!"

"I came home rather quicker than Ulysses did."

The girl laughed: "I'm sure you have business to talk with my father. I'm going for a swim before dinner." She disappeared. Moments later Staples saw, from the terrace, a lithe brown naked body diving into the water from the rocks. He wished he could join her.

Georgios Karapolitis read his mind correctly.

"Why don't you swim too? You must be hot and tired after your long journey from England. You'll find a robe in your room. Of course you'll stay the night, won't you? You certainly can't get back to Athens this evening. The last hydrofoil has already gone."

"I'd love to."

"So you decided not to talk business after all." Iona smiled at him as he joined her in the clear blue water of the bay.

"Your father and I both thought that business could wait."

Iona broke into a lively crawl which took her fifty yards out to sea and fifty yards back again. She drew up alongside him and then flipped over onto her back so that her breasts were exposed to the sun. She rotated her arms backwards one after another, slowly, like the vanes of a windmill on a hot summer day.

"The sea is my number one priority." She flipped over again onto her stomach and ducked her head in the water.

Staples looked at his companion, looked at the little bay and the house above it with its view of the ocean, looked at the groves of olive trees rising on the headland behind the house, felt the wind in his face and the sun on his skin.

"Yes, I can see how the sea becomes a priority when you live in Greece."

"It's in our blood." The girl spoke matter of factly. "Talk to me, talk to my father about the sea, anything to do with the sea, and you'll find we'll listen. The Karapolitis are one of the great sea-going families in Greece. And Greece as you know is a nation of sea-farers."

Staples hoisted himself onto the jetty wishing he was a great deal fitter and trimmer. He pulled the robe firmly round him. Being naked in the water was one thing; being naked on land – unless it was for very specific purposes – seemed to him to be another matter entirely.

Iona had no such hesitations. She tossed her towel over her shoulder and ran back ahead of him up the steps to the house.

It wasn't finally till after dinner that Georgios Karapolitis and Brian Staples had the talk he'd come all the way to Greece to have. They sat on the terrace with a bottle of Metaxa brandy on the table in front of them and small cups of bitter-sweet Greek coffee to wash it down with.

"I remember when Greek coffee used to be called Turkish coffee even in Greece," said Staples.

Karapolitis shook his head. "Not now. We try not to talk about the Turks. Not with the Cyprus problem. And the Aegean problem."

Staples seized his cue. "I guess we all have our problems of one kind or another. I suppose you know what mine is?"

The two men looked at each other in the fading light. Both of them big wheels in their way. Channel Ferries could certainly hold a candle to Karapolitis Lines. The Greek might win on tonnage; but in terms of operating revenues there couldn't have been much in it.

"Don't tell me . . ." It was more a flippant suggestion than anything else. "The government are requisitioning more of your ships for the South Atlantic!"

Staples laughed. "No, it was bad enough last time. Imagine trying to operate your *Flying Dolphin* service to the Islands and then being told one day that all your boats are being sent off to the Black Sea."

It was Karapolitis' turn to laugh. "Our hydrofoils come from the Black Sea, you know, they are made in Odessa."

He turned serious.

"I suppose your problem is the Channel Tunnel Project?" Karapolitis pointed to a copy of the *International Herald Tribune* which was lying on the table next to the brandy and the coffee. "It's all in today's paper. It appears that this time your Government has finally and definitely made up its mind to go ahead with the project. In fact not just one government, both governments. Britain and France. That's correct, isn't it?"

"Exactly. This time they mean it. At least the British Government does. I heard the Prime Minister's statement in the House. She's giving the go-ahead to private enterprise. There won't be any government backing. That's not her way. She's convinced that the private sector can and should manage on its own."

Georgios Karapolitis walked over to the edge of the terrace. He laid his hands on the railings, knuckles upwards. He narrowed his eyes and gazed out across the sea. Way out there across the bay he could see the lights of the planes as they came in to land at Athens airport. Beyond the airport, to the east, was Cape Sounion. He was not an especially well educated man. He couldn't recite all the battles of the ancient world. But he knew that Greece had a long history and that Sounion was part of it. He liked to be able to stand on his own ground, purchased with good Greek drachmas, to look Cape Sounion straight in the eye.

There was a wind getting up and the waves were breaking around the sides of the bay. The launches, at anchor by the jetty, were bobbing around dangerously. Karapolitis shouted an order to the servants in the house, then watched as the two house boys, Apollo and Dionysos, ran down, switched on the electric winch and hauled the launches up the slipway until they were out of danger.

Georgios Karapolitis came back to his guest. He down down beside Brian Staples and poured himself another large glass of brandy.

"Cigar?"

"No thanks. My doctors told me to give it up."

"Never take any notice of what your doctors say," Karapolitis admonished him. "My father will be a hundred this summer and has never seen a doctor in his life." He took a long deep pull on the cigar. The smoke wafted out to sea. "So you want me to help, do you?"

Staples nodded. "Yes. The Chunnel project is going to go ahead. And it's going to do my business a great deal of damage. In fact, the Chunnel could kill Channel Ferries altogether. It will destroy all the investments we've built up over the years in ships and harbours and docks. We shall be a dead duck sitting out there in the water. We tried our damnedest to get the decision reversed. Now I want to try a different way."

"What way?"

It was Staple's turn to call in aid the theatrical props. "Perhaps I will have a cigar after all."

When the cigar was lit, he leaned towards his Greek host. His face came very close to that of Georgios Karapolitis. The white, rather pudgy, visage of the Tory MP for Felixstowe was a clear contrast to the bronzed good health evident in the Greek's features.

"We can still win, I believe," Staples said. "With your help, we can win."

"What do you want me to do?"

"I'm not sure yet. That's why I wanted us to talk."

"You're sure there *is* something I can do?"

"Quite sure."

"Let's drink to that anyway."

Both men laughed and raised their glasses.

Later that night Georgios' daughter Iona slipped into Brian Staples' room. He woke from a heavy sleep as he felt her hand on his groin. The moon had come up over the bay and the light shone on the water beyond the terrace. The sea had calmed down. With the windows of his room wide open Staples could hear the waves lapping the jetty.

Iona said in a straightforward, cheerful way: "Daddy wanted me to come." She laughed. "He's the boss. For the time being anyway."

"Bully for daddy."

Staples decided that, since he was now doing business in the Greek way, he had better learn to like it.

In the event, it wasn't a question of learning to like it. Staples didn't understand precisely why Iona Karapolitis had come to his bed. He knew he was not overwhelmingly attractive to women. Rather the reverse. And yet, somehow, there seemed to be an urgency, almost a viciousness, in Iona's ministrations. She might have been performing at "daddy's" behest – a bonus thrown in to cement the deal – but he had no doubt at all, as she forced herself onto him, that she was also serving her own peculiar interests and desires.

At one point, as she crushed his testicles with her hand, he thought she was trying to maim him.

"Don't do that!" he cried.

"I'll do what I like," she hissed in his ear.

And she did. On the whole, he enjoyed it.

She slipped away as silently as she had come. The next morning, when Staples woke, he wondered whether he had dreamt it. But when he saw her at breakfast, he knew he had not.

"I'm afraid daddy had to leave early for Athens."

"Bully for daddy," Staples smirked.

She smiled coldly, daring him to say more.

3

They made it to Lyons, having left Paris after breakfast, well before noon. Pierre Leroux, who was driving, turned to his companion.

"Shall we stop for lunch?"

Monique Delacourt nodded. "Why not?"

They left the autoroute at the first exit and stopped at a country restaurant. They ordered the simple set menu. Three courses for fifty francs not counting the wine.

"It's ridiculous how expensive Paris is," said Monique.

"It's ridiculous how cheap the country is," Pierre Leroux replied.

"That's a politician's answer. A socialist politician's answer. Always suggesting that someone isn't being paid what he deserves for what he produces."

"I *am* a socialist politician."

Monique Delacourt touched his hand. "I'm beginning to understand it."

They sat a few minutes over the coffee.

"I'm going to make it one day", Leroux said to her, "to the top. All the way to the top."

"Are you sure?"

"Quite sure."

"The waiter didn't recognize you when we came in," she teased.

"I wouldn't expect the waiter to look at me when I come in with you on my arm." And then he added, going beyond the predictable gallantry, "This isn't my area. And the national campaign hasn't begun yet. Just wait."

She smiled, drawn by his energy and ambition. Pierre Leroux was the youngest member of the Cabinet and many said the ablest as well. Mitterrand had made him Minister for Consumer Affairs first, and had then promoted him to Minister of Transport. There were those who suggested that Mitterrand had favoured him merely to have him fail. Others saw this as a grooming of the heir apparent.

When he first took office, Mitterrand had hinted that he would prefer to serve a five-, rather than a seven-, year term. "*Sept ans, c'est trop, n'est-ce pas?*" was the precise expression he had uttered. True to his word, he had recently announced that the Presidential elections would be held early and the Parliament had passed the necessary legislation. Some observers believed that the President's move arose, in part at least, from a desire to favour Leroux's candidacy. Whichever way it was (and no one apart from the President knew that for sure, not even Leroux), there was no question but that the Minister of Transport was a force in the land.

"What made you first come to Provence?" Monique asked him when they had rejoined the autoroute and were once more heading south. "Your roots are in the North, aren't they?"

"Precisely because my roots *are* in the North, I decided to come to Provence. There are people down here who count if you want to function at a national level."

Pierre Leroux did not elaborate on this rather cryptic remark and they drove on in silence.

Just past the Roman town of Orange the road divided. Right for Spain. Left for Marseilles. Leroux took the lefthand road, leaving Avignon on his right. Thirty minutes later, they turned off the autoroute onto the back roads behind Aix-en-Provence. Leroux's manner became more relaxed. He slowed down from a hundred and sixty or a hundred and seventy kilometres an hour, which is what he had been doing on the autoroute, to a speed more in keeping with the drowsy countryside.

"Like so many Frenchmen, I hate the autoroutes. But I couldn't do without them."

"The high-speed train – the TGV – will get you quicker to Lyons or to Marseilles than any car, no matter how fast you drive. You, of all people, must know that as Minister of Transport."

Leroux laughed. "You're right. I just can't get into the habit of using it."

"You ought to start promoting it a bit more."

They were driving now towards the foothills of the Lubéron. In the little Provençal villages, the flags were out for the next day's July 14th celebrations. The wayside stalls of peaches and melons, aubergines and tomatoes bespoke the wealth of the region. Leroux pulled over to make way for a herd of pigs that was finding its own way home, in its own good time, along the road ahead of them.

A sixteenth-century castle, set on an outcrop of rock on a plain in the shadow of the Lubéron mountains, indicated that they had reached the village of Lourmarin. They took a dirt track running behind the village and followed it two or three kilometres into the pine forest. The low-slung Mercedes bounced on the ruts and once the exhaust jarred as it came into contact with a stone on the road.

"That's the only trouble with these Mercedes," Leroux complained, "the carriage is too low."

"Two strikes against you. First, as a French minister you should be driving a French car, surely. Second, as a socialist, you shouldn't be driving a Mercedes!"

"You may be right on the first count," Leroux laughed as he replied, "although I haven't noticed that any of my colleagues are particularly prone to French cars. But you're dead wrong to suggest that as a socialist I shouldn't drive a Mercedes. The whole point about socialism is to prove, and I mean prove, that *anyone* can make it. Not merely those that were born with a silver spoon in their mouth."

"And you have proved that?"

They rounded a bend in the pine forest. Leroux braked. The car came to a stop on a ridge commanding a distant view of the Montagne Sainte Victoire. In the foreground, looking out over the plain, was an old Provençal farmhouse, surrounded by a grove of trees: olives and oaks, cherries and peaches. It nestled on the hillside, looking down into the plain. In front of the house was a garden of plants and flowers, and terraces full of climbing things.

"There's the answer to your question," Leroux said.

Monique Delacourt said nothing. She had seldom seen a more beautiful place in her life.

They parked the car in the shade of the pine trees and walked down the short slope the last fifty yards to the house.

"I hope Yvette has been in. I warned her I was coming."

Yvette had indeed been in. A salad and a ratatouille, cold meats and cheeses had been prepared for supper. The windows had been thrown open in the house. The pump had been turned on and the water was circulating in the swimming pool below the terrace.

They ate at an old stone table outside. Monique Delacourt couldn't believe that the colours of Provence were real. The blue was so clear; the green of the pine trees so sharp and dark. Fields of lavender dropped away below the house, shimmering blue and purple in the evening light. A gentle breeze came up off the plain and enveloped them as they sat there.

"I bought the place twenty years ago," Leroux explained, "at the beginning of my political career. I was on one of those long bicycling tours in the South; you know how keen young Frenchmen are on bicycling. I decided to cut through on a back road from Aix to Avignon and I came across Lourmarin. I spent two nights in the village, camping below the castle. One morning when I was exploring the countryside I discovered this place. It was almost a ruin then. A lot of the stonework was in very bad repair and of course the land was totally overgrown. But it was charming beyond belief. Exactly what I wanted as a place to get away to, when it was time to get away. I found the owners. Rather a well-off couple who had other property in the area, but were reluctant to sell this one. It had romantic associations for them; apparently, fifty years or so earlier, they met there and fell in love."

"How did you persuade them to sell?"

Leroux looked embarrassed. "I told them that I too was hoping to get married and that I was looking for a place my fiancée and I could live in after the wedding."

"And of course that touched their heart strings?"

"I think it was the money I offered which finally moved them," Leroux laughed.

"And the fiancée?"

"Never was one." He looked at her. "I've always been too busy to get married. You have to understand that."

Monique sighed. She wondered why it was that men were always telling her they were too busy to get married. What was it about her? As a "career woman" was she supposed to be above marriage and that kind of thing? Sometimes she wished she had been rather less successful at her career and rather more successful at managing her personal life. The trouble was that she loved her work, revelled in it, adored the daily contact she had with all sorts of people, from bankers to engineers to ordinary workmen shovelling earth from one place to another. She loved the intellectual challenge that any project, large or small, could present. Recently she had been working desperately hard. As the part of the multinational consortium which had just been awarded the contract to build and operate the Channel Tunnel, Falaise et Cie had just entered a phase of particularly hectic activity. And much of the work, Monique found, was devolving on her in the role as Falaise's Chief Project Engineer. Though construction could not start until the treaty had been formally signed between Britain and France, already the preparations had entered an intensive phase.

So when Leroux had called her and invited her down to his place in

Provence for the 14th July weekend, she had hesitated about accepting. There was so much on her plate. But Leroux had insisted.

"You need the break, Monique," he had told her, "and you'll love Provence."

If Monique Delacourt had accepted, the reason wasn't so much Provence, it was more Pierre Leroux. She had first met him two months earlier, at an official function in Paris. He had been there as Minister of Transport; she, as a senior employee of a major French engineering company involved in transport projects. Leroux had gravitated naturally towards her. One of the things that frustrated him most about his life as a French politician was how male-dominated the whole business was. Political meetings, political lunches, political speeches – it was always a question, or so it seemed, of men in suits talking to other men in suits. What he liked about Monique Delacourt was that in spite of all the difficulties, all the obstacles, she had made it to the top – and managed to remain very feminine at the same time. Monique had been flattered by, and had responded to, his interest.

They had been seen together at restaurants in Paris. Their photograph had appeared in *Paris-Match* and *L'Express*. She had stayed at his flat in Paris on more than one occasion. But this was the first time that they had spent the weekend together.

With a touch of asperity in her voice, Monique Delacourt commented on Leroux's remark about marriage.

"Of course I understand you may be too busy for marriage. But you're not too busy to be here today. That's all I care about."

Leroux touched her hand. "And tomorrow. And the next day. Let's make the most of it."

He showed her around the house after their meal.

"I tried to keep the character in every possible way." He pointed to an oak-panelled cupboard in the bedroom upstairs. "When I had time I scoured the markets in Nice and Cannes for old pieces like this which would fit into the style and period. The old people are on the coast. And when they die, their possessions are sold. You find some lovely old pieces in Nice and Cannes if you look for them."

They made love upstairs in a dark, cool room, heavily shuttered against the bright evening. They left just one window open, a small square window which gave out onto a grove of cypress trees, set amid a vineyard with the mountains of the Lubéron rising in the background.

Leroux was a gentle lover. He knew when to give and when to receive.

He was both delicate and inventive. Monique lay on her back while he explored her body. She listened to the wind play about the house and watched the tips of the cypresses sway across the open window. From time to time swallows and martins darted into view, swooping in mid-air to catch flies and other insects. He roused her to a quiet and controlled passion. She wanted him to continue and then she didn't want him to continue.

Half an hour later, he brought her a *citron pressé*.

"I thought we might go into Cucuron. Tomorrow is the 14th and all the shops will be shut. We had better get supplies today, particularly since we have people coming."

She roused herself reluctantly and took the drink.

"What people?"

"Political, I'm afraid. But they may interest you anyway."

"I'm sure they will."

The heat of the day had passed by the time they reached the market in Cucuron. They bought what they needed and then sat at a café table. Monique Delacourt ordered a beer.

"I'll have a glass of red wine from the co-operative," said Leroux. "The co-operative makes a good a wine as any," he laughed, "as long as you drink it *sur place*."

When finally they returned to the farmhouse, it was well after midnight. The stars shone from a clear sky.

"Do you know that painting of Van Gogh's, 'La Nuit Etoilée'?" Leroux asked, as they stood outside.

"Of course I do."

"This is it, isn't it?"

As they watched, a satellite crossed the sky from left to right.

"Van Gogh never saw the satellites," Leroux said.

"Was he missing something?" Monique Delacourt wasn't sure.

They swam in the pool by the light of the stars. Later, they sat on the terrace.

"You know, Pierre, up till now I've always thought of you as a ruthless, ambitious politician who is going to be President one day."

"And now?"

"I think of you as a ruthless, ambitious politician who is going to be President one day, but who can show *occasional* sparks of feeling."

"Don't be deceived," Leroux laughed, "I'm even nastier than I seem."

The following day, being July 14th, saw the opening shots fired in Pierre Leroux's campaign to become President of France. He had chosen the date deliberately. The tricolor was flying over the castle in the valley and the guns had sounded that morning to mark the anniversary of the Revolution. The Quatorze Juillet was a day people tended to remember. That was the way Leroux wanted it. The detail counted.

In many ways, he modelled himself on the Kennedy family. He was fascinated by the Kennedy myth. And by the reality. One summer he had found himself with a day to spare in Boston. He had hired a light aeroplane at Logan airport and had flown over to Cape Cod. As they neared Hyannis, he had asked the pilot to take him down low over the Kennedy compound.

"Which was Jack Kennedy's house?" he had asked.

The pilot had pointed to a large white building, surrounded by a square fence and set beside the water's edge.

"That was the President's," the pilot said. "There are other houses down there belonging to members of the Kennedy family . . . Teddy . . . Ethel . . ."

They had banked and turned back to Boston. For Leroux, it was a small but significant pilgrimage. In his own mind he saw his Provençal farmhouse, with its land and terraces, as a kind of French Cape Cod, a place where Presidential dreams might be dreamed and campaign strategies worked out.

In spite of the fact that it was July 14th, and a national holiday, Yvette the maid showed up promptly for work. She had brought her young man with her. He gazed in patent adoration as she busied herself with the lunch.

"We shall only be four, Yvette. Do you think you can manage?" Leroux said.

She was a friendly, buxom girl who spoke with a strong Provençal twang.

"Jules can help me."

Jules seemed only too delighted to be asked.

While Yvette was preparing lunch, Pierre Leroux spent half an hour trimming back some trees so as to improve the view from the terrace.

Then he called on Monique to help him draw some wine from the thirty-litre bottles in which he had bought it from the co-operative. They filled three large carafes and set them on the table.

"It costs you ten francs more per litre if you buy it in bottles," Leroux told her, "and it's the same wine. Absolutely the same. Côtes du Lubéron. It just doesn't have the fancy label."

At the edge of the terrace was a cherry tree, heavy with fruit. Monique filled a basket. Yvette, somehow, had already managed to pick a quantity of apricots and these too were piled on the table.

"Who's coming to lunch?" Monique asked Leroux.

"Oh," he replied with some nonchalance, "a couple of local mayors. Marseilles and Lyons, to be precise." And he went on to explain why. "Marseilles is vital. If you're trying to devise a strategy to capture the heart and soul of the socialist party in France, you have to begin with the two key regions. One is the Pas-de-Calais, which of course is where I come from, so that's more or less wrapped up – or at least I hope so. The other is the Bouches-du-Rhône, which means Marseilles. If you have the Pas-de-Calais and Marseilles behind you, then you have a real chance of gaining the support of the party as a whole. Without them, you may as well not begin."

"And Claude Genet in Marseilles is important?"

"He's crucial."

Monique nodded. Claude Genet had swept through to an impressive victory in the recent local elections. He was the new broom, cleaning up after decades of Gaston Deferre. It made sense to bring Genet on board right from the start.

"And was that one of the reasons you bicycled down here twenty years ago and bought yourself this house? So you could have a base here too?"

Leroux smiled. "I won't say it didn't have something to do with it."

"You think ahead, don't you?"

"That is what life is about. Thinking ahead."

Monique Delacourt returned to the subject of the guests. "You have the Mayor of Lyons coming too?"

"Yes. Louis Baudin is an old friend of mine. You'll like him. He brought me into politics in the first place. He had real *piston*. Clout. Lyons was the heart of the resistance movement during the war. All the threads came together there; all the groups of the *maquis*. That's where the centre of co-ordination was. Louis Baudin was one of the key figures in organizing the opposition to the Germans. I met him when I was attending my first party congress, in the '60s. He was then and still is something of a hero. We took a liking to each other and have been friends ever since. Lyons has changed since he took over as mayor from the Gaullists."

"It's a long way to come to lunch." Monique Delacourt remembered the previous day's drive down from Lyons.

"I think he'll find the journey was worth it."

They heard the sound of cars coming up the sandy track through the pine trees. Pierre Leroux went out to greet his guests. The mayors of Marseilles and Lyons had arrived together.

"Ah, *bonjour* Claude, *bonjour* Louis. How was the journey? Not too hot I hope?"

"Fine. Absolutely fine," Louis Baudin replied. "The Quatorze is a good day to travel. Everyone is sleeping late. The roads were almost empty."

Leroux turned to Claude Genet. "And coming from Marseilles? Was there much traffic?"

"No problem. Nothing to it."

Pierre Leroux led his guests back to the house. Monique was waiting on the terrace. He introduced her to his political allies.

Louis Baudin, the old man from Lyons, war hero, one time darling of the people, bent over and raised her fingers, almost, but not quite, to his lips. The shock of white hair fell forward across his forehead.

"*Bonjour madame. Enchanté.*"

Claude Genet, Marseilles' new broom, nodded stiffly. He had not expected Leroux to have some female in tow. That was something they would have to discuss. The candidate's image was all-important. He would remind Leroux that French socialism still had a pronounced moral streak to it.

Leroux sensed what the Mayor of Marseilles was thinking. As they drank their pre-lunch aperitifs on the terrace, he found a moment to take him aside.

"Behind every man, there is a woman, *n'est-ce pas?*"

Claude Genet shrugged somewhat ungraciously. "*Il faut toujours être prudent.*"

There were, as Leroux had promised the maid Yvette, only four of them there that day at lunch on the terrace of the old farmhouse at Lourmarin. Four of them to chart a new path for a new candidate. Much was said; and much, also, was left unsaid. Louis Baudin and Claude Genet pledged their help, and the help of their people. That was important. They were explicit about this. This was one of the things that was said.

"We know you can do it, Pierre." Louis Baudin had lifted his glass.

Leroux had replied: "I'll do my best."

The things that were left unsaid, of course, were even more important. They had to do with what a Leroux victory would bring to Lyons and Marseilles. To Baudin and Genet. And to the people whom they worked with. Such things were not said, because they went without saying.

Lunch took a long time. After lunch, they all had a short siesta; and then they swam. By five o'clock in the evening, it was time for Leroux's guests to go.

"I have to be back for the fireworks," Louis Baudin said. "We're having a massive display to mark the Quatorze. The biggest ever."

The tall avuncular man laughed. He wrapped his arm around Leroux's shoulders as they made for the car.

"That's the way it is with socialism, my boy. Always extravagance of one kind or another. That's what the people expect. And we certainly give it to them!"

Claude Genet, the Mayor of Marseilles, broke into a smile.

"That's your way, Louis. Down in Marseilles, we're trying to do things differently now. A parade on the Canebière and that's about it."

Louis Baudin paused in front of his black Peugeot.

"You think you'll change things, Claude, but you won't. If you give the people fireworks on July 14th, there'll always be one or two who complain about the extravagance. But if you *don't* give them fireworks, there'll be many more who'll attack you for failing to show the necessary respect for the Republic!"

The two men drove off together, Peugeot following Peugeot, down the bumpy track into the plain. Pierre Leroux and Monique Delacourt stood side by side, watching the cars until they were out of sight.

They turned to walk back to the house.

"Did it go well?"

Monique Delacourt wasn't sure she had grasped all the nuances of the afternoon's discussion. There had been talk of "timetables" and "pressure-points", of "options" and "alternative strategies" which could be adopted in the event of this or that happening.

"Yes. It did go well," Leroux replied. "Better than you could have ever imagined."

Yvette departed with her fiancé. The motorcycle roared away down the track, leaving a sudden silence behind.

Leroux looked at his watch.

"In half an hour the crickets will start. They make the devil of a din. Why don't we go for a walk while it's cool and quiet?"

They walked up into the mountains behind the farm. Sat on the rocks high above the house. Saw the tricolor lowered on the great castle below. Dusk gathered, but still they sat there. Then the first fireworks blossomed in the darkness, showering sparks of light on to the plain.

He took her hand and held it, tight. He spoke fiercely, passionately.

"Most Frenchmen think of them only as fireworks. An excuse to celebrate. When I see the fireworks on this day I think of the revolution which we have now betrayed so terribly."

Pierre Leroux recovered himself quickly. For a moment he knew he had shown his true colours. That was dangerous. It was something a politician should never do.

He stood up and pulled her to her feet. "Come on. Let's have a last swim before we head back to Paris."

"We are going tonight?"

"I'm afraid we must. I have to be at my desk tomorrow morning. Don't forget I'm a minister. And ministers have to set an example even in M. Mitterrand's government," Leroux laughed.

She laughed too. *"Bien sûr, monsieur le Ministre."*

4

Oliver Grantham had first come to know and love the Black Forest when he was stationed at Freiburg with the British Army of the Rhine. It was not much more than an hour's drive into the mountains. Sometimes he would take the family with him: his wife, Lily; the two boys if they were home from school; the yellow Labrador – Sally – which they had acquired as a puppy on first coming to Freiburg. The problem of finding a new home for Sally before they returned to England would come up on such occasions.

"I love England," Grantham once told his wife when they were out walking with the dog, "and I hope I'll die there. But if there's one thing I do think they exaggerate about, it's the rule on dogs coming into the country." He would look at the Labrador running free beside them. "How can you ask a dog like this to spend six long months in kennels in quarantine? Do you realize what a chunk of a dog's life six months is? It's the equivalent of five years in prison."

Lily took a more responsible view of the problem.

"Britain has been free of rabies for hundreds of years. Why risk it now?"

Looking back at their time in Germany after their return – without Sally – to England, the Granthams realized that the Black Forest had become a kind of home from home for them. One place they had liked in particular. It was a large, modern hotel, known as the Hetzel, built high up above Lake Schluchsee. Almost every room had its own balcony looking out over the forest and field. The facilities were unrivalled: indoor and outdoor swimming pools; indoor and outdoor tennis; squash; sauna and massage; and fitness classes designed to meet all needs. The hotel also offered a complete selection of guided "Wanderungs". These were hikes for those who wanted to walk briskly through the mountains without necessarily knowing at every moment where precisely they were, or where they were going.

In winter, for sometimes the Granthams came in winter as well as in summer, life went on much the same. Instead of the hikes in the forest, there was quite passable skiing and, for a British army officer with a passion for all things physical, to be able to ski on real mountains in the course of a weekend pass was cheering indeed.

Lily Grantham had readily agreed when her husband told her, soon after he had taken up his new job, that he intended to spend the weekend in the Black Forest before going on to Paris and a meeting of the board of Chunnel Consortium.

"Of course I understand," she had said. "It will do you good to take a break, darling. Get some air into your lungs. Stretch your legs. I sometimes think civilian life can be a little too tame for you. You're not used to it."

So Grantham had flown to Basel-Mulhouse airport, where he had hired a car to drive down to the Black Forest late on Friday night. A bottle of champagne was waiting for him in his room, courtesy of the hotel management. Peter Drexner, who had been running the Hetzel since it was built, did not easily forget a name. Or a face for that matter.

By 7 a.m. the next morning, Grantham had already swum sixteen times around the great pentagonal indoor pool, and ten times around the connecting, slightly smaller, outdoor pool. Afterwards he had gone to the gymnasium for his first workout of the day.

Oliver Grantham was a methodical man anywhere. He was especially methodical in the gym. He began with the bicycle. Pedalled three minutes; paused ten seconds; moved on to the weights. Four minutes with fifteen kilograms, then a quick three kilometres on the moving belt. He worked up a gentle sweat, dropping his hands to his side so that the arms hung long and loose; concentrating on maintaining an even pace. The control button was by his right hand. He took the last few hundred yards at a sprint, then slowed the band down, and walked off knowing that he was not quite as fit today as he had been when he 'yomped' from Port San Carlos to Goose Green with a 150-pound pack on his back, just to show his men that he could do it as well as they could.

From the running track to the wall bars. He hooked his feet firmly under the third rung, lay back on the bench, then proceeded to sit up and touch the toes of each foot in turn with a wide swinging motion that had each hip swivelling through one hundred and eighty degrees.

Normally Grantham allowed himself a minute's rest between rounds. That morning as he paused before the next set of exercises, the door of the gym swung open and a blonde, sun-tanned woman came in, nodded him a greeting and then proceeded to do some efficient-looking warming-up exercises.

In the middle of a knees-bend-and-stretch which Oliver Grantham found a particularly appealing sight at that early hour of the morning, she looked over, and asked him in German:

"Are you going round the course? May I follow you around?"

Grantham's German was perfectly serviceable. You didn't hold a senior post with the British Army of the Rhine without acquiring a good deal more than a smattering of the language of the host country.

"Come along. I'm just starting on the second round."

It was more of the same, only faster. This time he took the twenty kilo bar and was amazed, not only when she followed suit, but when she matched him lift for lift.

Her hair came down from the bun in which it had been tied. She tossed it over her shoulders without interrupting the flow of movement.

A sense of courtesy, if not old-fashioned gallantry, suggested to Grantham that he should let the blonde woman, whoever she was, take the lead on the running track. He motioned to her to step up ahead of him.

"*Danke schön.*"

"*Bitte sehr.*"

They started off fairly slowly. A steady ten kilometres per hour. Grantham focused on the flowing golden hair in front of him and on the contrast it made with the black of the woman's leotard.

Without warning, the woman increased the speed of the running track to twelve to fifteen and then to eighteen kilometres per hour. Grantham found himself running at full stretch. He lengthened his stride, kicking his feet out in front of him. He was sprinting. And it wasn't just a hundred-metres sprint. It wasn't two hundred metres. She kept it up for four hundred metres altogether and might have gone on if Grantham hadn't tapped her sharply on the shoulder and shouted:

"*Das genügt!*"

It was indeed enough. He finished the second round of exercises with rather less enthusiasm than the first.

She walked out of the gym behind him.

Grantham looked at her. Her chest was heaving, but less than his.

"You're a fit lady." He introduced himself.

"*Auf Wiedersehen.*"

The good news that morning was that when he returned to his room, breakfast was already waiting.

He had a rapid shower and then went out on the balcony with a towel wrapped round his waist. The morning mist which earlier had shrouded the pine trees had now disappeared and even though it was not yet eight o'clock the sun was clear of the line of hills.

Grantham set to work. He dealt with the eggs first. Two lightly boiled eggs, as he had ordered. He moved on to the salted herring. God only knew where the Germans got their herring from, now that the North Sea was fished out; but somehow they managed it. After the herring came the part of a German breakfast which he really liked: the *Ausschnitz-platte*: cold meats – ham and tongue, beef and sausage, garnished with pickles and herbs, and served with an assortment of breads, including some fine white rolls which would have done credit to a Victorian tea party.

There was only one drawback, he thought, about the German breakfast, or at least about the modern German breakfast, and that was the way they served the milk in those damn silly little plastic cartons which were so hard to open. And when you did finally get them open, if you did, you discovered it wasn't milk at all. It was cream. If there was one thing Oliver Grantham couldn't stand, it was cream in his coffee. Coffee either had to be *au lait* or else black as Iago's heart. Today, thank God, all was well. Someone had got the message. Grantham removed the linen napkin from a large white jug and poured hot milk into his coffee. He lifted it to his lips, mentally toasting the mountains and the day.

He heard the buzzer ring and went to open the door. The room maid was standing there. He still had the towel wrapped around his hips; but she didn't seem to mind in the least. She had seen worse, or maybe better, things in her time. She smiled at him, a cheeky smile, cheeky as the bosom which thrust out at him beneath the starch of her uniform.

"A lady asked me to give you this message."

"Thank you."

He took a sealed envelope from her.

The girl still stood there. Still smiled.

Assuming that she was waiting for a tip, Grantham walked back into the room and rummaged among the change which he had left on the table until he found a five-mark piece.

He turned to find that the girl had followed him in.

"Thank you," Grantham said. He tried to put the money in her hand but for some reason she seemed determined to stay and talk.

"*Bist du ein Englander?*"

Grantham realized as he replied that the girl was surprisingly pretty. She had short fair hair, light blue eyes and a warm, generous mouth.

"Yes, I am English."

The girl seemed delighted to be reassured on that score. She sat on the bed, straightening her skirt as she did so. The idea briefly crossed Grantham's mind that she was acting a part, playing a role, though he couldn't for the life of him think why.

Natural curiosity, not to say lust, got the better of him.

"Do you know many English people?" He realized with some sadness that the coffee would get cold. But then he had second thoughts. What did it matter if the coffee *did* get cold?

A psychologist might have called it a random sexual encounter. Grantham would have agreed up to a point. As far as place and time were concerned, it certainly was random. But it was not random in the sense of being unimportant. It mattered a good deal to Grantham to know that he was still capable of attracting women. He had long ago given up trying to come to terms with the rights or wrongs of the matter. He didn't agonize. He didn't see that there was anything to agonize about. He was an ordinary, sane, healthy individual who found it much easier to say "yes" than "no".

So Grantham took the German maid – *das Zimmermädchen* – for what she was. A bouncy, nubile peasant girl, who had seen more of life in the last six months working at the Hetzel Hotel than she had during twenty years on her father's farm.

"*Wie ist Ihr Name?*"

Before replying, the girl dropped her skirt to the floor and stepped out of it and then, in virtually the same movement, pulled her blouse off over her head. She stood there facing him, with the light behind her. She had a broad chest, with thick rubbery nipples. Her belly was just a bit fatter than it ought to have been. Not gently swelling like Cranach, thought Grantham; more like Renoir. He noticed that the edges of her pubic hair had turned a lighter colour than the rest. Grantham supposed that she had been sunbathing in her off-duty hours in a too-skimpy bikini. There was no stopping them, he reflected, once you brought them off the farm and showed them the bright side of life.

The girl put her hands on her hips. "*Greta. Ich heisse Greta.*"

"I'm Peter."

Grantham pronounced the name the German way, like a Victorian schoolboy addressing his father. He felt tempted to add that his full name was Peter Drexner, but he decided against it. Even a simple country girl might think there was something odd about that. He wondered which of his friends, in similar circumstances, had called themselves Oliver. Or even Oliver Grantham. He could think of one or two who might have. He was pleased by the idea. It was a kind of compliment.

He pulled her to him, still wearing the towel, and kissed her. Then he pushed her, quite roughly, down onto the bed. He pulled her over on top of him so that her breasts hung down towards his face. He crushed first one, then the other, against him.

"*Schnell!*" she said. "*Ich habe nicht zu viel Zeit.*"

Not much time; but time enough, thought Grantham. The artillery had done its work. The softening up process was over. The brigade moved forward into the attack.

When the girl had gone, Grantham remembered to read the note she had brought. It was written in English.

"I enjoyed your company in the gym this morning. Are you free for tennis or a walk through the forest? Please give your answer to the room maid or else ring me on extension 292."

The note was signed, with a flourish, Ingrid Lubbeke.

As Grantham picked up the telephone and dialled the number, he wondered vaguely why the name Ingrid Lubbeke seemed familiar to him.

He used his own name now; no point in trivial deceptions.

"This is Oliver Grantham here."

"Ah, the *Zimmermädchen* brought you my message?"

"Yes." As a statement of fact it was the truth, but not the whole truth.

"I do hope you will be able to join me this morning." Over the telephone Ingrid Lubbeke's voice had a rich, throaty timbre.

"That would be very nice."

"Tennis? Or the walk in the forest?"

"Why not both?"

He beat her at tennis easily. He was essentially a serve-and-volley player. And since his first service was hard and accurate, her return was little more than a lob to his smash. After his minor humiliation in the gym, Grantham enjoyed being able to turn the tables.

Ingrid Lubbeke came off the court after a 6-2 6-1 defeat looking rueful.

"I don't usually lose so completely."

"Tennis is my game."

"I can see that."

As they walked back into the hotel, Grantham caught sight of a row of magazines on a news-stand. He was surprised to realize that the face of his tennis partner was the same as the face on the cover of that week's *Stern* magazine. He knew now why the name Ingrid Lubbeke was familiar.

He pointed to the magazine. "That's you, isn't it? You're an actress, aren't you?"

She shrugged. "I came here to get away from all that for a week or two."

"Have you succeeded?"

"More or less. The Black Forest is a little world of its own you know. They don't see much beyond the pine trees."

She turned to him as they reached the lift. "I'm here for a rest. Why are you here?"

Grantham replied quickly, casually. "You could say the same for me."

For the second time, he told the truth, but not the whole truth.

Later that morning, they met again and walked through the forest towards Bonndorf. It was about ten kilometres altogether.

"The problem about pines," Ingrid Lubbeke volunteered after they had been walking for half an hour, "is that they don't make a rich ecological system." She pointed to the trees at either side of them. "Too many pines here. See how the mat of pine needles almost kills the undergrowth. You won't find a diversified plant life or animal life in pure pine forest. You need a variety of trees, ecologically speaking."

"How do you know about ecology?" Grantham asked. "I thought you were an actress."

"I *am* an actress. But I'm also 'into ecology', as they say. That's what the *Stern* magazine feature is about. You've heard of the Green movement in Germany? Remember how it began in the early eighties by capturing seats in Hamburg and Hesse and elsewhere? Well, it has gone from strength to strength. The Greens have identified with certain public figures; one of them is me."

Oliver Grantham made a mental note to read the *Stern* piece later.

Even without reading it, he could see that the idea made sense. Ingrid Lubbeke's performance in the gymnasium that morning had had more than a touch of professionalism about it. It was also in its way a statement of belief.

"You're a kind of cross between Jane Fonda and Brigitte Bardot?"

She laughed. "I wouldn't say that. But I have my point of view. And in Germany it's respected."

Over lunch at a café in the village of Bonndorf, Grantham came back to the question.

"The Greens are an important political force in Germany today. Do you identify with them completely?"

Ingrid Lubbeke answered the question in a roundabout way. They were sitting at an outside table at one of the high points of the Black Forest. On all sides a panorama of pine trees and pasture could be seen. It was dramatic, spectacular scenery.

"Look at that sweep of hills," Ingrid said. "Look at the forests. Look at the fields and houses. You know that the Black Forest, as you see it now, is virtually unique in Germany. If supporting the Greens means supporting all this, of course I support the Greens wholeheartedly."

She poured herself some more wine. The local white wine of the area. She passed him the carafe and he filled his own glass.

"But if you mean," she continued, "do I support absolutely everything the Greens say or do, the answer is of course 'no'. There are some crazy men involved – and women too."

Grantham waited for her to elaborate but she did not. He wondered if she was telling the truth about the extent of her involvement with the Greens.

They walked back to Schluchsee by a different route. By the time they reached the hotel, it was well after five o'clock. It had been a long and as far as Grantham was concerned a very enjoyable day.

"You sent me a little message this morning and I was glad to receive it. May I return the compliment? Would you have dinner with me this evening?"

The language was a little stilted; too much of the soldier in it. But the meaning was clear.

Ingrid Lubbeke smiled at him. "Haven't you seen enough of me for today?"

"I'd like to see a lot more of you. No *double-entendre* intended."

"Are you sure?"

"Sure about what?"

"Sure about the 'no *double-entendre*'?"

Grantham laughed. "Well, not entirely sure!"

Back in his room, he rang for the maid and wondered whether Greta would still be on duty. If she was, he decided he would indicate gently but firmly that once was quite enough.

But Greta was not on duty. Another girl came to the door. Grantham asked her to go down to the lobby and buy him the current issue of *Stern* magazine. He spent half an hour reading a two-thousand-word article, with photographs, on Ingrid Lubbeke. Though he missed some of the nuances, he got the gist of the piece. And the photographs in any case spoke for themselves.

Over dinner, she asked him: "What do *you* do in real life? I mean when you're not getting fit in the gym, or playing tennis, or walking twenty kilometres through the woods?"

"I was a soldier. Now I'm a civilian."

"Just that? A full time professional civilian?"

"You could call it that."

Grantham hated answering a direct question about himself. It made him acutely nervous. His experience of life was that if you told people things, then somehow, one way or another, they managed to use them against you. He remembered once, as a child, he had admitted to his mother that he did not like parsnips; and his mother, who believed in the principle that children should like whatever was set before them, had never let him forget it. In later life, he was often guided by what he came to refer to as the "parsnip principle": never say anything about yourself, or about anything else for that matter, which you don't absolutely need to say.

In this particular case he deviated to a trifling extent from his normally strict application of the parsnips principle.

"Do tunnels bore you?" he asked.

"No. Do you bore tunnels?"

He was delighted by the quickness of her wit. "Yes, as a matter of fact, I do. Or I will."

By the end of the evening, he had told her a good deal about the project. She was fascinated.

"Of course," she told him, "I know about the scheme. Everybody does. I knew the political decision had been taken. But even so, I don't think I've ever quite realized that this is something that is really going to happen. At last, after hundreds of years, England is going to be linked with the Continent!" She looked at him in an open, innocent way. "What about terrorists? Won't the tunnel under the Channel be a sitting target? How can you guard against a terrorist attack?"

Grantham sensed a wind of caution blowing somewhere behind his left ear. There was much that he admired about the woman who sat opposite him. Not least, he reflected, the generous cleavage that he had kept in view most of the evening. But that did not mean to say you gave away trade secrets just for the hell of it.

"We've thought about the terrorist problem," he mumbled. "We've got some ideas on it. But these are early days, you know."

He was not to be drawn further on that particular subject.

After dinner they went outside. She put her arm in his.

"I'm glad I met you, Oliver. There's a lot of nonsense in an actress's life. You rush around from here to there. Spend hours on make-up, hours – sometimes days – on one take. You look back at the year and ask yourself: did I do anything I really wanted to do? Did I meet anyone I really wanted to meet?"

She was about four inches shorter than he was, and she had to raise herself on her toes to reach him. She kissed him on the mouth. Pulled him towards her. Her arm circled the back of his head, and her fingers took hold of the hair on his neck – fiercely, almost viciously.

She pulled away to look at him.

"When I met you this morning in the gym, I knew at once that you were something special. And I'm not just saying that. I mean it. Sometimes you can tell."

She had one of the Hetzel Hotel's ultra-large apartments – fifty-five cubic metres of it altogether – looking south over the lake. It was strewn with her things.

"This is my holiday," she explained, as she saw him making a mental note of the disorder. "I don't get much holiday a year. Believe it or not, we actresses work very hard. But when I'm on holiday, I want to do just as I like. I don't want to bother about my husband or children. I don't want to tidy up. I don't really even want them to know where I am."

Grantham had seen pictures of the husband and children in the magazine article. From what he'd been able to gather, Mr Schwarz was a successful business man in Cologne and the children, whose names he had now forgotten, were at school there. Ingrid Lubbeke, like so many other professional women, used her maiden name.

For a moment, Grantham wondered who was seducing whom. Then he decided that wasn't the question. Married people, when they met other married people, did not have time for seduction. Not normally anyway. They just had to get on with it.

They got on with it.

At one point, when he called her Greta by mistake, she rebuked him.

"My name is Ingrid, not Greta."

"I didn't call you Greta," he lied, "I said: 'that's better'."

And, of course, it *was* better.

She put her legs round his back and he buried his face in her neck. They rose and fell together. He shut his eyes and saw a clear firebreak leading upwards through the pine trees, with shafts of sunlight filtering through the branches. He smelt the scents of the wood, as he had known them that morning on the way to Bonndorf. He was prepared to believe at that moment that she was someone worth caring for.

At one point, determined to make it last – it was so good – he pulled away from her. She cried out in real anger: "Not now! for God's sake!"

So he concentrated on the trees, and on the clearing through the trees, and on the light filtering through the branches, so that later he could remember what it had all been about.

In the morning, he rang his wife from his hotel room. He still had Ingrid's scent on him, but that was not something that Lily would know at a distance of five hundred miles. He felt no remorse, no regret – just the feeling that last night had not been like other nights.

"Hello darling, how are you?" Lily spoke cheerfully, as soon as she heard his voice.

"Much restored, thank you. The place is the same as ever."

"Did you get some walking in?"

"Yes, lots."

They talked for a few minutes with the ease and confidence of people who had been talking to each other for years.

"Ring me from Paris, won't you? Will you be staying at the Lancaster?"

"Of course. Oh, by the way," Grantham added, "I'll be seeing Konrad von Rilke for lunch today. I'll send him your regards."

"Oh, do! I was always very fond of Konrad."

Grantham replaced his receiver. He smiled. There had been more than one reason for his journey to the Black Forest. Yes, he had needed a break. But, even more important than that, now that he was back in civilian life he wanted to pick up the threads with one or two of his old mates from NATO days. Like, for example, Lieutenant General Konrad von Rilke, former Commander of the German Army's Third Panzer Division, and now a leading banker.

5

It was pouring with rain when he left the hotel around mid morning. He drove up past Titisee into the Hollenthal Gorge with the strains of Wagner coming from the car radio. The mood of the music matched the mood of the place. The mist had not yet lifted from the pine trees; the defile was narrow and foreboding. The cars crawled nose to bumper, each driver following the lights in front of him. Road signs warned of falling rocks.

After one particularly long hold-up, Grantham consulted his road map and decided to try to find a back way through the mountains. He pulled off to the right onto a narrow metalled road which appeared to lead in the right direction. After two miles the surface crumbled into a bare dirt track. It was an eerie experience. Visibility was down to forty metres. Grantham began to feel disoriented. It was like flying without instruments.

He halted the car; switched off the engine; sat there waiting for the mist to clear. He didn't wish to plunge over a precipice. When the mist didn't clear, he drove on slower than before. Zigzagging upwards, he sensed rather than saw the sun breaking through the mist. Moments later, the great alluvial plain of the Rhine lay spread out below him. From Freiburg to Karlsruhe the land shone with noonday brightness. In escaping from the Hollenthal Gorge he had – it seemed – escaped the micro-climate that affected it as well.

Like a rivulet running into a stream which then becomes a river, the dirt track on which Grantham had been driving for the last hour turned into a minor road which in due course joined a major road. The sun told Grantham he was heading in the right direction. He looked at his watch. This was one occasion when it would not do to be late.

The Auberge de l'Ill at Illhaeusern is the proud possessor of three stars in the Michelin. Lying north of Colmar, and south of Strasbourg, west of the Rhine and east of the Vosges, Illhaeusern is an unpretentious village in an unpretentious area. This is not a great gastronomic centre like, say, Lyons. But the food rates the guide's highest testimonial: "*vaut le voyage*".

This was something Grantham had discovered during his time in Germany. He had also discovered, after a couple of fruitless trips across the Rhine into France, that booking ahead, preferably booking months ahead, was the only way of being sure of a table. In January, he had booked for July.

He drove fast, making up for lost time. At eighteen minutes past noon he crossed the Rhine into France. There were no border formalities; he was merely waved on through by a bored guard. At ten minutes to one he parked outside the Auberge de l'Ill knowing that, at least, he hadn't lost the table.

The tall German, who had been standing by the river with a glass of Kir Royal in his hand, turned when he saw Grantham enter the garden of the inn. He strode over and greeted him warmly.

"Ah, Oliver, my dear fellow. How good to see you! I was beginning to wonder whether you'd forgotten our date. Six months is a long time, and I know you've been very busy since then."

Oliver Grantham smiled. "I said I'd be here and I am here, am I not? I'm sorry I'm a few minutes late. Some awful weather in the Black Forest delayed me."

They went straight to the table. Menu in hand, Grantham looked his old friend over.

"You're looking well, Konrad. It's four years since I've seen you, but you haven't changed."

"I told you civilian life was fun," replied von Rilke. "I've been with the Dresdner Bank for three years now, Oliver, and I can assure you, I've never felt better."

Grantham knew that the Dresdner Bank was one of Germany's largest banks. He also knew that von Rilke, on retiring from the army four years earlier, had moved into a very senior position in that bank. An aristocrat by birth and outlook, von Rilke had in the few short years which had intervened since he left the West German army become a key figure in that small tightly knit banking-industrial circle which, with occasional help from the politicians, directed the destinies of the country. He was also a close friend of Chancellor Kohl.

Like Grantham, von Rilke was fit; like Grantham, he was in his fifties. Unlike Grantham, he was an immensely rich man, his wealth residing mainly in large estates situated on both banks of the lower Rhine.

He leaned across the table and took the menu from Grantham. "You booked the table, let me order the food. I've been coming here longer than you have. And by the way," von Rilke continued, "lunch is on me. We're celebrating. It's four years to the day since I left the army."

Grantham protested, but was overruled. He accepted with good grace. What difference did it make, who paid for whom? Things always evened themselves out in the end.

They sat there for well over an hour. Towards the end of the meal, when he had said most of the things he had come to say, Grantham mentioned his new job.

"I know, my dear Oliver. Everyone knows. We follow these things. We're very envious of you. You ought to know that Chancellor Kohl is entirely behind the Chunnel project. He has personally told me so. He talked with your Prime Minister about it at the last Anglo-German summit. Germany may not be directly involved; but, believe me, there is no one in government circles who doesn't understand how important this scheme is for us. And I'm not just talking in terms of binding Britain tighter into the Common Market." Von Rilke lowered his voice. "No, I'm talking about the military aspects too. Britain still has forty thousand troops in West Germany. But they will not be there forever. The pressure is on to bring them back to Britain. You can't afford to keep them on the Continent."

"But . . ." Grantham began to protest.

Von Rilke wouldn't accept the interruption.

"No, Oliver, let me finish. There will be a retrenchment. That's why it's doubly important, trebly important, for there to be this fixed link into Europe; some means of conveying vast quantities of men and material over to the Continent in a very short space of time."

"And back again?"

Von Rilke took his point; he smiled. "I thought that, in the British history-books, Dunkirk was not a defeat; merely an orderly retreat."

Grantham smiled with him. How long ago that particular war seemed! He pushed his plate aside.

"Do we have different enemies today?"

"We both have the *same* enemy and, because we have the same enemy, we don't need to fight each other any longer."

They drank to that.

As they walked to their cars, von Rilke asked him: "Where are you heading now?"

"Paris. We have a meeting of the board of Chunnel Consortium. It's the first time we've all come together since the go-ahead was given. And it's the first time that I shall meet these gentlemen in my role of managing director."

"Try to see Maximilien, if you have time, while you're in Paris."

"Maximilien Miguet?" Grantham knew of only one Maximilien.

"Of course. He thinks like us. And, unlike us, he's still on the active list."

Grantham nodded. "I'll certainly try."

Displaying unaccustomed warmth (after all he was a Prussian and Prussians are not given to displays of emotion) von Rilke pulled Grantham towards him and embraced him on both cheeks.

"It's been good to see you, old friend."

"You too."

Von Rilke's driver saluted smartly as the tall German reached his car. Grantham watched him drive away.

6

Sir David Blakely brought the meeting to order.

"It's 11 a.m.," he said. "I think we had better begin."

He was a perfect chairman. Solid. Serious. Irresistibly polite. Without being in any way flashy or mercurial, he could bring eight people around a table and get the best out of them. The trick, as he saw it, was simple. Concentrate on the business in hand. As his collection of major chairmanships grew, less successful business colleagues would sometimes ask him how he did it. His advice was invariably the same:

"Simple, old boy," he would say. "Stick to the point. And always remember, there's no business, however important it may be, which cannot be concluded before lunch."

David Blakely turned to the agenda in front of him.

"Our first item is the chairman's introduction." He smiled. "I promise to be brief. If I asked for a chance to say a few words this morning, it was quite simply because this is an historic occasion and I did not think we should let it pass unnoticed."

He paused. When he saw that he had their full attention, he went on:

"This is the first time that we have met together as a board since the governments of France and the United Kingdom took the historic decision to go ahead with the Cross Channel Tunnel Project or Chunnel. Moreover, it is the first time we have met as a board since the decision was taken, by those same governments, to award the contract for the construction and operation of the Chunnel to our consortium. I think, as our first order of business, that we should record our approval of these decisions."

A round of applause greeted these words.

"I believe we should also, at this moment of history, pay tribute to those engineers and visionaries who first thought of the Channel Tunnel scheme and who, despite all setbacks, have kept it alive in the public mind. I refer, for example, to the great French engineer Albert Mathieu who in 1802 proposed a tunnel to link France at Cap Gris Nez with England at East Wear Bay near Folkestone. Or that remarkable Frenchman, Thomé de Gamond, who in the 1830s came up with various plans for tunnel and bridge schemes. We may recall also Britain's Sir Edward Watkin, one of the last great railway barons of the nineteenth century, who fought so long for a Channel tunnel; and another British engineer, Colonel Beaumont, who actually designed a machine which could bore through the chalk. In fact, Beaumont's machine, used by Watkin, may be called the grandparent of present-day tunnelling machines."

He turned to the dark-haired, expensively dressed woman who sat half way down the table on his left. "Isn't that so, Miss Delacourt?"

"Certainly." Monique Delacourt felt relaxed and invigorated by her brief holiday in Provence. Even though this was strictly Blakely's moment, she felt confident enough to venture a contribution of her own.

"As I recall, Chairman," Monique's English was stylish, yet subtly accented, "it was Baron Emile d'Erlanger who said – I hope I remember it accurately – 'The impervious grey chalk, extending from shore to shore, is as tempting a material for the engineer to bore through as Stilton would be to a mouse.' "

There was a ripple of laughter around the table.

Monique Delacourt was glad she had spoken. She had made her present felt early on. In an otherwise all-male gathering, that could be important.

"Thank you." David Blakely smiled at her. "I'm so glad you mentioned the d'Erlangers. I never knew Baron Emile. But of course I knew his nephew Leo, who became chairman of the old Channel Tunnel Company."

The smile became patently insincere.

"The Channel Tunnel Company, of course, was too far ahead of its time. Chunnel Consortium has been awarded the contract which fifty years earlier, perhaps even twenty years earlier, would have gone to them. But what a charming civilized man Leo was! My wife and I visited him just before he died. I ought to tell you, ladies and gentlemen, that one of the stipulations of Leo's will was that his coffin – and presumably its contents – should be carried on the first train which passes through the Chunnel."

His voice had grown sombre; there was the hint of a tear in the corner of one eye. Blakely knew when to lay it on.

"He told me of this when we met him. I promised him that I would do everything in my power to ensure that this wish was carried out."

David Blakely bowed his head in a brief tribute to a great man. The others followed suit. Oliver Grantham, sitting on the chairman's right, made a mental note to check on whether coffins could or should be carried on the Inaugural Train.

Sir David was nearing the end of his brief statement.

"I don't want to abuse my time. We have a lot of business to get through." He peered over his spectacles at his colleagues. "It is right that we should celebrate today. But I should like to utter one word of warning. None of us should think that the political battle is over merely because the necessary decisions have been taken by the French and British governments." He pulled out a sheet of paper from a file. "Miss Delacourt has quoted Baron Emile d'Erlanger. I, in my turn, would like to quote Winston Churchill. I'll read you his words: 'There are', Churchill said, 'few projects against which there exists a deeper and more enduring prejudice than the construction of a tunnel between Dover and Calais. Again and again it has been put forward under powerful and influential sponsorship. Again and again it has been prevented . . . To those who have consistently favoured the idea this ponderous and overwhelming resistance has always been a mystery.' "

Sir David Blakely decided, at this point, to be pretty ponderous and overwhelming himself.

"We are none of us innocents," he warned. "Watch out for opposition. For there will certainly *be* opposition. Be sure of that. Remember what Winston Churchill said."

Blakely took a sip of a glass of water. He smiled broadly around the room.

"I shall now hand over to Oliver Grantham. You are all, of course, aware of Mr Grantham's military record. Today he faces a civilian challenge equal to any that he may have faced in the past. Grantham's job is to pull this project together. To make sure it gets completed on time. As you know, Chunnel Consortium is a multi-national grouping. We have the tunnel engineers, Falaise et Cie from France. Miss Delacourt, their Chief Engineer, has already made a contribution to the discussion this morning and you will be hearing from her again later. We have the Dutch firm, Sonders N.V., who will concentrate on the complex electronic equipment necessary to ensure the proper functioning of the Chunnel." He nodded towards a long, lanky Dutchman who sat next to Monique Delacourt. "It's good to have you with us today, Tom."

Tom Anders replied: "It's a great occasion, Chairman; I'm honoured."

David Blakely continued: "And, of course, we have the two great construction companies, Marchmain Limited from Britain, and Hoffman Algemeine AG from Germany. These are the companies who are going to be responsible for undertaking the construction of the port installations and facilities on both sides of the Channel, including of course all the major work of earth-moving and clearance."

He looked up. "There you have it, ladies and gentlemen. A massive multi-national undertaking. And Oliver Grantham is the man who is going to manage the whole thing. Believe me, we will need him!"

There was a burst of spontaneous applause as Grantham rose to his feet. None of them were in any doubt that Sir David Blakely's selection of Oliver Grantham as the managing director of the Chunnel Project was inspired. In the time since he had been appointed, Grantham had already imposed his mark, and his own approach to doing business. He was a man used to leading from the front.

Looking even fitter than usual after his weekend in the Black Forest, Grantham moved down to the other end of the ornate boardroom. (They were meeting in the Avenue d'Iéna offices of the French partner, Falaise et Cie.) He referred to the first of several charts which had been pinned up on the wall.

"Phase One of the project," he began, "will be limited to conventional rail-only traffic. The single main running tunnel will be seven metres in diameter with a 4.5 metre diameter service tunnel. Phase Two will be the first stage construction of the rail track circuit and terminal facilities at each portal. This will be completed so as to permit the introduction of road vehicle ferry train services. Phase Three construction will include the building of a second seven-metre main running tunnel and the completion of the train ferry track circuit and terminal facilities. Our bankers, Browning Brothers, are confident that the required funds will be readily forthcoming from the private sector. They have advised that to raise resources from the outset to cover the cost of all three phases would be an extremely expensive operation and would result in our having to pay heavy charges on money we would not actually be using. They take the view that we should go to the market as and when we need funds."

Tom Anders, the tall Dutchman, looked sceptical. "Is that altogether prudent? I can understand the point about having capital tied up without revenue being generated to pay for it. But what happens if this market situation changes? We don't want to find ourselves with a tunnel half-dug and no money left to complete!"

David Blakely interrupted. There was a touch of menace in his voice as though to suggest that the Dutchman's point was almost, if not quite, out of order.

"I really don't think it would be right at this moment to question the wisdom of our financial advisers. I'm sure they know what they are doing. I have dealt with Browning Brothers for a quarter of a century. They know their business. I might point out that Brownings stepped in and financed the construction of the Suez Canal on a private basis when neither the French or the British governments could find the money!"

Laughter greeted this last point. Even Tom Anders joined in.

"I defer to you, Chairman," he said.

After the interruption, Grantham continued with his exposé. "I think you all know," he said, "that Chunnel Consortium, in making its bid for this project, did *not* ask for any government guarantees. In fact this was probably a crucial element in the two governments' decision to award us the contract. All the other bidders or potential bidders insisted on being indemnified at the very least against cancellation of the project for *political* reasons, that is to say by one or other of the contracting governments. But our judgement was, and remains, that the political climate is ripe for this project and that the will exists both in London and Paris to see it completed. So we will be going ahead without government completion guarantees. As I have said, our bankers are confident that the private sector will be able to generate the necessary resources."

He looked around at his audience.

"On the whole, things look pretty good. Our bankers tell us that as long as we're projecting returns above 14 per cent, we'll have no difficulty in attracting capital – whether debt or equity.

"There's only one thing that could knock the figures right down and that's *delay in construction*." He paused. They were still listening, which was a good sign. Sometimes numbers could put people to sleep quicker than Mogadon.

"When we ran these sensitivity tests, ladies and gentlemen, it became apparent that construction delay was an even more important factor as far as the rate of return was concerned than cost-overruns or revenue shortfall." He pointed to the chart. "If you build in a three-year delay, we immediately drop down to single figures. That's why timing is crucial. *We have to keep to schedule*."

Tom Anders, who was obviously in a fractious mood, again interrupted: "What happens if we run into a major geological problem? Delay may be forced upon us."

"We're not going to run into major geological problems," Grantham replied shortly. He was beginning to be irritated with Anders. He turned to David Blakely. "May I, with your permission, Chairman, invite Professor Giuseppe Finzi to address us at this point?"

David Blakely readily agreed to the suggestion. He had been personally responsible for the choice of Professor Giuseppe Finzi as the geological consultant on the Chunnel Project. Blakely had first met Finzi, one of Italy's most eminent scientists, in Rome in the 1960s. Since then Finzi had been a frequent visitor at Sir David's Tuscan villa.

Professor Finzi was well prepared. A white-haired man, now well into his sixties, he scurried down the table to stand next to Grantham.

"I will try to say what I have to say in any case with the aid of charts. This will be more intelligible."

There were chuckles from several members of the board. Finzi was an eccentric character, with a good deal of charm.

"Tom Anders," Professor Finzi resumed, "has raised the question of what will happen if we run into a major geological snag. I am quite convinced, as Mr Grantham has already said, that we will not run into such snags. Let me try to explain why."

He turned to the first of his charts.

"What you see here is the representation of the geology below the sea bed near Dover. The Lower Chalk rests directly on the Gault clay, because the Upper Greensand is missing here. The presence of similar chalk cliffs on both sides of the straits suggests continuity beneath the sea and this has indeed been confirmed on numerous occasions by borings and surveys. The Lower Chalk is also known as the Cenomanian, or 'Grey' chalk. Its thickness ranges from two hundred and sixty feet on the English side to two hundred and ten feet on the French side. It is a chalk marl with substantial clay content. This contributes plasticity and low permeability. In fact it is easily excavated, and self-supporting at the tunnel face at least for the necessary time. I would point out," Professor Finzi continued, "that the pilot tunnels of 1882 still remain sound."

"What you're saying, Professor," commented Blakely from the other end of the table, "is that a tunnel line driven through the Lower Chalk below the sea bed should encounter no major geological problems?"

"Precisely. I would go further even," said Finzi. "I have been studying tunnelling conditions in different parts of the world for many years. From a technical point of view, I do not believe you could ask for a more favourable stratum than the Lower Chalk."

"Stilton to a mouse?" Blakely reminded them of the quotation Monique had used earlier. They all laughed. It had been a good morning so far. Even Tom Anders seemed satisfied with Professor Finzi's replies.

The meeting ended with champagne. Grantham circulated among the members of the board. Blakely was right. Nothing could be more important than getting to know each and every one of them individually.

Forgetting his earlier irritation, he went up to Tom Anders. "I'm glad you pressed Finzi on the geology point. Were you satisfied with the answer?"

"I think so. Finzi seems to know his stuff." Tom Anders smiled. "Of course, the proof of the pudding will be in eating. Isn't that what you British say?"

Momentarily Grantham wondered whether in fact Anders still had doubts, but was diplomatically keeping them to himself. The mood at the meeting that morning had not been one of caution; no one liked to be a spoil-sport.

Grantham returned to his hotel later that evening, after dining with friends. He was staying at the Lancaster, just off the Champs-Elysées. He usually stayed there when he was in Paris. It was a small, friendly hotel. He had complete confidence in the discretion of the management. Not, he thought ruefully, that there was any need for discretion under the present circumstances.

He saw the large brown envelope propped against the elegant Louis XVI looking-glass as soon as he entered his room. Since he was not expecting anything to be delivered to him at the hotel, he examined it carefully from a distance. His full name, correctly spelt, had been typed on the label. There was no other marking of any kind.

He called down to the desk and asked to be put through to the security officer.

"There's a package in my room. I'm not sure where it comes from. Would you possibly make enquiries and call me back?"

A few minutes later, the security officer called back.

"The envelope was delivered this evening, by messenger, while you were out."

"Despatch rider?"

"Yes."

"Do you know the firm?"

"I'm afraid not."

Grantham decided to play it safe. He asked the security officer to come and remove the envelope and to subject it to a proper scrutiny.

"You have machines for that, I suppose?"

"Of course, sir."

The man came and collected the envelope. Grantham handed him fifty francs. It seemed a small price to pay to avoid the risk of being blown up.

Ten minutes later the man was back. There was a smirk on his face which Grantham found distasteful.

"Just photographs, sir." The man laid the envelope on the table.

"Photographs?" Grantham was surprised. There was no reason why anyone should be sending him photographs. Certainly not now.

When the man had left, still smirking, Grantham picked up the envelope. Inside were four glossy six-by-eight-inch black-and-white photographs. He recognized the man in the photographs as himself. He recognized the girl as Greta, the German room maid who had made his bed, and lain in it, at the Hetzel Hotel in the Black Forest a few days earlier. And without being unduly imaginative he could recognize, too, what he and Greta were up to.

He picked up the telephone again. Within seconds he had dialled through to the Hetzel Hotel.

"Can I speak to the manager, please, Peter Drexner?"

The manager come on the line.

"Mr Drexner? This is Oliver Grantham here. No, I'm in Paris. A quick question – I'll tell you the reason some other time. Do you still have a girl called Greta working for you? She was on the sixth floor while I was there last weekend."

"I'll check."

It took Peter Drexner only a few moments to establish that Greta Gottlieb had left the service of the hotel at the end of the previous week.

"If you find out where she's gone, can you let me know? You've got a note of my office address and the phone number. Call me anyway."

After he had replaced the receiver, Grantham examined the photographs once again. He smiled. Why were some people so silly as to imagine that a man could be blackmailed by photographs depicting him indulging, to the evident enjoyment of both parties, in some perfectly innocent heterosexual activity? He sighed. The problem with blackmailers was that they were so old-fashioned. Didn't they know that life had moved on? Adultery wasn't on the list any longer. Not in his view, anyway.

He tossed the envelope and its contents into the waste-paper basket. On the whole, he thought, as he got ready for bed, the other side – whoever the other side was – had made a mistake.

He was just about to turn the light off when he had second thoughts. He got out of bed, walked across the room and removed the envelope from the bin. He then sat down at the *escritoire*, picked up the ivory-handled pen which the Hotel Lancaster thoughtfully provided for its guests and readdressed the package to: Greta Gottlieb, Sixth Floor, the Hetzel Hotel, Hochschwarzwald, Schluchsee, Germany. He wrote: PLEASE FORWARD on the envelope. Inside, he scribbled a short note: "Thanks so much for letting me see these. Please keep them as a memento of a wonderful morning." He signed and dated the note, taking care that both signature and date were legible.

Grantham returned to his bed. The old truisms, he mused, as he drifted off to sleep, were often the best. Attack was always a good method of defence.

General Maximilien Miguet had invited Grantham to breakfast at the Travellers Club on the Champs-Elysées.

"Any friend of von Rilke is a friend of mine," he had told Grantham over the telephone.

Grantham walked over from the Lancaster and arrived, as planned, at half past eight. He had been to the Travellers Club before. It was an imposing building of classical design set back from the main thoroughfare.

The doorman was expecting him. "The General is in the library."

A short, wiry man was standing by a table in the middle of the cavernous room looking over the morning's newspapers. He turned as Grantham came in. "General Grantham?"

Grantham had almost forgotten how it felt to be called "General", since he had dropped his military title when he left the army. That phase of his life now seemed far away and long ago.

"General Miguet?"

The two men shook hands.

"Of course I've heard a lot about you," Maximilien Miguet said over breakfast. "You had a 'good war', isn't that what you say?"

"I was lucky," replied Grantham. "I think we were all lucky. The Falklands campaign could have been a fiasco. Fortunately, it wasn't."

Maximilien Miguet cast a professional soldier's eye over his guest and obviously approved of what he saw. "I'm sorry you left the army. Britain needs men like you, I'm sure."

"I've got other work to do now." Oliver Grantham had gone on to explain his current assignment. Miguet had been impressed.

"What a massive undertaking!" the Frenchman had exclaimed. "If you pull it off, your name will go down in the history books. Like de Lesseps."

"I'm no de Lesseps. I'm just part of a team." Grantham had shrugged modestly.

It was an agreeable breakfast which passed quickly. Before the two men separated, Grantham put a question to Maximilien Miguet which had been in the forefront of his mind since the previous evening.

"I know that, as a military man, you're above politics, General; so don't answer this unless you feel you can. But I'd like to find out how you see the current political situation in France. Take, for example, my own pet concern: the Channel Tunnel project. Your government seems to be committed today. But what about two or three years from now? Will the political determination still be there? Remember, it may take years for the Chunnel to be completed. The record of Anglo-French co-operation on major projects is not very encouraging. Forgive me for being frank."

"The Concorde is still flying, isn't it?"

"Only just," Grantham replied. "And in any case, the way the Concorde treaty was written made it virtually impossible for either government to pull out. But that is not the case with the Chunnel."

General Miguet brushed a crumb of croissant from his trim, black moustache. He folded his napkin and then drained a last mouthful of coffee.

"I don't mind answering your question." He looked Grantham straight in the eye. "But, of course, I would not care to be quoted. My own belief is that under the Socialists things are going from bad to worse. I do not care to predict the future for my country. Build your tunnel! We need it. But, for God's sake, build it fast!"

General Miguet walked Grantham to the door. "I shall stay at the club a few minutes longer," he explained. "I have some telephoning to do."

Grantham walked out onto the Champs-Elysées with the powerful feeling that neither he nor France had heard the last of General Maximilien Miguet. General de Gaulle had waited twelve years on the sidelines at Colombey-les-Deux-Eglises before taking up the reins of power. There had been echoes of de Gaulle in Miguet's last remarks. Was he, too, waiting on the sidelines?

He looked left, up the great avenue, towards the Arc de Triomphe. He looked right, down the avenue, towards the Place de la Concorde. What a city Paris was! What a country was France! By Jove, he thought,

Miguet was right. Something had gone wrong with the natural order of things. Socialism was too gross a penalty to be inflicted on such a great and glorious land! France's destiny surely lay elsewhere!

7

For Oliver Grantham and David Blakely the third day of the Lords Test was not to be missed unless there were very good reasons. Both men had been members of the MCC for almost as long as they could wield a bat. Grantham remembered wearing the orange and yellow MCC tie knotted nonchalantly around his waist when he'd walked out to the wicket on the afternoon of the Eton and Harrow match to score his first (and, as it happened, last) half century at Lords.

Grantham had taken his seat in the Pavilion soon after lunch. He had been joined by Blakely half an hour later. Grantham summarized the position.

"It's fairly even at the moment, I'd say. England had a first innings lead of thirty runs. Now they're sixty for two in the second innings. Botham has just gone in. He's batting now."

As he spoke, the ball – hit mightily by Botham from the Nursery end – soared toward the Pavilion and bounced against the side of the commentator's box.

"Yes, I rather imagined that might be Ian Botham." David Blakely smiled and settled down beside his friend to enjoy an afternoon's cricket.

By tea, England were a hundred and fifty for two. Botham had already scored fifty and was racing towards his century. There was a flurry of interest in the Pavilion as the Queen arrived to meet the players on both sides.

"She'll probably stay at least till Botham's out," Grantham overheard one old boy saying to another.

"She'll stay anyway, I expect," the second man replied. "She usually does when we're playing Australia."

After meeting the players, the Queen came into the Members' tea room. She was escorted by the President of the MCC, Lord Coulton.

"Donald Coulton is a very old friend of mine," said Blakely. "I think we might go and say hello. Come along."

It was the first time that Oliver Grantham had seen Her Majesty at close quarters since that brief but memorable ceremony at Buckingham Palace when she had presented him with the DSO for his part in the Falklands campaign. And he certainly didn't expect the Queen to remember him.

But she did. "Goose Green, wasn't it?" she asked.

"Exactly, Ma'am," Grantham replied.

"And what are you doing now?" It was not a *pro forma* question. There was real interest in her voice.

"The Channel Tunnel," he answered. "I've been appointed managing director of the Chunnel Consortium."

"Oh, really? That's going to keep you busy for years, isn't it? I hope I shall ride through it one day when it's finished."

"I promise you, Ma'am, you will be receiving an invitation to the Great Inaugural!"

The Queen gave a warm little laugh and moved on, her small retinue going with her. Grantham looked round to see that Sir David Blakely had disappeared. Probably gone for a pee, he thought. No sense in going for a pee later, with Botham at the crease. You might miss the best six of the afternoon.

He stood by the open window, gazing down onto the green sward as the umpires walked slowly out after the tea interval. He had just about decided not to wait for Blakely any longer but to take his seat on the benches outside, when Lord Coulton came up to him.

"I didn't have a chance back there to say how awfully glad I am to meet you. As you can imagine, I've been rather busy making sure Her Majesty isn't mobbed by small boys seeking autographs."

Grantham laughed, taking an instant liking to the tall peer whose reputation in Britain's business community was every bit as high as that of Sir David Blakely himself. But whereas Blakely was essentially a chairman, a boardroom heavyweight, Donald Coulton had a more mercurial personality altogether. His mind thrived best at the frontiers of science. There were many areas of modern technological development where Donald Coulton had played a part, and often a major part.

On the field below, the umpires had now been joined by the players. The match was about to resume. Coulton peered out of the window, spectacles perched on his long thin nose and dark hair receding sharply from the high bronzed dome of his head.

"I had better be getting along," he said. "The Queen is bound to be thinking up some tricky question about the no-ball rule to ask me." He turned serious. "Do give me a call at my office, won't you? I feel sure we have things to talk about."

Grantham returned to his seat next to Blakely in time to see Ian Botham caught on the boundary for seventy-five. There was much applause for the returning hero. When things had calmed down again, Blakely said:

"I saw you talking to Don Coulton back there in the pavilion."

"Yes. He said we should meet."

"So you should. There's no finer mind than Coulton's. It was largely because of Coulton that Marchmain joined the Consortium. Of course, he has a finger in just about every pie. But Marchmain is one of his main interests."

They watched for a further hour. With Botham's departure, some of the fire and fun seemed to have gone out of the game.

"It looks as though England's heading for a draw." Blakely gathered up his things. "We might make tracks, don't you think?"

Grantham agreed.

They stood at the gate by Lord's Tavern waiting for the chauffeur to bring up the Rolls.

"The problem about five-day cricket," said Grantham, "is that it takes five days. There simply isn't time."

The car drew up beside them and they got in.

"You don't have to watch five-day cricket," commented Blakely. "You can watch three-day matches or one-day matches if you like. They have a different flavour, but they're still recognizably cricket. You *compress the time-frame*. That's all."

An hour later, when Grantham walked through the door of his suburban house in Fleet, Hants (so far he had resisted all Sir David Blakely's blandishments about moving to London), the words "compress the time-frame" hit him with a sudden overwhelming force. You could change from five-day matches to one-day matches and still play cricket. Couldn't you build a tunnel in one year, say, instead of five years? Wouldn't it still be a tunnel? All you needed to do was "compress the time-frame". All?

Grantham was silent throughout most of supper.

"What's the matter, darling?" his wife asked him. "Didn't you have a good day?"

"I had a very good day. I met the Queen and Botham scored a

splendid seventy-five. I'm just thinking." Grantham smiled at his wife. "You suppose I'm a keep-fit fanatic. But I do think sometimes, you know."

Lily could get nothing more out of him. Good-humouredly she cleared the table and left him to it.

Half an hour later Grantham came into the sitting room, where his wife was watching television, with a triumphant look on his face.

"I've got it! You know, Lily, I think I've got it!"

"Got what?"

"How to compress the time-frame! How to build the tunnel in one year, not five!"

"Well?" She sounded sceptical.

Grantham seized her by the shoulder. "You stand over there and be France," he said. "I'll stand over here and be England. In between us is the Straits of Dover, do you understand?"

Feeling like a child in a school play, Lily went to stand at the other side of the room.

"Now," Grantham continued. "You want to dig a tunnel under the sea. What do you do?"

Lily looked down at the fine Persian carpet bought in their pre-school-fee days, which now separated her from her husband. She seemed to be puzzled.

"I guess you start on one side and come out the other side," she replied. "That's what you normally do with tunnels, don't you?"

"No, my girl," Grantham said firmly. "That's just what you don't do. Not if you want to compress the time-frame. You don't start on one side and dig through to the other side. That's the typical, traditional way of going about things and it will take you an age. *You start in the middle.* That's what you do. Start in the middle!"

She looked at him with concern. "You didn't sit out in the sun too long today at Lords?"

But Grantham was halfway out of the room.

"Where are you going?" she called after him.

"More thinking," he called back.

She did not see him again until well after midnight when he crawled into bed beside her.

"How did the thinking go?"

"It went very well," Grantham grunted and went to sleep.

8

Less than a week later, Oliver Grantham flew in a Marchmain plane to Dyce airport, Aberdeen, where a Westland helicopter also belonging to Marchmain was waiting to take him out to the oil-field. Visibility was poor, a summer mist enveloping the North Sea. After an hour's level flight during which time Grantham could tell he was over water but not much else besides, the helicopter banked and dropped.

A reception party was waiting for him at the pad. Grantham stepped down from the helicopter, ducking his head instinctively to avoid the still turning rotor-blades.

A bearded young man wearing a blue Marchmain anorak and over it an orange life-jacket came forward to greet him.

"My name is Michael Prestwick. I'm the chief research scientist on board Marchmain 58 – that's the number we've given to the production platform here. I'll show you round on top and then, if you don't mind, we'll go below. It's a bit blowy up here today." He handed Grantham an anorak and a lifejacket. "Please wear the lifejacket", Prestwick said, "whenever you're in an open area. We're very strict on safety regulations. We have to be. Ninety-nine per cent of all accidents are due to a failure to observe elementary safety precautions."

Grantham nodded. "It's just the same in the army."

They went below into the living area.

"We can use the cinema," Prestwick said. "There'll be no one there at this time."

The "cinema" was a large room, capable of seating forty in comfort.

"What I'm going to show you", Prestwick began, "is a film which Marchmain have just made under my responsibility. We have called it *The Total Subsea Production Concept*. Some of the experimental work which is described in the film has been carried out from Marchmain 58.

We have a recorded commentary," Prestwick added, "but it may be simpler if I give it myself."

"Any way you like."

Prestwick started the film. "The first five minutes or so", he said, "deal with existing systems of offshore oil production, mainly in the North Sea. As I explained a moment ago, both the first-generation and second-generation structures were fixed or bottom-mounted structures. But towards the end of the 1970s a new concept was introduced, namely the floating system. You can call this the third generation if you like. Basically you have a buoyant platform moored over subsea well-heads. This enables the structure to rise and fall with the tides.

"What Marchprod – our new system – does is to combine the essential features of both the fixed and the floating production systems. You have a bottom-mounted platform, but at the same time the platform can adjust to the action of waves, currents and windforces."

Grantham watched with growing fascination. This was not science fiction, he had to remind himself. This was the reality. The frontiers of exploration had moved on. The oil men nowadays were not tall Texans with five-gallon hats, but promising-looking youths from Newcastle and Glasgow with doctorates in geology or computer science.

As the film came to an end, Michael Prestwick addressed himself directly to Grantham.

"Our major challenge, Mr Grantham – and it's one we're fairly sure we've solved – was to combine the essential features of the subsea production complex with the articulated buoyant column which we saw earlier in the film. In summary, we have linked the compliant Marchprod column, running down from the surface plinth, to the subsea production complex itself. That column will house a one-atmosphere access shaft to be used for personnel or material transport or for the export of product."

He switched on the lights. "Do you have any questions?"

Oliver Grantham did have a question but this was not the time or the place to ask it. He stood up.

"I can't tell you how grateful I am to have had a chance to see this," he said. "I do hope I haven't taken up too much of your time."

Michael Prestwick also stood up. "We're all part of the same team."

The weather had cleared by the early afternoon. The helicopter flew back into Aberdeen at a height of about three thousand feet. Grantham could see the oil platforms spread out below in the different fields. Once again, he thought what a rough environment it was. The surge and swell of the sea seemed to be increasing by the minute. There were white-topped breakers everywhere.

Something about the pilot's manner of flying made Grantham suspect that he had a military background.

"Were you in the Navy?" he asked.

"Ten years." The pilot nodded. "I joined Marchmain when I came out. They needed helicopter pilots for their North Sea operations."

"Did you go to the Falklands?"

"I did. A rum show, that was. I was flying Sea King helicopters then, of course."

"I did a bit of flying myself, when I had time."

"I thought I recognized you, General, when I picked you up," the pilot said. "Good to have you on board, sir!"

Grantham took over the controls for the next twenty minutes, only relinquishing them on the approach to Dyce airport. The Lear executive jet was waiting on the runway, engines running.

Grantham shook hands with the pilot. "Thanks for the ride."

"Any time."

Grantham hit the ground running.

On board the executive jet, the steward offered him a drink and the evening paper. A news item, tucked away on an inside page, caught his attention. The headline read: GREEK SHIPOWNER IN CHANNEL FERRY TAKEOVER. Datelined Athens, the *Standard* story announced that Georgios Karapolitis, owner and founder of Karapolitis Lines, had made a successful bid for Channel Ferries. Mr Karapolitis was reported as saying: "I have great faith in the cross-Channel business. Karapolitis Lines are wholly international in outlook and this is one of the most important international shipping routes in the world." The story went on to add that Mr Karapolitis had been asked at a press conference whether or not he thought that the construction of a Channel Tunnel would make a difference to his business. The Greek shipowner, according to the *Standard* story, was reported to have expressed considerable scepticism about the possibility of the Channel Tunnel being finally constructed. "And in any case," Mr Karapolitis had continued, "even if it is built, we do not expect it to have more than a marginal impact on our operation."

At the end of the story was a report of a statement made in London, at the same time as the Athens announcement, by Brian Staples, owner and operator of Channel Ferries. Staples had apparently said that he was "thrilled and delighted by the recent move by Karapolitis Lines. This will put the long-term operations of Channel Ferries on a much sounder basis." Grantham read that Staples had expressed the conviction that he himself would be retaining a key role in the new business.

As they came in to land at Heathrow, he folded the paper and put it in his briefcase. The time had come, he thought, to find out a bit more about Mr Karapolitis.

Iona Karapolitis stayed on after her father had returned to Athens at the end of his brief unannounced visit to Britain. Brian Staples took her to lunch at the Ritz. He also booked a room for the night under an assumed name and warned his wife that, even though Parliament had risen for the summer, he would probably be delayed by business in town and would not therefore be returning to Felixstowe that evening.

Lunch, as it turned out, was a strictly business affair. There was no hint of remembered intimacy in Iona's manner. Staples quickly learned that the young woman was more than the heir apparent to the Karapolitis empire; she was also the force behind the throne. Now that Karapolitis had taken over Channel Ferries, Brian Staples had become just another employee. Talking to Iona over lunch that day at the Ritz, Staples had the unpleasant sensation that he was being eaten alive, like the oysters they had just consumed.

As they neared the end of the meal, he grew increasingly depressed. He desperately wanted to go to bed again with the lovely creature who sat opposite him. But she gave no sign at all of having similar ideas. Staples realized with considerable bitterness that he was getting precisely nowhere and would continue to get precisely nowhere. He might as well not have booked the room. In his heart he was not surprised at the way things had turned out. However good he might or might not have been at making money, he had never had much of a way with women. Other men, more physically unprepossessing than he, did not have much trouble. But Staples not only lacked beauty; he lacked charm as well.

Wiping sweaty palms on the table cloth out of sight, he asked her: "Would you care to see the sights afterwards?"

Her reply was cool, almost icy. "No, thank you. I spent two years in London. I know the sights."

"Can I drop you anywhere, then?"

"Actually, you could. Paddington."

On their way to the station, Iona Karapolitis told Staples the reason for her planned excursion to the West Country. She did so, however, not because of any inherent warmth of feeling towards the man; simply because she knew she might need him later, if only for logistical support. She might be able to stay in England for several days, or even weeks, at a time; but she would never be able to stay on a permanent basis given the other demands on her time and given, too, her natural preference for the Mediterranean way of life.

She had more or less finished what she had to say as they drove down the ramp into the station.

He looked at her with grudging admiration. "Who thought of that idea?"

"Actually I did. I told daddy and he agreed. We put our people to work making enquiries as soon as you left Poros. It's a matter of exploring all the angles, not just the obvious ones. Sometimes, you have to be nasty. I've learned that from daddy too."

He could not resist saying: "Bully for daddy!"

For the first time since his visit to Greece, she gave him the warm, dazzling smile that he remembered so well.

As she got out of the car, still smiling, she handed him a large brown envelope, "Could you post this for me? I've got to rush for the train."

"Of course."

The envelope was already stamped. After Iona had left, Staples put it into a letter-box at the station. He was surprised to notice the address. How nasty could the Karapolitises, father and daughter, be, he wondered?

She took a taxi at Taunton station. Iona Karapolitis told the driver where to go.

"That's about forty miles from here," the man said in a broad Somerset accent. "We can go over the Brendons."

"I don't mind which way we go."

As they drove past Bishops Lydeard and up into the Brendon Hills, Iona Karapolitis recalled the last time she had visited England for an extended stay. She had told Staples she had spent two years in London. That was the truth. Two years in the sixth form at St Paul's Girls School under the tutelage of its celebrated High Mistress Julia Swanson, or "Swanny" as she was more familiarly known to her pupils, had given her more poise and intellectual punch than her arch-rival, Christina Onassis, had acquired in a lifetime of jet-setting. She had worked hard; and she had played hard too.

It was during her stay in London that she had fallen in love for the first time. Deeply, irrevocably in love.

While the car rolled along the narrow, windy road with its high uncut hedges, Iona Karapolitis cast her mind back across the gap of almost ten years to Tommy Plowright, the man she had wanted to marry. She remembered the passionate affair they had had, how he used to come and wait for her after class, parking his red MG the other side of Brook Green opposite the school gates, so that he could watch her emerge. And she remembered how she would feel a little jump of joy every time she saw him sitting there with his gloved hands resting lightly on the steering wheel and his light brown hair just falling over his collar.

Then one day the little red MG wasn't there; and Tommy Plowright wasn't there. Instead there were whispers in the school corridors and sympathetic looks from knowing friends and finally a talk from "Swanny" herself. "Swanny" had been firm but kind. She could not condone – serious boyfriends were always discouraged – but she could understand and sympathize. She refused to let Iona go to the inquest.

Tommy Plowright's death through an overdose (the inquest left open the matter of whether it was accidental or deliberate) left a deep mark on Iona. Amongst other things, it put her off men. She was prepared to use them, as they used women, for sexual gratification. But she did not wish ever again to become emotionally involved with them. Iona Karapolitis was charming and beautiful but underneath – as Brian Staples had found out – she was hard. For her, it was a matter of self-defence.

Half an hour out of Taunton, the driver pulled the car into a clearing at the top of a hill and pointed out the view.

"That's the Bristol Channel. And over there is Wales. It usually means rain if you can see Wales from here."

Iona Karapolitis roused herself from her daydreams. She looked at the sweep of land running down from where they were to the water's edge five miles away. In the distance, the combine-harvesters were working their way through the standing corn. The wheat-fields were interspersed with clumps of trees. What a green and golden land England was, thought Iona, at least when the sun shone. She got out of the car, grateful to stretch her legs. The driver followed suit. He lit a cigarette and offered her one. "Are you from these parts, miss?"

"No, I'm from Athens."

"Well, that's a long way from Taunton, I'm sure."

The Brendon Hills ran into Exmoor itself. Winsford, Iona's destination, lay in the heart of the moor.

"It's a pretty little place," the driver said. "I haven't had a run over this way for quite a few weeks. It makes a nice change."

They stopped to ask the way at the local store-*cum*-post office. Iona noticed on the house opposite, a plaque which said: ERNEST BEVIN STATESMAN LIVED HERE. There were geese on the village green and peacocks outside the pub, the Royal Oak.

The driver emerged from the store. "Apparently the turning off is a mile or two beyond the village," he told her. "On the road to Exford."

Before driving on Iona decided she ought to book a room for the night somewhere, just in case her business took a long time and she was unable to catch the last train back to London from Taunton.

"Do you think they have rooms at the Royal Oak?" she asked the driver.

"They do. But you'd be lucky to get one now. This is the busy season."

She was lucky. The burly, jovial landlord of the Royal Oak liked the look of her and found her a room under the thatch. She left her bags as an earnest of her return.

Two miles past Winsford, the road swung round to the right in a wide bend, leaving the river Exe which it had been following for the past few miles. As it did so, another, much smaller road, nothing more than a farm track, turned away left-handed to follow the river upwards through a steep sided valley in the direction of its source. Iona had all the time in the world to observe and absorb the scenery since the pot-holed state of the road made speed impossible. On the right hand side of the track as they drove along it, the Exe sparkled and bubbled crystal clear. Like a mountain stream in Greece, thought Iona.

"What kind of bird is that?" she asked as a large grey bird, with long legs which it had tucked up in flight, flapped away ahead of them.

"That's a heron," the driver said. "And over there's a pair of buzzards." He pointed to two large birds which hung with wings outstretched almost motionless above the valley.

Iona saw one of the birds stoop and fall through the air like a stone. Seconds later, the other followed suit.

"Picked up a vole or a rabbit, I'd say," the driver commented. "You can see deer here too if you're lucky."

"What kind of deer?"

"Red deer. The wild red deer of Exmoor. The stags are great big fellows with horns. Antlers we call them."

After a mile and half the valley broadened. The farm-track crossed the river over a narrow rickety wooden bridge and rose a hundred feet or so.

"I think that's the house you're looking for." The driver pointed to a pretty, white-fronted cottage set apart from a group of buildings which was obviously the main farm. "That's where Mrs Potter lives, or so they said in the village."

Iona paid the man, adding a generous tip, and walked up the path towards the cottage. Some terriers ran out to meet her, barking and yapping. A woman, well into her seventies, but sprightly of step, followed the dogs.

"Down, Sheba! Down, Scrumpy! I'm sorry about the dogs," Mrs Potter apologized, taking Iona's hand. "But I live on my own here. Since I'm rather hard of hearing, they let me know when someone is coming!"

She beamed at her guest and took her into the sitting room while she busied herself in the kitchen making tea.

"We ought to have a proper cream tea," she called cheerfully through the open door. "But I don't have any cream and I don't have any scones. I've some cake though. Would you like some cake?"

Raising her voice so as to be sure of being heard, Iona replied that, yes, she would love some cake.

Tea, when it finally arrived, was surprisingly elegant. Mrs Potter had dug out her family silver in honour of the occasion.

"It's not often I have a chance to use the Watkin tea set, living here the way I do. I'm glad you've given me an excuse. I believe in keeping up standards."

The woman shot Iona a challenging glance and Iona hastily agreed that she too believed in keeping up standards. There was, she decided, just the right note of conviction in her voice. The High Mistress of St Paul's would have been proud of her.

Mention of the Watkin tea set reminded Mrs Potter of the purpose of Iona's visit.

"You want to talk about great-grandfather Edward, don't you? Did you say you are writing a book?"

"No, not a book. Just an article."

Mrs Potter seemed disappointed. "I think you ought to do a book. There's masses of material. He was a fascinating old boy."

"Perhaps I will be able to expand the article," Iona replied judiciously. "In any case I'm most anxious to find out what I can about Sir Edward Watkin. Now that the government has taken a decision in favour of the Channel Tunnel, there is going to be a great deal of public interest in the early pioneers."

"Well, great-grandfather would have been pleased about that." Mrs

Potter poured herself another cup of tea. "Building the tunnel was his dream, you know. You could almost say it was his life work."

"Did you ever meet him?"

Mrs Potter laughed at Iona Karapolitis' question. "I'm not that old! I was born in 1907. Edward Watkin died in 1901."

"How old was he when he died?"

"He was in his 82nd year. He was born in Manchester in 1819. The Watkins were a wealthy Manchester textile family. He gave up the family business to enter the railway industry." She laughed. "If Edward Watkin hadn't devoted all his energies to a project which never came off, the Channel Tunnel, I as his great-granddaughter might be living in a castle, not a modest little country cottage in the heart of Exmoor!

"The tragedy was, my dear," she continued, "that great-grandfather never got his way in Parliament. He persuaded Gladstone all right. Gladstone once told a public meeting: 'Sir Edward Watkin is one of those men who is wicked enough to desire that a tunnel should be constructed under the Channel to France, and I am one of those men who are wicked enough to agree with him.' "

Iona laughed. "I'm glad you remembered that."

"Yes," said Mrs Potter. "He persuaded Gladstone but he never persuaded Parliament. The problem was, people continued to believe that the existence of a Channel Tunnel would be a threat to the security of England."

"Do you think they were right?" Iona asked.

"Of course not." Mrs Potter shook her head derisively. "A lot of old fools and old women! Great-grandfather had no time for any of them."

"You really know the history of it all, don't you?"

Mrs Potter threw the dogs some scraps of cake.

"When you get to my age," she said, "you tend to live in the past. My father was very proud of his grandfather. I am very proud of my great-grandfather. Of course, his dream failed. We might have been rich and we are not. Even before great-grandfather's death, the capital of the Channel Tunnel Company had been reduced from £275,000 to £93,000. That was in 1897. In the following year all shares of nominal value greater than four shillings were sub-divided into shares of four shillings. Then you had the first World War which knocked them down even more. No one was going to build a Channel Tunnel which the Germans might use to invade Britain. The same applied in the Second World War as well."

After tea, the two women went for a walk with the dogs up the valley. They followed the river.

"What a beautiful place this is," Iona said.

"Isn't it?" Mrs Potter agreed. "I don't think I could ever leave it. It's a matter of hoping the money will last."

"I'm sure you'll never have to leave."

Mrs Potter seemed both surprised and gratified to hear Iona's confident statement.

The sun was setting as they came back to the cottage. The shadows had fallen on the river. Sheep were calling from the hills.

Iona thanked the old woman profusely for giving up so much of her time. As she turned to go she asked casually: "By the way, do you still happen to have any shares in the Channel Tunnel Company? People collect the old certificates nowadays in much the same way that they collect stamps. You might find they're worth something."

"Good heavens," the old lady exclaimed. "I never thought of that. Yes, of course I've got some of the old certificates. Thousands of them. My father inherited them from his father who in turn inherited them from great-grandfather Ted, and now I've got them." Again there was that rueful smile. "They were meant to be the pot of gold at the end of the rainbow, weren't they?"

"They still could be," Iona said.

The old woman stopped and looked at her with surprise.

"What do you mean?"

Iona smiled her warmest, most dazzling smile.

"You don't mind if I come in for a few more minutes? It wouldn't take me very long to explain."

An hour later, Iona Karapolitis left the cottage in the valley to walk back down the farm-track towards the village of Winsford. The valley was magically quiet. Only the ripple of the river running beside the track, the distant bleating of sheep and the swoop and rush of swallows heading home for the night, marked the silence. She had almost reached the end of the valley, where the farm track debouched onto the main road, when a herd of twenty deer came down the hill in front of her, splashed across the river and went on up the other side. She had never seen the red deer of Exmoor before. She stood stock still while they passed. One huge stag bringing up the rear caught sight or scent of her as he forded the stream. He stopped in his tracks holding his head into the wind so the great antlers lay almost flat against his neck. Then he trotted on and after the others.

She dined alone that night in the Royal Oak. Afterwards, she had a drink in the bar. The landlord, recognizing her, asked her if she'd had a good afternoon. She told him about the deer and he replied:

"You were lucky. Not everyone gets to see deer their first afternoon on Exmoor."

Iona Karapolitis knew she had been lucky in more ways than one that day.

9

Grantham came early the next morning to the offices of Chunnel Consortium in Victoria Street. It was ironic, he thought, that the headquarters of the old Channel Tunnel Company had been just a few doors down the road. He had read somewhere that, at one stage in the checkered history of the cross-Channel project, an irate crowd, incensed by the idea of French *cuirassiers* emerging from a hole in the ground near Dover to take over the country, had stormed or at least stoned the Channel Tunnel Company's premises. He hoped the gleaming new offices of Chunnel Consortium would manage to escape a similar fate.

In spite of his early arrival, his secretary, Sandra Furlong, was there ahead of him.

"Good morning, Mr Grantham."

"Good morning, Sandra."

As far as the mode of address was concerned, it was a non-reciprocal relationship and Grantham intended to keep it that way. There was no point being on too familiar terms with people you might one day have to fire.

Not that he had any intention of firing Sandra Furlong. She was not only extremely competent; her competence was allied with an exuberant personality and an optimistic disposition that enabled her to spot unerringly the silver lining in the darkest of thunder-clouds.

Sandra Furlong had been in England for the last ten years. Her childhood and adolescence had been spent in the Caribbean island of Barbados. Her father had been a well-to-do lawyer, practising at the Bridgetown bar. Her mother had been mainly occupied in bringing up a large family. When she was eighteen, Sandra had gone to the University of the West Indies in Jamaica and thence to England, where she had had no difficulty in finding gainful employment. The letter of introduction written by her father to Sir David Blakely, who regularly visited Barbados on holiday and who had established more than a nodding acquaintance with old Fred Furlong at the bars and beaches of the luxurious Sandy Lane hotel north of Bridgetown, had helped.

Sandra Furlong had never found her colour, which was a rich creamy brown, to be a barrier to a successful career in England. On the contrary, if anything it had helped. She was an exotic plant in sometimes drab surroundings and was appreciated as such.

With the establishment of Chunnel Consortium and the appointment of Oliver Grantham as the managing director, Sandra Furlong had been the natural choice among several contenders for the post of secretary-*cum*-executive assistant. Grantham and she had moved in together to the top-floor suite opposite the Department of Industry. There had been only one moment of friction and that was when, good-naturedly, Grantham had suggested to her that she should cut back on the tropical plants which were sprouting in every crack and corner.

"I think we ought to be able to see the view," he had said. "After all we do *have* a view." He had waved his hand in the direction of the Thames half a mile beyond the plate glass windows, and at the Palace of Westminster and the London skyline. Earth had not anything to show more fair.

Sandra had reluctantly agreed to prune her jungle.

That morning, after he had gone through his mail, Grantham called Sandra Furlong in. He looked at her approvingly. She had more zap, he thought, than a hundred English girls he had known. Quite apart from being a darn sight better looking. Maybe one day . . .

Grantham pulled himself up short. That line of thought would get him nowhere. If there was one cardinal rule in office life, it was 'don't dip your pen in the company inkwell'.

"Sandra," he said, "do you think you could find out whether Georgios Karapolitis was in town recently? I read in the paper that Karapolitis Lines have just taken over Channel Ferries."

"I saw that too. I cut it out for you. It didn't mention his being in London."

"Try and find out anyway, will you?"

While they were talking, the telephone rang. Sandra Furlong picked it up. She listened, then held her hand across the mouthpiece while she told Grantham:

"A man wants to come and see you. He says he's got some historical information about the old Channel Tunnel Company which you ought to know about. He says it could be important."

Grantham looked at his watch. It was still only 10 o'clock and he had no appointments until lunch. "If he's in London, tell him to come on over. I'll be happy to talk to him."

Sandra Furlong smiled. She liked her boss to be positive.

An hour later, she ushered into Grantham's office a middle-aged, balding man with a distinctly professorial air about him.

"In real life", Arthur Jones began, "I'm the librarian at Newham, down in the East End. That's why it took me over an hour to get here. But I'm also the secretary and chairman of the Channel Tunnel Association." He coughed modestly. "In fact you might almost say I *am* the Channel Tunnel Association. Our membership had fallen off greatly in recent years and now that the government has taken the decision to go ahead with the project, there doesn't seem to be much need any longer for a society like ours. So I'm a bit of a one-man-band at the moment."

"Go ahead, anyway," Grantham encouraged him. "One-man-bands often make the best music."

Arthur Jones marshalled his arguments. "How much do you know of the history of the Channel Tunnel project in the last century?" he asked. "Have you heard for example of Sir Edward Watkin?"

"Of course," Grantham replied. "Watkin was the man who actually started digging. He was the chairman, if I remember right, of the Submarine Continental Railway Company which took over the old Channel Tunnel Company."

"Exactly. He was also, as I'm sure you know, a Member of Parliament."

Grantham nodded: "I knew that too. I've heard that he was a respected figure in the House of Commons. He even persuaded Gladstone to back him in the end. Not that it did him much good. I mean the House of Commons never voted to approve a Channel Tunnel bill presented by Watkin or anyone else for that matter, did they?"

Arthur Jones hesitated before replying. "I don't think it's quite as simple as that," he finally said. "The crucial year, though, was 1892. That was the year Watkin introduced his tunnel bill for the last time in the House of Commons. I read the speech he made in the House on that occasion. It was clear from the start that he didn't expect the bill to succeed."

For the first time the Newham librarian opened the brief case which he had brought with him and took out some papers. "I've brought with me a copy of the Hansard for 14 November 1892, which was the day Watkin introduced his last tunnel bill. It's the unofficial Hansard because the series didn't become official until 1909. We don't have the full verbatim till then either. But even the unofficial Hansard makes it quite clear," Jones continued, "that the House of Commons did not vote just once on Watkin's bill that evening. It voted *three times*."

Once again Arthur Jones paused. "Even though the record is incomplete," he explained, "the atmosphere of the occasion comes over quite clearly. Everyone in the House that evening – and from the voting figures there were probably 200 members present – knew that Watkin's bill was bound to be defeated. But they wanted to throw the old boy a consolation prize. *Honoris causa*, if you see what I mean. After all, he had been trying so hard for so long. So, at Gladstone's suggestion, they split the motion into two parts and voted on each part separately before voting on the motion as a whole."

"Do you have the actual text of the motion?" Grantham asked.

"I do." Jones read it out: "The motion was 'that this House approves the proposal for the construction of a tunnel beneath the Channel between Dover and Sangatte and grants to the Channel Tunnel Company the sole concession for the construction and operation of the said tunnel, such concession to run for ninety-nine years'."

"That seems fairly clear," said Grantham.

"The original motion was clear," Arthur Jones replied, "but what happened after that doesn't seem to be at all clear. As far as I can see from the record the House rejected the first part of the motion, that is to say the principle of building the Channel tunnel, by 90 votes. But they then went on to *accept* the idea of granting the ninety-nine year concession to the Channel Tunnel Company. Procedurally, of course, it was a nonsense. But that's what they did. You know what parliaments are. It was the House's way of paying a last tribute to Sir Edward Watkin as the chairman of the Channel Tunnel Company."

"And what did the House do about the motion as a whole?" Grantham asked. "You say they voted three times."

"Oh, sanity had returned by then. The motion as a whole was rejected by 94 votes, and that was that."

Grantham was puzzled. "I don't see what the problem is, then," he said.

"The problem", Arthur Jones explained, "is not with the motion as voted. It's what happened after that, as far as I can see. Mr Gladstone immediately rose on a point of order which the Speaker accepted. He suggested that it would surely be the will of the House – I'm paraphrasing because we don't have the verbatim – that the second part of the motion which they had just voted be deemed by the House to be a substantive motion standing in its own right. Hansard notes that the speaker saw fit to accept Mr Gladstone's proposal (and here I quote) 'in the spirit in which it was intended and in the light of the fact the present session would see the retirement of the Member for Hythe, namely Sir Edward Watkin, more than a quarter of a century after he had first entered the House of Commons'. The House then proceeded to vote on Mr Gladstone's proposal without dividing. It was carried with acclaim."

Arthur Jones put his papers back in his briefcase.

"I've told you this because I thought you ought to know it. I'm probably as interested as you are, Mr Grantham, in seeing this tunnel built. The Channel Tunnel has been more than a hobby of mine for years. It's been something of a passion. I don't want it to go wrong now. And it *could* go wrong, you know."

Oliver Grantham still was not sure he entirely understood what the other man was driving at.

"But that's almost a hundred years ago," he protested.

Arthur Jones sighed. "If it was a hundred years ago, it wouldn't matter. But it's not. The House of Commons voted in 1892. It gave a ninety-nine year concession for the construction and operation of the Channel Tunnel to the Channel Tunnel Company. It's not yet 1992, not by my reckoning anyway."

When the librarian had gone, Grantham – feeling that he had taken a heavy punch on the jaw – spoke into the intercom.

"Sandra, I wonder if you can try to get me an appointment with Sir Giles Morgan QC, today in his chambers. Perhaps you can tell the clerk that it is rather urgent and that we very much hope that learned counsel will oblige."

Grantham lunched at the Garrick with a friend and afterwards walked over to Lincoln's Inn. Sir Giles Morgan's chambers were at the top of the staircase in Stone Buildings, on the far side of the quadrangle. Sir Giles himself was a polished, urbane man who had been Solicitor-General in the previous administration and was still a Member of Parliament as well as being a QC.

"I'm glad we were able to fit you in. Don't tell the Law Society, or they'll be after me for not going through solicitors," he said only half in jest. He extended a hand of welcome to Grantham as the latter entered the book-lined room. "I'm afraid I shall have to leave for the House in about half an hour."

"It shouldn't take more than half an hour. It's your advice I want."

"That's what counsel is for." Sir Giles Morgan smiled benignly. It worked out that his own particular brand of advice, balancing things out throughout the year, was worth about £500 an hour. Cheap at the price, he reckoned.

He listened without interrupting while Grantham outlined the situation, then leaned back in his chair and pressed his fingertips together.

"You will appreciate that I can only give you a preliminary opinion now. I shall have to see the papers. On the face of it, I think you have a problem but not a major problem. It's a matter of standing, *locus standi*, as we would say. I tend to the view," here he picked his words very carefully, "that only the Channel Tunnel Company itself would have standing in this particular case, that is to say the Channel Tunnel Company would have to maintain that its legal and juridical personality, not to speak of its financial prospects, was being infringed by the decision of the government to promote the tunnel via Chunnel Consortium. So we will need to establish: does the Channel Tunnel Company itself actually exist today in a legal form? Who controls it? Who, in other words, are the principal shareholders? All that should be a matter of record. Your financial advisers should be able to track that down. Who are they, by the way?"

"Brownings."

"Hmmm . . ." Sir Giles Morgan seemed momentarily doubtful about the wisdom of Chunnel Consortium's choice. "A trifle . . . er . . . *upright*, I'd say. But I expect you know what you are doing. Anyway," he checked his watch and continued briskly, "Brownings or someone else will give you the facts. We may discover there is no possibility whatsoever of the Channel Tunnel Company initiating an action either because it's been wound up, or because the shares are all held by people, like your friend the librarian, who wouldn't have the slightest interest in starting such an action. And if the Channel Tunnel Company doesn't intervene then I tend to the view that no one else could. And besides," Sir Giles concluded, "your librarian fellow does seem to have stumbled on all this rather by chance, doesn't he? There's no reason, is there, why anyone else should find out? You could always let sleeping dogs lie."

Back in his office, Grantham got through to Brownings just before they all went home for the day. He spoke to George Browning, who was the eldest of the four brothers who still ran the family firm. He told him precisely what he wanted.

"I'll do my best. We will probably have to dig around."

When, a couple of days later, Grantham received Brownings' confidential report on the Channel Tunnel Company, the doubts he had about the bank's competence were at least partially assuaged. The bank had clearly worked quickly and well. The twenty-page document went into the background and history of the Channel Tunnel Company, the takeover by Submarine Continental, the issue of shares and developments in the early twentieth century, with a concluding section on the recent past. Some bright young man, just down from Oxford – or so Grantham surmised – had permitted himself, on behalf of the bank, a concluding witticism: "Like Milton's Lycidas, the Channel Tunnel Company is not dead; it doth but sleep. However, there is no possibility that it will reawake in any recognizable form; still less, is there a possibility that it could be reconstituted in a form which would threaten the interests of Chunnel Consortium."

Grantham flipped through the report until he came to a short paragraph headed 'Current Ownership of Shares in the Channel Tunnel Company'. He read what the bank had to say on the subject:

"Notwithstanding the moribund nature of the company, we have tried to establish present ownership of the shares. The chief shareholder appears to be a Mrs Eileen Potter, who is the great-granddaughter of Sir Edward Watkin, former chairman of the Channel Tunnel Company. Mrs Eileen Potter is believed to retain almost all the shares once held by Sir Edward Watkin and members of his family. These probably account for over 40 per cent of the nominal capital. The bank has made enquiries as to the present whereabouts of Mrs Potter. We have learned that aged and somewhat infirm, she lives on Exmoor; address can be supplied. She is not known to have professional financial advisers."

As he put down the report, Grantham breathed an audible sigh of relief. So it was a red herring after all, he thought. Some old lady, living in the depths of the country, who had never heard of Hansard, let alone read it, was sitting on a truckload of worthless share certificates. He scribbled a note to Sir Giles Morgan QC. "Thank you so much", he wrote, "for sparing the time to see me the other afternoon. On reflection, I think you were right. It's better to let sleeping dogs lie."

He took the note through to Sandra Furlong.

"Don't bother to type it out," he said, "just be sure Sir Giles gets his fee promptly. You never know when we may need him again, and he did put himself out."

Sandra gave him a cheerful smile. "I'd put myself out for £500 an hour."

"I'd rephrase that, Sandra, if I were you." Grantham smiled back at her. "Some people might get the wrong idea."

He walked back to his office. A moment later he re-emerged.

"I've just had an idea," he said. "You wouldn't like to take a day off, would you? I'd like you to run down to the country."

10

When Oliver Grantham, soon after his return from Scotland and his visit to Marchmain 58, telephoned Donald Coulton at his office, the latter had clearly been pleased.

"How good of you to call!" Coulton purred. "I would have contacted you myself, otherwise. When can we meet?"

After a certain amount of good-natured sparring over dates and places, it was finally agreed that Grantham should drive over to Berkshire for Sunday lunch. Berkshire meant Donald Coulton's Queen Anne mansion a few miles from Hungerford. Here, Lord Coulton indulged what was – apart from cricket – his other great love: horses. He kept a string of thoroughbreds at Lambourne under the competent eye of Rex Withers, who was also trainer to the Queen. As a matter of fact, Coulton had switched to Withers on Her Majesty's advice ten years previously. That advice had been sound. In recent years, horses carrying Coulton colours had been consistent winners. The personal friendship which had developed between the Sovereign and Donald Coulton, partly as a result of their shared love of the Turf, was not something that Coulton spoke about.

Donald Coulton had mentioned, when inviting Grantham over for lunch, that his daughter would be there too. "Candida's just down from Oxford," he had said. "It'll do her good to meet you. Give her a taste of real life."

As Grantham pulled into the driveway and parked in the courtyard (the chauffeur had the day off), a young woman with startlingly fair hair and pale, almost translucent skin, came out of the house to greet him.

"You must be Oliver Grantham." She twiddled a tennis racket in her hand and smiled at him. "I'm Candida Coulton. Donald's on the telephone to New York. He likes to wake them up early, particularly when it's Sunday. He said he'll be through by lunch. Would you care for a game of tennis?"

Grantham shook hands with the young woman. He had on occasion seen pictures of the Honourable Candida Coulton in glossy magazines or in the gossip columns of the press. He remembered that she had been described as one of Oxford's 'bright young things', a kind of modern-day Zuleika Dobson. Nothing that he had so far read had made him specially wish to meet the lady in question. He realized now, as he took her hand in his, that the newspapers had probably got it wrong. After approximately ten seconds acquaintanceship Oliver Grantham was prepared to say that Candida Coulton had a natural charm that no amount of money or success would spoil.

"Of course I'd like a game of tennis," he replied, taking his bag from the back of the car.

"You can change at the court," she said. "We've got showers and things there."

The last time he had played tennis, Grantham recalled as they knocked up on the court, had been in Germany at the Hetzel Hotel where he had defeated the actress, Ingrid Lubbeke (he warmed at the memory). This time, against a worthier opponent, he found himself stretched to win a game, let alone a set. Candida Coulton was not merely good at tennis. She was very good.

When he finally came off the court after a 2-1 defeat Grantham asked her, "Did you get a tennis blue at Oxford?"

"Actually I did."

"You might have told me."

"You didn't tell me you had the DSO."

"That wasn't my DSO," Grantham replied. "That was the regiment's. I was merely the recipient. Anyway, I am a civilian now. You don't talk about gongs in civilian life."

They walked back to the house together.

"I suppose you got a first too at Oxford, did you?" Grantham thought he might as well learn all the bad news at once.

"I'm afraid I did. Maths and physics, that kind of thing. But it wasn't a starred first," she added to soften the blow.

Grantham grunted. He wondered whether or not he might have to revise that snap judgement about 'natural charm'. The girl seemed almost too good to be true. She played tennis like a dream; had a first class degree; was rich to boot.

"Do you have any drawbacks?" he asked, only half-joking.

She took a swipe at a passing rosebush with her tennis racket.

"Yes, I do," she replied. "I'm Donald's daughter. That's a drawback. I want to do things for myself. In my own way. It's difficult to do that when your father's probably the most famous industrialist in the country."

The most famous industrialist in the country was waiting for them in the drawing room. He stood with his back to the fireplace. Grantham had seen photographs of that fireplace, just as he had seen photographs of the Honourable Candida Coulton. They both could be listed as Coulton assets, movable and immovable.

"I'm so sorry I wasn't here when you arrived. Did you have a good game?"

"I was soundly defeated," Grantham replied.

"Nonsense!", Candida protested. "His eye wasn't in. He had just got out of the car."

"Why don't you say what you mean, that I'm an old boy of fifty who ought not to be playing singles with sprightly young things?"

Coulton looked at him sympathetically. "Have a drink anyway."

Grantham asked for a gin and tonic without the gin. "I'll have something stronger later," he explained. "Just now I want something cool and long."

Donald Coulton laughed and turned to his daughter. "You'll have to give him a return match another time."

"I'd love to." Candida Coulton spoke as if she meant what she said.

Grantham noticed that her eyes were grey.

The dining room looked out over the Berkshire Downs. In the distance, Grantham saw a tall post standing starkly against the sky.

"That's Coombe Gibbet, isn't it?" he asked.

"It is," Lord Coulton replied. "They last hanged a man there less than a century ago. His name was Ben Smith and his end, I suspect, was well-deserved. He was an old-fashioned highway robber."

Grantham reflected that old-fashioned highway robbers came in different shapes and sizes and that Coulton himself was a skilled practitioner of the art. However, he kept his thoughts to himself and merely commented: "What one generation sees as highway robbery, another may call political terrorism."

For a time the conversation turned to violence of various kinds, especially political violence.

"Public figures nowadays are so exposed," said Donald Coulton. "There's no way they can avoid running risks. Queen Victoria went into seclusion for years after Albert's death; but nowadays the public wouldn't stand for it."

"What do you mean, Donald?" Candida Coulton asked. She sat between the two men, with her back towards the window.

"I mean," replied Coulton, "that the public expects Royalty to perform nowadays; to earn its keep, as it were. They want value for money. It's a sad fact, but I'm afraid it's true."

He turned to Grantham. "Take this tunnel under the Channel you're building. If you're successful, the Chunnel is going to be one of the great projects of this century. Perhaps of any century. The day is going to come when the first train from London to Paris is going to roll through that tunnel without stopping. That will be an extraordinary occasion. And the Queen will have to be there. Just as the French President will have to be there. On show. That's what I mean when I speak of the inevitability of exposure of public figures nowadays."

Grantham found himself agreeing with everything Coulton said.

After lunch, Candida Coulton disappeared in the direction of the swimming pool. The two men drove over to Lambourne to see Coulton's horses.

"They will have been out first thing this morning," Coulton explained. "But Withers may be organizing some gentle exercise this afternoon. He generally does. That keeps the stable-lads busy at least. Otherwise they'd be roaring around on their motorcycles."

Rex Withers, a weather-beaten man of medium height who looked as though he wore his soft brown trilby even in bed, was waiting for them in the yard.

"They'll be going out in a minute or two," he told them. "We can follow them in the Land Rover if you like. You'll get a better view that way."

They sat three abreast in Rex Withers' new diesel Land-Rover and when the horses came out into the yard, they followed them on to the downs. The lads, thought Grantham, seemed cheerful enough. If they were suffering from motorcycle deprivation, they didn't show it.

"Four of my horses are out today," Coulton explained. "I've got a couple more with Withers, but they're not here at the moment."

They had driven about a mile on to the downs, when Rex Withers brought the Land-Rover to a halt.

"If you and Mr Grantham would care to stand up on that hillock," he said, "you'll get a fine view. I'll stay here in the car, if you don't mind. I'm getting a bit creaky with age now."

Donald Coulton smiled. "Nonsense, Rex. You're the fittest man I know."

Coulton and Grantham walked up to the vantage-point. The string of horses, spread out below them, had broken from a trot into a gentle canter.

Coulton pointed. "See the dark chestnut lying third. That's my newest acquisition: March Joy. I paid more money for him than I ever paid for a horse before. I paid for blood. He's got Derby winners on both sides."

They watched for a quarter of an hour as the horses exercised on the downs. At one point, the string broke into a gallop, not a flat-out gallop but enough for a good horse to show its paces.

Coulton watched through binoculars. When he lowered them he said: "I think March Joy is going to be all right. I like the look of him."

As they walked back to the Land-Rover, Coulton added: "Racing is like looking for oil – a bit of a gamble. You try not to talk too much about your prospects. You just have to hope you're onto a winner." He turned to Grantham, as they neared the car. "I'll give you an example. You've heard about our Marchprod units and the total subsea production concept, or whatever they call it. It's a gamble for us. If the gamble pays off, it will transform oil exploration. But the system still has to be proved."

The Land-Rover was only a hundred yards away. Grantham knew that this was his moment.

"I can think of a way of proving the system which could be the most important venture Marchmain has ever undertaken. I'm talking about using the Marchprod and its related system on the Chunnel project."

Grantham waved his hand to take in the sweep of the Berkshire Downs and the horses still exercising below.

"Of course it's a gamble. Like your horses are a gamble. But the pay-off could be immense. Literally unimaginable. *We could be lopping years off our construction times.*"

As they reached the Land-Rover, Donald Coulton paused. He stood a few feet away from Grantham, looking at him steadily and, so it seemed, sizing him up. Did the man, Coulton seemed to be thinking, have Derby winners on both sides, dam and sire? Could he run? Could he win?

Ten or twenty seconds must have passed while Lord Coulton remained deep in thought. Finally he smiled and twitched his spectacles on the bridge of his nose.

"Perhaps we had better talk this over at home," he said.

Over tea in the library, Grantham outlined his basic idea.

"As you know," he began, "we – that is to say Chunnel Consortium – had a board meeting in Paris the other day. I was able to show them the results of the sensitivity tests which we had pulled off the computer only a couple of days earlier. What the tests showed very clearly indeed, was that any *delay in construction* would have a very serious impact on the projected rate of return, much more serious an impact than, say, a cost overrun or a revenue shortfall. In fact, I was able to show the board that a three-year delay in construction would immediately bring the rate of return down to the single-figure range. And that of course would be completely disastrous for us. No one is going to put money into a project with a six or eight per cent rate of return, when you can get twelve or fifteen per cent just by leaving it in the bank."

Coulton nodded somewhat impatiently. He hadn't been in business over thirty years only to be told by a relative novice what was or was not an acceptable investment.

"What I didn't tell the board that morning in Paris," Grantham continued quickly, sensing the other man's mood, "was that we'd run another program on the computer. We asked the computer to tell us what the effects on the internal rate of return would be not of the three-year delay in construction, but of a three-year *advance* in the construction timetable!"

"And what did the figures show?"

This time Coulton spoke with evident interest. Grantham hesitated before replying. He did not want to seem naïve. He knew as well as anyone that results always depended on assumptions.

"What we got," he replied slowly, "was a range of values depending on the assumptions made about the cost of capital, the phasing of major items like the purchase of tunnel-boring machines and so on. But in every case, even when we had built in the worst possible assumptions about revenue shortfall or cost overruns, we came out with a projected internal rate of return of over *twenty-five* per cent!"

Donald Coulton got up and walked to the open French windows. He stood there looking out, his tall figure silhouetted against the afternoon light.

When finally he swung round to face Grantham again, there was a gleam in his eye as though he'd just spotted a winner at the bloodstock sales in County Kerry.

"Twenty-five per cent and you're talking!" He beamed at Grantham. Coulton was a gambling man at heart. This was the kind of gamble he liked.

"Don't think that this is altruism. The oil business is pretty slow at the moment. We're still feeling the effects of the recession. There's an oil-glut, not an oil-shortage. People aren't opening up fields the way they used to. And in any case, as a major partner in Chunnel Consortium, Marchmain has as much an interest as anyone in the success of the operation. If we can prove the technology in the Channel, it will serve in the North Sea as well. We are talking about similar depths and similar operating environments. I'll see what we can do."

Grantham also rose to his feet. Later, he would remember that moment in the library of Donald Coulton's Queen Anne mansion in Berkshire as one of the high points.

"*Compress the time-frame!*" That was what David Blakely had said. Grantham knew now that he could do it.

Coulton walked with him to the courtyard, where he had parked the car.

"If it works, you think you'll lop three years off the construction time, then?"

Grantham felt himself filled with an unbounded, unqualified optimism.

"We'll do better than that," he replied. "We'll not only halve construction time. We'll quarter it!"

"Steady on now!" Coulton laid a restraining hand on Grantham's shoulder. "Don't let's run before we can walk."

As they stood talking together in the courtyard, Candida Coulton emerged from the direction of the pool in a bikini. She held a towel in her hand which she now used to pat her hair dry. She smiled at the two men as she came up to them.

"What have you been doing with him all afternoon, Donald? I was waiting for you at the pool."

It was clear from Donald Coulton's expression that he was the original doting father.

"I'm sorry, darling," he said. "We went to take a look at the horses. But I'm sure Mr Grantham will be back another time. He can swim then. It's getting a bit late now."

"I do hope so." Candida Coulton smiled at Grantham sweetly, draped the towel around her shoulders and went on into the house.

Coulton gazed fondly after her. "Her mother died three years ago. We've grown rather close since then."

"I can imagine," Grantham replied. He had two sons but no daughter. Sometimes he felt the lack.

Grantham drove back slowly across country to Fleet. He was in a reflective mood. How much his life had changed in the six short months since he had left the army! He had never been so busy, so fulfilled.

*

Back home Lily greeted him with, it seemed to Grantham, something less than her usual warmth.

"You were a long time," she said. "I thought it was just a business lunch."

"Lunch doesn't always mean just lunch." Grantham realized that his reply had sounded sharper than he had intended. "I'm sorry, darling," he added. "I seem to be getting caught up in this job far more than I imagined."

Later, when they were halfway through dinner, Lily said to him *à propos* of nothing in particular: "You know, Oliver, I followed you around for twenty years when you were in the army. It wasn't that easy with the children growing up. Now you've got this new job and it looks as though it's going to be the same thing all over again. I'm not sure I don't want some life of my own. Before it's too late. If you see what I mean."

Grantham gazed at her absent-mindedly. He was thinking about the maximum desirable number of buoyant articulated columns.

"I'm sorry, darling," he said again. "What did you say?"

"Oh, never mind." Lily sighed and got up to fetch the cheese from the sideboard.

When she came back to the table she said: "I mean it, you know."

Grantham helped himself to cheese. He took her hand. He was fond of his wife. He hoped she was fond of him. He wasn't exactly sure what Lily had said. He certainly wasn't sure what she had meant. But he knew that this was the moment to sound reassuring.

"Don't worry, dear. It will all sort itself out in the end."

It was a meaningless kind of remark, Grantham knew. But it had served in the past. Presumably it would serve in the future as well.

"I don't believe you've been listening," Lily said. And then, suddenly, she burst into tears.

11

A few days after his meeting with Donald Coulton, Grantham went back to Paris. He asked Monique Delacourt to make available one of the conference rooms in the Falaise building, together with a projector and a technician to operate it.

"I want to show you a film," Grantham had said. "When you've seen it, I think you'll understand very clearly indeed what I'm driving at."

Whereas Michael Prestwick, at the time of Grantham's visit to Marchmain 58, had provided his own narration, Grantham was content to let the film's recorded commentary speak for itself.

Running-time altogether was twenty minutes. At the end, Grantham said, "Basically, you see, it's a matter of simple arithmetic. The original scheme put up by Chunnel Consortium involves – does it not? – the use of two tunnel-boring machines – TBMs – on the main Phase One Tunnel. Of course, there's the service tunnel as well to consider. But for the moment I'll leave that out, since with its much smaller diameter that's less of a problem."

He walked over to a blackboard and picked up some chalk.

"Two TBMs – one starting in France, the other starting in Britain and both of them hoping and expecting to meet in the middle somewhere – is what most engineers, indeed most knowledgeable laymen, assume you are talking about when you speak of boring a tunnel from England to France. As I remember the figures we put up, assuming a boring rate of seventy-to-eighty feet per day . . ." He wrote the figures up on the blackboard . . . "And assuming also a total tunnel length of some thirty-two miles, our two TBMs boring for twenty four-hours a day, seven days a week, fifty-two weeks a year would take three years to meet in the middle. As I recall, we allowed some latitude, since a boring rate of seventy to eighty feet per day could be pretty optimistic. We might not be able to achieve that in day-in, day-out operation. Which means that instead of talking about three years tunnelling time we've been planning at least four."

Again he wrote the figures on the blackboard.

"Now let's assume," he continued, "that instead of two TBMs, we use four TBMs. Put a Marchprod in mid-channel with associated subsea units, sink a shaft below the seabed, then excavate along the tunnel line in *both* directions, that is to say, towards France on the one hand and towards England on the other. You halve your construction time because you have four machines working, not two!

"Now," said Grantham, "let's take the argument one step further, and use *two* Marchprods instead of one."

On the blackboard he drew a rough diagram showing the coast of England and the coast of France, with Dover and Folkestone on the left and Calais on the right and a thick chalk line denoting the course which the Chunnel would take. Under the first diagram he drew another, showing a cross-section of the Chunnel along its whole line from portal to portal.

"On the English side the portal is several miles inland from Dover because of the problem of the gradient as we descend beneath the cliffs and under the seabed. Since the landward access is therefore longer on the English side than on the French side, and since we want to share the load more or less equally between the six tunnelling machines, we will probably want to position our first Marchprod a bit nearer the coast on the English side than we will on the French side. By the time we've finished," he made some crosses on both lower and upper diagrams to indicate the positioning of the Marchprods, "we will have effectively divided the 32-mile tunnel into six separate sections, each handled by a separate TBM. TBM 1 starts at Dover, drives five miles under sea along the tunnel line to meet TBM 2 which will have driven five miles from Marchprod One in the Dover direction. TMB 3 starts from Marchprod One and drives five miles towards Calais to meet up with TBM 4 coming from Marchprod Two. TBM 5 starts from Marchprod Two and bores towards Calais until it meets up with TBM 6 which will have driven five miles seaward having started on the French side."

Grantham paused. He wanted to give her time to absorb the facts and the figures. He wanted her to understand that what he was advancing was not a minor modification of the plan, but a radical change.

"I rang you, Monique" – it was the first time he had called her Monique, but somehow it seemed appropriate at that particular moment – "because, as you know, I'm not the tunnel engineer. That's your concern and Falaise's concern. I had an idea and I spent a little time seeing if there was any technical possibility of that idea being made to work. I went to Scotland, as I told you, and visited the installations in the North Sea. I tried to appreciate whether the technology which had been developed for one set of circumstances, namely oil-exploration, could be used for the kind of purposes I had in mind. There's no point in putting this kind of thing to our board, whatever the political and financial advantages may be, if it's not *technically* feasible. What you see here," he concluded, "is the gist of a plan, the germ of an idea. What I want you to do now is to tear it apart."

After Grantham had finished speaking, Monique Delacourt said precisely nothing at all for two and a half minutes. Grantham calculated that one of the more efficient tunnel-boring machines could have proceeded three or four inches towards its destination during that space of time.

When she did finally say something, she spoke softly, in a voice that hardly rose above a whisper.

"I'm not going to tear your scheme apart, Mr Grantham," – Grantham noted that she very deliberately had not called him by his first name – "because I think it's a brave bold concept and, like you, I understand the need for speed. Of course I would want to know a great deal more about the Marchprod technology and the undersea production system of which you speak. But I'm prepared to accept that Marchmain knows what it's doing and to be convinced by Marchmain engineers that they have a system which works."

She lit another Gauloise and made a big play of checking the tip to see that it was glowing a nice warm red colour and that the used match was safely stowed in the ashtray.

"No," she said, still in an ultra-quiet voice, "I'm not going to tear your scheme apart. It's probably a good scheme in theory. It may even be a great scheme."

And then she added, with a note of complete finality:

"The problem is, it won't work!"

She stood up, brushed some cigarette ash from her skirt and spoke to him with the kind of direct and deliberate rudeness which was characteristically French.

"You may have been a great soldier, Mr Grantham, in your bloody stupid war in the Falklands. I know nothing about that and frankly I don't want to know. *Je n'en sais rien!* But I do know you've just wasted my afternoon and I'm not amused. You crash around like a Boy Scout having great ideas, so you think. You suppose you're going to be a hero, knocking years off the construction time of the Chunnel. The trouble is, you don't check the elementary facts first, do you?"

She was trembling as she spoke.

"You speak of six TBMs. Six TBMs! Where in hell do you think we're going to get six TBMs from? Don't you know there aren't six TBMs in the whole wide world that can do the job we want them to? They don't grow on trees, you know. We're going to be digging a seven-metre diameter tunnel. We've got to drive that tunnel to hair-breadth accuracy. The kind of TBM we need is about the largest, most complicated, precision tool ever built. It takes as long to build a TBM as it does to build a tunnel!"

Grantham went white beneath his habitual tan as Monique Delacourt continued to rail at him. He gritted his teeth. He couldn't remember when he had last been addressed in such a fashion. I'll get you for this, you silly little bitch, he thought. He was savagely angry.

Finally he said, icily: "Are you sure you're right?"

"Quite sure." She was still excited but the worst of the eruption was over. "If you care to come to my office for a few minutes before you catch the plane back to London, I'll prove it to you," she said.

They picked up their papers and left the conference room together in silence. At the door, a complicated little minuet took place with Grantham waving her on through ahead of him, with elaborate irony, while Monique Delacourt refused, equally deliberately, to take precedence. Finally, they walked through the door simultaneously, bumped into each other and burst out laughing.

Monique turned to him, smiled very prettily and said: "I'm sorry I called you a Boy Scout."

"I called you worse things than that," Grantham replied. "Only you didn't hear them." His anger too, had subsided. "I guess we'll learn to work together. I've grown too used to pushing people around."

"That's what being a soldier is, isn't it?"

"Was," replied Grantham.

It took her well over an hour to persuade him, as they sat together in her office, that the game simply wasn't worth a candle. He was a stubborn man, was Grantham. He wasn't simply going to take her word for it. He wanted to be convinced; wanted to have the evidence for her statement placed before him. She contended that there were more just men in Sodom and Gomorrah than there were TBMs for use on the Channel Tunnel Project. Then let her demonstrate that contention unassailably!

And that, more or less, was precisely was what Monique Delacourt proceeded to do.

"Basically," she explained, "there are only a handful of companies in the world making tunnelling machines. The Robbins Company of Seattle, in the United States, has manufactured more than one hundred machines, the majority of these being designed for medium or hard rock. Robbins built one of the largest machines yet used with a diameter of thirty-six feet eight inches for driving the combined diversion and power tunnels for the Mangla Dam in Pakistan. That machine, by the way, was later modified for driving the twin road tunnels under the Mersey river in England."

Grantham nodded. He remembered the Mersey project.

"Other companies," Monique Delacourt continued, "include Jarva Incorporated, who have manufactured a number of machines, including a twenty-foot diameter mole used in San Francisco on a section of the Bay Area Rapid Transit Project. Two Ingersoll Rand machines drove the Cookhouse tunnel in South Africa and the sewer tunnel in Rochester, New York. One of their largest machines was used on the Port Huron tunnel in Michigan, where it bored an eighteen-foot, four-inch diameter hole through shale and limestone boulders. The Fairmont Tool Company has produced several tunnelling machines. Their largest was used on the Navajo Irrigation Project, New Mexico, when it drove a nineteen-foot, ten-inch diameter tunnel two miles long through sandstone. Fairmont machines also worked on the Seikan Tunnel in Japan which, as you probably know, carries an undersea railway line under a 13.5 mile wide strait between the islands of Honshu and Hokkaido."

Monique Delacourt spoke without stopping for five minutes. Then she summarized.

"In short, you have a handful of manufacturers who over the years have made a handful of machines. Each one of those machines has been tailor-made for the particular project, with the exception of the machine which bored the Mersey Tunnel which, as I told you, was brought over from Pakistan and adapted. Now, as you know," she continued, "the dimensions of the cross-Channel tunnel are quite specific. They are dictated by the need to carry Berne gauge rolling-stock and also, since the passage of freight is going to be a major function of the tunnel, the trains will have to be able to carry containers of the internationally agreed dimensions, whether as individual items or as part of truck-trailer combinations. So our bored tunnel is seven metres in diameter. No more, no less. Translate that into feet, remembering that the diameter of your TMB must correspond exactly to the desired diameter for the tunnel, and you see that we need a machine with a diameter of" – she did a quick calculation – "twenty-two feet eleven inches. To my knowledge," she concluded, "there are no rotary-face tunnelling machines of that diameter available to us. And, believe me, Mr Grantham, I follow these things."

Grantham did not doubt it. He had been more impressed than he could say by the mastery, the sheer virtuosity the Frenchwoman had just demonstrated.

"Don't look surprised." Monique Delacourt sensed his reaction. "Falaise's business is tunnelling. I'm the *ingénieur en chef*. If I don't know this kind of fact, I shouldn't be where I am."

Grantham looked out of the window. He could see the river Seine in the distance and beyond it the Eiffel Tower soaring skyward. He had seldom felt such an acute sense of disappointment. If there was one thing he hated, it was to be told that something he wanted to do couldn't be done. Had they said that to Monsieur Eiffel too, when he first produced his plans?

"What I don't understand," he said to Monique Delacourt, "is how we're going to start tunnelling at all. From what you say, we don't even have two TBMs, let alone six. I agree it was naïve of me to suppose that you could buy TBMs off the shelf, as it were. But if we can't buy them off the shelf, how do we start? Do we wait two years for someone to build them for us?"

Monique Delacourt smiled. "It's not as bad as all that," she replied. "Four years ago, even before Chunnel Consortium was formed, Falaise placed an order with Fairmont Tool of Tucson, Arizona, for two TBMs of the appropriate diameter, namely twenty-two feet eleven inches, capable of generating 900,000 pounds of thrust. We placed that order on spec, as you say. Falaise had no certain knowledge that the governments of Britain and France would decide to go ahead with the Channel Tunnel Project; nor did we know that Falaise would be part of a successful bid for the contract. But it was a risk we decided to take, a finely calculated business risk. And it paid off in the event. The Fairmont Tool Company should now have two TBMs ready for us. They have promised delivery at the end of the month.

"So we have two TBMs lined up, but not six. The board of Channel Consortium may decide they like your scheme. I hope they do. I like your scheme. I think it is bold and imaginative. But say we placed an order today for four additional TBMs like the two we have already ordered. By the time those extra TBMs are built and delivered, and by the time you've got your undersea structures in place, we ought to be so far along with construction as to make it questionable whether the extra expense and the extra risk, because I am sure there *will* be a risk," – she emphasized the last word – "*will* be worthwhile."

There was a certain finality in her voice. Grantham felt as though he had just been awarded a *proxime accessit*. He was being commended for a good try.

He was sitting there wondering what to say next, when Monique Delacourt's telephone rang. Overhearing her side of the conversation, conducted entirely in French, Grantham deduced that she had just been stood up for dinner. His surmise proved correct. Putting the receiver down, Monique said to him:

"That was my friend, Pierre Leroux, the Minister for Transport. He's just launched his campaign for President and he has to go to a meeting tonight. We were planning to have dinner."

Grantham made a quick decision. He was going to have to work with Monique Delacourt. It was important to build up a relationship of trust. She had to have confidence in his judgement and vice-versa. They hadn't made a very good start.

"I'm sorry Leroux is not able to have dinner with you tonight. Will you allow me to step into the breach? That is, if you haven't seen quite enough of me for one day."

Monique Delacourt appeared to be charmed by his almost Gallic gallantry. She laughed.

"If you mean: can you take me out to dinner? the answer is no. But if you mean: can we have dinner together? the answer is yes. I love cooking and nowadays I don't get enough chance to practise."

She had an apartment on the Ile St-Louis with a view of Notre Dame. It was a light, airy place, full of books and of music.

They ate at a table by the window. Monique Delacourt lit candles. Inevitably, the conversation reverted to tunnels and tunnelling.

"Are you sure", Grantham pressed her, "that there are no more TBMs available?"

"If there *were* others of the right dimension and characteristics, then they would be in use somewhere else, wouldn't they? They didn't interrupt work on the Mangla Dam in order to build the Mersey Road Tunnel. They waited for Mangla to be completed first – and that took six years!"

Grantham took her point. He said nothing further on the subject. Somewhere, at the back of his mind, a tiny idea had formed. Not an idea that would, with any certainty, come to fruition. Just an off-chance idea; something to be looked into.

Later she asked him why he had given up being a soldier. "Don't you miss it?"

"Of course I miss it," Grantham replied. "When you've done something or been something for thirty years and then you stop, of course you miss it. But I haven't lost touch with the army altogether, you know. I have a lot of good friends there. And not just in Britain."

Mellowing with the food and the wine, he told her something about his army career.

"I missed World War II and I missed the Korean War. In the late fifties I was with our mission in Washington and I did a spell in Brussels with NATO and another in Germany. I also served in Aden, Borneo and Northern Ireland."

"That must have been nasty."

"Political terrorism is always particularly nasty."

"We have our share of it here," Monique said. "Paris has become something of a centre for international terrorism. Hardly a week passes without a bombing incident of some kind. We have Arab terrorist groups; we have Corsican extremists; we have the Armenians. Someone told me the other day that the Germans too are moving back to Paris – they're finding that things are getting too hot for them at home. Apparently the German 'Greens' have established an international arm based in Paris, dedicated to what they call 'direct action'."

"How do you know?" Grantham was intrigued.

"Oh, this kind of knowledge becomes common currency after a time," she replied. "Paris is a very small city."

"Is Mitterrand's government deliberately soft on terrorism?"

Monique Delacourt was unwilling to be drawn. She shrugged. "Socialism usually has other priorities than the maintenance of law and order."

Still later, he tried to draw her on the subject of Pierre Leroux.

"Is he really a viable candidate to succeed Mitterrand?" he asked.

"He really is," she replied. "They are making preparations now for the Party Congress in Marseilles. It's not quite the same as a nominating convention in the United States. But still, it's important."

"Do you think he's going to be the candidate of the Socialist Party?"

Monique Delacourt thought before replying.

"I'm no political expert," she said. "But I think much will depend on how much support Leroux gets in the big centres like Marseilles and Lyons and the Pas-de-Calais region. Leroux tells me that things are looking good in Marseilles and Lyons. Apparently the mayors in both those cities have come out strongly for him. Oddly enough, he appears to be running into real trouble in the Pas-de-Calais area. I say, oddly enough, because of course Leroux comes from that region and you would expect them to be solidly behind him."

"What's the problem there?" Having been a soldier for most of his life, Grantham was just beginning to discover the fascinations of politics.

Monique Delacourt hesitated.

"I'm not absolutely clear," she replied. "And I don't think Pierre is clear either. The Pas-de-Calais has always been a particularly radical area. I suppose you could describe it as the 'hotbed of socialism' in France. I don't think they like Pierre's Mercedes!"

She laughed. Grantham laughed too.

It was a good evening. Grantham didn't return to the Lancaster until nearly midnight. This time, to his relief, there were no brown envelopes waiting for him propped against the looking-glass.

His eye fell on the telephone by the bed. He remembered that he had not called his wife to tell her of his change of plan. She was still expecting him home that evening and by now she would be wondering why he had not appeared. He looked at his watch. It was an hour earlier in England. Lily would probably still be up and waiting for him.

He dialled the number of his house. There was no answer. He dialled a second time, thinking that he had perhaps made a mistake the first time. There was again no reply.

Puzzled, Grantham replaced the telephone.

He tried the call a third time, first thing next morning before he left for the airport, with no greater success. On arrival, instead of driving into London, he told the chauffeur to take him home.

He found a note on the kitchen table. It carried the previous day's date.

"Dear Oliver," Grantham read. "I've gone away for a few days. I want to think things through. I don't think you need me much at home. Perhaps you never have needed me. Not, at any rate, the way that I have needed you. I'll telephone as soon as I can. Perhaps we will be able to talk, though I doubt it."

She had signed it simply "Lily".

There was a postscript to the letter.

"PS. Someone sent some photographs. They are not very pretty I'm afraid. Of course I mind about that, but there is all the rest as well."

Grantham found the photographs in the waste-bin. She hadn't even bothered to tear them up. He pulled them out of the bin, read the facetious inscription and recognized his own distinctive signature. This time, he tore the photographs up into small pieces and thrust them back into the receptacle.

Ten minutes later, he was on his way back to London. The chauffeur drove fast but carefully, as he always did. The Rolls hit the M3 with the rush hour long since past. The road was clear and the sun shone. For some reason a Latin tag came into Grantham's mind. Something left over from his schooldays. *Etiam si labitur orbis, impavidum ferient ruinae.* Even if the whole world collapses, the ruins will strike him unafraid. Was it Horace? He couldn't remember.

By the time he had reached the river at Kew, he had more or less sorted things out in his own mind. Subconsciously, he knew, he must have been preparing for a moment such as this. Lily had gone. Perhaps she had gone for good. Was it better for partings to be long drawn out or should one recognize the inevitable when it came?

One thing Grantham knew for sure. He would not cry over spilt milk, not even for gallons of it. He could not now afford to divert his energies from the mainstream. He would find out where Lily was. He would go to her. They would talk and, perhaps, they would work something out.

But it was also possible that they wouldn't work things out. In that case, Grantham knew in his heart that he would have to let go. There were just too many other things to do in life. Marriage was a useful framework; but it was not indispensable.

"You look a bit down this morning," Sandra Furlong said to him as he walked into the office shortly before noon.

"Nonsense," Grantham replied briskly.

She brought him a gin and tonic anyway and he drank it.

"A Mr Peter Drexner called from Germany," Sandra said as Grantham sat there wondering whether the world hadn't, after all, come to pieces that morning.

He pulled himself together. The gin and tonic helped.

"Drexner? Good. I'll call him back. Did he leave a number?"

Until that morning, Grantham had almost forgotten that he had asked Drexner to try and find out where the girl Greta had gone. Now it all came back to him with a vengeance. Damn the girl! And damn whoever it was behind her! If there ever was anyone behind her! He had a personal as well as a professional score to settle. He picked up the telephone.

"I'll get him myself," he said.

Sandra Furlong could read the signs. She walked out of the room, closing the door behind her.

Grantham got through to Schluchsee on the first try. Peter Drexner sounded apologetic, almost embarrassed.

"I'm afraid we can't trace Greta Gottlieb anywhere. She left no forwarding address."

"Are you sure?"

"Absolutely."

Grantham thanked the hotel manager for his pains. For a moment or two after he had finished the conversation, he sat at his desk thinking. Somebody somewhere was lying. If Greta Gottlieb had not received the envelope with the photographs inside it which he had mailed in Paris, then someone else had. Someone who knew his home address. He looked at his watch and saw that it was almost lunch-time. He swore under his breath. The cleaning lady would probably have emptied the rubbish by now. It was Tuesday, and the dustmen came on Tuesdays.

He rang through to his home in Fleet. Perhaps he might just catch Mrs Ladd before she left. He was lucky.

"Oh Mrs Ladd, I'm glad I got you." Grantham tried to sound casual. "I wondered if you had emptied the rubbish in the kitchen yet. I'm afraid I've been rather stupid and thrown some papers away which I need."

Mrs Ladd, who had been the Granthams' daily for the last ten years, was obviously pleased to hear his voice.

"I was just going to do it. I'll leave it if you like."

"Thank you so much."

Before he could put the phone down, Mrs Ladd had asked him the question that he feared was coming.

"I wonder where Mrs Grantham is?"

"Oh, didn't she tell you?" Grantham knew that the note of casualness sounded forced but there was nothing he could do about it. "She's had to go away for a few days. Her sister is ill."

"I'm sorry to hear that," Mrs Ladd replied. "Shall I leave you some supper?"

"No, don't bother. I shall probably eat in town."

In the event, he didn't eat in town. At the end of the afternoon, he went to the gym at the Institute of Directors and had a strenuous three-quarter hour session.

He pushed himself to the limit. The ex-Marine supervisor who was on duty that afternoon warned him not to overdo it. But Grantham, halfway through a punishing schedule, took no notice. There were times when you had to overdo things.

He had a sauna and a shower and drove back to Fleet just ahead of the evening rush-hour traffic. As he had hoped it would be, the envelope was still in the waste-bin. He smoothed it out and looked at the postmark. To his surprise, he saw that the letter had been posted in England. The postmark was Paddington. Both the date and the time of posting were clearly legible.

Two Scotches later, Grantham burned the envelope and the torn-up photographs which he fished out of the bin. He was sitting there at the kitchen table wondering whether to burn the letter from his wife as well when the telephone rang. It was Lily.

"I'm in Ireland," she said. "Did you get my note?"

"I think we ought to talk."

"Can't we talk now?"

"No, darling." Grantham felt he could risk a 'darling'. "Of course you can't talk these things over on the phone."

Lily sighed. "You will have to meet me here then."

"Can't you come back?"

"Not now, Oliver," Lily said. "I'm not sure that I will ever be able to come back."

He met her the next day in the Arran Islands. He still had her note in his pocket and he had reread it on the plane from Heathrow to Shannon. He was a man of action. On the whole, he believed in doing, not being. He was sure he could win her back. He hired a car at Shannon Airport and drove north up the coast past the cliffs of Moher to Galway. He was lucky with his timing. The afternoon flight run by Arran Air to the islands in the six-seater Beechcraft was on the point of departure as he arrived. There was one seat left and Grantham scrambled in. They took off moments later and headed out over Galway Bay.

They flew quite low over the water. The coast of Connemara stretched away on the right. Looking back over the port wing he could see the majestic cliffs of Moher. It was so beautiful he wanted to cry.

They flew straight to Inishmore, the largest of the islands. The tiny airport was set a couple of miles from the main harbour.

She wasn't there to meet him, so he set off on foot into the village. The road ran along the water's edge. From time to time he passed small stone fishermen's houses, with the nets spread out along low walls and lobster pots stacked in front of the door.

He was about half a mile from the village when he saw Lily walking towards him. She had a scarf around her head and was wearing her gaberdine macintosh and stout brown walking shoes. Her face was lined. It had been for years. To Grantham it was a familiar country.

"I wasn't sure what time the plane came in," she explained as she came up to him. "Otherwise I would have been at the airport."

"It doesn't matter."

There was a degree of constraint between them which had never been there before. It was as though some door had been shut which could not now be reopened.

"We could walk if you like," she suggested.

"Let's."

They walked away from the airport, away from the village towards the northern end of the island of Inishmore. The road climbed and the wind blew against them.

Lily chose her words carefully. She knew what she had to say.

"Of course I mind. Anyone would mind. No one likes to have their noses rubbed in it." And she added matter-of-factly, "I'm sure it's not the first time. And I'm sure it wouldn't be the last time either."

Grantham said nothing. There was nothing to say.

"I mind," Lily continued. "But I don't think that is the fundamental point. What matters is that you have your life and whatever happens you are going to get on with it, and if I can manage to tag along and fit in with whatever it is that you want to do, well, that's fine. But if I can't fit in, you're going to just go on and do what you want to do anyway."

She stopped. Turned to face him. He looked at her, her face set against the outcrops of rock with the narrow rough road winding away behind her.

He loved her. But he also knew that she was right. He could see that she was crying now, and he put his arm around her shoulder. She let it rest there for a moment and then she moved away.

"Shall we walk on, or shall we go back?" he asked.

She broke down then. Sat in the road, put her arms around her knees and buried her head. Her shoulders shook.

"Oh God," thought Grantham. "I can't handle this. I thought I could but I can't."

"We could try again, Lily." He didn't want to say it, but he knew he had to. He waited for her reply. Whatever it was, he knew he would go along with it. He owed her that.

Finally she lifted her head. Her face was glistening with tears.

"I don't want to lose you," she said, choking back the anguish. "We've been through too much together. But I know I can't keep you either,

Oliver. You're fifty. You're running against time. I can sense it. I can't stand in your way. We would both suffer."

He helped her to her feet. He had never felt so rotten in his life. Not because she was wrong. But because she was right.

They could have gone on together. They could have followed the island road up and over towards the great cliffs of Inishmore wreathed in mystery and legend, where a man might gaze out towards America if he had a mind to, or else look down and watch the ocean crash against the rocks hundreds of feet below, while seabirds swooped and plunged in the wind.

They could have gone on together but they didn't. They turned, then, and walked back the way they had come towards the village and the airport.

"Perhaps I had better move into a flat in London for a while," Grantham suggested. "Blakely is always suggesting it."

She nodded. "I think that might be a good idea. I could stay on in Fleet. Someone has to take care of the garden."

He was in time to catch the evening flight back to the mainland. They stood together on the perimeter of the little airstrip with a couple of other passengers, watching the small blue and white craft being buffeted by the strong winds as it came in to land. The plane taxied over towards them.

"You go," she said to him. "I'll stay on here for a couple of days. I want to walk and to think."

He kissed her on the mouth.

"We may come through this, you know," he said.

"I don't know," she answered.

The plane circled once to gain height after it had taken off. Grantham saw her standing there in her scarf and mackintosh looking up at the sky. He waved once, but doubted whether she had seen him.

12

When he came back to his office the next day, Sandra Furlong's welcome seemed to be especially warm. He had told her nothing about the crisis in his marriage; but she obviously sensed that something was wrong. She plonked the large mug of coffee in front of him as soon as he had sat down at his desk.

"You look as through you need this," she said.

He drank it greedily. Then asked her: "Anything happen while I was gone?"

"Yes." Sandra Furlong seemed pleased with herself. "You asked me to check whether Mr Karapolitis was in Britain the other day. Well, he was. I called Claridge's on the off chance and asked to speak to him and they told me he had left over a week ago. Then I remembered that his daughter was in business with him, and so I asked whether by any chance Miss Karapolitis was still there."

"What did they say?"

"They checked on the records and told me that Miss Karapolitis had stayed on a few days after her father but that she too had now left."

"They didn't by any chance indicate where she had gone?"

"No. And I didn't ask them," Sandra Furlong replied. "But I think I know."

Grantham looked at her in surprise. "What do you mean?"

Sandra sat down the other side of Grantham's desk. Mini-skirts were back in fashion and as she hooked one shapely brown leg over the other, Grantham had one brief, inspiring glimpse of panty. With all the recent fuss and drama, he reflected wryly, it was quite some time since he had given the matter of panties and such-like the attention it deserved. He found himself thinking about Ingrid Lubbeke and that brief, glorious encounter in the Black Forest. He would have to get in touch with Ingrid soon . . . for a number of reasons. . . .

His mind returned to the present when he heard Sandra say:

"I was picked up at Taunton by a taxi driver who was waiting in the rank there beside the station. He was a talkative fellow. When I told him where I wanted to go, he said that was funny, he had taken a young lady out there only a week or so earlier. 'Attractive woman,' the taxi driver said. 'Came from Greece or some such place.' Then, later on," Sandra continued, "when we drove up the river to where Mrs Potter lived I realized that the young lady from Greece was probably Iona Karapolitis herself. She just got there ahead of us."

"What do you mean?" Alarm bells were ringing in Grantham's mind.

"I made friends with the old lady," Sandra explained. "Had tea with her, told her how beautiful the valley was and how lucky she was to live there. I could tell that her circumstances were, as they used to stay in the more genteel quarters of Barbados, 'rather straitened'. So after beating about the bush for a polite length of time, I came out with the proposition you told me to put."

"And what did she say?"

"She looked surprised. And then she looked suspicious. She told me that she didn't have any share certificates in the Channel Tunnel Company. So I thought it best to beat a strategic retreat and I said that we must have had the wrong information and what a pity it was, because if she did happen to have any Channel Tunnel Company share certificates she could get a very good price for them indeed.

"She admitted it then. She said that only the other day she had shown them to another young lady who also looked a bit foreign and she had learned they were worth quite a bit of money, really. So I nudged her along a bit at this point and asked, then, was it true she probably did have some certificates after all? And, after that, she admitted, somewhat shamefacedly because, as she explained, she had always thought of them as family heirlooms of a sort, that she used to have some but that she had just parted with a whole trunkful and that she wouldn't have believed that a nice young lady arriving like that out of the blue could possibly have brought so much money with her."

Grantham swore. "What makes you sure the girl was Iona Karapolitis? That's only an hypothesis, isn't it?"

"No." Sandra Furlong was adamant. 'I called in at the local village pub, The Royal Oak, on the way back. It lets rooms as well. I talked to the landlord. In fact, I chatted him up a bit. Kept the taxi waiting while I had a few drinks in the bar. I was about the only person there, since it was early evening. I said that I didn't expect he got many Barbadians visiting Winsford. And he said, quite cheerily, that though the blacks didn't go much west of Taunton" – Sandra Furlong laughed as she recalled the scene – "on the whole, they got all sorts of visitors. And then he mentioned a young Greek woman who had stayed a few days earlier, so I knew I was on the right track. Before I left, I took a look at the hotel registration book which he kept just behind the bar and there her name was, large as life: 'Iona Karapolitis – Athens, Greece'."

"Then what did you do?"

"The taxi took me on to Taunton and I took the train back to Paddington."

The word Paddington rang a bell in Grantham's memory.

"Do you remember what day Iona Karapolitis stayed at The Royal Oak?"

"Yes, of course. It was the 27th."

Grantham nodded. It made sense. It was the same date as the postmark on the letter. He stood up and walked over to the window. There was a heavy barge laden with crates plying its way steadily up the Thames. Like that barge's progress towards Teddington, it had all once seemed plain sailing. And now, suddenly, it wasn't plain sailing at all.

Sandra Furlong was still sitting by the desk. Grantham turned back to her.

"Did the old lady say she had sold *all* her shares?"

"I think so. She wasn't specific."

Grantham pulled the telephone towards him, looked up a number in his book, and dialled Robin Dawson, senior partner in a long-established firm of City stockbrokers. Dawson came on the line almost at once.

"Good to hear from you, Oliver. What can I do for you?"

Stockbrokers don't waste words when they are trading. Grantham didn't either.

"Can you tell me if the old Channel Tunnel Company shares are still quoted? Call me back if you like."

"I don't have to call you back," Dawson replied. "I can tell you now."

Sitting in his City office, Dawson tapped the keyboard of the desk computer in front of him. The information he wanted was projected instantaneously onto the screen.

"CTC shares," he told Grantham, "have a face value of four shillings. If you can remember what four shillings are." He laughed. "There are about half a million of them in circulation somewhere. You can buy them today for about a tenth of a penny each. If you can find them. In my view, that's expensive!" He laughed again.

Grantham spoke quietly into the mouthpiece. It might have been a field telephone, with the force commander giving final, precise instructions for battle.

"I want you to buy every single CTC share you can lay your hands on. I don't mind what you have to pay."

"Your own account?"

"Yes. Buy them in my name." Grantham's reply was immediate. If there was ever a time to gamble, this was it.

"But don't buy so fast, Robin, that it looks as though something is up. We don't want other people getting interested."

"Perhaps you'll tell me one day why *we* should be getting interested." Robin Dawson sounded caustic.

"I will one day, Robin. Not now."

They spoke for a few seconds longer. Dawson was about to finish talking and start buying when a change in the numbers on the screen in front of him caught his eye.

"Now that's very strange, Oliver," he said. "It looks as though someone else is buying CTC today. They have just gone up from .1p per share to .15p per share. I know you're starting low, but that's a 50 per cent increase! What's going on? Do you all know something I don't know?"

"Just buy, Robin, would you?"

Grantham put down the receiver and turned to Sandra.

"What's the name of that big stamp-dealing company? The one with offices in the Strand?"

"Stanley Gibbons?"

"That's the one. Will you get them on the phone for me, please?"

Sandra Furlong retreated to her desk in the ante-room, muttering under her breath, like Alice: "Curiouser and curiouser".

Later that day Grantham went round to Stanley Gibbons' sales-rooms and offices in the Strand. The managing director, a brisk efficient-looking young man called Giles Lowe, was waiting for him.

"You were right to call," he said. 'Most people think Stanley Gibbons only means stamps. Philately and nothing else. They're wrong. The business we have been doing in recent months and years in old certificates has grown more rapidly than anything else. People seem to feel they're buying a slice of history."

They were talking in Lowe's upstairs office. As he spoke, Lowe walked over to the wall and pulled open the drawer of a metal cabinet. He took out some wide, heavy sheets of paper.

"And, of course, they're right," he continued. "In their way, these certificates *do* have historical significance. Look at this one, for example. It's a bond issue organized for Argentina's first loan in 1824. As a matter of fact, Argentina defaulted four years later; but that didn't deter the money-men."

He pushed the drawer shut and pulled another open. He held up a fistful of paper.

"You've got to remember that the last decade of the nineteenth century in particular was a perilous time for bankers and investors. American railroads went bankrupt. Australia was hit by drought. Latin American governments, not only Argentina, defaulted; Tsarist Russia was trying desperately to industrialize; South African goldmines were being sunk in the wrong places."

Grantham examined some of the certificates. He could understand immediately what Giles Lowe meant when he spoke of "historical significance". These pieces of paper represented hopes and dreams which, for one reason or another, had foundered.

"What about old Channel Tunnel Company share certificates?" he asked. "Do you have them? Could you obtain them?"

Some time later as Grantham left the Stanley Gibbons building and walked out again into the Street, he thought about one minor practical matter which he had not yet resolved. Before noon the next day, he would have to let Stanley Gibbons have his cheque for £50,000. In the normal course of events he could, as it were, have raided Chunnel Consortium's petty cash. He could have rung up David Blakely, explained the problem and Blakely would certainly have covered him. When you were building a one-billion-pound-plus project, you didn't quibble about the odd fifty thousand. But this was one occasion where he couldn't use Chunnel Consortium; couldn't rely on Sir David Blakely. This time, he was on his own. That was the way it had to be.

He walked along The Strand, rounded the lower edge of Trafalgar Square, and then continued along Pall Mall until he reached the Army and Navy Club. By the time he got there he knew exactly what he was going to do.

The porter recognized him as he came in.

"Good evening, General."

"Good evening, Smithson."

There was a telephone kiosk for the use of members and their guests below the stairs.

Grantham wrote out a number on a piece of paper and asked the porter to get it for him.

"I'll take the call in the cabin," Grantham said.

As he waited in the stuffy cubicle for the call to be put through, Grantham realized that his heart was beating a fraction over its normal seventy-two. It was as though he had just done three minutes on the exercise-bicycle in the gym with the weights set at 30 kilos. He steadied himself by breathing out slowly and deliberately.

The telephone rang in the booth. "Your call to Germany, sir," said the porter.

Grantham recognized the voice at the other end of the line immediately.

"Konrad! I'm so glad I found you in."

Grantham talked for fifteen minutes. When he emerged from the cabin, the gong was sounding for dinner. He walked up to the dining-room with a small, happy smile on his face.

The smile broadened and turned into a positive beam when he saw emerging from the bar and also heading for the dining-room his old friend and comrade-in-arms, "Buffy" Watson.

Grantham greeted the other man warmly. "What's an SAS man doing here? I thought they kept you penned up in Hereford with the cattle!"

Buffy Watson laughed. "Oh, they let us out from time to time. Or else, we blast our way out!"

The two men picked a table in the corner.

"I've been wondering what happened to you, Oliver."

"Ditto," said Grantham.

As he unfolded the starched linen napkin and spread it on his knees, Grantham realized that there were pluses as well as minuses in the present situation. If he hadn't had that spat with Lily – it *was* just a spat, wasn't it? – he'd be on his way back home to Fleet now and he wouldn't have met Buffy Watson in the Club.

As things turned out, Grantham would reflect later, it was one of the happiest chance encounters since the Egyptian princess found Moses in the bullrushes.

"It has to be somebody's birthday somewhere," said Blakely, opening up a bottle of champagne.

Grantham had never known a time when his friend would not produce champagne at the slightest excuse. He remembered that

Blakely, even when he was a boy at Eton, always kept a bottle handy; in later life he kept several bottles handy.

Lydia Blakely, Sir David's Italian wife, came to join them. She was a dark-haired, attractive woman, in her mid forties, and probably the main reason why Sir David maintained his expensive establishment in Tuscany. One way or another, Lady Blakely found a reason or an excuse to visit Italy several times a year. Sir David was happy to let her go. Anything that was good for her was good for him.

"Oliver! How good to see you! It's been too long. I'm sorry I was away last time you were here."

She kissed him, Italian-fashion, on both cheeks.

"And how is Lily?" Lydia Blakely said. "You must bring her up to town one day. We don't see enough of her."

Grantham was not a man who believed in beating about the bush.

"Lily and I are separated at the moment," he said. "Things may work out. Or they may not. Time will tell."

There was real concern in Lydia Blakely's voice as she replied, "I'm so sorry. Is there anything I can do to help?"

"Not at the moment, but thanks."

When his wife had gone, David Blakely turned to Grantham. "I had no idea. Rather sudden, wasn't it?"

"Things are always sudden when they happen."

And then he had decided that he had better, after all, say something. He told Blakely about the photographs.

"What is interesting," he said, "apart from the banality of it all, is that someone has obviously decided that I am a target. I've always believed that the best method of defence is attack. That's why I sent the photographs back. I wanted to draw them out into the open straightaway and, I suppose, I succeeded, though" – there was a rueful note in his voice as he continued – "the cost in personal terms has been rather higher than I expected."

If Grantham left out of his account the most convincing piece of evidence, namely that the photographs had been posted from Paddington on the very same day that Iona Karapolitis had taken her train from Paddington to Taunton, it was for a very good reason. He did not at this stage want to tell Blakely anything at all about the business of the old Channel Tunnel Company and where his investigations were leading. If he had told Blakely that Iona had been at Paddington, Blakely would have asked him how he knew and where she was going. And then the cat would have been out of the bag.

Blakely refilled both their glasses. "Shall we spike their guns?"

Grantham smiled a broad confident smile. "I tell you, David," he said, "we shall not only spike their guns, we shall ram them right up their backsides."

They talked for another half hour. It was the first opportunity Grantham had had to inform Blakely in detail about the recent developments on the Chunnel project. He told him about his excursion to Scotland to the site of the oil rig; of his visit to Lord Coulton's place in Berkshire and of his subsequent trip to Paris.

As he described the incident with Monique Delacourt, Grantham felt some of his own anger and humiliation returning.

"She called me a Boy Scout!" he told Blakely, "except she pronounced it 'scoot'."

Blakely almost collapsed with laughter.

"You are having a hard time of it, Oliver, aren't you?" Then he turned serious. "Are you sure she's right? I'll tell you what I think, Oliver, and you can do what you like with it. I think you've got a damned good idea there and you shouldn't let it go just because some little trumped-up French graduate from the Ecole des Mines has her nose out of joint because she didn't think of it herself!"

Blakely's words fell on Grantham's ears like the gentle rain from heaven. He knew he had been about to give up; and now he wasn't about to give it up at all. Blakely, it came to him, had never been a great cricketer himself; but he had been a damn good captain. He had known when to change the bowler; but he had known, too, when to keep a bowler on.

"Thanks," Grantham said. "I needed that piece of advice and encouragement just then. When somebody calls you a Boy Scout, it hurts. You start wondering whether you aren't, after all, getting carried away by your own enthusiasm. I was about to let the idea drop."

"And now that you're not about to let it drop, what's your next step?"

When Grantham told him, Blakely said: "You can't go to the States just as managing director. They wouldn't understand that. They would think you were some kind of low-level flunky."

Sir David Blakely broke open another bottle of champagne. He lifted his glass.

"I'll keep on the chairmanship but I'm going to get the board to name you president. And frankly, Oliver, I think you've deserved it. I don't know of any other man who could have pulled this thing together in so short a time."

They drank to that.

Before Grantham left, Blakely asked him where he planned to live, now that his domestic life had suffered a sea-change.

"You'll want to get a flat in town for the time being," Blakely said. "You can put the lease in the company's name."

For the first time, Blakely's remark caught Grantham on the raw. "I'm not a charity case, you know," he replied stiffly. "I shall probably buy something for myself." Then a flicker of a smile crossed his face. "What's two or three hundred thousand pounds on a fine day? I've been out of the army a couple of years already, you know, David. I'm learning fast how the game's played."

Blakely gave a him a long, searching look. You could know a man for thirty-five years and still not know all that there was to know about him.

13

Grantham flew direct from Heathrow to Tucson, Arizona. The opening up of the American South-west to direct intercontinental travel was one of the phenomena of the 1980s. The Sun Belt States, particularly Arizona and Nevada, had gone on growing at a time when the rest of the country was in the throes of recession. When companies like Fairmont Tool moved to a place like Tucson, they did so for sound business reasons. Locating in the Sun Belt made sense. You could serve the domestic market, particularly the market which was growing up within a few hundred miles' radius; you could serve the export market as well. Mexico and Latin America lay just south of the border. And over there to the west, beyond the Pacific, were the new burgeoning economies of Asia.

On and off over the last twenty years, Grantham had travelled a good deal in the United States. This was his first visit to Tucson. Fairmont Tool sent a senior vice-president out to the airport to meet him.

"Hi, I'm Howard Leeming."

Grantham warmed immediately to the tall, bronzed man who walked towards him with arms outstretched.

"Good to meet you," Grantham said. "Thanks for coming out."

"We're putting you up at the Desert Inn," Leeming said, as they drove off. "We thought you'd like it there. The downtown hotels have really passed their prime. Nowadays, it's the desert or nowhere. As long as you've got transportation, who cares about being ten miles out? And who hasn't got transportation nowadays?"

Grantham watched the scenery unfold. Cactus plants of every shape and size lined the road.

"Our cacti are protected now," Leeming told him. "People used to drive out from town, dig one up and plant it in their back yard. That would be a violation now, and darn right too! It's the environment of the desert that makes this place what it is." He gestured out of the car window. "You think that's dead out there, don't you? That desert's teeming with life. Ever see the Walt Disney film *The Living Desert*?"

Grantham shook his head. "No, but I'm prepared to believe you anyway."

Leeming waited while Grantham checked in. "Don't worry about the bill," he said. "Fairmont will take care of that. I'll see you in the morning."

Grantham was grateful to have a chance to unwind. It had been a long day. God knows how many time-zones he had crossed in his flight west.

He found his room, unpacked his things, walked twenty minutes in the surroundings of the hotel, had dinner by himself and, finally, was in bed and asleep before nine o'clock.

Leeming came for him early the next morning.

'We have an eight-thirty appointment with Matt Ericson, Fairmont's chief executive. He interrupted his vacation to be with you today."

"So I should think," said Grantham.

When the President of the Consortium which was about to undertake one of the largest construction projects in the history of the world came into town expecting to do business with one of its major suppliers, you certainly anticipated that someone would be minding the shop.

"I'll tell you something, Mr Leeming," he commented drily, "I'm not sure that Mr Ericson will want to resume his vacation once he has heard the proposition I'm going to put to him today."

"Call me Howard," Leeming said.

Matt Ericson was a florid, heavy-set man. Around sixty years old, he was on the telephone when Grantham and Leeming arrived in his office and they had to wait two or three minutes before he was free. When, finally, Ericson came out to get them, there was – Grantham thought – more than a hint of cavalierness in his manner.

He motioned his visitor to a seat.

"I'm afraid there's nothing we can do. Absolutely nothing. We consulted our lawyers and they tell us that the Administration has a watertight case."

"I don't understand what you're getting at," said Grantham.

Matt Ericson appeared surprised. "What the heck! I thought the telex notifying you had gone out at the end of last week." He turned to Howard Leeming who was sitting on his right. "Howard, you ought to check that one out, you know. Falaise should have been informed as soon as the rule-making was finalized." He pronounced Falaise like phallus.

"Perhaps you had better explain now that I am here," Grantham intervened quietly. He could see that Leeming was looking both embarrassed and suspicious. Was his boss playing some funny game which Leeming knew nothing about?

Ericson pulled a sheet of paper towards him. "I guess we've got caught up in the escalating trade dispute between the United States and Europe," he said. "On August 18th last, the Department of Commerce, at the direction of the President and pursuant to Section 6 of the Export Administration Act, amended Sections 376.12, 379.8, and 358.2 of the Export Administration Regulation. The Department of Commerce isn't saying so, but you and I know that these moves on the part of the Administration are in retaliation for the continued expansion of European trade with the Soviet Union, including, of course, but not limited to, the second pipeline project. What these amendments amount to is an expansion of the existing US controls on the export of goods and technical data, not just to European firms trading with the Soviet Union, but to European firms period."

Grantham was incredulous. "Are you telling me," he protested, "that Fairmont's contract to supply tunnel-boring machines to Falaise is covered by these amendments? I thought they related purely to oil and gas exploration, exploitation, transmission, and refinement."

"Look, Mr Grantham," Ericson spoke with increasing irritation. "I'm as distressed with this situation as you are. I hate to cancel a contract as much as I hate anything. I agree that the main thrust of the regulations relate to oil or natural gas technology. But our lawyers have looked at the language of the schedules. It clearly covers compressors and they reckon it covers TBMs as well. Fairmont Tool may be missing out on a few million dollars worth of business in Europe, but, believe me, we do billions of dollars worth of business with Uncle Sam. We've considered this matter rather deeply. We are not prepared to risk Administration penalties by violating the amendments. You can sue us for breach of contract if you like. That's your prerogative. In those circumstances we would expect the US government to indemnify us."

Grantham didn't want to let it go at that. Suddenly the whole thing seemed to be falling apart around his ears. It seemed as though it wasn't a question now of finding six TBMs or even four TBMs. He wasn't even going to get the two that they had been counting on from the start.

"Goddammit!" he exploded, crashing his hand on the desk top in front of him. "You've built the machines, haven't you? They're standing there, waiting to be shipped to us. What the hell are you going to do with them?"

Matt Ericson had stood up to indicate that the interview was at an end. "That's our problem, I think, not yours," he replied.

Grantham left the room fuming.

As they walked out to the car he said to Howard Leeming, who was still escorting him, "I don't believe you even built those machines. I think you've been stringing us along."

Howard Leeming stopped in mid-stride. He shook his head. "No, sir. You're dead wrong there. We built those machines all right. They're ready to go digging."

"I'd like to see them." There was a note of grim determination in Grantham's voice. "You never know, the political situation between the US and Europe might change and the Administration might reverse its decision. After all, our money is on the nail. I'd like to have a first-hand look at the product."

"Sure thing. You want to see them right now?"

They got into the car. "No point in walking in this heat," said Leeming. Grantham agreed. It was not yet nine o'clock but the desert temperatures were rising rapidly towards the nineties.

Security had been tight at the office headquarters; it was even tighter at the manufacturing complex.

"You're talking about industrial secrets," Leeming explained as they passed one security fence and checkpoint, then another, "which are, literally, the lifeline of a company like ours. You let those secrets go one way or another, and you've lost your principal asset."

They parked the car outside a shed as big as an aircraft hangar and went inside. The TBMs were there all right. As Leeming had promised, they were built and ready to go. As he saw the giant machines, Grantham felt a surge of excitement inside him. Procedurally speaking, there had obviously been some god-awful cockup. But in terms of sheer technology he could see, just by standing where he was, that Fairmont Tool had delivered the goods in no uncertain terms.

Howard Leeming, too, was obviously proud of Fairmont's achievements.

"I'm as sorry as you are, believe me, about the way things have turned out." Leeming, unlike Ericson, spoke with evident sincerity. "There's nothing I'd like better than to see these babies put to work on the Channel Tunnel. As an engineer, I'm proud of them."

As they walked around the shed, Leeming gave Grantham a running commentary. "There are only four other machines like these in the whole world. Two of them were being used on the Helmand Valley Irrigation Project in Afghanistan until the Soviets invaded and everything came to a stop out there. Another pair is actually being used today on the extension of the Rome Subway. These six machines are known as our 'F' Series. You've got a cutting head torque of five and a quarter million pounds per foot. Thrust is 600,000 pounds. The cutting head has forty-four cutters. Most of these are toothed roller cutters; some are disc cutters."

Grantham noticed that in the operator's cabin, which they reached by climbing some metal stairs, a panel had been fixed giving the specifications of the machine – torque, thrust, number of cutters and so forth – more or less as Leeming had described. What puzzled him was why the data should be given in a language which he took to be Japanese, as well as English. He asked Leeming to explain.

The American was clearly taken aback by Grantham's question.

"You're right. It *is* Japanese," he admitted. "Now that they can't go to Europe, these machines are being shipped to Japan. They leave next week."

"Lucky for you, eh? Lose one customer, find another."

Grantham felt his suspicions rising. There was something funny going on at Fairmont Tool and he wanted to find out what it was.

"Hell!" Leeming looked even more embarrassed than he had been earlier. "The Japanese have been putting on a lot of pressure ever since they decided to build the second Seikan Tunnel. That's the tunnel," he explained, "which connects Honshu to Hokkaido by crossing under the Tsugaru Strait."

Grantham stood there in silence, inspecting the data panel.

"You move fast, don't you? The Department of Commerce issues its amendments on 18th August. By 28th August you've got all the data and instructions written up in Japanese and the freighter's waiting in Los Angeles."

Leeming stood his ground, loyal to the company no matter what crooked dealing might have been going on behind his back.

"Fairmont is in business. We didn't become the biggest tool makers in the world for nothing. We have to move fast."

Later that afternoon, Grantham made some calls from his room at the Desert Inn. He rang Washington, DC first of all. Prescot Brown Jr, who was a partner in the prestigious Washington law firm of Bovington, Tracy, was about to leave for the day when the call came through.

"Good to hear you, General," Prescot Brown spoke in a slow Ivy League drawl. He had been an undergraduate at Harvard and then gone on to Law School at Princeton. With his button-down irts, pale blue eyes and gold-rimmed spectacles, he was, to Grantham, the archetypal WASP.

"I'm not a general any more, Prescot," Grantham laughed. He could clearly visualize his friend sitting there in his office in the Federal Triangle Building just across the road from the World Bank and only two blocks away from the White House. Then he said, "Do you have a moment? I'm in Arizona. There's something I need to ask you about."

"You catch me on my way home, Oliver, but it won't hurt if I'm a few minutes late. Fire away."

Grantham gave a succinct outline of the situation, before coming to the key question. "Basically, what I want to know is this: is Fairmont pulling a fast one on us while at the same time sheltering behind the amendments to the Export Administration Act? Do those amendments cover equipment such as TBMs or not? If they're using the amendments as an excuse to sell stuff we've ordered to the Japanese, what can we do about it?"

While Grantham talked, Prescot Brown had been scribbling notes on a yellow legal pad. And, when Grantham had finished, the Washington lawyer took his time before replying. If there was one thing he had learned in fifteen years on the treadmill between corporation boardroom, White House and Capitol Hill, it was that you thought first, and spoke later.

At last Prescot Brown said: "You'll have to give us a bit of time on this one. You've posed an interesting problem there. I can't give you an off-the-cuff answer. At first sight, I'd say that you've been taken for a ride, as you surmised, but that there's nothing much you can do. My recollection is that the schedule says nothing specifically about TBMs. But if the Administration chooses to take a broad interpretation, they can probably make it stick."

"Shit!" Grantham swore into the telephone. But before he could give vent to his feelings any further, the other man had continued:

"This is just a first reaction. Can you look in here on your way home? I might have something more for you."

Grantham made a quick decision. It was Friday. He had been planning to catch the overnight flight back to Europe. It was the ritual reflex of the married man. Get back to the wife and kids at the weekend. But then he thought: what the hell! The kids had flown the nest long ago and it looked as though Lily had departed as well. A busy man sometimes needed a break. He could visit the Grand Canyon before flying East. It was something he had always wanted to do.

"Sure," he replied. "How about 3 p.m. Monday?"

"3 p.m. Monday would suit me fine," replied Prescot Brown. "If you have anything else we ought to see, bring it with you."

The telephone rang as soon as Grantham replaced the receiver.

"You won't know me." It was a woman speaking with a marked Spanish accent. "My name is Dolores Garcia. I work for Mr Ericson. I saw you today when you came into the office. There's something I need to tell you. Something about the contract."

"Can't you tell me now?" Grantham had a mental image of a woman with light brown skin, jet black hair and a vivid slash of red lipstick smiling at him earlier that morning as he walked, with Howard Leeming, into Matt Ericson's office at the desert headquarters of Fairmont Tool Company.

"No. Not now, not over the phone. Meet me at the bar in OK Corral exactly one hour from now."

"Where's that?"

"Everybody knows OK Corral."

An hour later, having caught a cab out to old Tucson, Grantham was waiting for Dolores Garcia to walk through the swing-doors. There were two or three other customers at the bar, dressed in traditional cowboy clothes. He realized, as he overheard their conversation, that – unlike him – they were dedicated movie buffs.

"Burt Lancaster played Wyatt Earp," one of them said. "Earp was dying of TB. A bit like John Wayne in *The Shootist*."

"Wasn't Kirk Douglas in the movie too?" a second man asked.

"Sure he was. He played Doc Holliday."

The make-believe cowboys drifted out into the mean street where makebelieve tumbleweed blew at regular intervals to frighten a couple of tired-looking horses tied up outside the general store.

The barman came over and asked him if he wanted another drink. Grantham said yes. He looked at his watch. The girl was late. Or maybe he was a fraction early.

"Who killed Liberty Valance?" Grantham asked the barman, entering into the spirit of the place.

"How the hell should I know?" the man replied. "I just work here."

Dolores Garcia overheard the question as she slipped onto the bar stool next to Grantham.

"Everyone thinks Jimmy Stewart shot Liberty Valance. He has this gunfight on a dark night with Valance, played by Lee Marvin, and Valance dies. Jimmy Stewart becomes a big hero in the town. Then right at the end of the film, we learn that Jimmy Stewart didn't shoot Liberty Valance after all. John Wayne did!"

Grantham laughed. "I should have guessed."

"You should have known!" Dolores Garcia replied severely. "John Ford made that movie right here in old Tucson. That's a part of our heritage."

The barman had moved off again down to the other end of the bar. Out of earshot he busied himself polishing glasses and waiting for the bad guys to burst in and shoot out the lights.

Grantham admired Dolores' professionalism. As far as anyone could tell, he was an out-of-town visitor; she was just showing him the sights.

They went out into the sunlight of the late afternoon. She took his arm as they walked down the wide, empty street towards the small, white adobe church with a cross on top situated at the very edge of the town where the fantasy world of the 1880s ended and the real living desert began.

"Sergio Leone filmed *Once upon a Time in the West* here, too," she told him. "I come from Mexico, you know, from across the border. That film meant a lot to me. Do you remember it?"

Grantham was not quite sure if he remembered it or not. He was not really into films.

They stood in front of the little white church and she told him about Sergio Leone's film.

"You have this poor Mexican family living outside of the town," she said. "It's a couple with their son. The gang of four nasty men ride in. Henry Fonda, Jack Elam and so on. They kill the parents, rape and mutilate the mother. The son sees it all. The gang rides off again. In later life, the son grows up. He's played by Charles Bronson. He tracks the men down and kills them. First one, then two together. He ends up by killing Henry Fonda. A great film. We Mexicans have had to fight for our place in the sun."

They walked on, beyond the church, into the desert. Finally she said:

"You see, it's a matter of honesty. We may be poor but we're honest. When you're secretary to a man like Ericson, you get to see and hear a lot about what goes on. I don't like Ericson. I never have liked him. But that's not the point. He's a crook and you ought to know. You need to know."

"Why do you say that?"

"The Japanese got to him over that contract. They bribed him. They offered him half a million dollars, personally, if he'd let them have the two Series F machines which your people ordered four years ago. A couple of them came into his office one day. They talked about extreme political pressure back in Japan to get the second Seikan Tunnel built after the ferry accident."

"You're sure they bribed him?"

"Quite sure. Ericson left the money in the office safe overnight. I counted it. I took a note of the serial numbers too."

Grantham let out a long low whistle. "How did you hear the conversation in Ericson's office? Didn't he shut the door?"

"He left the intercom switched on. He quite often does that when he wants me to take notes without being in the room. I guess this time he just forgot."

Grantham stopped at a clump of cacti and examined the thick, spiky leaves. Others had been this way too, he noted. Names had been carved onto the plants like graffiti on subway walls.

They turned and walked back the way they had come.

"Would you testify?" Grantham asked. "It could cost you your job."

She shrugged. "Sometimes you have to do what you think is right. . . . I have my car here," she added. "I can give you a lift back to the Desert Inn."

They didn't go straight back to Grantham's hotel. Like the good guys in the westerns which had been turned out by the dozen in old Tucson's heyday, they drove off into the sunset. As the sun began to dip behind the giant cacti Dolores swung the car off the road onto the hard surface of the desert.

"Look over there." She pointed. "You can see the moon rise even before it's dark."

She switched off the engine, leaned over and kissed Grantham on the mouth. Then she opened the car door and beckoned him out. She had a blanket in the back and she spread it on the ground some way from the car. Grantham wondered, as he lay down next to her, whether he wasn't getting a bit old for this kind of thing.

"I think I'm getting a bit old for this kind of thing," he said. "Anyway what about scorpions, rattlesnakes?"

She laughed. "I grew up in the village just across the border not so far from here. Poor people, village people don't make love in hotel rooms. If you want to be alone together, you go out into the desert after the heat of the day. The scorpions and the puff adders and the rattlesnakes have gone to bed by then. It's too cold for them."

He buried his head in her breast. She felt the muscles of his arm and back. Fingered the hard, firm flesh.

"My God, you're in shape," she exclaimed.

"I have to be."

She swung her leg over his and pulled herself onto him. For the first time he kissed her properly. Kissing was such an intimate thing. Sometimes, thought Grantham, it was even more intimate than the act of love itself. He kissed her mouth. He kissed her breast. And then, as she lay back beneath the moon and opened her legs, he kissed her there as well, gently, delicately. Surprisingly so, for so hard a man.

When she moaned and moved on the blanket, he knew that she was ready. At the height of it, she lapsed into Spanish. "*Que bueno!*" she cried.

Grantham could only agree.

They lay there afterwards, looking at the stars.

"I saw just the same sky when I was a child, and a young woman, before I came to the United States. In Mexico, we see the same sky and the same stars as they do here in Tucson, but it is a world apart."

"Where exactly were you from in Mexico?"

"I came from Sonora, from a place called Siete Cerros. It means the Seven Hills."

"That's a beautiful name."

"It's a beautiful country."

After a while, they gathered up their things and drove back into town.

For Grantham, the weekend that followed had a certain magical quality about it. It was but the latest in a long series of encounters. But it still meant something. He hired a car at the hotel and picked her up at her apartment in downtown Tucson. Then they drove north.

"I'm glad I decided to stay," he said.

"I'm glad too."

They stopped for lunch in a town called Show-Low.

Dolores explained: "Two partners wanted to split their land but they couldn't think of a way of doing it. So they drew cards, the winner being the one who showed low. That's how the town got its name."

Later in the afternoon, still driving north, they visited the Petrified Forest, a primeval jungle first flooded, then invaded by silicate deposits so that the wood remained perfectly preserved after millions of years.

Then they continued through Navajo country until they reached a motel.

"Do you have a reservation?" the tall Indian at the reception desk asked.

"I thought this *was* a Reservation," Grantham replied.

The Indian remained totally impassive. He, and his race, had learned the hard way about the white man's sense of humour.

They had dinner in the hotel dining room. They were the only white couple there. The rest of the diners were Indians.

"You shouldn't make jokes, like you did when we arrived," Dolores warned him. "These people are still bitter about what the white man did to them."

Grantham took the point. At about the same time, he reflected, that Sir Edward Watkin was trying to get his Channel Tunnel scheme going, on the other side of the Atlantic they were committing genocide on an unprecedented scale.

After dinner, they went for a walk through Indian territory, turning back to the motel only as night fell. As they walked, Grantham could feel his shoulder blades tingling. He could imagine what it would be like to be shot in the back by an arrow.

They made love that night, and again in the morning before they left. It occurred to Grantham, as they lay in bed together with the early sun streaming in through the window, that no one else, as far as he knew, had any idea where he was or what he was doing. He didn't have to ring up Lily and tell her where she could get hold of him in an emergency. He didn't have to ring up and tell Lily anything at all. And if Blakely, or anyone else, wanted to communicate with him, well, they would just have to wait. The freedom to be out of touch was important, Grantham thought. He had never had it in the army. Someone always had to know where you were.

The car had an automatic speed regulator. They cruised on through a landscape which, with its mesas and buttes, grew progressively more lunar.

"The astronauts trained here," Dolores told him.

Grantham could well believe it. The scenery was, literally, out of this world. They had their first full-scale view of the Grand Canyon at a place called, appropriately enough, Desert Lookout.

"I've seen it before," Dolores said. "It's still unbelievable."

"It's unbelievably unbelievable," Grantham replied. He meant it. Of course he had seen pictures of the Grand Canyon. Everyone had. But the reality was a hundred times more impressive than the pictures.

He wanted to climb down the trail to the bottom of the gorge. But she told him it would take the whole day to go there and back, even on mules, and they didn't have the whole day.

"Can't we spend the night at the bottom and come back in the morning?" he asked.

"There's only one lodge down there and that'll be full. You have to book months ahead."

Finally they compromised, and walked down the trail as far as the Indian Gardens. The summer visitors were thinning out at the end of the season. America was getting ready for the Fall. But there were still enough people around to make Grantham wish he had been born a century or two earlier.

They climbed on down through geological time. Towers and turrets, pinnacles and alcoves, cliffs, ledges, crags of every shape and size abounded. The limestone at the top of the canyon gave way, as they descended, to bright red sandstone beds, which extended for some eight hundred feet on the vertical plane, and then below them came greenish sandstone beds and a series of sandstone and limestone strata.

They were standing at a vantage point, looking deep down into the canyon floor, still almost a vertical mile beneath them, when Dolores Garcia stiffened like a gun-dog scenting a bird.

She pointed to a couple of Japanese who were climbing back up the track towards them. She swore in Spanish "*Merda!* They're going to see us."

But the Japanese, who were puffing heavily from the uphill climb, appeared not to pay any attention to the man and the woman who, with exaggerated courtesy, flattened themselves into the canyon wall, so as to let the climbers pass.

A few seconds later, when the Japanese were forty or fifty feet above them, Grantham glanced back. He saw that the pair had stopped. Both had raised binoculars and appeared to be gazing intently at the spectacular display presented by the sheer face of the canyon wall on the other side of the gorge.

Later that evening, Dolores Garcia dropped Grantham off at the airport in Flagstaff.

"I'll take the car back," she said. "You're better off flying from here now."

They kissed in the car.

"We seem to be making quite a habit of this," Grantham laughed as he drew away.

"I don't call twice a habit!" She seemed really sad to see him go.

"Hell," thought Grantham as he boarded a plane for Washington D.C., "I seem to spend my time nowadays being seen off at airports."

Instinctively, he checked his breast pocket to see if he still had the items she had given him.

At precisely three o'clock on Monday afternoon, Grantham arrived at Prescot Brown's office in the Federal Triangle Building.

"It's so good to see you, Oliver." There was genuine warmth in the other man's greeting.

"Good to see you too."

They got down to business straightaway.

"I think there's no doubt," Prescot said, "that this is a retaliatory measure on the part of the Administration, the retaliation – of course – being on account of the expansion of European trade with the Soviet Union. So the first question that has to be asked is a general question, that is to say, it applies to the amendments as a whole; and that is, is the retaliation justified in law?"

Prescot Brown consulted his notes.

"I was pessimistic when I spoke to you over the telephone last Friday. I'm still pessimistic. We could, if you like, seek to maintain that the Administration's amendments are not consistent with the export Administration Act itself. For example, Section 6 of that Act requires the President to 'consider the reaction of other countries to the imposition or expansion of Export Controls by the United States'. It also requires the President to 'determine that reasonable efforts have been made to achieve the purposes of the controls through negotiations or other alternative means'. We could try to make the case in the courts both in terms of consistency with the underlying Export Administration Act or in terms of the admissibility of the amendments, given the basic principles of international law."

Prescot Brown paused and looked at his guest across the desk.

"I'll tell you quite frankly," he said. "We can try, but I don't think we will necessarily win. I was brought up to believe in the principle of the separation of powers. The judiciary and the executive are meant to act independently of each other. But the reality isn't quite like that, you know. We are likely to be seeking a ruling before a Federal District Judge who is himself a Presidential nominee and if the issue went all the way to the Supreme Court, again I am not sure how it would go. There has been a tendency in recent years for the Supreme Court to side with the Administration more often than not."

"What about the schedule?" Grantham asked. "It doesn't specifically mention TBMs?"

"It doesn't specifically exclude them, that's the problem," Prescot Brown replied. "Once the courts have accepted the legality of the Administration's actions at all in enacting the amendments, it's quite unlikely that they will then take a restrictive view of them."

Grantham nodded. What the lawyer had said made sense.

"Those machines are ready to leave," Grantham said. "There's a ship out on the Coast waiting to load them up. Can we seek a temporary injunction preventing their export, while we test the matter in the courts? As far as I'm concerned, it's a clear breach of contract."

"Don't get me wrong, Oliver," Prescot Brown said. "I think it's a breach of contract too. I think that you're right in supposing Matt Ericson played a fast one on you and is trying to get away with it by pleading the amendments. But that's going to be darn difficult to pin down."

It was the moment that Grantham had been waiting for. He passed over the paper which Dolores Garcia had given him the previous evening.

"Ericson was bribed. By the Japanese. That's a list of the banknote numbers. I have a tape of the conversation too."

Grantham explained the circumstances in which this particular evidence of corruption had come into his possession. Prescot Brown seemed suddenly much less pessimistic. Corporate venality was meat and drink to him. He dealt with it every day in one form or another.

There was one question in which he showed a special interest.

"This man Leeming, you say he's the Senior Vice-President. Is he to be trusted?"

Grantham had been sizing up men all his life and he had not often been wrong in his judgement. He remembered the embarrassment Leeming had shown during the interview with Matt Ericson. He was convinced that, though Leeming might have suspected something strange was going on, he had absolutely no knowledge of the bribery attempt by the Japanese.

"I'd say Leeming is straight. As straight as you can be in the rank world of Fairmont Tool."

Prescot Brown nodded in a satisfied way. "Good. We may need him."

Grantham was happy to leave matters in Prescot Brown's capable hands. That was what one paid lawyers for. Prescot would get to work, either directly, or through an associate firm in Tucson, and one way or another he would produce results.

"I think we can shift this one now," Brown assured him. "I wasn't so certain when you first came in this afternoon."

As Grantham was about to leave, the telephone rang on Prescot Brown's desk.

"Yes, he's here," the lawyer answered. "He can talk to you now."

Grantham took the receiver.

"I'm glad I got hold of you," Sandra Furlong said from London. "Hertz International have been on to me today. Apparently you rented a car from them in Tucson and it wasn't returned. You put the Company address on the form. I just thought you'd like to know."

"Thanks, Sandra. I'll talk to you later."

Grantham turned to Prescot Brown with a puzzled expression on his face.

"That's funny. Dolores Garcia was driving that car. She dropped me at Flagstaff so I could catch the plane to Washington. She was going to take the car on to Tucson. She said she'd turn it in that night."

"We'll look into that too if you like," Brown said. "All part of the service."

"Would you?" Grantham sounded relieved. "I'll be staying at the Mayflower."

Grantham had dinner that evening with an old friend from the Pentagon, Bill Peabody and his wife, Judy. They lived in a pretty period house on the waterfront in Alexandria, Virginia.

During the meal they talked, as people tend to do on such occasions, about mutual friends. Like diplomats, senior military men were always meeting each other in different parts of the world. Soldiering had its own forms of free-masonry. Bill Peabody had been intrigued to learn that, in spite of the fact that Grantham had now left the armed services, he was still in touch with men like General Maximilien Miguet.

"I tell you," said Peabody, as they sat after dinner, smoking cigars and looking at the lights of Washington across the Potomac. "That man could go very far indeed. At least in a French context."

Grantham nodded. He knew that when Peabody spoke of a "French context" this was really a shorthand way of saying that the French, if the situation demanded it, were quite prepared to throw democracy out of the window along with the kitchen sink. Grantham suspected that Peabody approved of the "French context". Generals in the United States Army, and Peabody was a very senior general indeed, were quite prepared to believe that democracy, like good wine, did not always travel well.

"France needed Charles de Gaulle," Peabody added. "Someday it may need Maximilien Miguet."

The conversation turned to Pierre Leroux.

"I don't know too much about him," Peabody said. "I'm told he's a rising star."

Judy Peabody slipped out to "do the dishes" as she put it. She knew that the two men would want to be alone together.

Grantham took advantage of her absence. "You can shoot this one down if you like, Bill, but I'd like your help if you can give it. One of my key people, her name is Monique Delacourt, is fairly closely involved with Leroux. I'd like to know that she's not stepping on some minefield. If you have anything on him, could you let me know?"

Bill Peabody laughed. "Is that an official request under the Anglo-American Defense Cooperation Agreement? If so, it has to come through the proper channels. You've got forty-one people, so I'm told, working with your Defense Attaché in your Embassy. One of them ought to know which form to fill in."

Grantham laughed too. "No, of course it's not an official request. I don't have status any longer anyway. I just wondered if you could help."

Bill Peabody poured himself a tumbler of neat bourbon.

"How am I going to get the information to you, if I can't pass it through channels? It may take a few days."

"Aren't you going to be at the NATO anniversary celebrations in Brussels later this month? Even ex-generals like me have been invited to that! We could find a moment to talk then."

"Far from the madding crowd, eh?" Peabody laughed again. "That decides it for me, I hadn't made up my mind whether to go over to Europe or not. But if you are going to be there, Oliver, I certainly shall!"

When he got back to the Mayflower, Grantham found that Prescot Brown had called. The message urged him to call back any time, no matter how late.

Prescot Brown, when he came on the line, was succinct and to the point.

"They found the car. They found the girl too. She was dead. She drove off the road into the desert about twenty miles outside of Flagstaff and hit a rock. The car turned over. She was still inside. Apparently a wheel came off. Hertz are maintaining that the car had been properly serviced. Do you think someone loosened the wheel nuts?"

Grantham told Prescot about the Japanese.

"Dolores saw them on the trail. They were coming up as we were going down. She thought they didn't see her. They could have found the car at the top if they were looking for it."

"I'll think about that," Prescot Brown said. "It would be good to get those Japs for homicide as well as bribery."

When he had finished the conversation, Grantham felt so angry and disturbed that he walked out into the street and down towards Lafayette Park. His mind raced. Probably, almost certainly, it was homicide, not an accident. Probably, almost certainly, the Japanese wanted to eliminate not just one, but both of them. He hated to think that he was the last person to have seen Dolores Garcia alive. Was Ericson involved?

He walked for half an hour around the streets. When he finally returned to his hotel, it was with the grim determination that heads should roll at Fairmont Tool. One way or another Dolores Garcia's death would be avenged. He remembered lying with her beneath the stars while she spoke to him about her childhood in Sonora and the Seven hills – "Siete Cerros". The cunts, he thought, the pricks, the absolute bastards!

14

Two years out of three the Sheraton Hotel off Connecticut Avenue in Washington, DC is the home of the World Bank and the International Monetary Fund's annual meeting. Delegates jet in from the four corners of the world and for a week congregate in the Sheraton's myriad suites and cocktail lounges, buffets and bars.

Officially, the meeting is for the nations who make up the membership of the Bank and Fund. The finance ministers of the rich Western countries pat each other on the back and rub shoulders (often, in the most literal sense, in the Sheraton's crowded elevators) with their counterparts from Asia, Africa, and Latin America. And the finance ministers will, as is their wont, have brought with them their own delegations of monetary experts. Most would take care to observe the golden rule: the smaller and poorer the country, the larger and more conspicuously expensive the delegation should be.

Certainly, as Grantham got out of his cab early the next morning and walked into the foyer, he could not help remarking on the crush of people fitted out in Savile Row suits. "That's the way the money goes!" he muttered to himself as he bounded up the steps towards the main conference hall.

He noted, as he pushed his way inside, that the international bankers, having recovered from the momentary scare created by the prospect of a Mexican and other defaults, were now back in force. And why not? he reflected. Nowadays, co-financing was the name of the game. You picked a developing country. The Fund underwrote the balance of payments while the Bank put up some longer term money for major projects. And major projects, now that McNamara had gone with his trendy ideas (like financing rural development and family planning), meant above all, hardware: machinery and equipment of every kind. Which in turn meant big fat contracts for Western industrial firms.

That's where the private bankers came in. A nice little topping up loan to finance half a dozen turbines on a major irrigation project in a country like Sri Lanka could help to ensure that, whatever the World Bank rules on competitive bidding in theory might say, the contract for those turbines went to some thrusting US company whose president might just conceivably have had lunch on Wall Street not a million years earlier. It was all pretty incestuous, Grantham thought. But at least it worked. That's why the bankers were there. As long as they could keep lending, they could show the debts as an asset in the balance sheets. If the developing countries couldn't pay the debts back, that didn't matter either. You just lent them some more. That way the merry-go-round could keep on spinning.

Grantham followed the crowd into the main hall. He spotted Anthony Hitchcock, the tough, able young man who had been appointed Britain's Chancellor of the Exchequer, making a late entrance accompanied by two officials. Treasury men, Grantham supposed. Letting his eye rove over the ranks of delegates who were now seated and fiddling with their earphones, Grantham noted that the French delegation was there in force. He half expected to see Pierre Leroux leading France's team. It would have been just like that thrusting ambitious politician to have elbowed Jacques Deshormes, the veteran Socialist who served as France's economics minister, aside. But Deshormes, he saw, was in his place, his grizzled, short-cropped head bent over his papers.

The delegates were seated in alphabetical order. Two or three seats down from France came Japan. Sitting at the back, as he was, Grantham did not have much of a view of the faces of the Japanese delegation. Not that he minded much. One Jap, he always thought, looked like any other Jap. Seconds later, he realized he was wrong about this. One of the men sitting towards the end of the row of Japanese turned round in his seat and looked behind him so that Grantham had a clear view of his face. It was only a brief glimpse but it was enough. Grantham was virtually certain that the Japanese delegate sitting four seats away from Takahashi Yasamoto, the Japanese finance minister, was one of the men whom he, and poor Dolores Garcia, had met on the trail down to the Indian Gardens at the Grand Canyon two days earlier.

For the moment there was nothing he could do except speculate. The President of the World Bank, Jim Clarkson, a tough Californian who modelled himself, if he modelled himself on anyone, more on Tom Clausen than on Bob McNamara, had begun his speech. Grantham listened with only half an ear to the dry parade of facts and figures.

"During the Financial Year which ended on the 30th of June last,"

Clarkson told the gathering, "the amount of loans from the World Bank and the International Development Association, as well as investment commitments of the International Finance Corporation, came to $15.6 billion. . . ."

The President of the World Bank droned on. The larger the sums of money described, the drier became his tone of voice. He described the distribution of bank loans and IDA credits by sector and then he outlined their distribution by region and by country.

"India," said Clarkson, "remains the most active borrower at $1.6 billion, followed by Indonesia at $926 million and Brazil at $722 million." And he added as almost a throw-away line, "World Bank operations in Afghanistan remain, of course, suspended for the duration. There has been no new lending to that country since 1980."

At this point, Jim Clarkson allowed his glance to fall deliberately on the front row of the stalls where an empty seat marked the place which should have been occupied by Afghanistan.

It was a long speech. Clarkson gave them their money's worth. They broke up for coffee afterwards.

Coming out into the foyer well ahead of the crowd, Grantham ran into Alex Lyons, the burly *Daily Mail* correspondent whom he had last seen – it seemed months ago now – in the House of Commons' Press Gallery on the day when the Prime Minister announced that the government was going to go ahead with the Channel Tunnel project.

But, before that, their paths had crossed quite frequently. They had got to know each other well when Alex Lyons had been in Brussels as the *Daily Mail* Common Market correspondent at the same time as Grantham had been there for NATO. Acquaintanceship had developed into friendship. Grantham appreciated Lyon's flair and almost unerring instinct for a good story. Lyons was deceptively soft-spoken; a world away from the chain-smoking, heavy-drinking, journalistic stereotype.

The *Daily Mail* correspondent had for his part appreciated Grantham's sheer professionalism. He knew a good soldier when he saw one. And when Grantham had made the switch to civilian life and had taken on the organization of the Channel Tunnel project, Lyons had run two 'exclusives' in the *Mail* which had ended up by portraying the man almost as much as the enterprise.

There was ten years difference in age between them.

Grantham looked at the younger man's freckled, open face. "Alex, fancy seeing you here! I thought you were covering the domestic scene nowadays."

"When you're as important as I am on the *Mail*," Alex Lyons smiled immodestly, "you get to pick and choose your own stories. What about you? Looking for finance?"

Lyons' question was only half in jest. He was always on the look-out for a story.

"Nothing for us here," Grantham shook his head. "I'm just an observer."

Lyons didn't press it. The two men helped themselves to coffee from urns that had been set up on the sideboard in the foyer. They went to sit on the sofa at the far end of the room.

"I see that Hitchcock is here for Britain," Grantham said, keeping his eye out for the Japanese as he spoke.

"Yes, I've got an interview with him this afternoon. For tomorrow's paper."

Grantham was interested. "How do you do that? Do you take notes? Do you rely on the famous journalistic photographic memory?"

"Oh, I pretend to," Alex Lyons laughed. "In practice, I'll tape him. That's what we all do nowadays." He tapped his lapel. "It's all in there. Microrecorders, microcassettes, the lot. It's a marvellous back-up system. Instead of scribbling away like mad, you can concentrate on what a man is actually saying."

Grantham at last saw the Japanese emerge from the hall, trailing, with typical Japanese politeness, a few paces behind their country's finance minister.

"Do me a favour, Alex," Grantham said urgently. "See that fat Jap coming out now, behind Yasamoto? Can you get him on tape? You may be able to use it yourself later. There's a story there."

"You don't have to do deals with me, Oliver. What do you want me to say to him?"

"Anything. Say you're doing a 'colour' feature for the *Mail* and you haven't got any yellow yet!"

Sometimes being famous helped, Grantham reflected as he rode up in the elevator to the 8th floor of the World Bank's "G" Street building. Dick Jordan, the World Bank's now underemployed loan officer for Afghanistan, had been only too delighted to see him.

"I admired what your country did in the Falklands, Mr Grantham, and I know that you personally were involved," Jordan had said over the telephone. And he repeated the sentiment when he ushered Grantham into his office.

Jordan was a thin, gangling American who had joined the World Bank ten years earlier, after graduate school, on its Young Professional Program. He had done a spell in the Projects Department followed by a couple of years as an economist; his promotion to loan officer for Afghanistan had come two years before the Soviet invasion of that country.

"What can I do for you? As you can see, we're not too busy at the moment," Dick Jordan laughed. It was a warm, relaxed laugh.

Grantham took an instinctive liking to the man. He came to the point straightaway.

"As I understand it," he began, "you were disbursing on a $200 million IDA credit for Afghanistan for the Helmand Irrigation Project when the Soviets took over."

"That's right," Dick Jordan waved his hand on the map of the wall. "The Helmand is one of the major rivers in Afghanistan. The project was multi-purpose. It had an irrigation component. We were going to get water to over a hundred thousand hectares. It also had a power generation side. By the end of it we would have had six turbines each with a 600 megawatt rating. That's a hell of a lot of power, you could keep half the country going on that. We had got most of the equipment in there but that was about all. The dam isn't built. The turbines aren't in place and the diversion tunnel wasn't even begun."

"That's what I wanted to ask you about," said Grantham. "Off the record of course. And I mean that."

"I understand."

"Specifically", Grantham continued, "I want to know what happened to the TBMs. My information – that's from Fairmont Tool who supplied them – is that you had two TBMs on the project and that they're probably still there."

"Not probably, certainly. Those TBMs, to the best of my knowledge, are still in their crates on the site. There's no way the Russians could have removed them even if they had wanted to. That's still rebel-held territory. Why do you ask?"

So Grantham told him.

Grantham had one more errand to run that day, after they had left the restaurant. Prescot Brown was waiting for him in his office.

Together they listened to the tape which Alex Lyons had so efficiently supplied.

"It's the same voice. I'm sure of that."

"We'll check the voice-prints anyway. We don't want to make mistakes."

Two hours later, Prescot Brown called Grantham at the Mayflower as the latter was preparing to leave for Dulles International Airport and the night flight to London.

By nature a cool, laconic figure, the attorney tried his best to keep the note of satisfaction out of his voice. The best lines, he had always found, were the throw-away lines.

"I can tell you, all hell has broken out in the last couple of hours. Out there in Arizona, you've got the sheriff running around, you've got the State Police running around. Now the Bureau has come in because the Japs clearly crossed State lines."

"Did the voice-prints match?"

"Sure they matched. The only question is, can we make the homicide charge stick? It turns out your friend is a Mitsikawa operative, seconded to MITI, that's the Japanese trade ministry, for the duration of the Bank-Fund meeting. The Japs are claiming diplomatic immunity at the moment. Mitsikawa by the way, in case you didn't know, are the main contractors on the Seikan Tunnel. That's why they need the TBMs. They're looking for funds too. That's why they're in town."

"What about Ericson?"

"He's been fired from Fairmont Tool. He'll probably be charged as well. Howard Leeming has taken over as chief executive. He called me a moment ago to tell me that the freighter is being diverted through Panama. You ought to have your machines within two weeks."

Grantham felt the surge of relief flood through him. Thank God for the full-time lawyers like Prescot Brown, he thought. There was no way he himself could have sorted all that out. Chunnel Consortium paid the man a hefty fee. But, by God, he got results!

The limousine was waiting at the door of the hotel. An hour later, he had checked in at the Pan Am desk. The girl told him that his flight would be called in forty minutes.

Grantham went up to the Executive Lounge at Dulles Airport, poured himself a tall Scotch and stood glass-in-hand, looking out onto the runway and at the Virginia countryside beyond. The sun was just dropping behind the Blue Ridge mountains. Once as a boy in one of the school holidays, Grantham remembered, he had gone camping up there, in the country beyond the Shenandoah River. How many years ago was that now? It seemed like only yesterday.

He put his glass down as his flight was called. Why was it, he wondered, that he always seemed to be on the move? But what kind of man would he be if he stopped?

The truth of it, Grantham decided as he boarded the plane for the seven-hour flight back home, was that he probably didn't dare to find out.

15

If there had been a helicopter service from Athens to Paros, Brian Staples would have taken it. The *Lemnos* was a sturdy boat, built on the Clyde between the wars, and her crew was an experienced crew; but there was nothing that either boat or crew could do to diminish the force of the summer gale which, blowing up out of a clear blue sky, was now lashing the seas of the Cyclades into white-topped fury.

On the Beaufort Scale the wind was Force 9, or higher. Brian Staples had imagined that he would enjoy the six-hour crossing from Piraeus to the Islands. He had imagined himself sitting on deck in the sun counting the rugged outcrops of land as they passed and absorbing, drinking in, the atmosphere. In the event, he had had to make a hurried rush from Athens Airport so as to catch the *Lemnos* moments before her departure.

Four hours out, the gale had struck them. Instead of absorbing the sun, Staples had found himself clinging to the railings on a wildly plunging deck.

The physical circumstances aggravated his already fractious state of mind. He could understand the reasons which had led Iona Karapolitis to set up her own place away from that of her father. He could also understand that Iona had wished to demonstrate that her way of doing things was not necessarily the same as Christina Onassis's way of doing things. Paros was not Scorpios. But the upshot of it all, Staples reflected, was that obeying a summons from Iona Karapolitis to attend a weekend strategy session was a great deal more difficult than going to a constituency meeting.

By the time the *Lemnos* had fought its way into the little harbour of Paroikia to disgorge its load onto the quayside, Brian Staples' temper had, if anything, worsened. Instead of drinking in the beauty of the place, with its whitewashed houses, windmills by the water's edge and Venetian ramparts which bespoke the island's chequered history,

Staples fussed about his luggage and shouted offensively at small boys who tried to help him with it.

Perversely, the wind dropped almost as soon as he set foot on land. Though it was mid-September, the temperature was high in the eighties. Without the wind, Staples found himself sweating profusely as he walked off the quay, past the fruit stalls and ticket booths, in search of a taxi. It was only when he had at last found a battered old Citroën to take him up the mountain, where at least it would be cooler, that he felt at all capable of registering the spectacular natural beauty which surrounded him.

Three quarters of an hour later Staples was nearing his destination in considerably better humour. The taxi had taken him out of town and up into the hills which formed the centre of the island towards a village called Marathi. As they climbed, he had had a magnificent view of Antiparos and the small islands which were clustered around it. He had observed the caiques of the local fishermen coming back into port; the small boys tending sheep; donkeys braying in the late afternoon; hobbled goats moving erratically from one pasture to the next.

They had passed ten or twenty little white churches, and as many scattered homesteads. Marathi itself, when they reached it, was nothing more than a grouping of houses, half a dozen altogether, representing the highest settlement on the island. The taxi driver swung the car under the shade of a fig tree.

"Marathi," he said. And then he pointed to a rough track which led on up the mountain. His manner made it clear that this was a road unsuitable for taxis.

Reluctantly Staples got out of the car. At least they might have sent a donkey for me, he thought, as an enthusiastic hee-haw broke the stillness of the late afternoon. He picked up his bag and began to walk.

After about half a mile of heavy, up-hill going, Staples found his stride and realized he was quite enjoying himself. Looking at the tracks he'd climbed, he could quite understand the reluctance of the taxi driver to proceed. This was a path for a Jeep or a Land-Rover or, better still, a tracked vehicle.

The scenery grew more spectacular as each minute passed. Staples realized that Iona Karapolitis, in her peculiarly individual way, had managed to select a site for her own retreat every bit as unique as that chosen by her father.

An hour later, totally recovered from his climb and from the ill-temper with which he had begun the day, Brian Staples listened to Iona Karapolitis's account of how she had come to Paros.

"All my life," she said, "I've been fascinated by marble. Parian marble is the finest in the world."

They were sitting on the terrace of Iona's house, high on the mountain. Straight ahead of them, on the island of Naxos across the water, loomed Mount Zeus. To the north lay the distant outlines of Tinos and Mykonos, the central islands of the Cyclades and, beyond them, the ring of outer islands.

Iona had appeared to be deeply apologetic that no one had come to meet him at the quayside.

"I sent Stavros down with the Jeep, but they said the boat was indefinitely delayed. I felt sure you'd find your way."

Staples had said nothing at that point. The reason there was no one to meet him by the quayside, he suspected, had nothing to do with the weather. It was more of a question of Iona Karapolitis demonstrating yet again that she was in charge now. He was grateful in any case to arrive, even on foot carrying his luggage. Doubly grateful for the large Ouzo which was thrust into his hand.

"I built this house out of marble, as you can see." Iona, with a sweep of her hand, indicated the gleaming building which seemed to grow right out of the mountainside.

"I opened up the quarry again. The last time marble was mined here was when the French came to get it for Napoleon's tomb at Les Invalides in Paris. And that was 150 years ago. Did you know that the Venus de Milo or, as we say, the Aphrodite of Melos, is made of Parian marble? It's translucent to a depth of 3.5 millimetres. Compare that to 2.5 for Carrara marble and only 1.5 for Athenian Pentelic! No wonder they wanted to make sculptures from it."

"You don't feel cut off?" Staples asked.

"Not at all. Sitting high up on the hill like this with sea for miles around, I have magnificent radio reception and transmission. I can communicate, instantaneously, with almost anywhere in the world if I want to."

Staples was wondering whether or not to express interest in her radio equipment (he didn't want to be interpreted in the wrong way) when a man whose face was familiar to him, but whom he knew he had not seen in years, walked out onto the terrace to join them. Iona rose to her feet.

"You two must know each other, surely?" she said.

Looking at the tall, stooped figure Brian Staples suddenly realized who he was.

"Professor Dummett?" he ventured. "I'm Brian Staples. The last time I met you it was when you were giving your valedictory lecture as the President of the Royal Society, before you went off to Australia."

"What a good memory!" Dummett spoke crisply. "Of course, I expect politicians to have a good memory."

Iona Karapolitis interrupted. "Professor Dummett is an old friend of ours. He's holidaying in the Mediterranean this summer. We were delighted he could spend a few days on Paros." She went inside, leaving the two men alone on the terrace.

Staples wasn't sure whether the presence of Professor Sir Michael Dummett, ex-President of the Royal Society and now occupier of the Chair of Geology at the University of Sydney, Australia, was planned or accidental. He suspected it was planned, Iona Karapolitis being what she was.

For a few minutes, before Iona returned, they made polite conversation.

"How is Australia? Do you ever regret leaving England?"

"I never really felt I *had* left England," Dummett replied. "Science is universal, you know. Geology, especially so. We geologists all know each other; we all see each other at international conferences and congresses here and there. The friends I have now are the friends I've always had."

"What about the life? Do you enjoy the life in Australia?"

"Of course. That's why I went. And remember, I'm over seventy now. I like to see the sun when I wake up in the morning and I like to see it set in the evening too."

Iona Karapolitis and Brian Staples drove down the mountain into Naoussa for dinner. The little port, the island's northernmost, was crowded gunwale to gunwale with red, green, yellow and blue caiques. They sat at an outside table in the harbour, watching the boats ride the evening swell.

"You must have had quite a gale today, coming over from Athens," Iona commented.

"We did."

Professor Dummett had decided not to come into the village with them. The old man was tired. Staples probed gently, hoping to discover the reason for the man's presence on Paros.

But Iona wasn't giving much away.

"Let's just say that Professor Alexander Dummett has great scientific integrity and, of course, an international reputation as a geologist specializing, at least in his heyday, in sub-sea formations. Shall we leave it at that?"

They ate and drank simply. Souvlaki and dry red Parian wine.

"There's no point going for anything fancy here," said Iona. "If you want a fancy place and fancy people, go to Mykonos. Go to Scorpios. I don't want any of that. Most of Paros is as unspoiled today as it was twenty years ago."

They were drinking little cups of dark, bitter-sweet Greek coffee after the meal when two men joined them. Iona Karapolitis introduced the newcomers as Hans Kruger and Stephanos Ypsilantis.

"They're part of my team," she explained cryptically.

The four of them sat there until almost midnight. They covered the ground. Iona was the first to admit that the attempt to hit Grantham where it hurt, as it were, had probably been a mistake.

"That business in the hotel in Germany was crude," she said, "and I'm not sure it was effective. We should have known better. We should have known that Grantham would respond in the way he did. If someone tries to kick you in the balls, you kick them in the balls. You ought to tell Drexner he made a mess of that one, Hans. He's a friend of yours, isn't he?"

The blond, tanned German looked crestfallen. "It seemed like a good idea at the time," he explained. "Drexner was angry later. He said we risked compromising him professionally. The girl apparently enjoyed it, though."

"Where is she now?" Iona asked.

"We're not sure. She left the hotel. Someone said she joined the Green party. Maybe the experience with Grantham 'radicalized' her, as they say."

Iona Karapolitis cut him off brusquely as she saw the beginnings of a smirk on Hans Kruger's handsome Teutonic face.

"We paid them both well enough, anyway," she said.

Brian Staples was not quite so pessimistic in his evaluation of the ploy.

"I don't know Grantham," he said, "I only know of him. I'm told he's now separated from his wife. If you can disorganize a man's personal life, you can affect his professional life too."

But Iona didn't seem interested in pursuing that line of thought any further.

"I wanted you here today, Brian, because we have to move ahead. Daddy wants results. I want to give him results."

Iona Karapolitis didn't say that her success in this particular operation would probably affect the willingness of her father to hand over to her, at a date in the not too distant future, total control of the Karapolitis empire. But the others took her meaning anyway and realized that their own interest in a successful outcome was almost as great as hers. Sitting there at the table, in the harbour café, away from other diners, they decided upon the next steps of the campaign.

"We have to knock the Chunnel project on the head before it gets started." Iona was emphatic. "It will be much more difficult later. We now have over forty per cent of the outstanding shares in the Channel Tunnel Company. That gives us the right to insist on a shareholders' meeting. Something for you to arrange, Brian."

"There'll have to be notice of such a meeting," Staples commented. "That's the law, even if the Company is virtually defunct."

"Make it the legal minimum," Iona instructed. "I doubt if more than a handful of people will attend. And none of those will have large holdings. It will be a walkover."

Staples decided to mention at this point a matter which had been worrying him.

"The market in CTC shares has been fairly busy recently in London," he said. "It looks as though someone else is buying."

Iona Karapolitis brushed the objection aside.

"Someone may be buying. It may even be Grantham. He may have picked a hint of what we're trying to do. But there's no way Grantham or anyone else can pick up enough shares on the market to out-vote us. We found Mrs Potter. He didn't."

Kruger and Ypsilantis came back up the mountain with them. Were they going to stay the night? Staples wondered.

When they reached the house, Iona disappeared after nodding a curt good night to Staples. She looked, he thought, as beautiful as ever. She dwelt in marble halls and it suited her. He wished he could glide after her but he knew he wasn't the gliding kind. And anyway it was clear that she had no such ideas in mind – at least as far as he was concerned.

Not long after Iona had gone off to bed, the two young men – the German and the Greek – excused themselves. Staples had not yet mastered the geography of the house but it seemed to him, from the direction they took, that they would end up either on the bare mountainside or else in Iona Karapolitis' bedroom.

There was no sign of the two young men at breakfast the next morning. Iona, however, appeared looking particularly cheerful and healthy. Staples thought he knew what the reason was. Had she had them one after another, he wondered? Or had she had them together?

Not for the first time in his life he wished he was younger and prettier.

The helicopter came around ten o'clock to take him off the island. After an hour and a half's flight over the blue Aegean and the islands dotted about below, they hit the mainland at Cape Sounion. He caught a glimpse below of the columns of the ruined Temple of Poseidon where, he remembered, Byron had once carved his name. Then they flew on down the coast to Attica, over the beach resorts of Lagonissi and Vouliagmeni, to land at Athens airport.

Thirty minutes later, Staples was boarding a plane for London.

16

The Kacha Garhi camp, some five miles from the centre of Peshawar, consisted of low squat dwellings made out of baked mud, interspersed with lines of brown tents.

It was not the only such camp in Pakistan; but because the Khyber Pass and the frontier post at Torkham was only thirty miles away, Kacha Garhi had a special significance. Among the two thousand refugees from Afghanistan was more than a fair proportion of fighting men. And, of these fighting men, most were Pathans.

Their leader, Bashir Khan, was a tall, black-haired man, with a hooked nose, flowing beard and a fierce, piercing gaze which would have been intimidating just by itself. As it was, Bashir Khan tended to go about the camp with a rifle slung over his shoulder, a curved sword hanging from his belt, a dagger and a grenade or two thrown in for good measure.

Warned of Grantham's impending visit, Bashir Khan decided to organize a display of tribal dancing. Like all Pathans, he was a proud man. They might call Kacha Garhi a refugee camp; but, as far as he was concerned, it was a parade ground for fighting men.

Buffy Watson, Grantham's companion that day, was fluent in Pashtu, the language of the Pathans. As a young man, he had done a spell on the North West Frontier (those were the days when exchanges between the British army and the Pakistan army were still frequent). He had picked up the "lingo" quickly and it had never left him since.

Taking the Pathan by the hand, Buffy Watson explained how delighted both he and his friend General Grantham were to visit the chieftain and his men. It turned out that Buffy Watson had known several members of Khan's family, including the Afghan cousins. Watson explained to Grantham that the Pathans had for centuries moved freely between Afghanistan and Pakistan. They were no respecters of frontiers. As they saw it, their country – Pashtunistan – extended on both sides of the border. It was only since the Russian invasion that the barriers to movement had finally gone up.

Delighted to be renewing, if only in an indirect way, an old acquaintanceship, Bashir Khan offered to slit a sheep's throat or two before the dancing.

"Later," Buffy Watson counselled. They had a long evening ahead of them. In good time they would need all the sustenance they could get, both solid and liquid.

For Grantham, who had never been in that part of the world before, although he had been almost everywhere else, the display of tribal dancing which Bashir Khan organized that afternoon was a very special occasion. His "refugees" – over a hundred of them – danced in full tribal regalia – flowing white robes, embroidered leather waistcoats, sashes and bandoliers – with coloured dusters in one hand and antique rifles in the other.

As Watson and Grantham sat on folding chairs in front of the tents the Pathans flashed the dusters, stamped their feet and whirled the rifles around their heads, with amazing stamina and dexterity. The dance was punctuated by the volley-firing of blanks and the quick, almost simultaneous working of the breech; then each tribesman in turn, as a virtuoso, would perform some special steps while his fellow-dancers stamped, clapped and swayed to the rhythm of wood-pipe and drums.

In another dance the tribesmen used swords and, in yet another, each man held a thin strip of metal at either end. A circle of these strips made up by the dancers would twine in and out upon itself in weird intricacies of pattern until, at a sharp command from the drummer, the whole complexity would dissolve.

"I've never seen anything like it, Buffy." Grantham clapped vigorously as the dance came to an end.

"They don't just dance; they fight as well," Watson replied.

When the dance was over and dusk had fallen, they built a fire on the hard-baked earth. True to his word, Bashir Khan slaughtered a sheep and they skinned and roasted it. With a dozen of his men, the Pathan sat cross-legged in front of the fire. He sipped dark-black tea from a glass. When he spoke he did not mince his words.

"What we need is arms. Arms to fight the Russians, to get them out of our land."

There was no mistaking the passion with which Bashir Khan spoke. Medicines and blankets they had in plenty. It was the hard stuff that they needed now.

Buffy Watson looked at Grantham and Grantham nodded. Watson took the list from his pocket.

"We've thrown in a couple of Pucaras," he said. "The Argentines left them behind in the Falklands. There's other Argentine weaponry here too. But it's all in good order."

Bashir Khan's great gaunt visage broke into a smile. His white teeth flashed.

"Show me the list," he said.

Buffy Watson handed it over.

They stayed at the Peshawar club. Their host, a lieutenant colonel in the Pakistan army called Mumtaz Kalim, showed them round with evident pleasure. He pointed out the names written up on the ceiling of the mess.

"The ladies climbed up the chandeliers on guest nights," he told them, "to add their own signatures. The officers tried to look in another direction while they did so." He giggled. "I'm afraid they did not always succeed."

"I remember that story," Buffy Watson laughed. "I stayed here before. I once played squash with Roshan Khan when he was world champion. I only got two points in half an hour."

"You did better when you played me last, Buffy," Grantham said.

After dinner Buffy Watson and Grantham had a moment alone together on the veranda of the Peshawar club. They looked out at the lights of the lines.

"It's still very much a cantonment town isn't it?" remarked Watson. "It hasn't changed much in twenty years."

"Did you expect to come back in this way?" Grantham asked elliptically.

"Not really," Watson replied. "I still don't quite understand how you swung it. You have to have political cover for something like this, believe me."

"We have the cover."

Grantham knew, as he said this, that it had been a close-run thing in Whitehall. Finally, he had gone to see the Prime Minister herself.

Philip Maitland, the PM's private secretary, had tried to sound him out first before agreeing to the meeting. But Grantham had insisted. He did not want to be fobbed off with standard civil service tactics. In the end, he had gone round to Downing Street to be shown into the PM's study, had waited for Sir John Markham, the head of the home civil service, to try to make the case against, before he had swept the board with a series of closely reasoned arguments.

The idea of paying the rebels off with captured Argentine arms, currently stockpiled in the south of England, originated with the PM.

"We've got to do something with them," she said. "We may as well give them to the Afghan rebels, if they'll have them."

The fourth person at that meeting in the PM's study overlooking St James's Park was Sir Morley Gibson, an elegant silver-haired gentleman who had been a professional diplomat with the Foreign Office before being moved across to head Britain's intelligence service, MI6. Professionally, he was known simply as "C".

"Oh, they'll have them all right," Morley had said; "they're desperately short of arms."

No, thought Grantham as he sat there drinking what Buffy Watson referred to as a chota peg, political cover was not the problem. The problem was: could they do it?"

The decision, go or no-go, had finally to be Buffy Watson's. That was obvious. He was going to be the man in charge. If things went wrong, his neck would be on the line.

"How much experience does the SAS have of this kind of flying?" Grantham asked.

"Some. Given the weights involved, we're going to be at the frontiers of our capability, I'd say, both human and technical."

"Can't we get them out by road? That would be safer, wouldn't it?"

Buffy Watson shook his head. "Not a hope. The Kandahar road is out of the question. And you couldn't get a convoy through the Khyber; the Russians would make sure of that. Besides, you're talking about a seven-metre diameter for those machines, so I understand. I know that road through the Khyber. In places it's little more than a rocky, mountainous track. No, it has to be air. It has to be helicopters. That's the only way."

Later on their host came out to joint them. Mumtaz Kalim was a cheerful fellow whose happiest days had been spent at Sandhurst. They had a last drink together before turning in.

"You know we want to be all possible help, don't you?" he told them. "General Zia is a great admirer of your Prime Minister. He approves of the resolute approach. He has sent a message, or so I understand."

Grantham nodded. "He has indeed. I must say that I am very grateful for it. This kind of cooperation between our two countries is important. In the end, we want the same thing, don't we?"

They drank to that.

*

The SAS team flew in after dark. The first briefing took place almost immediately. There were a dozen men altogether, dressed in civilian clothes. Ostensibly they were a team of technicians to check on the communications facilities of the base.

Buffy Watson took them through the operation step by step.

"You must take the politics as read," he began. "All I'm going to say on that score is that it has been decided at the highest level that this operation is in HMG's interest."

He didn't introduce Grantham, who sat next to him in the briefing room. It was a case of no names, no pack-drill. Buffy Watson knew that a handful of his men would certainly recognize the former commander of the Parachute Regiment, but he also knew that even if they did, none of them would show it.

"As I said," Buffy Watson continued, "the political side is not our concern. We know through channels that we have the support of the Pakistan Government, though there will, for obvious reasons, be no active Pakistan participation. And we shall have local support on the ground, I can assure you of that."

The map was pinned to the wall behind him.

"We're going up to the top end of the valley. As you can see from the map," he pointed with his stick, "that's about eighty miles northwest of Kabul. This is rebel-held territory. As you know, the Soviet presence in Afghanistan is still limited to the main towns and strategic areas, like the Khyber and other frontier zones. So we expect the cooperation of the tribesmen; indeed, without their cooperation, this operation wouldn't have a snowball's chance in hell of success, if I may coin a phrase."

Again he pointed at the map.

"It's very rugged country. I've been there. When you're building a dam, you don't build it in the flood-plain. You build it in the mountains, so that the sides of the river valley itself form the reservoir. The TBMs – Tunnel Boring Machines – came in originally on the new US-built highway from Kandahar. We have the satellite picture and we know that they are still there, freighted up at the project site headquarters. The TBMs," he explained, "were to be used to drive the diversion tunnel through twelve miles of solid rock, just about here," – he pointed again at the map. "You have to be able to divert the river, in order to build the dam."

He looked around. "Any questions so far?"

"How do we get in and out?" The man who spoke was a tall, tough Irishman, Sergeant Gallagher by name but known to his mates – inevitably – as "Paddy".

"By helicopter, Paddy," Buffy Watson replied. "They're waiting for us at Peshawar. I only hope to God you can fly the brutes."

"You name it," said Paddy Gallagher, "we'll fly it. What are they? Sea Kings? Chinooks?"

Buffy Watson paused so that his words would have maximum impact.

"Not Sea Kings. Not Chinooks. Not Sikorskys. Not Agustas."

Gallagher looked puzzled. "What will we be flying then, sir? I'm no expert, but I'd say those TBMs must be as heavy as a sow in pig! There aren't many helicopters that can handle those kinds of load."

Buffy Watson couldn't resist flashing a quick smile at Grantham, as he played his trump card.

"Ever heard of the MI-10, Paddy?"

What was news to Paddy Gallagher and the men of 22 SAS was not – of course – news to Oliver Grantham. As Buffy Watson spoke, Grantham's mind went back yet again to that hard-fought day when 3 Para finally took Goose Green after their brutal slog down from San Carlos Bay. Goose Green had been the main Argentine base on the Falklands islands except for Port Stanley itself. The quantity of arms and ammunition they had captured that day had been staggering.

Much of the booty had been brought back to Britain. For months after the Falklands War the Press had been filled with pictures of Argentine ground attack aircraft being unloaded from freighters at Southampton; of rifles stockpiled in Gosport; of hundreds of thousands of rounds of shells and other ammunition being sorted through at one army depot or another so that compatible material could be retained and the rest destroyed.

Much Argentine equipment had, of course, been lost in the battle for Goose Green itself. Brian Hanrahan and Robert Falk, reporting for BBC television, had described the scenes of devastation for viewers throughout the world. On June 2nd 1982, for example, Robert Falk had spoken of how "piles of ammunition, field artillery and machine-guns, the skeletons of wrecked Pucara aircraft, are still strewn across the little port of Goose Green". They had also heard him describe how "two huge Soviet built military helicopters, the largest in the world, which the Argentines had been using to ferry troops and material throughout the islands, have also been destroyed". Viewers were shown pictures of wreckage which clearly seemed to come from the Soviet machines.

"I think there's no doubt," Buffy Watson had continued, "that the MI-10s will be able to do the job for us. In case you don't know, we're talking about the largest helicopter in the world. Weight empty: 60,185 lbs. Maximum take-off weight: 96,340 lbs. Maximum load on platform

– there's an external platform under the undercarriage – 33,070 lbs. Maximum slung load: 17,635 lbs."

"What's the range with full payload?" Gallagher asked.

"155 miles, that's 250 kms," Buffy Watson replied. "It's not a lot, I know, but as you look at the distances on the map you will see it's enough."

Buffy Watson turned in Grantham's direction. "Those who've flown in it," he said, "tell me the MI-10's not a fast machine, either. Cruising speed is about 112 mph with full load. But, there again, that should be enough for us. Both machines will be done up again in Soviet military markings. They will have a distinctive radar profile which the Soviets will recognize. After all, there are other MI-10s operating in Afghanistan today. They're not going to start shooting down one of their own."

"What about the tribesmen, sir?" It was Paddy Gallagher's last question of the day. "They tend to take pot shots at Ivan's helicopters when they see them!"

Buffy Watson smiled. Again he nodded in Grantham's direction and for the first time gave a clue as to his identity.

"The General and I have been working on the tribesmen. I'm fairly sure the natives will be friendly. There ought to be a beacon in position to give us a clear run in to the head of the valley provided our Pathan friends on this side of the frontier have been able to link up as planned with their people over there. We should be in radio contact with them from this evening."

The helicopter, homing in on the beacon, dropped out of the sky like a giant moth. The contractors, before they left, had cleared the area. The first MI-10 came down in the middle of the landing ground, huge rotors – 114 feet 10 inches in diameter – still whirring. Seconds later, the second MI-10 also landed. Ideally the pilot would have liked to have left a clear gap, of at least the width of the rotors, between the two machines but circumstances did not permit this kind of luxury.

If there was to be an ambush, Watson knew this was the moment for it. This was the time when both men and machines were at their most vulnerable. But the signal had come through; the beacon had been switched on; sometimes you had to rely on arrangements actually working. Even so, the men, Grantham among them – leapt down from the machines, ducking beneath the still-turning rotors, with their guns at the ready.

A light flashed at the edge of the clearing. From the shadows, a group of tribesmen emerged. With relief Watson and Grantham saw that Bashir Khan – who had gone ahead – was among them.

The exchange, guns for tunnelling machines, took place swiftly and silently. The MI-10s were surrounded by swarthy Pathans who swarmed around and over the Russian helicopters, unloading the arms with great speed and dexterity. Like ants, when each man had what he wanted, he disappeared again into the night.

The SAS men tried to keep some semblance of order as the unloading took place, but it was not easy. These men thirsted for weapons; they had been thirsting for weapons for years, and would now brook no delay. In all, the unloading took half an hour. Once or twice, the moon had darted behind the cloud and operations had been momentarily interrupted but on the whole, they had kept to the timing.

The difficult part came next.

Prudently, Buffy Watson had kept on board the last several crates of arms. He had wanted to be sure that he still had some counters to bargain with just in case Bashir had not retained a sufficient squad of volunteers.

In the event, he need not have worried. While the disposal of the arms was going on, Bashir and his men had given stalwart assistance to the six SAS men assigned to the cradles. The principle of each cradle was simple, the same as the claw of a giant crane. Once dropped over the target, whatever it was, the cradle would be drawn tight by the upward pull of the crane – or, in this case, the helicopter. The steel hawsers were designed to withstand the strains of over a hundred tonnes; the margin of error was ample.

An hour after the helicopters had first arrived the arms had been unloaded and the cradles had been fixed into place. It remained only to start the engines – each helicopter had a 26500shp Solvievd-25v turbo shaft power system – and hover over the loads until the tow was fixed.

With most of his men on board, Buffy Watson had one last conversation – always in Pashtu – with Bashir.

"Are you sure you and your men want to stay, Bashir?" he asked. "I can take you back to the camp if you like. There's plenty of room."

Bashir shook his head, his long locks moving from side to side.

"We have a war to fight."

Two of the men stayed on the ground to supervise the hitching of the tows. Bashir Khan and his men helped to place the hawsers in position, while first one, then the other MI-10 hovered overhead. The down draft from the giant rotors blew a gale through the turbans of the Afghans and through their loose flowing robes. It created a storm of dust which made the operation trickier than it otherwise would have been.

At last they were ready. The SAS men who had remained on the ground were pulled back on board. One after the other the MI-10s lifted off.

One of the features of the Soviet helicopter was that it had a rear-facing control cabin which enabled the load to be surveyed at all times.

An SAS man sitting next to Grantham told him, "One of the things you have to watch out for in this kind of job is oscillation. When you're carrying heavy loads like this, it's easy to set up oscillations and they can destabilize the helicopter rapidly. That's why the rear-facing cabin helps. You can see what's happening, and give the pilot instructions about checking it before it gets out of hand."

They went back down the valley the way they had come. As soon as they could, they flew in line abreast rather than line astern.

"You watch each other's tail whenever you can," the SAS man sitting next to Grantham explained. "If a tribesman down there looses off at us with a rifle, he won't do much harm unless he's lucky enough to hit the pilot. But if he has an SA-7 shoulder-fired missile, as some of them do, he could do a lot of damage. The only thing we can do then is to drop an infra-red trailer and hope that decoys the missile. That's what the Israelis did in the Lebanon. They waited until they saw Syrian missiles coming and they dropped trailers."

Grantham nodded. He wanted to tell the man sitting next to him that he had fought a war or two in his time but he refrained. When the man asked him, by way of making polite conversation, what his interest in the operation was, Grantham had replied:

"Oh, I'm just along for the ride."

"Some ride."

The banter disguised the tension. Quite apart from Afghan tribesmen, with or without shoulder-held anti-aircraft missiles, they all knew they might be being picked up, somewhere, on Soviet radar. They were flying as low as they dared but with the load slung beneath the helicopters that was not as low as it had been on the outward journey. Home-bound they had to gain height.

"But if we do appear on the radar," the SAS man said, "we shall look like a helicopter all right. Our height and speed will tell them that. We'll probably look like a Soviet helicopter. Like an MI-10 in fact. There isn't another machine in the world that has a radar profile like the MI-10. This machine gives off a pretty big blip, as you can imagine."

Grantham remembered what Buffy Watson had said at the briefing. How soon in fact would it be, he wondered, before Soviet intelligence put two and two together? A day, a week, a month? How soon would someone make the connection between two MI-10s apparently destroyed at Goose Green and two big blips appearing one moonlight night on Kabul radar?

Once again they skirted the capital city, flying in a wide arc over the westerly plains. Then they were climbing again, up towards Jalalabad and into the defile which had seen the massacre in the last century of one British army and the decimation of others.

Ten minutes later they were over the Khyber Pass itself, and dropping rapidly into the plains of Pakistan. Grantham permitted himself one terse comment.

"Phew!" he said.

"Same from me in spades!" his companion added.

The giant US C-5 Galaxy had landed that same night at Peshawar airport. Long ago, Grantham had realized that there was only one plane in the world which could carry two TBMs back to England: the Lockheed Galaxy. Thank God the US Administration had seen the point. Once the President had realized that his allies, those weak-kneed, flabby Europeans were actually getting off their butts and helping the Afghans instead of just talking about what an awful thing the Russian invasion was, he had come through in no uncertain terms. He had told the ranking Pentagon general who first broached the subject: "The Brits need a Galaxy? They'll have a Galaxy!"

It turned out that there was one flying back from the Far East to Germany anyway, and it made sense to stop overnight in Peshawar. As dawn broke, the great plane rolled down the runway and took off over the cantonment, banked above the Karcha Garhi camp, and headed west, towards the Indian Ocean.

Buffy Watson, like any well-trained commanding officer, checked that his men were happy, and then came over and had breakfast with Grantham.

"An A-OK success," he commented. "The Afghans are happy, they've got their arms. The Pakistanis are happy. We've left them two perfectly serviceable Soviet helicopters which they can use for any purpose they like including firewood. You're happy because you've got your TBMs. We're happy. The Americans are happy. Who isn't happy?"

"Maybe the Russians?" Grantham ventured.

"Hell!" replied Buffy Watson. "You overrate Russian Intelligence. Ivan was probably asleep all the time."

17

It seemed an age since he had seen her. She was as beautiful as ever. He looked at her as she walked past the barrier towards him and he could see, in his mind's eye, the sweep of the Black Forest behind her. It was a good day to remember.

"Ingrid!" He embraced her warmly on both cheeks. "How good of you to come!"

"How good of you to ask me, Oliver. It looks like it's going to be a great occasion."

He had brought his car out to Zaventem, Brussels National Airport.

"I'm afraid the schedule is fairly tight," he explained. "We're staying at the Amigo. The ball starts at around eight o'clock. That gives us about an hour and a half."

Grantham took the ring road west until he hit the E5 motorway. Twenty minutes later Grantham parked his car in the Amigo's underground garage.

"People prefer the Amigo," Grantham explained as they rode up to the fourth floor, "because the lift goes straight from the garage to the rooms. You don't need to pass through the lobby if you don't want to."

"So you've checked in already for the both of us, have you?" Ingrid laughed.

In the end, they were late for the ball. While Grantham dressed, Ingrid decided to have a bath. He heard the water running; and she called to him to bring her a drink. There was champagne in the ice bucket. Grantham opened the bottle, poured out two glasses, and carried them into the bathroom on a silver tray.

She had her hair pinned back, was leaning back in the bath, surrounded by foaming bubbles, just the way – thought Grantham – actresses were meant to. Her breasts rose clear of the water. She took the glass of champagne in one hand.

"Could you scrub my back for me?" she asked. "For you, it would be easier."

When they got out of the bath, he told her firmly: "We are going to be late and I don't want to be late."

"Does it really matter?"

Grantham was adamant. "Not more than half an hour."

She bargained with him good humouredly. "Forty minutes," she insisted.

He remembered her body, the way a man remembers a road he has taken before, even though he may not have consciously marked the route. He remembered the contours of her flesh; the lift of the breasts; the gentleness of the belly.

"I've been waiting for this," she said.

"*Ich auch*," he replied.

Down in the square below, the great medieval square – La Grand' Place – which was Brussels' pride and joy – a band had been playing. The good people of the city were beginning to stroll across the cobbles in front of the Hôtel de Ville.

Grantham registered the sights and sounds below. The setting was always important.

She lay face down on the bed and he ran his fingers down her spine. "I wondered if I would hear from you again," she said. Then she moaned as his hand fluttered, probing. She turned over suddenly onto her back. "I want you now."

He was still lean and fit and he could feel the muscles in his lower abdomen tense with anticipation. He entered her kneeling and then pulled her up off the bed towards him. He buried his face in her hair, which was still damp from the bath. He crushed her soft breasts against his chest while she threw her arms around him and raked her fingers down his back.

"That is so good. *Das ist gut!*" she said.

He pulled her right over then so that their positions were suddenly reversed. He realized that she was fighting and laughing at once. He remembered how he had seen her in the gym at Schluchsee.

"Pin me then," he dared.

She was stronger than he ever had imagined. She kept him inside her as she forced his shoulders back on the pillow but he beat her away, straining, and then as he was about to explode inside her he threw her back into the pillows and pinioned her with his own body. He felt the force of her orgasm merging with his own.

They were forty-five minutes late altogether by the time they reached

Val Duchesse, the splendid château where the ball was being held. Nobody seemed to mind. The chauffeured cars were still streaming in through the gates and up the long gravelled drive. The reception lines were still ten or twenty persons long. The King of the Belgians himself had yet to arrive, though other royalty was already present.

" 'There was a sound of revelry by night'." Grantham quoted as they inched their way forward in the line. "That's how Byron described Brussels on the eve of the battle of Waterloo."

"I know," Ingrid Lubekke smiled at him. "They taught us that one."

Grantham took her arm. He felt proud of her. It was the first time he had appeared at a public occasion with a woman since he had separated from Lily. He had warned her earlier that there would be photographers present.

"Won't your husband mind?" he had asked her.

She had explained that her marriage was more of a fiction than a reality. "We hardly see each other now. I expect we shall divorce soon." She had spoken so matter-of-factly that Grantham had not pressed the matter. It was her affair, not his.

The major-domo announced them to the array of dignitaries that made up the receiving line and then they moved quickly on. Grantham found himself surrounded by familiar faces. Soldiers and ex-soldiers whom he had known on one continent or another, diplomats and ex-diplomats, politicians and ex-politicians. With Ingrid on his arm he moved around the room.

When she heard the strains of music coming from across the courtyard, and saw that people were already making their way towards the ballroom, she said to him: "Shall we dance, Oliver? I've never danced with a British general before."

"You mean you want more exercise? I'm not much of a dancer, you know."

"Let's find out anyway." She guided him towards the band.

Grantham was about to sweep Ingrid Lubekke onto the floor for what seemed to him to be a waltz when he felt a hand on his shoulder and turned to see the broad, smiling face of General Peabody.

"Bill!" Grantham exclaimed. "So you made it over here after all!"

"Once I heard you were coming I couldn't resist it."

Peabody was resplendent in full dress uniform. A row of medals clanked on his chest and the bars of campaign ribbons covered most of the left hand side of his tunic.

"May I have the honour of being presented?" Peabody looked at the German actress who hung on Grantham's arm.

When Grantham introduced her by name, he was conscious that Peabody's gaze flickered momentarily as though he was absorbing the implications of that particular information.

"I'm delighted to meet you, madam." Peabody bowed and brought his heels together in an almost Prussian manner.

As the three of them stood there talking together at the edge of the dance floor, they were joined by a tall, suave, dark-haired German who introduced himself as Count von Rimsdorf. He was immediately greeted by Ingrid Lubekke as a long-lost friend.

"Heinrich, what are you doing here?"

"My dear Ingrid, how good to see you!" the German replied. "I'm with NATO now."

After a new round of introductions had taken place the German bowed deeply in Grantham's direction.

"May I have your permission, dear sir, to borrow this lady for a brief tour of the dance floor?"

Grantham laughed. "Willingly. As long as you bring her back in one piece."

Ingrid smiled at him prettily. "Don't worry, Oliver, I shall be back." She laid her hand lightly on his arm as if to indicate the proprietary nature of their relationship.

Left alone, the two men were able to fill in the gaps.

"No Lily?" Bill Peabody asked.

"Not now, now yet," Grantham replied, and he added, "No Judy?"

Peabody laughed. "No Ingrid, either, as far as I'm concerned. Good luck to you, though." And he added as though as an after-thought; "She's quite involved with the Greens, isn't she? I remember reading about her in *Time* magazine not so long back. You ought to watch that one. Some of the Greens have pretty strange friends as bed-fellows."

Grantham nodded. "I know," he said. "I can assure you our relationship is strictly non-political."

Peabody turned it into a joke. "I wouldn't mind a strictly non-political relationship with Ingrid Lubekke!"

At the far side of the room Grantham caught a glimpse of the actress waltzing with verve and vigour in the arms of the German diplomat.

Grantham and Peabody moved out of the crush of people towards the floodlit courtyard of the château. There was still the occasional scrunch of a long black Mercedes on the gravel drive as the late arrivals made for the now much-diminished reception line. The buzz of music and dancing could be heard, but less insistently outside. There was a chance to talk. It was a chance that both men had been waiting for.

"I found out what you wanted about Pierre Leroux," Peabody told Grantham as they walked toward the great spreading oak tree in the middle of the courtyard. "We had to probe. What we have is dynamite, I'd say."

Grantham looked at him sharply. "You mean it?"

"Sure, I mean it. I know a sleeper when I see one."

They stood against the tree in the middle of the courtyard, while the American told Grantham what he had learned. He summarized the information, cutting out the non-essential details.

"Some of the evidence," Peabody explained, "is circumstantial. Our people have had to put two and two together. But we can document enough of it to be sure. The key was Louis Baudin in Lyons. He still *is* the key."

"Baudin? Isn't he a war hero?"

"Sure, he's a war hero. He fought the Germans. Now he's a Socialist mayor. Philby fought the Germans too, didn't he?"

"Is money involved?"

"More than you can ever imagine. Leroux's campaign is going to be the best-financed Presidential campaign in French history, you wait. They'll launder it, of course. They're already doing so."

Grantham looked Peabody straight in the eyes. "Let's be clear about this, Bill. You're telling me in so many words that Leroux is a Soviet agent. An active Soviet agent, recruited after the war by Louis Baudin and now he's bidding fair to be President of France."

"That's about the long and short of it." As they walked back towards the ballroom, Peabody commented: "We're watching this one, Oliver. I don't think we need get too excited just yet. Leroux has a long way to go before he gets elected. Our political experts don't think he can get elected in any case. They say he doesn't have the support where he most needs it, up north, in the Pas-de-Calais region. If you're going to be the Socialist Party candidate in France, you've got to have Marseilles and the north."

"Don't underestimate Leroux," Grantham replied. "He has gone far, fast. Thanks, anyway, for the tip-off. We ought to keep in touch on this one, you know."

Peabody put a friendly arm on Grantham's shoulder. "Let's do that."

As they came back into the dance hall, Ingrid and her German escort waltzed over towards them. She looked flushed and animated.

"What have you two been talking about? Old times, I'll bet."

Peabody beamed at her. "Sure. Whenever Oliver and I get together we talk about old times. Old times are often the best, aren't they, Count?"

General Peabody and Count von Rimsdorf drifted off, leaving Grantham and Ingrid alone together.

"Let's dance now," said Grantham, "before someone else grabs you."

She leaned into him as they danced and he caught the fragrance of her hair. He put his lips to her temple and whispered in her ear. "I'm glad you came back, Ingrid. I don't like being a wallflower."

"You could never be a wallflower: you're not made that way."

"No, I suppose I'm not."

He shut his eyes for a moment and let the music and the place get to him. What a strange way to celebrate NATO's anniversary, he thought. And then he thought, perhaps it wasn't so strange after all. In Europe, they had been dancing their way through war and through peace for hundreds of years.

"I only came because of you," Ingrid whispered in his ear. "NATO is not really my scene. But I haven't seen you in so long. Next time you can come with me somewhere. March in a Save the Seals rally in Hamburg, for example!"

He held her body against his as they moved to the music.

"Ingrid, I'll even wear a T-shirt if you ask me to."

Coming up for air at the end of a dog-leg which had taken them down one side of the room, round the end of it, and back the other side, Grantham caught a glimpse of the tall figure of Konrad von Rilke. He broke off in the middle of the movement.

"I want you to meet another old friend of mine."

Konrad von Rilke turned as Grantham tapped him on the shoulder. His face broke into a smile.

"Ah, Oliver, I saw you a moment ago but you were dancing with this delightful actress whom I know by reputation," he bowed low as he said it. "I didn't dare interrupt. You were dancing with such grace and elegance."

The three of them sat down together at a table, while a waiter served them drinks. Later, when Ingrid Lubekke excused herself for a moment, von Rilke asked:

"Where did you meet her? She's quite a star in Germany you know."

"So I am beginning to realize," Grantham replied. "I keep on having to fend people off." Then he explained: "I met her in the Black Forest, a few months back. Remember the time we had lunch at Illhaeusern?"

"How could I ever forget that lunch?" von Rilke laughed.

They raised their glasses. "To all of us!"

"You know Bill Peabody is here, don't you?" asked Grantham.

Von Rilke nodded. "So is Maximilien. It's quite a gathering of the clan, isn't it?"

There was one personal message which Grantham wanted to convey. He spoke from the heart.

"Konrad, I haven't had a chance to thank you properly for what you did the other day when I rang you from London. Give me a week or two more and you will have the money back with interest."

"British rate of interest or German rate of interest?" von Rilke asked jokingly. "There is a difference you know!" Then he added, more seriously, "So your scheme is working out, is it?"

"Beautifully," Grantham replied.

Ingrid Lubekke returned to the table. Both men rose from their seats as she joined them. It was getting to be quite an evening for bowing and scraping, thought Grantham.

They didn't return to the hotel until 3 o'clock in the morning. By the time they had left Val Duchesse, Grantham had met almost everyone he had ever wanted to meet, including General Maximilien Miguet, who had expressed himself absolutely delighted to renew their brief acquaintance.

"Let's walk in the Grand' Place before going up," Ingrid had suggested. He took her arm and they wandered into the magnificent square, quiet now and deserted except for a couple of policemen. They walked up on to the empty bandstand.

"I feel sometimes sad. Look at this square, how wonderful it is! Now it is almost the only thing left in Brussels. They have destroyed the rest. That's the problem," she spoke with a sudden vehemence and anger. "We spend our time destroying things. We destroy beauty when we see it."

"Is that why you spend so much time with your ecologist friends?" Grantham asked.

She turned to him. "I suppose so. At least they offer hope."

As they walked back to the Amigo, Grantham said: "I think I know what you mean. The trouble is, as a soldier I tend to think in different terms."

"It's not too late to change." There was a sharpness, a hint of steel in her voice which he had not noticed before.

What was she really, he wondered? An actress masquerading as a radical? Or a radical masquerading as an actress?

18

James Thornton had been the director of the British School at Rome for the last six years. He liked the job, and he liked the life, immensely. The School was set outside the traffic-ridden heart of the city on a hill above the Viale delle Belle Arti. It was a light, airy place, full of trees and open space with the Borghese gardens a few minutes' walk away.

Thornton was a vital, dynamic man in his early forties. He had brought the School, which over the past twenty years had occasionally seemed to be floundering, a new sense of dynamism and direction. He believed in active, rather than passive archaeology. He took the view that sites and landscapes were disappearing so fast that nothing short of drastic measures would suffice. He spoke of "rescue archaeology" and "fast-digging techniques" and believed that the British School, and indeed all archaeologists, should be much more closely involved with the political process. In his view, archaeology was as politically charged as any other subject.

As director, Thornton was responsible not only for the running of the School, but also – in a general sense – for its scholarly output. The series "Papers of the British School in Rome" was well respected in academic circles and there were always scholars in residence who, in one way or another, contributed to the maintenance of the School's reputation. Thornton prided himself in particular for having persuaded the eccentric but amiable Professor Morris Herbert to spend two or three years in Rome immediately following his retirement from the Regius Professorship at Oxford University. Sitting at his desk on the first floor of the building and looking out the window in the direction of the Borghese gardens, Thornton reflected on how close he and Morris Herbert had grown during the time the old man had been staying at the School. Thornton was not a classical archaeologist himself; he was a mediaevalist. But he could recognize outstanding scholarship when he saw it. That was part of the job. Both he and his wife delighted also in the personality which went with the scholarship. Morris Herbert's whole life seemed like a highly polished epigram. His urbanity, his felicity of phrase, his sometimes quirky humour had brought light and life to many an Oxford commonroom; now it was the turn of another institution to profit.

Thornton and Herbert had fallen into the habit of walking together at the end of the morning in the gardens of the School. Flowers gave the old professor almost as much pleasure as a neatly turned phrase. And he loved the sun, too.

"It was the sun that got me out here, James," he once confided to the director as they strolled amongst the statuary. "I always said that when I retired I would head for the warm south. Oxford is fine, but it doesn't have enough sun."

"Their loss is our gain," James Thornton had replied. And he meant it.

One morning in mid-November, with the sun streaming down as though to defy the coming of winter, the two men met together at the top of the steps for their pre-lunch constitutional.

Thornton slowed his pace to accommodate the more deliberate gait of the older man. Not that Professor Herbert was in any way decrepit; simply cautious.

"When you get to my age, James," he would say, "you don't want to slip on any banana skins. There's a Great Banana Skin in the Sky waiting for all of us and that's enough for me!"

They reached the far end of the gardens and sat together on a stone bench looking out over the valley. Morris Herbert was in a ruminating mood. He had reached the time of life when it was a pleasure to let the mind wander off on what might seem to be tangents.

"It's funny, isn't it," he said, "how much of our knowledge of ancient Rome depends on Renaissance writers like Onofrio Panvinio and Pirro Ligorio. In the mid-1500s and throughout the 1600s they were recording what they saw, or what they knew from other sources to have been in existence in classical times. They were writing about monuments and sites which have long since been obliterated. I'll give you an example."

He reached into a pocket and took out a slim leather-bound volume.

"This, as you will realize, is one of the famous treatises of Pirro Ligorio. I borrowed it from the library this morning. Don't worry." Herbert smiled as he saw Thornton's look of alarm. "I signed for it in the correct way and it will be back under lock and key after lunch. I just wanted to have a chance to show it to you this morning. Have a look at the title page."

Thornton opened the book and looked at the title page.

LIBRO
Di M. Pyrrho
LIGORI NAPOLITANO,
DELLE ANTICHITA DI ROMA,
NELQVALE SI TRATTA DE
Circi Theatri, & Anfitheatri.
CON LE PARADOSSE DEL MEDESIMO
auttore, quai confutano na commune opinione
sopra uarii luoghi della citta di Roma.

"It's beautiful, isn't it?" Thornton said.

"Yes, it is." Professor Herbert took the book back from the Director.

Thornton waited for the old man to continue. He knew Morris Herbert well enough by now to realize that the Professor was leading up to something and that sooner or later, in his own good time, he would get there.

"Of course," Herbert continued, puffing on his pipe, "Ligorio was one of the greatest Renaissance historians. Time and again we've discovered that Ligorio's speculations turn out to be well-founded."

The old Professor appeared to change the subject abruptly.

"I took the subway the other day," he said. "The new line which runs up from the Spanish steps to Termini station. Actually, I wanted to get to the Piazza Bologna but the subway doesn't go that far yet. So I got out at Termini and decided to walk the rest of the way since it was a fine day. Just outside the station, there's one of those large maps which show all the bus and underground routes and if you press a button you can find out where you're going and how to get there. Just for fun, I pressed the button marked Piazza Bologna and the map told me that I ought to take bus 310. It also told me that, one day when the subway is finished, you'll be able to go by underground from Termini to Piazza Bologna with one intermediary stop at Policlinico. That set me thinking. Do you know why?"

Thornton hazarded a guess. "You're wondering if the new subway line is going to smash through some ancient Roman ruin. You're thinking about the Fellini film *Roma*, where the tunnelling machine bores through into some magnificent palace covered with frescoes which immediately disintegrate on being exposed to the air." He laughed. "The trouble is: they've learnt their lesson nowadays. The new subway lines in Rome are driven deep, deep as the Piccadilly line in London, well below any possible Roman remains."

Herbert took another puff at his pipe. "Not a bad guess. You're half right and half wrong. It's not so much the subway I was worried about, it's the station." Out of another pocket, he pulled a plan of Rome and spread it out on the bench between them.

"You know as well as I do," he said, "that the original Roman wall, known as the Servian wall after Servius Tullius, sixth king of Rome, surrounded the Palatine, the Subura, the Esquiline and the Collina, which included the Quirinal. The Servian wall dates from about 378 BC. Not a great deal of it is left. When people nowadays think of the walls of the City of Rome they talk about the Aurelian Wall, built by the Emperor Aurelian in the 3rd century AD, most of which survives to this day."

He pointed at the map with his finger.

"If you walk approximately four hundred yards northeast from the main entrance of Stazione Termini you come to the National Library. That library, as you know, has been built on the site of the old Castro Pretorio, which was the quarters of the Praetorian Guard. The eastern boundary of the Castro Pretorio is itself formed by the Aurelian Wall. At the same time this was the beginning of the Via Tiburtina, the ancient Roman road which led out to Tivoli."

The director of the British School could not quite see what Professor Herbert was driving at.

"The Castro Pretorio was excavated, I thought, before they built the National Library there. In any case, as I understand it, the Policlinico station will be at Policlinico itself, which is outside the wall and outside the Castro Pretorio."

Morris Herbert's ancient leathery face, so much like one of the papyri he spent his days with, broke into a smile.

"Exactly. The Policlinico subway station will certainly be outside the wall, about two hundred yards outside it, to be precise, along the old Via Tiburtina. And in my view, James," he came suddenly to the point, "to locate a subway station at that spot would be to commit archaeological sacrilege. And I mean sacrilege in the most literal, as well as metaphorical, way."

He still had the leather-bound treatise by Pirro Ligorio in his hand. He tapped the book sharply with his finger as he spoke.

"Ever since I went up there that day," the Professor continued, "I had the feeling that something was wrong. A hunch, if you like. I read in the paper that the tunnelling machines were about to start work on the extension of the line from Termini to Piazza Bologna. All the necessary permissions seemed to have been obtained. As you yourself said, the fact that the new lines will run so deep under the city has lulled all those who are concerned with the preservation of antiquity into a false sense of security. I felt that day in my bones that something was wrong and ever since then I've been looking for some way of proving it. This morning," he held up the book triumphantly, "I think I found it."

James Thornton could sense, within himself, a rising excitement. This, he thought, was what archaeology should be all about. This was what the British School of Rome should be all about. This was the kind of thing that the director of the British School ought to be concerned with.

Once again, Morris Herbert consulted the little book from his pocket. This time he turned, not to the title page, but to the end.

"Ligorio finishes his work with a description of the Castro Pretorio as he knew it at the time he was writing. Let me read you what he says. My Italian I know is not as perfect as yours, but I'm sure you'll understand."

Thornton smiled at the old man's unbecoming modesty. He knew very well that Morris Herbert was a perfect linguist, just as at home with mediaeval Italian as he was with ancient Latin.

Herbert read out the relevant passage in his fruity Oxonian voice:

" 'Nel luogo, dove era quel dempio, fu fatta una chiesa dedicita a uno di nostri santi (ma secondo che'l dembo e solito di fare) hura e annullata l'antica, e la moderna chiesa; e gutto'l sito e occupato di vitne, e, fatto pino.' "

Thornton whistled. "So Pirro says there was a church there on the Policlinico site in ancient times and Pirro is not often wrong."

Professor Morris Herbert's smile had become positively complacent.

"There's more to it than that," he said. He passed the little book over. "See what some contemporary reader has scribbled in the margin, at the point where Pirro is talking about the church. He's written '*anche catacombi*'. Catacombs existed there as well!"

Thornton took the book from Professor Herbert's hands. He peered at the marginal inscription. Herbert gazed at him intently as he did so.

"It's not the only marginal note," he said almost defensively. "You'll find that there are others as well, certainly by the same hand."

Thornton flipped through the pages of the book. He could see what Herbert meant. Someone in the dim and distant past had obviously gone through Pirro's work rather carefully, comparing his own observations with that of the historian, and making notes in the margin where appropriate.

Thornton passed the book back to Professor Herbert.

"You'd better keep that under lock and key, Morris," he said, "we may need it."

The old man kept a deliberately straight face. He knew the fish was hooked, but he also knew that he had to play the fish home.

"You're the politician, James," he flattered him, "if any of us are politicians here."

Thornton leaned back in his seat, closed his eyes and let his fantasies run wild. He could see the headlines even now in his mind's eye. *La Stampa*, the *Corriere della Sera*, *Il Giorno*, *Il Tempo* – they would all want the story. British School of Rome Masterminds Major Discovery – Subway Construction Halted to Permit Investigation of Catacomb Site!

He brought himself back to earth with a jolt. Opening his eyes, he said to the Professor, "We'll have to move fast. I'll get on to the local archaeological superintendent. We can try and get work stopped pending an investigation. They have extraordinary powers, these local archaeological superintendents. A telegram to the local police station does the trick usually. They've been stopping the subway construction for years in Rome. It's a game they know how to play."

Professor Herbert interrupted gently. "I hate to intrude at this point, James, but surely the Vatican has to be involved as well, doesn't it? Don't we have to go back to the Concordat of 1929 which made the Vatican and – more particularly – the Pontifical Commission responsible for the catacombs? So, if the archaeological superintendent won't stop the subway, I'm sure that the Pope will. You don't find a new catacomb every day of the week."

Thornton gazed at the professor with admiration. What a professional the man was!

"I'll get on to the Vatican as well," he said.

They talked for a further half an hour in James Thornton's office. When Professor Herbert had finally left, he was well satisfied with the results of his efforts. He knew that things would move and move fast. Once Thornton was convinced, as he was convinced in this case, that a certain goal needed to be pursued, he went after it with all his energy. Herbert was confident that the necessary results would be achieved. Somebody somewhere would object. After all, not only were different ministries involved, such as the Ministries of Transport and Culture;

there was the Vatican too, which could be relied upon to stand up for the departed souls of the faithful.

The warm sunny morning had turned into a warm sunny afternoon. Leaving the School, he walked across the Borghese gardens towards the Porta Pinciana. He passed through the old walls and ambled on down the Via Veneto making for a favourite haunt, the bar of the hotel Excelsior.

"Oliver, my dear boy, how very good to see you!"

Morris Herbert spotted his old pupil (he had taught classics at Eton before taking up his fellowship at Oxford) as soon as he walked into the lobby of the hotel.

"Morris! Punctual as always!" There was real warmth in Grantham's greeting.

"I've ordered you a Campari soda."

Grantham raised his glass and Professor Herbert in turn raised his.

"*Salute!*"

There was a twinkle in the old man's eye. Grantham understood what it meant.

"Did he buy it?"

'Hook, line and sinker," Herbert replied. And then he went on to recount the details of his conversation that day with James Thornton, the Director of the British School.

When he had finished, Grantham said: "Thank God I remembered you were here in Rome and thank God, too, that you were ready to help."

The old man turned serious. "I'm a patriot too, Oliver. Don't ever forget that. *Dulce et decorum est pro patria mentiri.*"

Grantham laughed.

They sat together, looking out into the street as the crowds began to thicken in the Via Veneto.

"I don't regard it as fraud anyway," Grantham said. "Just a little gentle deception. In any case, the Italians can't afford that subway. It's much too expensive, their public finances being in the state they are. They'll love an excuse to cancel, or at least delay, the project."

"You'll have to work at the political level too, won't you?" Morris Herbert asked. "The Vatican and the archaeological superintendency may put in their formal complaints, but ultimately it's the politicians who'll decide."

Grantham looked indulgently at his old friend and mentor.

"We're working on that, I assure you."

Before they parted, Grantham had one last question.

"How did you know about the passage in the book by Pirro Ligorio?"

"Pure luck, my dear boy. I had a look at Onofrio Panvinio, who wrote a similar work, but I couldn't find anything there. Then there was Rofini who wrote the *Corpus Absolutissimum Antiquitatum Romanorum cum Notis*. There was a bit about the Castro Pretorio there, but not quite what we wanted. Ligorio was the third one I studied. I was thrilled when I found that reference to a church, now disappeared."

"And the marginal note about the catacombs?"

Morris Herbert looked sheepish. "I'm afraid that was a little invention all my own. Don't worry," he added quickly when he saw the look of alarm on Grantham's face, "I knew what I was doing. Vegetable dye in the ink, of course, not chemical dye. Only amateurs make that mistake."

"Will it stand up to expert examination?"

"Trust me, Oliver." And again he smiled his small impudent smile. "I rather specialize, you know, in Renaissance marginalia."

19

Sir David Blakely's Tuscan villa was set high up in the hills behind Gaioli. He had bought it in the early fifties when deserted farm houses in the Italian countryside were still going for a song. Under Lydia Blakely's loving care and attention, it had been extensively remodelled and refurbished: terraces built; a swimming pool put in; electricity brought from the nearby town and wells sunk to the depth of two hundred feet to find abundant supplies of crystalline water.

It was Chianti country. Blakely's villa commanded an extensive view of a magnificent Bellini landscape – Giovanni more than Gentile. A succession of little hills, each crowned with a farmhouse or church or grove of trees, spread away from the foreground into the middle distance. On the far horizon, the line of the Apennines loomed in more sombre tones, a distant reminder that life was not all a bowl of roses. On the slopes of the hillsides, both near and far, grew the abundant vines of the region. Chianti Classico was a full-bodied red wine; it reminded Blakely of the breasts of the peasant women whom he would see giving suck by the roadside or in the fields: dark and heavy and rich in promise.

The Tuscan villa had never meant as much to Blakely himself as it had to his wife Lydia. Possibly this was because he lacked her Italian origins; he did not relate to the soil of Italy in the same way that she did. More likely, it had to do with the differences between their two personalities. Blakely loved the place but, in his heart, grudged the time he spent there. Unlike Donald Coulton, his eminent rival, whose love for horses and cricket was as much therapeutic as anything else, David Blakely had never cultivated hobbies of any kind. He did not really know how to relax. He liked to keep on going; to keep on organizing things. Enforced idleness bothered him and, even though he had had telex and telephone facilities installed in the villa, he would always find – after a week or two in Italy – some reason for getting back to London.

That was why he especially welcomed Oliver Grantham's visit that autumn morning.

He strode out into the courtyard to greet his old friend.

"Ah, Oliver! So you remembered the way!"

"Like the back of my hand," Grantham replied. "Is Finzi here?"

Grantham was referring, of course, to the Italian professor who was the *éminence grise* behind the Channel Tunnel project (at least as far as its geological aspects were concerned) and whom Grantham had last seen in Paris at the time of the Chunnel Consortium's board meeting.

"Yes, he is," Blakely replied. "He's been staying the weekend with us. Anders is here too."

"Good." Grantham was genuinely pleased. It was always important to have a sceptic around. Crucial decisions would be taken that morning. Over-enthusiasm could be as dangerous in its way as faint heartedness. Anders had a way of pricking bubbles.

Lydia Blakely joined them for lunch beside the pool. She was as pleased as ever to see Grantham. But this time she made no allusions to his marriage. Grantham was grateful for this. The state of his marriage was his own business. Well-meaning enquiries never helped much.

After lunch, Lydia went back into the house for the traditional siesta. The four men swam in the pool and then continued the discussion where they had left off.

Grantham summarized the situation.

"In short, we have the machines. Six of them." He laughed. "I can tell you now, gentlemen, that at one stage it looked as though we weren't going to get any. Fairmont were about to send the two we had on order to Japan and I had no idea whether or not we would succeed in getting the others."

Sir David Blakely said in his measured chairman's way: "You've worked miracles, Oliver. We all recognize that."

Even Tom Anders was impressed.

"I congratulate you, sir. You have certainly pulled the rabbit out of the hat. The question is now: what are we going to do with it?"

"I think this is the moment where we all have to turn to Professor Finzi for his professional guidance," Grantham said.

Pressed in this way, Giuseppe Finzi had no hesitation in proffering his opinion. He had been proffering opinions of one sort or another ever since he first graduated from the University of Rome. As his academic career had progressed, those opinions had been listened to with ever-increasing respect. He had received accolades from a dozen Italian universities and technical institutes, as well as honorary degrees from a number of European and American institutions. Italians tended to bandy words like *egregio* and *dottorissimo* around rather lightly, but in Finzi's case there was no doubt that these honorifics were well-merited.

After swimming, Giuseppe Finzi had once again dressed in his city clothes. He had brushed his grey hair carefully back from his temples. His tie was knotted with precision and somehow he had managed to remove every trace of Tuscan dust from the surface of his highly polished black shoes.

His voice, when he spoke, was as clipped and precise as his general appearance.

"I agree," he began, "that the acquisition by Chunnel Consortium of six tunnel-boring machines is a stroke of great technical brilliance. I also agree, though I am no expert in these matters, that the opportunity of achieving a construction schedule which extends over one year, rather than five, justifies the risks inherent in using undersea technology, including the Marchprod units. In geological terms, of course, this radical change in plan – important though it is for all other aspects of our work – is immaterial. When we met in Paris I explained the factors which circumscribe our choice of route. I said then, and I repeat now, that the lower half of the Lower Chalk is the *only* layer of rock beneath the Channel which has all the properties we require for boring a Channel Tunnel with the greatest speed, greatest safety and greatest economy. That being so, it will simply be a question of positioning the Marchprod units on the chosen line and of sinking vertical shafts in each case to the necessary depth. The geological problems remain the same whether we are driving a tunnel from A to B or from B to A or – as in this case – in a series of segments to make, ultimately, one continuous link."

Professor Giuseppe Finzi rested his case. For him the suitability of the Lower Chalk as a medium through which to drive a message, in this case the Channel Tunnel, had become almost an article of faith. Men had died for less. Finzi had devoted a lifetime to propounding and justifying his hypothesis; nothing would shift him from it.

Tom Anders, who had tried once before to test the Professor, made one last attempt. He had done some homework since that Paris meeting.

"Don't the layers tilt as well as dip? Couldn't that mean, if we stick to the shortest line, that we risk passing from the Lower Chalk into the Middle Chalk near the French coast?"

Finzi pooh-poohed the suggestion. "That's the Dummett hypothesis," he snapped. "I exploded that idea ten years ago with my paper to the British Academy of Sciences. Surely you know that?"

Anders subsided, crestfallen. He realized he should have known better than to have challenged Finzi on his own ground and, moreover, at his own game.

"I'm sorry, Professor," the tall Dutchman said good-humouredly. "I'm just a layman you know."

Towards the end of the afternoon, Blakely summarized where they stood:

"As I understand it," he said, "the two Marchprod units will be in position and ready to start drilling by the spring of next year. Our six tunnel-boring machines should be in place soon after. If all goes to plan, no more than twelve months will elapse between the commencement of drilling and the completion of the tunnel. That extraordinary fact, that is to say the prospect of having a Chunnel completed and in operation in, let's say, eighteen months from now, is going to be the central feature of our presentation when we go to the market for funds as we will in the spring of next year. Am I right, Oliver?"

"Absolutely right, David," Grantham replied. "My view is that, when the moment comes, we may even be able to revise the fifty:fifty debt:equity ratio which is what we are working on at the moment. I'm pretty sure that the public will know a winner when it sees one."

"Let's cross that bridge when we come to it, if you'll forgive the expression," Blakely laughed.

Lady Blakely came back out of the house to join them once more.

"Ah Lydia!" Blakely looked at his wife fondly. "Come and join us. There's time for a drink before dinner."

20

Mrs Potter arrived at Paddington in a flustered mood. She was three-quarters of an hour late and she had promised, absolutely promised, to be on time. It had not been her fault. The train had been delayed at Westbury – not for the first time, as she remembered. Fellow-passengers had muttered about "engineering works on the line"; but explanations as to the cause of the hold-up did not help.

Sandra Furlong hustled her into a taxi.

"The meeting is starting just about now," Sandra said, "but we may still be in time."

"Where are we going?" Mrs Potter asked. "You told me, but I'm afraid I've already forgotten."

Sandra Furlong smiled indulgently. She had been down to Exmoor on two separate occasions to rehearse the old lady in her role. She had spent many hours with her in that little white cottage at the end of the farm track. Mrs Potter had seemed to grasp it all quite clearly. But Sandra knew better than to count her chickens before they hatched.

"We're going to St Ermine's hotel near Victoria," she replied. "That's where the AGM is taking place."

"Some AGM." There was both scorn and indignation in Eileen Potter's voice. "To my knowledge, they haven't had a shareholders' meeting in twenty years. And I should know."

Twenty minutes later, the taxi pulled up in front of the hotel in Caxton Street. The Channel Tunnel Company's annual general meeting – the first, as Mrs Potter had pointed out, for a good many years – was taking place in one of the St Ermine's hotel's smaller meeting rooms. As she slipped in with the old lady on her arm, Sandra Furlong noticed that there were about twenty people present altogether. Grantham, who was sitting near the front, noticed them arrive and gave a welcoming wink. Sandra breathed a sigh of relief. Obviously they were still in time.

Brian Staples himself had taken the chair. He had explained this action to the small gathering at the beginning of the meeting.

"I am sure you will all know," he had said, "that the Companies Act provides, in situations like this where there is no board of directors sitting, for the major shareholder to take the chair as acting chairman till confirmed in that position by the meeting itself. This I now propose to do. As our first act of business, therefore, I would like the meeting to confirm me as chairman of this meeting. I should add that I propose to vote the forty-two per cent shareholding in the Channel Tunnel Company which is now held by Channel Ferries in favour of the proposition I have just enunciated."

He had, at this point, stared straight at Grantham. "Mr Grantham," he had said, "I am given to understand that you in your personal capacity dispose of thirty-five per cent of the voting shares of Channel Tunnel Company. Is that correct?"

Grantham had nodded. He had not expected Staples to challenge him so directly, so soon. The man's intelligence, he thought, must have been better than he supposed. Staples had been precisely correct in suggesting that Grantham disposed of thirty-five per cent of the shares of the Channel Tunnel Company. They had cost him a fortune but he regarded every penny as being well-spent. That brisk, efficient young man at Stanley Gibbons – Giles Lowe – had done a marvellous job. Over the last few weeks, the share certificates had flooded in to the offices in the Strand from every nook and corner. Of course Grantham had been disappointed when finally they had to call a halt having acquired only thirty-five per cent of the outstanding shares. He had known that thirty-five per cent by itself was not enough to defeat Staples.

"Mr Staples," Grantham had said, smiling benignly, "I should hate you, or anyone else in this meeting room, to think that we are here today in an adversary position. I shall be happy to second the proposition that you should act as chairman of this meeting."

Brian Staples had looked at him in surprise. That surprise had grown even more pronounced when Grantham raised no objection at all to the proposition which Staples then proceeded to put to the meeting.

"In a nutshell," Staples had said, "I am proposing that the Channel Tunnel Company institute proceedings in the necessary quarters with a view to having the Channel Tunnel Company's one-hundred-year concession to build and operate a tunnel under the Channel confirmed and ratified. I have explained the historical situation," he had told them. "I have indicated what Counsel's preliminary opinion has been as to the validity of that crucial vote in the House of Commons in 1892, when the claims of Sir Edward Watkin's company were recognized even though the House did not approve the idea of constructing the Channel Tunnel itself. It remains for us today to draw the necessary consequences." And he had added again, looking straight at Grantham, "it goes without saying that one aspect of such an action must be to seek, and to obtain, the cancellation by the Governments of both France and the United Kingdom of any concessions made – illegal concessions, I maintain – in favour of Chunnel Consortium."

Throughout all of this Grantham had remained silent. He was, he liked to think, biding his time. It was not, however, until he saw Mrs Potter enter the room with Sandra that Grantham felt in any way confident of meeting, and mastering, Staples' frontal attack.

"I put that proposition to the meeting, therefore," Staples repeated. "It is a clear proposition. I think we ought to vote on it."

By now the handful of the members of the public present had realized that an intricate power play was being enacted. A couple of financial journalists who had found themselves with nothing better to do on a wet afternoon began busily scribbling notes. Alex Lyons of the *Daily Mail*, who had been tipped off by Grantham (it was a sort of *quid pro quo* for Lyons's help in Washington) was mentally composing the opening paragraph of his 'exclusive' for the Business section of his paper.

"We can certainly vote, Mr Chairman, if that is the wish of the meeting." Grantham shrugged. "I am not much of a voting man myself. It seems to me that what you have said is entirely reasonable and fair. I second the proposition that the Channel Tunnel Company, as represented by the shareholders in this room, should assert its rightful claim to the Channel Tunnel concession!"

There was a stir in the room as he spoke. Staples looked frankly flabbergasted. If ever there was a turn-up for the books, this was it. Ever since he had found out from Fairmont Tool in Tucson, Arizona of Grantham's visit there; ever since the first rumours had reached him, as they were bound to, that Chunnel Consortium had dramatic plans for shortening the construction schedule; ever since it had become apparent that Grantham was going to any lengths to match the shareholding that Channel Ferries had managed to acquire in the old Channel Tunnel Company, Brian Staples had been preparing himself for a major confrontation. That the possibility of this confrontation now seemed to have evaporated was something he found very difficult to understand. He decided to test the water.

"Let me be absolutely clear," he said. "Are you, as minority shareholder, speaking in favour of my proposal?"

"Precisely," Grantham replied. "If you put it to the vote, I shall vote in favour."

Brian Staples looked around the room. "In that case, ladies and gentlemen," he said, "it does not seem necessary to put the proposal to the vote. Agreed?"

There were nods of agreement. Sandra Furlong laid a restraining hand upon Mrs Potter's arm.

"Not yet," she said.

Brian Staples, sitting at the front of the room on the dais, shuffled his papers as though preparing to bring the meeting to a close.

Grantham raised his hand.

"On a point of order, Chairman," he said.

"By all means, Mr Grantham." Having won a total and resounding victory, Brian Staples was all smiles and affability.

Sandra Furlong whispered urgently to Mrs Potter: "Go on, this is the moment. That was the signal!"

The old lady realized her moment had come. She rose in her place.

"The point of order is really mine, Mr Chairman," she began. "That kind gentleman was, I know, merely catching your attention on my behalf."

Brian Staples' smile had lost nothing of its warmth. He turned his attention to the back of the room where Mrs Potter stood.

"By all means. Would you care to give your name?"

"I should be very proud to." Mrs Potter spoke in a clear, firm voice. "My name is Eileen Potter; I am the great-granddaughter of Sir Edward Watkin, whom everyone in this room will know as the chief originator of the Channel Tunnel idea. He is the only man indeed who ever got down to digging as opposed to talking."

There was a small round of applause at this sally. The journalists present pricked up their ears. They realized they were not only getting a good financial story; there was some human interest as well. It was not every day that they came across the descendants of the great railway barons of the nineteenth century.

Staples' smile was wearing thin. So far, everything had gone swimmingly. He had been in complete control of the meeting. But now he could sense that things were beginning to slip away from him.

"I am sure we are all of us delighted," he said, "to meet the great-granddaughter of the great Sir Edward Watkin. I certainly am. But I fear we must if we can stick to the order of business. What was your point of order, madam?"

Sandra Furlong crossed her fingers. She hoped the old lady would not forget her lines.

But Eileen Potter was not for nothing Sir Edward Watkin's great-granddaughter. She knew when to rise to an occasion. The old lady spoke quietly, knowing she had the attention of the meeting.

"I'm afraid I was late arriving. My train was held up at Westbury. But, as I understand it, you were elected chairman at the outset of the meeting. Is that correct?"

"Quite correct," Staples replied. "There were no opposing votes."

"May I ask," the old lady continued, "now that the Channel Tunnel Company has decided once more to be active, what your plans for the future management of the Channel Tunnel Company will be?"

She looked fiercely, almost accusingly, at Brian Staples.

"You, sir, I am told, are deeply involved in the Channel Ferry operation. I am sure you have presided over our meeting today in a very effective manner. I cannot however believe that it would necessarily be in the long-term interests of the Channel Tunnel Company for its fortunes to be directed by a man who clearly has other interests at heart, rival interests if I may put it that way. Speaking as the great-granddaughter of Sir Edward Watkin, who never lived to see his lifetime ambition fulfilled, I must add that I would regard it as being extremely unfortunate if the Channel Tunnel Company were to win its claim to the concession only, if I may phrase it thus, to sit on it and do nothing, thus effectively ensuring that the status quo remains precisely as it is today."

The old lady had almost finished. Staples had turned a whiter shade of pale; but she pressed home her attack relentlessly.

"It is not clear to me," she continued, "whether in appointing Mr Staples chairman of this meeting, we also appointed him chairman of our company. But if, by any accident, that is what we did, then I move that we undo it as fast as we can."

Brian Staples found the words to interrupt her at this point. "Are you a shareholder, madam?" He spoke in icy tones. "Only shareholders may move motions at annual general meetings."

"I am indeed, sir. And I have brought the certificates along to prove it." Eileen Potter flourished a fistful of certificates triumphantly.

Brian Staples realized that he would have to let her have a run for her money. He had been in business long enough to know that each AGM had its share of nuts. The best thing a chairman could do was to let them talk themselves out. The worst thing a chairman could do was to try to shut them up. That was a sure-fire way of antagonizing the meeting. From where he sat, he could not see what certificates the old lady was waving. But he felt completely sure of his sums. When you had forty-two per cent of a defunct company, you had as many votes as you could possibly need. He spoke to her now with elaborate politeness.

"What precisely is your motion, madam?"

"I move a vote of no confidence in the chair, owing to conflicting interests," Mrs Potter said. "I further move that we elect as our chairman and managing director Mr Oliver Grantham whose interest in fulfilling Sir Edward Watkin's dream must be well known to all of us." She sat down.

There was a ripple of applause.

Later that afternoon, the three of them had tea together in the hotel lobby. Mrs Potter was still visibly elated.

"It's so different from the country. Sometimes I think I rather vegetate down there, my dears."

Sandra Furlong patted her on the arm. "I don't think you could ever vegetate, Mrs Potter. You're much too full of bounce and energy."

The old lady smiled at her. "Oh, I'm getting a bit vague, you know. I thought for a moment I might forget what I had to say."

Grantham beamed at her. "You did absolutely splendidly," he told her. "It was a marvellous performance. Did you see Staples' face when he found that your share certificates added up to an extra sixteen per cent and that you and I together therefore held the majority of the shares? I've never seen a man look so angry. But what I don't understand," Grantham continued, "is why you didn't let that Greek girl have those shares too, when you let her have the others."

"I would have done, I'm sure." Mrs Potter smiled innocently. "Actually, I thought I *had* given her all my certificates. It wasn't until I was going through some cardboard boxes that I came across the other ones. And then, of course, Sandra explained that Staples was really the enemy and if he gained control of great-grandfather's old company, that would be the end of it!" She sighed. "I'm only sorry I got rid of so many of my shares. At least they might be worth something now that *you've* taken over."

Grantham spoke to her in quiet and reassuring tones. "I want you to understand one thing, Mrs Potter," he said. "From now on, your financial future is secure. You still own sixteen per cent in the Channel Tunnel Company. That sixteen per cent is going to be worth a very great deal of money to you."

The old lady looked at him with wonderment. "How can you be so sure?" she asked. "I know I'm rather simple, but surely the Channel Tunnel Company shares are only worth something if the lawyers and the courts agree that the concession which was made to great-grandfather's company in the last century is still valid. If we don't win on that, then those shares are still just worthless pieces of paper, aren't they?"

Grantham helped himself to more muffins. It had been a long afternoon and he felt hungry. He passed over the plate to Mrs Potter.

"Have some," he insisted. "Your train may get stuck at Westbury again."

She was not to be fobbed off so easily. She had glimpsed the pot of gold at the end of the rainbow and she wanted to know whether it was real or not.

"Tell me, Mr Grantham," Mrs Potter insisted. "Am I right or not?"

Again Grantham spoke to her quietly and authoritatively.

"I give you my word," he said, "that whatever happens you will be a rich woman, Mrs Potter. Can I say fairer than that?"

There was something about his tone of voice which convinced her.

The Rolls took them back to the station. Grantham and Sandra Furlong saw the old lady to her seat in the train.

"This is not the end of our friendship," Grantham assured her. "This is just the beginning. No self-respecting Channel Tunnel Company can afford to be without the services, in an advisory capacity, of Sir Edward Watkin's great-granddaughter. You'll be hearing from us."

Sandra Furlong kissed the old lady on both cheeks. "I shall be down again soon. I'm growing rather fond of Exmoor."

As Sandra spoke, she thought of the jovial landlord at the Royal Oak, Winsford. A nodding acquaintanceship was fast blossoming into something more.

The train pulled out of the station. Grantham and Sandra walked back to the car together.

"Something's worrying you, Sandra, isn't it?" Grantham asked, seeing the frown on her usually serene brow.

Sandra turned to him. She spoke frankly.

"Mr Grantham, I just hope you weren't leading that little old lady up the garden path as far as the money was concerned. I couldn't forgive you if you were to do that."

Grantham smiled at her. "Sandra, a man has to tell a lot of lies between breakfast and tea time. That's the way life is. But I promise you I told Mrs Potter the truth. She's going to be a rich woman."

Sandra was still sceptical. "Surely that legal business could drag on for years."

"Forget about the legal business," Grantham told her. "Mrs Potter's going to be a rich woman by the weekend." And he added for good measure, to his secretary's evident amazement: "so am I!"

The chauffeur held the car door open for them.

"Home, James," Grantham instructed in high good humour. "Fast as you can. We have something to celebrate."

21

The following morning, David Blakely saw the reports in the newspapers of the much-delayed annual general meeting of the supposedly moribund, if not defunct, Channel Tunnel Company. He was surprised, thinking about it, not to have heard direct from Grantham on this score. This was surely something Grantham must have known about. Sir David found the whole development very worrying. Very worrying indeed.

He had tried to call Grantham straightaway. There had been no reply from Grantham's flat; at his office, Sandra Furlong informed Sir David with many apologies that Grantham was having lunch with Sir Giles Morgan at the House of Commons and would not be back until later in the afternoon. Sir David had put his telephone down wondering what the hell was going on.

When he finally got through to Grantham towards four o'clock that day, Sir David had detected – or so he thought – a note of considerable amusement in Grantham's voice.

"I'm not sure I see that there's much to be amused about in the present situation." David Blakely had spoken with some asperity.

"Can you meet me later?" Grantham had replied. "Come for a drink. I'd like you to see my new place."

He had given a Belgravia address and, once again, David Blakely could not suppress his sense of surprise.

"I didn't know you *had* a new place."

Later that evening, sitting in the drawing room of half a million pounds' worth of town-house in Chester Square, Grantham had laid his cards on the table.

"I'm not a greedy man, David, you know that. I've been a soldier all my life. Soldiers are not greedy men. They fight the wars which are made necessary because of the actions of greedy men, but they're not on the whole greedy themselves."

As he spoke, he had opened a bottle of champagne and poured his friend a drink. It was a strange reversal of roles. So much of their lives – indeed, ever since they had been schoolboys together – it had been David Blakely who poured the champagne, and paid for it too. Now Grantham was doing both the pouring and the paying.

"As I say," Grantham continued, "soldiers are not greedy men. But I'm not a soldier any longer. I'm a civilian now. I've got a few more years of productive life ahead of me and I want some of the good things." He waved a hand around the sitting room and out of the window at the square beyond. "Like this house for example."

David Blakely said nothing. He could see what was coming and he didn't like it at all.

Having gone as far as he had, Grantham didn't bother about mincing his words.

"I own thirty-five per cent of the shares of Channel Tunnel Company," he said. "I control a further sixteen per cent. That gives me the necessary fifty-one per cent interest in the company. Furthermore, I was yesterday appointed chairman and managing director of that company. I was authorized by a properly constituted annual general meeting to pursue a claim on behalf of the Channel Tunnel Company to the concession for the construction and operation of the Channel Tunnel voted in the last century by Parliament. Were the Channel Tunnel Company to pursue such a claim through the courts, I am convinced that we would stand a very good chance of winning. In any event, the mere fact that the company had brought such a claim with the possibility of extended litigation would effectively make it impossible for Chunnel Consortium to go ahead with its scheme. No government could push a hybrid bill through Parliament in favour of Chunnel Consortium, knowing full well that the courts might reach a different conclusion altogether."

"I'm sure you've taken legal advice on this point," Sir David said drily. "No doubt Sir Giles Morgan has been a mine of information. You *were* having lunch with Sir Giles today, weren't you?"

Grantham raised an eyebrow. He permitted himself a half-smile.

"Don't take it so hard, David. You play tough too. This house cost several hundred thousand pounds. I'll settle for three million. And Chunnel Consortium will have to buy out Mrs Potter's shares at the same rate."

"Mrs Potter?" Sir David Blakely was unfamiliar with the name.

"Mrs Eileen Potter," Grantham explained. "The great-granddaughter of Sir Edward Watkin."

David Blakely burst into a great guffaw of laughter.

"Bravo, Oliver! I take my hat off to you. I'd say three million is cheap at the price. You took one hell of a risk though, didn't you, with your own money? If you hadn't been able to outvote Staples, you would have spent good money acquiring shares in the Channel Tunnel Company and nothing to show for it."

"*Qui ne risque rien n'a rien*," Grantham replied. And then he added, for the record, "Friends helped."

And, as he spoke, he thought of the tall, aristocratic German, Konrad von Rilke, who had come through with the funds, both for the shares and for the Belgravia house, just at the time when he needed them.

"Cheap at the price, indeed, given the scale of our operation," Sir David repeated. "For a few million pounds Chunnel Consortium has acquired, as it were, absolute title. You *are* suggesting, aren't you, that Chunnel Consortium should buy out the majority shareholding in CTC? I do read you right, don't I?"

"The old lady comes on board too, in some form or another," Grantham insisted.

"Mrs Potter?"

Grantham nodded. "She was terrific at the meeting. She wiped the floor with Brian Staples."

David Blakely laughed again. "You certainly paid them back for those photographs."

"Believe me, David, I've only just begun."

Grantham looked around the room, felt the emptiness in the house. Vengeance was sweet, and he had not had his fill of it yet. He wondered whether Lily would come back to him when it was all over, or whether he would go back to her.

The following day Grantham wrote two letters from his office. One was to Mrs Eileen Potter at her home in Somerset, confirming their conversation the previous day. Mrs Eileen Potter was to join the board of Chunnel Consortium, incorporating as it now did the old Channel Tunnel Company, for a suitable and substantial fee. The other was to Mr Arthur Jones, the librarian at Newham in East London. Grantham took the opportunity of thanking Mr Jones on behalf of the board of Chunnel Consortium, and indeed on behalf of all those who wished to see the satisfactory completion of a great and historic project, for the signal services he had rendered. He invited Mr Jones to join the board of Chunnel Consortium as a non-executive director with special responsibilities for ensuring the necessary public participation and enthusiasm for the Chunnel project. Grantham pointed out that this was by no means a token responsibility. In any major enterprise, he wrote, the constructive support of the public was necessary. In the event that Mr Jones decided to accept the offer, Grantham invited him to come forward with a list of proposals whereby the Channel Tunnel venture could attract the greatest possible support from all sections of the public. He asked the librarian in particular to give some thought to side-issues which, though they seemed not to be of overwhelming importance at the moment, might at some stage require decisive action on the part of the Consortium.

"I am not the first soldier," Grantham wrote in his letter, "to believe that to be forewarned is to be forearmed."

He asked Mr Jones to submit to him, in order of importance, a short list of items which he, Jones, believed might at some stage or other require the board's attention.

"I feel confident," Grantham wrote in his concluding paragraph, "that you will bring both your unique knowledge of this project, and your imagination, to bear in pursuance of this task. Let us meet at an early date and talk things over."

22

It was not the first time that Her Majesty had visited a production platform. In the course of her long reign the sovereign had on more than one occasion inspected those North Sea installations responsible for producing the bulk of Britain's new-found wealth. But this was the first time she had visited a production platform which was concerned with sea-bed mining and whose command and control facilities were located not on the surface of the rig, as was typically the case, but on the sea-floor itself.

If Her Majesty felt the slightest uneasiness as she rode down the elevator in the access shaft, she gave no sign of it. She was much too well-trained for that. As they descended, Donald Coulton described the revolutionary Marchprod unit with proprietorial pride.

"What we have here," he said, "is a total sub-sea production complex. The first of its kind in the world. Today, and for the next twelve months, we will be using it on the Chunnel excavation. And of course a sister unit, as you know, ma'am, is installed a few miles from here towards the French coast."

Her Majesty nodded as they sank past the hundred-foot mark.

"We feel quite sure," Lord Coulton continued, "that these Marchprod units, once they have proved themselves here, will be able to be used on the ocean floor all over the world where conditions permit such operations."

"What is the maximum operating depth of these systems?"

It was not a pro-forma question. Her Majesty had always had a real interest in technical matters.

Donald Coulton turned to the bearded young engineer, Michael Prestwick, who rode down in the elevator with them.

"Dr Prestwick is the captain of this ship," he said. "I'll let him answer that."

"We're talking about one-atmosphere systems, ma'am." Prestwick gave the Queen the straightforward scientific case without embellishment or simplification. "By this I mean systems where people – even though they're on the ocean floor – can go on working as though they were in their own homes. We call it the shirt-sleeve environment and, as you can see, I'm dressed today as I would be if I were going to an office in London or, in my case, Aberdeen.

"In the Channel," Prestwick continued, "we are, as you know, operating at relatively shallow depths. At its deepest point, the sea floor does not lie more than two hundred and fifty feet below the surface. And this is fortunate since, as Lord Coulton has said, we are still very much in an experimental situation. But I feel quite confident that we shall be able to retain one-atmosphere conditions in water depth applications up to two thousand metres. That, as you can imagine, gives our total sub-sea production complex very great versatility indeed."

"Thank you very much."

The doors opened as they reached the bottom of the shaft and the royal party entered the control module. It was a long, brightly lit room, looking much like the nerve-centre of some nuclear command post or electricity-generating plant. A long bank of computers, discs clicking and whirring, had been placed in the centre of the room; to each side were consoles of various kinds and desks at which engineers and technicians were seated.

They walked on down the length of the control room. A pool photographer from *The Times* took photographs of the little group and Alex Lyons from the *Daily Mail*, who had received a personal invitation from Grantham to be present on that occasion, took notes for a story which would be syndicated the next day throughout the world.

At the far end of the command module, there was a bank of screens somewhat like the control room of a television studio.

"This young lady," Michael Prestwick explained, "has a fairly straightforward job. Her task is to monitor what is actually going on at the cutting face, approximately two hundred feet below us. She knows what to look for and when to report something unusual. The remote control cameras are actually mounted on the TBM itself. As you can see," Prestwick added, "boring seems to be progressing satisfactorily at the moment."

Donald Coulton realized with some surprise that the young lady to whom Michael Prestwick had just referred was none other than his daughter, Candida.

"My dear Candida!" he expostulated, ignoring for a moment the fact that he was in the presence of Her Majesty and that all remarks in such circumstances should either be addressed to the Sovereign or not at all, "you never told me!"

The young woman swivelled round on her seat. "Donald!" she exclaimed. Then, covered with confusion, she curtsied and rushed out an apology.

"I never told my father where I was working," she explained. "I wanted to make it on my own, if you see what I mean."

The Queen, who had met Candida Coulton on at least two occasions in the past in the company of her father, could not conceal her delight in witnessing the delicate little cameo which was taking place between father and daughter. She smiled.

"I sometimes think *my* children wish they could make it on their own too!"

Whatever slight tension might have been building, was instantly dissipated by this touch of humour.

As the party moved on, Donald Coulton found himself next to Michael Prestwick.

"Is she doing all right?" he asked. "I promise you, I knew absolutely nothing of this. Candida met Grantham at my house one day, but I had no idea she would apply to join you."

"She's doing fine. She's a real asset," Prestwick replied. "Quick and reliable. I didn't know she was your daughter. She signed in under another name."

Donald Coulton felt the faint thump of pride. Whatever name his daughter might have used, she was still his daughter. To make it on one's own was a very Coulton-like thing to do.

He took the young man's elbow and pressed it as the party moved on towards the next set of screens. "Keep your eye on her, won't you?"

The next bank of television screens revealed a large chamber occupied by half a dozen people in work clothes and hard hats. Michael Prestwick took up the tale.

"This module on the sea-floor is the control centre for the tunnelling operation. This is where all the key decisions are made, where the computers are located, where the detailed instructions are given about the direction and speed of the bore and so on. Tunnelling nowadays is probably as automated and as remote-controlled as any other industry – perhaps more so. But that doesn't mean you can totally do without people below the ground. You can steer a ship from the bridge; you can even control the engines; but you still need some engineers below decks."

They looked at the screen. Donald Coulton recognized Grantham in the chamber down below. He was obviously consulting with a colleague.

"Who's Grantham talking to?" Coulton asked.

"He's talking to Monique Delacourt," Prestwick replied. "She's Falaise's chief engineer, a very brilliant woman. She has the day-to-day responsibility for the actual tunnelling operation. Of course what goes on here is only one of her concerns. She just happens to be here on Marchprod One today; but she could have been on the other Marchprod unit, over there towards the French coast." Michael Prestwick gave a general wave in the direction where he suspected, without being sure, that France lay. "Or she might be at Dover with TBM number 3. Or at Sangatte where TBM number 4 is working. And Mr Grantham" (Michael Prestwick was quite unable to disguise the tone of admiration in his voice) "seems to be everywhere at once. He seems to have a knack of pulling things together."

"Can we talk to them?" Donald Coulton asked.

"Of course." Michael Prestwick pressed a switch beside one of the screens. "This is command centre to operation room. Can you hear me?"

On the screen in front of them they could see Grantham and Monique Delacourt break off their conversation.

"Sure we can hear you, Michael," Grantham replied. "I'm sorry we can't see you too since I know you can see us."

Coulton spoke into the intercom. "Her Majesty is in the command centre with us today, Oliver. Would you like to tell her briefly what you and Miss Delacourt are discussing? I'm sure she'd be interested."

Grantham smiled. "I apologize for not being able to report in person, ma'am. We'll be back on top half an hour from now. I don't know how tight your schedule is."

"Don't let me interrupt," the Queen insisted. "I'm sure you're doing more important work down there than you would be coming back up and talking to me."

"Thank you, ma'am." They could see Grantham nod respectfully in the direction of the camera.

While the royal party was being entertained on board Marchprod One before being helicoptered back to the mainland, Oliver Grantham and Monique Delacourt stayed below ground. They still had business to attend to. It was the first time that Monique had had an opportunity to give Grantham a detailed explanation of the operations in hand.

"Obviously, we can't go right up to the cutting face while the machine is running," she told him. "But we have our own back-up system of TV screens down here so we can see what's going on in much the same way as the people in the command centre can, though we don't have the computers or the other sophisticated tools for monitoring and regulation. And there's too much going on down here at any time for proper assessments to be made. It's rather like the space-shots, if you like. Of course the astronauts in their orbiting capsules have important tasks to perform. But the real control is exercised elsewhere."

Grantham saw exactly what Monique Delacourt meant when she had said that there was "too much going on" for proper on-the-spot control to be exercised. In the first place, there was the noise. Though the giant Fairmont TBM was equipped with the very latest in sound-suppression devices, the specifications of the job inevitably meant that noise would be generated. As they walked along the one hundred yards section of tunnel which had already been driven along the line towards the French coast, Monique Delacourt had to raise her voice to make herself heard.

"The power requirements tend to be much greater for rock machines", she shouted, "than for soft ground. That's because of the larger thrust forces required and also because of the greater expenditure of energy on cutting per unit volume."

Grantham had seen TBMs when he visited the Fairmont tool complex in Tucson, Arizona and again in Afghanistan. So the size of the machine came as no surprise to him. But this was the first time he had seen one in action.

"In essence," Monique Delacourt explained, still raising her voice, "the TBM has a fixed head, supported by jacks on shoes on the invert and at the sides, containing the drive motors and a rotating cutting head carried in a large heavy bearing. The diameter of the head exactly corresponds to the diameter of the tunnel. We can squeeze up behind the head if you like to inspect the rear section of the TBM. You'll have to wear ear-muffs and a hard hat when we go forward. That's just an elementary precaution. Whenever you're tunnelling in rock you work with shields behind the machines; but that doesn't mean you don't wear hard hats. The shields move forward with the machines. Until you've brought in the lining, there's always a risk."

"How soon will this section be lined?" Grantham asked.

"Ideally, we ought more or less to be able to keep up with the tunnelling. In other words we line as we go. That's a very sound principle. In the case of the Channel tunnel, we're dealing with the Lower Chalk which, as you know, is pretty ideal from a tunnelling point of view; it's self-supporting at the face. And of course, another great advantage of the TBM is that it cuts a smooth bore of the correct profile.

This not only gives a useful reduction in the amount of excavation – I mean, you're excavating precisely what you need to excavate and no more. It also means that you don't have to do a lot of grouting and filling, which would be the case if we were doing the classic 'blast and clear' operation. Any time you use explosives to tunnel, you're going to excavate more than you need. That's inevitable. Which means you have to fill in the holes later, and that costs money and time. With the TBM, you're making best use of the rock strength and facilitating the construction of the tunnel lining, whether it be *in situ* concrete or precast segmental lining, which is what we're using.

"As I say, 'line as you go' is the golden rule," Monique continued. "That way you can't be taken by surprise if the rock develops unexpected fissures. Ten days from now all this first section should be lined."

Grantham was intrigued. "If the segments exactly fit the dimensions of the tunnel, how do you get them into position?"

"The precast concrete segments come in two parts," Monique Delacourt replied. "We pass them through the lining which is already in place and then build on, following behind the TBM."

Grantham laughed. "You think of everything, don't you?"

A catwalk ran along the length of the machine. Monique led the way, continuing her remarks.

"Behind and attached to the fixed head is a chassis on which are mounted electro-hydraulic motors, conveyor, rear jack and expanded ring which can grip the tunnel walls and against which forward thrusts can be made."

She pointed out each item as they walked along the length of the machine.

As they stood there watching the machine in action, Grantham was filled with a sense of excitement. He had always believed in the Channel Tunnel project. He had always known that the thing was technically feasible, an idea whose time had come. But seeing the giant TBM in action, seeing the steady flow of rock and rubble coming back on the conveyor belt, convinced him – as nothing else could – that the tunnel would be built and would be built on time.

They walked back the way they had come. The conveyor belt, itself operating at walking-speed, moved with them.

"We could probably have got away with dumping the waste in the sea," Monique Delacourt said. "We did our homework on the tides and currents in the Channel and we were quite convinced that there would have been no threat to the marine eco-system or to navigation. But you know how the public can be stirred up on things like this. We decided it was better to play safe. The conveyor belt goes on up through the access shaft and right up to the loading platform on the Marchprod unit. The waste is taken away in boats and is being used in a construction project on the South Coast."

Grantham nodded. "I think that was very wise of you," he said. "Public opinion is something we simply have to be concerned about."

As he spoke, Grantham wondered how Arthur Jones was getting on with preparing his first report. How did the public see the Channel Tunnel project, disadvantages as well as advantages? It was important to know.

Monique Delacourt greeted the half dozen people who were still working in the subterranean chamber.

"We're splitting it about half and half," she said. "Normally there'll be about ten people down here; five of them will be British and five of them French. We try to keep the same ratio on the other tunnelling sections. At one stage we discussed the idea of having French engineers working on the French side up to the mid Channel point, and English engineers doing the same on the English side. But then we decided: this is a multi-national project, so let's keep it that way. And of course, up there in the command module, you've got Dutch technicians manning the communications equipment."

They had almost reached the bottom of the lift shaft. For a second, Grantham wondered whether he ought to ask Monique Delacourt about Pierre Leroux. It seemed such a simple, sensible thing to do. Or at least, he could warn her. He could let her know the kind of man she was associating with; advise her to keep her distance.

But then he realized that any such action would be lunacy. If the Delacourt–Leroux relationship was at all what it was cracked up to be, talking to Monique would be like flashing a mirror in the noonday sun. The news that certain people were interested in Leroux's political loyalties would get back to the man instantly.

No, Grantham reflected, this was something which would have to mature in its own time like a good Camembert.

Before he left, Grantham met Monique's deputy.

"This is Jean-Yves Lamonte," Monique introduced Grantham to a tough, bull-necked gentleman about thirty-five years old with a fierce crew-cut and red polo-necked sweater. "Jean-Yves was in the navy before he joined Falaise. He was an engineer then."

The Frenchman's leathery face cracked into a smile. "Still an engineer today. All machines are the same, even the TBM. It's just bigger."

"I'm a military man myself." Grantham shook hands with Jean-Yves Lamonte warmly. "Where were you based?"

"We were everywhere," Jean-Yves replied. "Off the coast of West Africa sometimes, sometimes in the Caribbean. Toulon. Marseilles."

Monique came back with him all the way to the lift-shaft.

"Talking about Marseilles," she said, "the French Socialist party is having its congress there."

Grantham's attention was aroused. "Forgive the direct question, but are you going with Leroux?"

"For Leroux this is the make-or-break meeting," Monique replied. "He has to get the nomination at Marseilles if he's to run in the Presidential election as the Socialist party candidate. Without the official nomination of the party, he may as well give up. I think I ought to be there. The project can spare me for a couple of days. Jean-Yves is a competent man. And there are plenty of back-up people, if anything goes wrong. Besides, I can be back within a few hours if I'm needed."

Grantham laid a hand on her arm. "Don't be so worried, Monique. I wouldn't dream of suggesting you shouldn't go to Marseilles. We're bang on schedule with the project. All the TBMs are working to full capacity. A good general knows when to retire from the scene. I'll tell you something," Grantham smiled at her. "I need a break too. I've been going at this project hammer and tongs for months now. As soon as we've got the share-offer well and truly launched, I'm going skiing. A week in the Alps will do me the world of good."

Monique Delacourt smiled back at him. Things had been difficult at the beginning, but she was learning to like the tough Englishman who had managed to show how comprehensively wrong she had been that day when they met in Paris but who nevertheless had not once sought to make capital out of her confusion.

"Have a good holiday, then." She reached up to give him a quick kiss on both cheeks, French-fashion. "Make sure it's the French Alps anyway," she counselled.

"You don't have to tell me," Grantham replied. "I've been going to Savoie since I was a boy."

"Is there anything you haven't done, Oliver?"

Grantham wasn't sure whether Monique's question was mischievous or not. He decided it was and, as such, better left unanswered.

"Look after yourself," he said. "Let's talk as soon as you're back."

Monique Delacourt stood there with Jean-Yves Lamonte for a second or two after the lift doors had closed and Grantham had disappeared. One day, she decided, she would ask Grantham about his marriage. The man had so much going for him. He was handsome, intelligent, funny, fit. And yet, somehow there was something missing. He didn't really seem to relate to people. He saw life in terms of doing, rather than being.

She sighed and turned back to her work. Perhaps all she was saying was that Grantham was a man, not a woman. And that kind of observation didn't get anyone very far.

Grantham didn't stop at the command module. He rode the lift straight up on to the surface. The helicopter was there waiting for him on the pad of Marchprod One. This time the pilot came out straightaway with his greeting: "Good to see you again, General."

Grantham immediately realized that this was the same pilot who had flown him in and out of Aberdeen, the day he had gone north to investigate the possibility of using undersea technology as a means of speeding up the construction schedules.

The helicopter took off almost immediately.

"You're about five minutes behind the royal party. But they're going straight to Windsor, or so they say on the RT. Mind you, that could be a piece of deliberate misinformation. They tend to do that with royal flights. It doesn't do for too many people to know where the Queen's flying and when."

Grantham looked down at the choppy waters of the Channel below. "It looks like it's blowing up into a storm," he said.

"Could be," the pilot replied laconically. "Beaufort 5 already."

Grantham sat back in his seat and thought about his afternoon. It all seemed to be going so splendidly. Could it last? Somewhere at the back of his mind something was niggling him. It had to do with what Monique Delacourt had said as they walked back from the rock-face. Something about the tunnelling procedure.

"We try to line as we go," she had said.

But what precisely did she mean? Was "trying" good enough? He thought back to one evening when his chauffeur had taken him to visit the old tunnel workings at Shakespeare Cliffs near Dover. He remembered how he had pushed the rotting planks aside to walk through the portal and into that dark hole which had been hollowed out over a hundred years ago. He remembered how he had felt the walls of the tunnel. They had been firm and dry. Nobody in those days had thought of putting in lining, certainly not pre-cast concrete segment lining. But life had moved on since then. In a battle, you had to take risks. But any soldier knew that the man who took risks when he didn't have to was a danger both to himself and others. Grantham decided that the Falaise people should be asked to ensure that the tunnelling and the lining operations didn't get out of phase.

The pilot interrupted his train of thought. "We're getting a gale warning now," he said. "Just as well we took off when we did. I wouldn't care to be out there on that rig, I can tell you, in a gale; not with all that shipping about. It's bad enough in the North Sea sometimes, and there you've got an ocean to play with. Out there in the Channel it's a very different story. Those rigs stand out like a sore thumb. I should know: I see the pattern of traffic as I fly out there. I'm surprised the shipping authorities in the Channel let Marchmain get away with it."

Grantham listened with half an ear. "They're temporary structures. This time next year they'll be gone and you'll never know they were there."

The pilot changed the subject. "We'll be landing in London in half an hour. Will the South-bank site do?"

"That's fine," Grantham replied. "My car's there."

Later that night, as Michael Prestwick and Candida Coulton lay in bed together, the sea surged against the Marchprod platform, buffeting the structure and the buoyant articulated column.

"It's like being on a boat at sea." Candida buried her face in the thick curly mat of hair on Michael Prestwick's chest. "We ride up and down with the waves."

"It *is* a boat in a way," Prestwick replied.

He pulled her closer, protecting her – it seemed – against the mounting roar of the wind. "I'm glad you came on board."

She laughed. "Donald was amazed to see me this afternoon. He had no idea this was where I was working. I just told him that I was going to leave home and would let him know as soon as I found my feet."

"You seem to have found my feet, as well as yours."

Outside the window of Michael Prestwick's cabin, as they made love, the lights of a late cross-Channel ferry could be seen. Michael Prestwick kept half an eye on it as he kissed her white neck and then pulled her onto him as he lay back, propped up at an angle, on the pillow.

He was a precise, methodical man. This was the sixth time, as he counted it, that he had made love to Candida Coulton. She had not been a virgin before they began their affair. He reckoned that, as far as previous sexual experience was concerned, they were about on a par with each other. On the whole, he thought, that was a good thing. And indeed, on the whole, he thought Candida Coulton was a good thing.

She had come into his life with about as much force as the gale presently raging outside. And for some reason which he could not fathom, she seemed to like him.

"I'm going to let the sea do the work for me," he said.

She giggled. "Lazy!"

Later, he said: "I don't really know why you like me. I doubt if we would have met socially, if you see what I mean."

She giggled again. "I've never been very fond of the people I meet socially. Anyway, I don't just like you, Michael. I love you. What's more, you're competent. I love competent people."

"Like your father, I suppose," said Michael Prestwick.

"I suppose so." Candida Coulton didn't seem to want to talk much about her relationship with her father.

Suddenly Prestwick sat up in bed and then, thrusting her roughly aside, bounded to the window.

"Jesus! Can't those idiots see us?"

As he spoke, the warning sirens on the rig sounded and the alarm lights flashed.

The cross-Channel ferry changed course when she was less than a quarter of a mile from the platform and finally passed about a hundred yards astern.

Candida joined him at the window. "Don't they know we're here? Can't they see our lights?"

"Yes, they do know we're here and yes, they should see our lights," Prestwick replied. "But the world is full of bloody fools. That's how accidents happen. Come back to bed, darling."

Candida Coulton climbed back into the bed next to him, feeling pleased. It was the first time Michael Prestwick had called her darling.

23

Grantham met Ingrid Lubbeke – who had flown in from Frankfurt – at Geneva. They hired a car and drove to Talloire, on the shores of Lake Annecy, for the night.

"The boys will be in Méribel," Grantham told Ingrid over dinner.

"Are you sure they'll want to meet me?"

"Why not? They're both grown up."

"Haven't they taken sides?"

"Not as far as I know. Of course, they still see their mother."

As he spoke, Grantham remembered the last time he had seen his wife. She had been standing there in her raincoat, looking up at the little plane as it took off from Inishmore. He knew her face as well as he knew her own.

Sitting there over dinner in the restaurant of the lakeside hotel which Grantham had known for twenty years, they talked about families and about family life. Both of them agreed that staying together was not easy, particularly when children grew up.

"Simon has finished Oxford now," Grantham said, "and Richard is half way through. They're in a chalet party for a week."

"We're lucky to get to Méribel at the same time."

Grantham put his hand over hers. "*I'm* lucky you were able to come. I needed a break. I needed you."

She smiled back at him.

After dinner, they walked along the shore of the lake. They could see the lights of Annecy in the distance. Directly across from them loomed the dark shape of the mountains.

"I've been coming to Talloire for years," Grantham told her. "I make a habit of spending the night here on the way to the mountains. It gives the body a chance to adjust to different rhythms."

They went to bed early in their room overlooking the lake. She undressed by the window, turned to him and he took her in his arms. She had undone her hair and it cascaded down her back. He was taller than she was; she lifted her mouth to be kissed.

"I've bought myself a house in London now," he told her. "I want you to see it."

"I'd love to."

Later, she said to him: "Do you know, Oliver, when I am with you, I feel quite happy. In Germany I'm a symbol; people write articles but they don't capture the real me. You've done something for me."

Grantham didn't want to go too far down that line. He understood what she meant but he wasn't ready for it. He made love to her.

"You make me happy," she told him. She moaned and then repeated, this time in German, "*Du machst mich so glücklich!*"

They left early next morning to drive through Albertville and Moûtiers and up the narrow winding road towards the picturesque village of Méribel.

"I've booked a room at the Belvédère," Grantham said. "It's right on the slopes. The lifts don't work in the evening, but I don't suppose we shall be going out much."

They hired boots and skis in the village and were out on the snow by the early afternoon.

Grantham thought he skied well but he realized, after the first couple of runs, that he couldn't hold a candle to Ingrid. He was twenty seconds behind her at the end of the long run down from La Saulire to Mottaret. She had to wait for him by the lifts. He came up to her, breathing heavily with the exertion, and asked:

"Where did you learn?"

"I grew up on skis," she replied. "I was a trialist in the German Olympic team, long ago now."

She had taken off her goggles and headband to throw her hair back and let the spring sun warm her face. "I love the mountains; I love the air." She skied over to him, leaned forward and kissed him on the lips. "I love you, Oliver. And I think you ski marvellously, anyway."

For Grantham, the next two days were as near heaven as anything he could imagine. They had bought the omnibus pass which allowed them to ski not just in the Méribel valley but also over in Courchevel to the east and Val Thorens to the west. The weather was fine and warm. It could have been Easter instead of February. Grantham, who thought he was familiar with most of the runs in the area, quickly came to realize that she knew the mountains even better than he did.

On the afternoon of the second day they skied on the Val Thorens side and then she led him, when it was already getting late, down from the Mont de Peclet, which towered over three thousand metres high, by an unmarked, unsupervised *piste* back towards Méribel. They came down at speed through a narrow defile which in summer carried a mountain stream. There were large pools of frozen water, grey-green in the late afternoon light, overhung with icicles and boulders piled deep in snow.

She motioned him with her hand not to make a noise. Avalanches could be set off by the sound of the human voice. They moved swiftly and silently down through the steep valley, fifty yards apart. On the final stretch, there were rocks and ice and the light had almost disappeared. For Ingrid Lubbeke, the conditions seemed to be a challenge. The worse they became, the faster she went.

At last, when it was quite dark, they burst down through the forest into Mottaret and Grantham heaved a quiet sigh of relief.

When he had found his breath again, he said to her: "I wouldn't have missed that for the world."

Grantham described the experience to the boys that evening when they came to dinner at the hotel.

"There's a poetry there," he told them. "No amount of ski-lifts and bubble-cars and tourists can take it away. If you catch the mountains at the right time, you can sense the poetry."

Grantham didn't say – because some things were better left unsaid – that it was also a matter of catching the mountains in the right company. But the boys understood anyway and were glad for him. The older one, Simon, who had just begun a career in merchant banking, asked Ingrid about the Greens.

"How important are they in German politics? Will they make a difference?"

"They already have," Ingrid replied.

She poured herself another glass of Crépy, the fine white wine of the mountains, and gave them a little lecture about the sea-change which Germany had suffered over the last two or three years.

"The Greens had already been active at the level of the States – the Lände. When the elections came in March 1983, they won twenty-seven seats in the Bundestag. That has had a profound impact on German politics."

Simon, a good-looking young man who had inherited much of his father's drive and directness, pressed her:

"I know you're associated with the Greens, at least in the public mind. I know that they began as an environmental party, an ecological party fighting against new runways and new roads – that kind of thing. I agree with all that. I'd like to see the forests and the mountains kept the way they are. But aren't they also heavily influenced by the communists? Making Germany a nuclear-free zone, which is what they seem to want, is surely playing straight into the hands of the Soviet Union."

Ingrid Lubbeke laughed. "Of course they are! Everybody knows that in Germany. We call it *Unterwanderung*."

"What does that mean?"

"It means subversion or infiltration. There's no doubt that the Greens are influenced politically by East Germany, for example. They also receive funds through the GDR."

"Doesn't that make you want to keep your distance from them?" This time it was Richard, slighter and darker than his brother, who took up the interrogation.

While Oliver Grantham sat back and watched with mild amusement as his two sons pursued an elusive quarry, Ingrid Lubbeke gave a measured, almost statesmanlike, reply.

"It boils down finally", she said slowly, "to the kind of score-sheet you believe in. If I look around Germany today, I still prefer the Greens to anybody else. They stand for some of the things I think are important. If I have a mission, it's to try to steer the party away from its nuclear hang-ups. The environmental case is a good one. It's good enough for me and I think it should be good enough for most people."

Grantham realized, as he listened to her, that there was more to Ingrid Lubbeke than even he had suspected. There were leadership qualities there. The question was: in what direction was she headed? He remembered Bill Peabody's raised eyebrow that evening in Brussels when he had turned up at the NATO ball with Ingrid Lubbeke on his arm.

Before Grantham's sons left, Ingrid tactfully suggested that they would probably want to ski alone with their father the next day.

"I know you haven't seen much of him in recent months," she said. "I shall rest and sunbathe."

*

The next morning Oliver Grantham and his two sons were on the slopes early. They skied in the Méribel valley in the morning, then towards lunchtime crossed over to Courchevel. Neither of the young men was as fit as the father, though both were competent skiers. By the time it was twelve-thirty, they were glad to have a break.

Grantham ordered three glasses of *vin chaud* and a bottle of Apremont as an apéritif, and the three of them sat together on the terrace of the café next to Courchevel's altiport.

"You can fly right into the mountains now," Richard Grantham said. "The nobs who have chalets at Courchevel drop in by helicopter or air-taxi. There's an hourly service from Geneva, Lyons or Chambéry."

As he spoke, a helicopter came in to land on the pad. A tall, craggy white-haired man got out, to be welcomed by a small official-looking party.

The Granthams observed the ceremony with interest. Oliver Grantham immediately recognized the tall man.

"That's Louis Baudin," he told his sons. "He was one of the great Resistance heroes in the war. Mayor of Lyons now, of course."

"French politicians love Courchevel," Simon Grantham commented. "My bank often tries to do business in Paris only to find that the relevant minister has gone skiing. Giscard still has a chalet here, you know."

A few minutes after Baudin's helicopter had arrived, a Cessna flew in low and fast to land at the altiport. This time a youngish-looking man, carrying a briefcase and wearing a sombre black suit, got out. He walked over to where Louis Baudin was still standing, surrounded by officials. The Granthams, sitting not more than fifty yards away, saw the two men shake hands in a manner which could be characterized as polite rather than cordial.

"I wonder who that is, then," Simon Grantham said.

"Another socialist, I'll bet." His younger brother was more cynical. "Socialists, particularly French socialists, love flying about in private planes."

A man sitting at the next table overheard the remark, turned to them and said, "*Vous avez raison.* That's Guillaume Mauplan; he's the big boss of the socialists up north."

He pushed over a copy of the local newspaper. Grantham read the headline, "Socialist mayors meet in Courchevel to plan presidential campaign. Official welcome today." He read the accompanying article with interest and then passed the newspaper back. It was odd, he reflected, how much politics came into everything. When he was a soldier, everything had seemed relatively simple. It had been a matter of saying to this man or to that man "go" or "do this". In the real world, politicians played a crucial role. You had to watch out for them.

By the time the *plat du jour* had arrived, the two socialist mayors and their entourage had been driven off in a Range Rover.

Grantham looked at his two sons. "I'm glad we managed to overlap out here a bit," he said. "How's your mother?"

As he spoke, Grantham saw behind the young men, now embarked on their wordly careers, the adolescents he had known so short a time ago; and behind the adolescents he saw the children whom he and Lily had brought up together. He knew his question would cause pain.

"You wouldn't expect us to criticize, dad," Simon said, speaking for both of them. "You're old enough to make your own decisions."

Grantham laughed at that. How often, he recalled, had he used the same expression himself.

"Thanks," he said wryly.

"Mother's well," Simon continued. "She hopes to see you – soon. She hopes you'll get back together again. So do we."

Grantham toyed with his *gigot d'agneau*.

"I can't explain it," he said at last, "and I'm not going to try. Thanks for not criticizing – at least in public. These things may work out, you know."

It was about as intimate a conversation as Grantham had ever had with his children.

The German went over the plan for one last time.

"You don't have to do any skiing," he assured Stephanos. "In fact, the less you look like a competent skier, the more realistic your performance is going to be. All you have to do is to count the number of 'eggs' – *télécabines*. The summit of la Vizelle – that's the lift they have to take on their way back to Méribel – is at two thousand two hundred and sixty-eight metres. The last two hundred metres before the summit the *télécabines* are rising almost vertically next to the mountain face. I shall be waiting, hidden behind the rocks, about sixty or eighty metres below the top. Your job is to make sure that the egg containing Grantham is halted on that final hoist. At a certain moment, just as you're about to enter the *télécabine* down below, you drop your skis down the crack – or drop one ski or something – anyway you cause a fuss and they halt the line of eggs long enough for me to do what I have to do."

"Just remind me of the mathematics again, would you?" the Greek said.

There was a touch of impatience in the German's voice as he replied: "The length of that particular lift up to the top of la Vizelle is 1650 metres. Each egg is 50 metres from the next egg. At any particular moment, therefore, there are 33 eggs strung out along the line of the lifts. Since we want the egg containing Grantham to be halted when it's one hundred metres from the top, you'll have to go into action just as egg no. 31 is about to leave the station."

Stephanos, though he still looked uneasy at the role he was being asked to perform, could no longer complain that the plan was not crystal clear to him.

"What will you do?" he asked.

"I shall just ski off round the back of the mountain. No one will see me. Or if they do, they won't suspect anything."

He stood up.

"Good luck, Stephanos. You'll have to hang around for a while. My guess is that Grantham and his sons will ski over this side and then take the *télécabines* back around four o'clock. I'll be waiting."

"Don't get the wrong egg. The *télécabines* might stop for some other reason."

The German laughed. "A *chasseur alpin* has field-glasses as well as his rifle, Stephanos. I shall be able to see what I'm doing."

Grantham noticed the fair-haired, suntanned man dressed in the uniform of a *chasseur alpin* with half an eye as he left the restaurant. He noticed the badge – 7 BCA. He wondered if the presence of these crack French troops at Courchevel had anything to do with the arrival of Louis Baudin and Guillaume Mauplan. Simon Grantham caught the direction of his father's glance.

"*Septième bataillon, chasseurs alpins,*" Grantham explained. "As far as I remember, their headquarters are at Bourg St Maurice. Apart from their activities in the mountains, their mission is to guard France's own nuclear deterrent on the Plateau d'Albion in the Massif Central."

The two Grantham boys looked at the man with interest as he walked out. They noted the fur hat.

"*Casquettes Fourrées*, is what they call them," Grantham explained.

*

Shortly after four o'clock Grantham and his two sons decided to call it a day.

"We don't want to leave it too late," Grantham said. "Ingrid will be wondering what has happened to us. And we've still got to ski back down the other side."

As they entered the "eggs" to ride up to the summit of la Vizelle, so as to be able to ski down into the Méribel valley, Grantham was dimly aware of seeing a man standing on the platform without actually entering the "eggs". He was also, even more dimly, aware that the man had probably been in the restaurant with him at lunchtime, eating at a table with the *chasseur alpin* whose distinctive white uniform and fur hat had attracted their attention earlier.

"No wonder they call these things eggs," Richard Grantham said. "They look like eggs and I bet they're just as fragile."

In theory, there was room for four in the little compartment. In practice, three Granthams occupied most of the space.

The valley, Grantham noticed as he looked out of the window, was now virtually empty. Courchevel was often deserted by the late afternoon because the sun – owing to the configuration of the mountains – left the slopes early. If you wanted the sun in the afternoon, you skied on the Méribel side.

"I've bought a new house," he told the boys. "Did you know?"

"Mother told us," Richard Grantham replied. He smiled. "I guess you've had a sudden access of funds, dad."

Grantham smiled back. He was enjoying this afternoon. "I suppose you could say so."

The egg in which they were travelling jerked to a halt about a hundred and fifty metres below the summit. As it did so, Grantham caught a glimpse of a man, wearing the white uniform of the *chasseur alpin* and the distinctive *casquette fourrée*, crouching behind the rock above and slightly to the right of the "egg" in which they were travelling. He saw that the man had a rifle in his hand.

"Look," he said to his sons. "There's another of those *chasseurs alpins* fellows. Hunting chamois, I suspect. They'll shoot anything in France, given half a chance."

As he spoke, the shell fired from the 5.56 Famas *fusil d'assaut*, which was the standard issue for the *chasseur alpin*, ripped through the fragile casing of the *télécabine*, blowing out the window on the left-hand side as it did so.

*

At about the same time as Grantham and his two sons took the *télécabine* to go back up the mountain and over to Méribel, Louis Baudin had begun a prolonged negotiating session with Guillaume Mauplan. They sat in the splendid sitting-room of Baudin's chalet high up above the village of Courchevel. In front of them stretched out a spectacular panorama consisting of the peaks and valleys of Savoie. Though much of the Courchevel "saucer" was in shade, the setting sun caught the mountain rims around them, endowing each peak with an iridescent halo.

Baudin had come straight to the point. He looked Mauplan fairly and squarely in the eye.

"You didn't come to Courchevel just for a holiday," he said. "You came because we need to talk, *n'est-ce pas*?"

"*Bien sûr.*" The other man nodded. And then he had said: "I'm not sure that Leroux can win in the Pas-de-Calais. It's not clear to me what a Leroux candidacy would bring us."

Old Louis Baudin had been playing politics long before Guillaume Mauplan was born. This was the kind of talk he understood.

"You mean he ought to be offering more than he seems to be offering."

The other man nodded again. "If our people are to be interested, yes."

"What kind of offer could he make which would make your people interested?"

Guillaume Mauplan had walked over to the plate-glass window and looked out onto the mountains. Instead of replying, he had drawn Louis Baudin's attention to the fact that the line of bubble-cars, running up to the summit of la Vizelle, appeared to have halted, even though it was apparent that there were still people in them. Mauplan turned back to his host:

"Do they ever get stuck all night?"

Baudin laughed. "Certainly not. This is one of the most efficient ski-stations in France." Then he repeated his question, determined not to be sidetracked: "What kind of offer would you be interested in? Tell me frankly. I'll tell you whether we can do it or not."

Mauplan resumed his seat, pulled out a Gauloise and lit it. It was a habit he had learned long ago when he had been working on the production line at Bioxyde's giant titanium-dioxide factory outside Calais. That was where his political career had begun, on the shop-floor. As far as Mauplan was concerned the shop-floor was the only place to begin.

"You know what we say where we come from up north, Louis. *Pas-de-Calais – pas de tunnel!*"

"Be more specific." The old man spoke sharply. "You can't mean Leroux should pledge himself to oppose the building of the Chunnel. Building the Chunnel is bringing a great deal of employment to the workers of your region."

"I'm not against building the tunnel," Mauplan replied quietly. "Leroux shouldn't be either. You're right, it's bringing jobs where we badly need jobs. I want to see the tunnel built. *But I don't want to see it working!* Nothing will kill the economy of my region more surely than the through-train to Paris! I know the coast, Louis. I know the whole Pas-de-Calais region. I know how much depends on the cross-Channel traffic. People who come in their cars spend the night in Calais and Dunkerque, in Dieppe and Boulogne. Take away that traffic and you'll kill those towns as surely as if you'd dropped an atomic bomb on them."

Baudin was listening attentively. "What precisely are you suggesting?"

Guillaume Mauplan took a long puff at his Gauloise.

"It's not so absurd as it may sound," he said. "The Socialist party in the Pas-de-Calais region will back the Leroux candidacy at the Marseilles convention next week on one condition – and on one condition only. Leroux must pledge himself, secretly of course, to cancel the Chunnel project at the earliest possible moment after his election to the Presidency of the Republic. That way my region will have all the benefit from the construction of the Chunnel and none of the drawbacks which would result from its actual operation."

Louis Baudin leaned back in his chair, looked up at the mountains as though praying for guidance and let out a long whistle:

"*Mon dieu – ça c'est quelque chose!*"

The German watched the bubbles swinging up the mountain towards him. He played a little game with himself. Was Grantham's 'egg' red, or orange, or green, or yellow? He decided it would be yellow; and he was right. Even without his field-glasses, he could distinguish the three occupants clearly. He wondered idly, as he raised the rifle to his shoulder and waited for the egg to stop moving, why Karapolitis had thought it necessary to do it this way as well as the other. Perhaps it was a question of making assurance doubly sure.

He saw Grantham glance down towards where he was crouching. The car swayed to a halt. Good, he thought, Stephanos had done his work. As he squeezed the trigger, his boot slipped an inch in the snow. He realized the shot had slapped into the egg without finding its mark. Damn, he swore, his finger tightening once again on the trigger. But he knew he had time. It would be ten, perhaps twenty seconds before the line of eggs started moving again. He could rely on Stephanos for that.

He had Grantham in his sight when the avalanche set off by the sound of the first shot struck him, knocking him off his perch and down the steep face of the mountain. It was not a large avalanche, as avalanches go, but it did its work. The snow, which had been piling up for days behind the boulders, suddenly exploded into movement.

Grantham watched the man fall; saw the snow and boulders roll over him; craned his head round in the cab of the egg to note the inert figure lying far below.

The line of eggs started moving again. They reached the lift-station at the summit of la Vizelle.

Neither of Grantham's sons spoke on the short swift run down to the Belvédère. However, as he was taking his boots off in the hall of the hotel, Simon asked: "Was that *chasseur alpin* really after chamois, dad? Someone could have got hurt."

Grantham shrugged his shoulders. "Someone did get hurt," he replied.

Not for nothing had he spent twenty years of his life as a soldier.

The "boys" stayed on for dinner at the hotel. Grantham was pleased. At the least, it meant they had decided not to take sides.

Ingrid Lubbeke, who had been waiting for them to return, had been discovered by a New York banker.

"Oliver, this is Ed Masterson. We've been having a drink in the bar. Ed Masterson runs Morgan Stanley. I've asked him to join us for dinner."

Grantham was delighted. The boys appeared to like Ingrid Lubbeke; but he wanted to avoid any suggestion that this was a new Mrs Grantham. Widening the party helped.

Grantham took to the New York banker from the start. He was a man after his own heart. A man of action. A man who liked the outdoor life. During the first part of the meal, Ed Masterson kept them all riveted with his account of a recent family vacation in Alaska.

"They flew us in there with a light aircraft, left us supplies. We fixed a rendezvous for three weeks forward. If we weren't there or they weren't there, well, that would have been the end of it."

Masterson was big in the Audubon Society. So Grantham told him about the chamois.

"Some hunter put a bullet through our *télécabine* this evening."

Ed Masterson took that with a pinch of salt. "What do you do for a living?" he asked.

Grantham told him. It was the first time the boys had heard, in detail, about the work on which he was engaged. And Ingrid, too, had never had much more than a rudimentary account. All of them in their different ways were fascinated and absorbed. Ed Masterson particularly so. When Grantham told him that the Chunnel Consortium had gone public for the first time that very day with an issue worth two billion pounds, his banker's instinct had come to the fore.

"Hell, I knew you people were going public soon; but I didn't realize today was the day. I guess my office didn't want to bother me with that since this is meant to be a vacation."

"We're expecting most of the issue to be taken up in Europe anyway," Grantham told him.

Ed Masterson, a short, blue-eyed man with a clear, open, honest face, was not to be deterred.

"I'd like to have a piece of the action too. That's an historic project!" He looked at his watch, one dial of which was set to New York time. "I'll just go and make a phone call," he said.

When Ed Masterson returned to the table, it was as though a balloon had been burst. He looked at Grantham in a serious, sympathetic way.

"Mr Grantham, I guess your people have gone home for the day or else" – and here he shot a quick glance in Ingrid Lubbeke's direction – "they don't know how to get hold of you. I've just been onto my office in New York. Of course they know about the Chunnel Consortium issue. I told them we ought to be in there somewhere. I said that this was a big and important project and I believe it is. But from what New York told me, your issue is running into trouble. The big boys, the institutional buyers, are apparently holding back. My people indicated that it wouldn't be right at this time for Morgan Stanley to get too closely involved."

Ed Masterson toyed with his empty coffee-cup. Then he looked at Grantham.

"I'm sure there's an explanation for the difficulty. And I'm sure that a man with your guts and vision is going to sort it out. I just thought you ought to know what they're saying in New York. The time difference helps, of course."

With that somewhat cryptic remark, Ed Masterson said good night and left the dining room.

Seconds later, the waiter came up to the table. "Mr Grantham, you're wanted on the telephone."

It was David Blakely. The tone of rich authority had gone from his voice. He sounded tired and dispirited.

"Oliver," he said, "I hate to interrupt your vacation. We're in trouble. Real trouble. The issue opened at ten o'clock this morning and nobody's buying."

"Does the City know something we don't know?" Grantham asked.

"The City knows that the *Sun* has a scoop on the Chunnel project and that it's going to be in tomorrow's paper. That's enough for them to hold back. Particularly the big boys. The pension funds and the insurance companies. Hell, I should know. I'm on the board of enough of them. I've talked to my friends and I can't move them. Not at the moment. Someone's done a good job of putting the word around even before the story appears."

"Do you know what the story says?"

"Does the name Dummett mean anything to you?"

Grantham searched his memory. Nowadays they had computers for searching memories, he thought. Perhaps a computer would have made a better job.

"Dummett . . ." he spoke slowly into the receiver. "I think Professor Finzi mentioned the name that afternoon in Italy, but I can't remember the context."

When he returned to the table, his face was solemn.

"I shall have to leave at the crack of dawn. We have a board meeting in Paris tomorrow afternoon." He turned to the boys. "Let's get together at the weekend. Come and see the new place."

Later, when Simon and Richard had left, Grantham said to Ingrid:

"Come with me to Lyons. You can fly to Frankfurt from there. I'm being purely selfish, of course. I'd just like to have you for a few more hours."

She smiled. "Why can't I come to Paris? I never turn down an excuse to go to Paris. There are people I can talk to while you're at meetings."

Grantham wondered what kind of people she meant.

They took an air-taxi from the alti-port at seven o'clock the next morning. The connections by air to Paris were bad, so they went by train instead.

"As a matter of fact," Grantham said as they boarded the TGV, "the train is quicker now even if you have got good connections. Station to station it takes under two hours to cover the four hundred kilometres from Lyons to Paris."

They had a long, leisurely breakfast on board the train. It was incredible, thought Grantham, how good the SNCF was. They were travelling at two hundred kilometres an hour and yet there was scarcely a vibration. In his imagination, he saw the train running straight on through past Paris, up towards Calais and then, barely pausing for breath, dipping down into the newly constructed Channel Tunnel to emerge less than thirty minutes later on the other side.

"Imagine running straight through to London like this," he said.

"Two hundred kilometres per hour beneath the Channel?"

"Probably not as fast as that. They haven't finished the upgrading of the track on the English side yet. The French built their high-speed trains and their high-speed tracks together. We didn't look quite so far ahead. But still, once these trains get going, you can be quite sure that they won't slow down more than they have to."

Ingrid Lubbeke stretched out her long, shapely legs diagonally across the compartment. She hooked her arms behind her head and leaned back languorously.

"I'd like to make love to you now, Oliver," she said, "on a train moving at two hundred kilometres an hour through France. Have you ever done it on a train?"

Grantham ducked that one. The parsnip principle. Anyway he wasn't in the mood. The news from the markets had depressed him.

"When you reach my age, Ingrid," he replied diplomatically, "novelty loses some of its attraction."

"Nonsense." She pulled him down on top of her and kissed him fiercely on the mouth. "You're so male, aren't you? So butch."

Grantham was not sure he liked being called butch. Laughing, he struggled out of her grasp and picked up the newspapers which they had bought on boarding the train at Lyons. On the third page of the *Figaro* was a long interview with Maximilien Miguet. It was entitled "La France et la Protection de l'Europe". Grantham read it with interest. In it General Miguet, interviewed at his country home outside Paris, expounded the basis of his philosophy. Europe, Miguet argued, could not be merely an appendage of America. Placing Pershing-2 and cruise missiles on European soil but under American control did nothing to increase Europe's security. On the contrary it diminished it to the extent that the United States might decide it was safe to fight a war with the

Soviet Union by proxy, i.e. through intermediate-range missiles based in Europe.

The conclusion followed with masterly Gallic logic. Europe had to look after its own defence. And since neither Germany nor Britain could be trusted with that responsibility, the glorious task must fall to France.

Grantham read the interview with care. Asked specifically by *Figaro*'s reporter what he was proposing, Maximilien Miguet had replied: "*Je propose que la France prenne l'initiative de dire aux pays européens: il faut parler de la défense européenne.*"

Miguet stated his firm belief that what Europe needed was a genuinely independent nuclear deterrent and this could only be based on France's own intermediate-range nuclear missiles, the French equivalent of the Pershing and cruise systems. The French independent nuclear deterrent was something, Miguet argued, to be maintained and strengthened at all costs. But those costs, of course, he went on to state, should be shared between those European countries which would benefit from the nuclear guarantee thus offered. The interview ended with Miguet making a passionate plea for all candidates in the forthcoming Presidential election to declare themselves positively in favour of the retention of the French independent nuclear deterrent as the basis of an independent European deterrent. At the same time, Miguet suggested that France should once again play a full part in NATO. The Alliance should consist of "truly equal partners".

Grantham read the article twice and found himself agreeing with every word of it. As each day passed, he was becoming more and more convinced that conventional wisdom was no longer appropriate. He could see what people meant when they spoke of the two super-powers using Europe as the battleground to fight out a nuclear war. The Miguet proposal for a *genuinely* independent nuclear deterrent, truly equal partnership with the Americans, was the only realistic option for Europe. And it was an option, Grantham realized, that would be fatally compromised if Pierre Leroux were to succeed with his Presidential bid.

The streamlined bullet-nosed train sped north through the valley of the Rhône. They passed Beaune and, once again, Grantham found himself reflecting on the greatness of France. What other country could produce a wine like one of the great Burgundies? What other country could produce men like General Maximilien Miguet, who recognized the truth when they saw it?

While Ingrid, who needed more sleep than Grantham, dozed in a corner of the compartment, Grantham himself continued his meditation. Time and again, he found his thoughts returning to Pierre Leroux.

Knowing what he knew about Leroux – what Peabody had told him that evening in Brussels – Grantham could only suppose that the selection of Leroux as the candidate of the Socialist party in the forthcoming French Presidential election, if that were to be followed by success at the polls, would be a disaster for France, for Europe and indeed for the Western world as a whole. Men like Miguet obviously perceived this clearly – and the General had said as much that day when Grantham had met him for breakfast at the Travellers Club in Paris. Men like Konrad von Rilke and Count von Rimsdorf saw it clearly. Peabody, whose heart was in the right place, unlike some of those American generals, knew what the score was and believed in a strong independent Europe standing alongside, without being subordinate to, the United States.

But was it enough merely to be aware of the danger? Shouldn't something be done to avert it? Shouldn't he, Oliver Grantham, a man endowed with both talent and energy, do something about it?

Later, he picked up the paper again. The main editorial was devoted to Pierre Leroux's prospects of emerging as the Socialist candidate in the forthcoming party congress at Marseilles. The leader-writer referred to some "deal" which had obviously been agreed between Louis Baudin, Mayor of Lyons and chief power-broker behind the scenes and Guillaume Mauplan, the socialist leader from the north of France. "Nobody knows what was said in secret between these two men", the editorial stated, "at their meeting yesterday in the Mayor's mountain retreat in Savoie. But it does seem as though the necessary breakthrough has been achieved as far as Leroux's Presidential prospects are concerned."

Grantham thrust the paper away and uttered a short, sharp, Gallic expletive: "Merde!"

"What's the matter?" Ingrid Lubbeke spoke without opening her eyes.

"The matter," Grantham replied with sudden viciousness, "is that the whole thing is going to go up the spout if that clever little shit Leroux gets in."

Ingrid was suddenly awake and interested. "Mitterrand often talks tough, doesn't he? I thought the French Socialist party was sound on defence. I thought Leroux was sound."

Grantham kept quiet. There was no conceivable way he could tell Ingrid the true facts about Leroux. Not now, anyway. Probably not ever. To cover up his indiscretion, he suggested that they should walk along to the restaurant-car for coffee.

There was a car waiting at the Gare de Lyon in Paris.

"I'm going to go straight to the office in the Avenue d'Iéna. The car can take you on to the hotel. I'll meet you later."

Grantham did not tell her that the car was a bullet-proof limousine provided by one of France's top security agencies. Nor did he say that the chauffeur doubled as a bodyguard. And he did not tell her, either, that since last night and the episode on the mountain he himself was carrying a gun in a shoulder holster. In Grantham's view, it was better not to worry women with this kind of detail. It made them nervous.

24

It was more or less the same cast of characters as before. But the atmosphere in the board room of the Falaise building in the Avenue d'Iéna was not at all the same. There was no hint of celebration this time, more a sense of shock and foreboding.

The meeting did not begin until half past four in the afternoon. Tom Anders had to come in from Eindhoven; Sir David Blakely and Bill Prendergast from London; Franz Kauffman from Frankfurt, representing Hoffman Allgemeine; and last but not least, Professor Giuseppe Finzi from Rome. Grantham noticed, as Finzi entered the room, that the little Italian was ashen-faced; he obviously knew that if there was one single person responsible for the fiasco, it was he.

At the last minute, just as they were about to sit down, the door opened and a little old white-haired lady bustled into the room. She spotted her name card at the table, walked quickly over and sat down. She nodded crisply in Sir David Blakely's direction.

"I'm sorry I'm late, Chairman. I only received notice of the meeting this morning and it took some time to get up from Exmoor. I caught the first available plane."

Sir David Blakely, who had been warned by Grantham to expect an elderly eccentric, was surprised and gratified by the businesslike attitude that Mrs Eileen Potter seemed to be showing towards the proceedings.

"We are all of us delighted to have you with us, Mrs Potter, at this and – I hope – other meetings of the board of Chunnel Consortium. We welcome you in your own right as a major shareholder in our enterprise; and of course we welcome you as the great-granddaughter of Sir Edward Watkin, whose vision and energy we had the pleasure of saluting when we first met in this room not so many months ago. If we may now proceed . . ."

Sir David surveyed the scene, the familiar faces, the less familiar faces – but all of them part of the team.

He caught Grantham's eye at the other end of the table. How much they all owed to that man, he thought. Six machines were now boring away beneath the Channel; records were being established every day as far as distances covered or rocks moved were concerned. Construction of the installations on either side of the Channel was well under way. The contractors were carving out the land for the yards and loading bays and loops, for the trans-shipment areas, parking facilities, shops, ticket-booths and so on. If they were months ahead of schedule, and not just on the tunnelling operation itself, it was he knew thanks to Grantham. And now without any warning it was coming unstuck. Blakely knew that in a few moments he would hand the floor over to Chunnel Consortium's president. He fervently hoped that somehow, between the time of their telephone conversation the previous night and the beginning of the board meeting, Grantham had been able to come up with some convincing scheme.

But he realized when Grantham caught his glance and shook his head despondently that this time they might be out of luck.

Blakely did not beat about the bush.

"I'm afraid to say that we meet today in a crisis situation. When I spoke, in this very room, as your chairman at our first board meeting I warned that we should expect opposition. That opposition has made itself felt. There have already been attacks of a personal or physical nature" – and he again nodded at Grantham – "there has been an attempt, happily thwarted, to challenge the legal validity of the Consortium's operation. But now we face a new challenge, a challenge to the basic concept and design of our project. Unless we meet that challenge head on within the next few hours, the damage to confidence – and particularly to the confidence of potential investors – may be irreparable." He turned to Grantham. "Perhaps you would care to comment."

Grantham was ready. Since he had arrived in the office earlier that day, he had been on the telephone non-stop. Telex messages had flashed between London and Paris and Paris and Sydney. He had already taken certain steps and he would be informing the board what those steps were. Other action was in train which, for one reason or another, Grantham decided it was best to keep quiet about for the moment.

He began with the personality involved. After all, the attack was credible not merely for the terms in which it was couched; the authorship was also crucially important.

"There can be no doubt at all", Grantham began, "about Professor Dummett's credentials. Before he went to Australia, Dummett was one of Britain's most respected scientists. Look him up in *Who's Who*. If they had given a Nobel prize in geology, Dummett would have won it. He was president of the Royal Society; author of three or four classic text books, dean of the Institute of Geological Sciences in London and now of course he holds the Chair at the University of New South Wales in Sydney." Grantham looked at Professor Finzi. "I am right, Professor, am I not, about Dummett's credentials?"

Finzi nodded with apparent reluctance. He still looked as though he had been coshed between the eyes. There was nothing a scientist valued more than his self-esteem and Finzi was rapidly in the process of losing it.

"I yield to no one in my admiration for Professor Dummett," he said bitterly. "As a geologist I have known Dummett, both the man and his work, for many years. And the fact that the article was accepted for publication by *Nature*, which remains the world's foremost scientific journal, is an additional reason for us to take it seriously."

Finzi waited a moment before continuing. It was important to have the board on his side and he would not achieve that with a flustered counter-attack.

"In spite of this, I am convinced that Dummett is wrong to have attacked the route we have selected. I believe that what I said in this room at our first meeting – I think it was Mr Anders who asked me a specific question about the alignment we proposed – still holds good.

"Let us take the facts first. As long ago as 1957, the Channel Tunnel Study Group organized and financed a comprehensive study covering traffic, geology, civil engineering and financial and legal aspects. In 1964, the governments of France and Britain asked the Channel Tunnel Study Group to organize further site investigations, which included seventy-three marine bore-holes, supplemented by geological profiling to provide fuller detail of the morphology and stratigraphy of the area, particularly on the proposed line of the bored tunnel.

"To make assurance doubly sure, in 1971 and 1972 a further seventeen marine bore-holes and eight land bore-holes in the Folkestone area were sunk in co-ordination with another comprehensive geophysical survey of the route using much improved equipment. This allowed particular attention to be given to zones of weathering in the chalk. This geophysical work was very successful. No major structural fault zones were detected on the route and it was concluded that conditions were favourable to tunnelling."

Finzi was about to proceed when Tom Anders, the lanky Dutchman, signalled to Sir David Blakely that he wished to interrupt.

"Go ahead, Tom," Sir David said.

Anders spoke in friendly tones. After all, he had just spent a weekend in Tuscany in Professor Finzi's company. He liked the man.

"The problem as I understand it, Professor, is our knowledge of geological conditions on the French side. You spoke of an initial programme of seventy-three marine bore-holes and a further programme of seventeen bore-holes. The point of bore-holes, as I understand it, is to enable you to establish the profile of the underground strata."

"That's right." Professor Finzi nodded.

"There seem," Anders continued, "to be two points at issue: do the underground strata, and in particular the Lower Chalk layer, 'dip' and 'strike' in the manner that Professor Dummett has suggested? Secondly, is there a chance that a fault might exist without having been detected by the exploratory operations which have so far been conducted? In other words, have the bore-holes which have already been drilled been of sufficient number and sufficiently close together for us to be able to say with certainty that the Dummett hypothesis is wrong?"

"Certainty", the Professor weighed his words carefully, "is a word scientists try never to use. Nothing in this life is certain. Of course, it is true, as you say, that you are using bore-holes to construct a three-dimensional picture of strata which lie underground. This is always a complicated and expensive operation. And it is particularly expensive and complicated in the case of marine bore-holes. Ideally, one would sink a bore-hole every few hundred yards, pull up the core, analyse the different lengths and relate these to the evidence of adjacent bore-holes. In practice, geologists have to make some assumptions about discontinuities. They have to look at the distance between bore-holes and at the results of any seismic surveys which may have been made, whether by refraction or by reflexion, and they have to draw their conclusions. I maintain my viewpoint that though there may indeed be 'dip' and 'strike' as far as the angle of the Lower Chalk plane is concerned, the line chosen is still a sound line. Indeed, I would venture to suggest that it is not only a sound line from the financial point of view, in that it is the shortest distance between the two points; it is also sound from a technical point of view. And I have spent a lifetime studying this problem whereas Professor Dummett, however eminent he may be, has merely looked at it from time to time."

"The question which interests me," Bill Prendergast intervened, "is why Dummett, who after all has gone off to live in Australia, should have decided to make his concern public at this time. Is it merely a sense of public-spiritedness? Is he really concerned with the prospect of a major mishap, either now or later? Or is there more in this than meets the eye?"

Sir David Blakely looked round the room, inviting contributions from others present. His eyes fell on Mrs Potter. A sense of courtesy made him ask for her opinion.

"Fossils," the old woman replied firmly. "That's what that fool Dummett has forgotten: the evidence of the fossils. Great-grandfather knew all about fossils. He was convinced that the line he had chosen was the correct one and that's the same line you're working on today."

For the first time in a long and gloomy day, Grantham felt a lightening of mood, not merely in himself but in those around him.

"Could you possibly explain a little further, Mrs Potter?" Sir David asked. And he smiled as he spoke. He had already begun to warm to the old woman.

"In my day," Mrs Potter began, "the Natural History Museum in Oxford had a wonderful collection of fossils. When I was up, I was studying the physical sciences. I often used to go along to Parks Road to look at the fossils. I discovered that you could learn as much about geology, and geological time, by studying fossil remains as you could by embarking on complicated programmes of measurement.

"You get different kinds of fossils in different geological layers. So if you're collecting fossils off the seabed, the kind of fossils you find – I remember they were called *Foraminiferida* – can indicate quite precisely which geological layer is at or near the surface. That, of course," the old lady concluded triumphantly, "is why great-grandfather placed such confidence in Thomé de Gamond."

Talking with ever-increasing assurance, she told them about Thomé de Gamond.

"Thomé de Gamond, like my great-grandfather, was a visionary. He was only twenty-six years old when he produced – in 1833 – his first scheme for a tunnel under the Channel. He believed, passionately, in the need for sound hydrographical and geological data. One of the things he did – I remember my grandfather telling me about it, but it's written up in history books anyway – was to go 'skin diving'. I suppose that's what you'd call it today. He used to have himself lowered from a small boat in the Channel, loaded with weights so that he could sink rapidly to the bottom where he could pick up all the geological samples he could find. He concentrated especially on the fossils, which he collected in different parts of the seabed, near the French coast as well as near the English coast. Thomé de Gamond argued that this was the surest and cheapest way of finding out about 'dip' and 'strike', as I've heard you gentlemen call these things today."

Mrs Potter paused. There was a touch of scorn in her voice.

"Of course, nowadays people like to have expensive methods. And complicated methods. I'm told they feed the results of all their bore-hole drillings into computers, programming they call it, and then see what comes out the other end. Perhaps that's what Professor Dummett has done. My suggestion, gentlemen, for what it is worth, is that one of your geological experts should make a comprehensive study of Thomé de Gamond's collection of fossils. You'll find it, I believe, in a little museum on the outskirts of Paris, near Neuilly. Of course, that was a village in the country then. Thomé de Gamond lived there most of his life. He left the fossil collection to the village in his will. I saw the collection once, you know, years ago. Each fossil was labelled with the exact location where it was found and its classification as being appropriate to the Lower Chalk, Middle Chalk, Upper Chalk layers and so on. I'm not suggesting that this is the whole answer to Professor Dummett by any means, but you may find something to go on."

They all looked at the old woman in amazement. Even Grantham, who had to some extent plumbed Mrs Potter's hidden depths, could not suppress his astonishment.

It didn't take very long for the meeting to decide to send a deputation, led by Professor Finzi, to Neuilly the following morning. It was a matter of being sure that no element of the riposte to Dummett was overlooked. If the fossils corroborated the thesis that the Lower Chalk was well below the seabed along the whole of the route selected, they would have a neat ball to bowl.

They would also re-run, for the umpteenth time, all the data they had from earlier drilling and sampling.

"I'm quite sure," Finzi told them, "that there'll be absolutely no change in our evaluation of the geology. I would also point out that the results of the borings which have been conducted so far during the actual excavation of the Channel tunnel merely confirm the assumptions we made in selecting the route."

"Thank you, Professor." Sir David Blakely decided it was time to draw this part of the proceedings to a conclusion. "I'm sure it is clear to everybody" – this was an understatement if it was anything – "that for us to change the route now would be next to impossible. Six tunnel-boring machines have been at work for several weeks. The line of the tunnel is already determined. The installations are being constructed on either side of the Channel. It is reassuring to know that nothing in the Dummett article could justify a change of plan. Our task now, therefore, is to neutralize as best we can the effects of that article. Lady Blakely and I will be giving a dinner this evening at Maxim's. We shall be inviting members of the French Government to it. Statements of support for the Chunnel Consortium operation will be forthcoming not merely from our friends in the French Government, here in Paris, but also from our friends in London. We are now on day three. Our hope is that by the end of the week the fuss will have died down, the institutions will come in, and that the issue which at the moment looks like being desperately under-subscribed, will in fact be a sell-out!"

There was a small, spontaneous burst of applause as Sir David finished speaking.

Bill Prendergast had one last question. In fact it was the same question that he had asked earlier.

"If we are right, and Dummett is wrong, then why did he write the article? Men like Dummett don't risk their reputations lightly. Can't we talk to Dummett somehow?" Prendergast looked at Grantham expectantly.

Grantham nodded. "I'm working on that."

Precisely how he was working on it, Grantham – just at that moment – did not care to reveal.

The dinner at Maxim's was a splendid affair. J. Walter Thompson handled the publicity and the guest-list. Photographers were present in force for the arrival of Pierre Leroux, the Minister for Transport and ranking member of the French Government, on the arm of Monique Delacourt, whose growing reputation as one of France's top women professionals had at least something to do with the fact that she had for months been seen in public with one of France's aspiring Presidential candidates.

In the course of the dinner, Sir David Blakely made a little speech expressing his complete confidence in the project, both as conceived and as it was now being carried out. Leroux, replying, toasted the vision of men on either side of the Channel, using much the same language as President Mitterrand himself had used on that first historic occasion when the treaty of Anglo-French co-operation was signed.

Grantham was seated next to Lydia Blakely. Always an attractive woman, that evening she had outdone herself. She wore a low-cut black dress, and a pearl choker round her throat which, Grantham reckoned, must have cost Sir David a fortune. Her black hair was piled high on top of her head and held in place with a simple gold clip. Lady Blakely knew when to rise to the occasion.

"I'm sorry you had to break off your holiday, Oliver. You deserved that holiday if anyone ever did. David was really worried that things were going to go badly wrong. I've never seen him so worried, in fact."

"We're not out of the woods yet," Grantham replied. "Everything we've done today is just a holding operation. Of course, we are going to put out statements to say that we are right and Dummett is wrong. But that's what people would expect us to do. They're not necessarily going to be convinced by that. We have to get the press on our side. That's the only way."

As he spoke, a waiter came up to his chair bearing a message on a plate.

"Forgive me." Grantham slit open the envelope. He saw David Blakely watching him from the other end of the table. He took out his pen and wrote a short message on the note which he had just read. The waiter was still hovering and Grantham told him to take the message on round to Sir David.

Sir David smiled with quiet satisfaction when he read the note. It was from Marchmain's Australian headquarters in Sydney. The message was headed: PERSONAL FOR GRANTHAM. IN RESPONSE TO YOURS OF TODAY PRELIMINARY ENQUIRIES INDICATE DUMMETT TOOK LATE SUMMER VACATION IN GREECE STOP DUMMETT GIVING NO INTERVIEWS OVER NATURE ARTICLE IN SPITE OF CONSIDERABLE JOURNALISTIC INTEREST BY NATIONAL AND INTERNATIONAL PRESS STOP WE ARE STILL PURSUING OUR ENQUIRIES AND HOPE TO HAVE MORE TO REPORT.

Sir David read what Grantham had scribbled at the bottom of the message. "I propose to take tomorrow's Concorde from Paris to Sydney. I hope that Alex Lyons from *Daily Mail* will accompany me, if available. O.G."

Sir David folded the paper neatly and tucked it into his breast pocket. He saw Grantham looking at him and gave him a quick thumbs-up sign.

"I wish we could go to Lourmarin again." Monique Delacourt sighed. "I felt so close to you then. You've become so involved now in your Presidential campaign that we hardly have any time together."

Pierre Leroux lay on his back next to her, pulling at his habitual cigarette and gazing out at the night sky of Paris over Notre Dame. He put out an arm.

"This only happens once in a lifetime, Monique," he said. "I have to give it everything now. The prize is so close."

She could sense that he was drawing away from her, wrapped in his own ambitions, and she tried to hold him.

"Do you want me to come to Marseilles?" she asked. "If this financial crisis is solved, I could probably get away. I'm sure Grantham and Blakely would understand. Even from a strictly professional point of view, my links with you have been vital for the Chunnel project. Just the fact that you were at Maxim's, and were seen to be there, will have made a great difference. And, anyway, I've never been to the Socialist Party congress before. It would be a good experience."

She laughed. She had spoken lightly, but in her heart she knew she desperately wanted this brilliant, attractive, ruthless young man, who was going to be the next President of France, to invite her to be with him at the nominating convention.

Pierre Leroux spent a long time not replying to her question. Two days earlier he would have said, without any hesitation at all, that he wanted Monique Delacourt to be there with him in Marseilles. Now he was not so sure. The previous Wednesday he had received from Louis Baudin, who had come to Paris specially for the purpose, a long and detailed briefing on the results of the conversations which Baudin had just held in Courchevel with the leader of the socialist party in the northern part of France, Guillaume Mauplan.

When he at first heard of the deal which Baudin had made on his behalf, Leroux had been furious. "You had no right to take such a position!" he had shouted. "I won't endorse it. It's pure cynicism."

Baudin had given him time to calm down. "That's what politics is all about," he had consoled him. And he had gone on to state in quite categorical terms that without such a deal over the Chunnel project, as proposed by Mauplan, there was no chance of those crucial votes from the Pas-de-Calais region being cast in Leroux's favour at the Marseilles meeting. He had reminded Leroux gently but firmly of where his long-term loyalties lay.

The two men had been walking together in the Bois de Boulogne. When you were a potential candidate for the presidency of France, conversations of the kind that Leroux tended to have with Louis Baudin, his mentor and backer, were best held out of doors and away from all means of surveillance.

"You can't imagine," Baudin had driven the nail firmly home, "that the Channel Tunnel project is in Moscow's long-term interests. They don't mind it being built, of course. It diverts resources which might be used elsewhere in the economies of Western Europe. But they certainly don't want to see it in operation. By agreeing to Mauplan's proposal, you are merely doing what Moscow would in any case expect you to do, when and if you are elected President."

Louis Baudin did not always take such a tough line with his protégé. But he had spent a lifetime waiting and working for this moment. He wasn't going to let it slip from him now merely because of some last-minute scruple on Leroux's part. Leroux should be in no doubt at all about who was paying the piper nor about the tune to be played.

The old man had slashed viciously with his walking-stick at a tree trunk:

"I know you're involved with Monique Delacourt. I like the woman, what I've seen of her. I liked her the first time I met her down at your place in Provence. But never muddle your personal affairs up with politics, my boy."

As Leroux lay there in the darkened room, wondering how to answer Monique's question, he realized that he was in danger of doing exactly what Louis Baudin had advised against: muddling his private and public lives. At the time when he ought to be persuading Mauplan that he would "buy" his proposal in exchange for support, it wouldn't do – it absolutely wouldn't do at all – to have the Chunnel's chief engineer trailing on his arm at public and possibly private meetings.

He put out his cigarette.

"Let's make love the way we did at Lourmarin," he said. "Remember when we were lying there, and the window was open, and the cypress trees were waving outside."

"Of course I remember. How could I ever forget?"

He kissed the inside of her thigh, then ran his tongue over her mound.

"Ah!" she gasped. "*J'aime ça; comme je l'aime!*"

He loved doing it too. It was a darkness of its own within the wider darkness of the room. He could lose himself there, he thought. Give up ambition.

She took hold of his shoulders, in the end, and lifted him on to her.

He hadn't answered her question. Because he hadn't, she knew the answer was no.

Professor Giuseppe Finzi got to the little museum, just by the river in Neuilly, ahead of the others. When Tom Anders and Bill Prendergast, the bluff and level-headed Marchmain man on the board, arrived by taxi, Finzi welcomed them and told them he had already had a chance to make an inspection of Thomé de Gamond's collection of fossils.

"I've spoken to the concierge of the museum. She's gone off to do some shopping, but she doesn't mind if we wander around. She says that nowadays she doesn't get many visitors to Thomé de Gamond's birthplace." He gave a brittle, nervous laugh.

Bill Prendergast noticed the suitcase standing in the hall with the Alitalia flight-labels attached to it. Finzi followed the direction of his glance.

"I'm going straight on from here to the airport," he explained.

As the little Italian led the two men on a brief tour, he explained the preliminary conclusions which he had already arrived at.

"I think we can say with absolute certainty," he said as they moved from one case of exhibits to another, "that every single fossil collected by Thomé de Gamond has its origin in the Upper Chalk. There isn't even any evidence of specimens from the Middle Chalk layers being found on the outcrops of rock on the seabed, let alone – of course – the Lower Chalk."

He spent some time explaining to them, naïve as they were, the differences between the fossils in the Thomé de Gamond collection.

"There are the short curly ones; there are long thin ones; there are the round flat ones. Each of them has its own history and tell its own story. Mrs Potter was right, completely right, to advise us to come here. It's an additional corroboration of the correctness of our decision about the work."

Looking at his watch, and muttering about flight-times, Finzi ushered them out once more into the hall of the museum. A taxi, which the Professor had obviously ordered, was waiting.

Bill Prendergast helped the Italian with his bag.

"My! that's heavy!" Prendergast placed the suitcase in the boot of the car.

"I'm afraid scientific papers are always heavy." Finzi gave a short laugh. "It's one of the occupational hazards of being an academic."

Giuseppe drove off in the direction of Roissy, leaving both Prendergast and Anders with a slightly uneasy feeling that it had all been a little too neat, a little too pat.

Later that week, when the concierge was flitting around with a duster in the small study which contained Thomé de Gamond's books and his collection of fossils, she had a feeling that not all the specimens were in their accustomed place. It also occurred to her, though she was not sure of this, that one or two pieces seemed to be missing. She decided to make a thorough check.

25

Leaving by Concorde from Charles de Gaulle Airport the following morning, Oliver Grantham experienced a momentary twinge of guilt. He remembered the protests which the fledgling environmental movement had made against the Australian Government's decision to allow the Concorde to overfly the country at supersonic speed. At the time, he had felt that the Australian Transport Minister, who had maintained – as he authorized the route from Perth to Sydney – that the only people who would be affected were "a couple of Abos and the kangaroos", had laid it on a bit thick. Aborigines and kangaroos had rights, after all. But now, with the prospect of reaching Sydney in under half the normal time, he was well aware that sheer convenience outweighed most other considerations.

Time was of the essence. There was no question of prolonging the offer period. That would make absolutely no difference to the take-up. On the contrary, an announcement that the offer would remain open longer than originally planned might have precisely the reverse effect. It would indicate a lack of confidence and the market would react accordingly.

Alex Lyons was sitting in the aisle seat across the gangway. Grantham explained the problem to him.

"We've done everything we can this end. But I need a retraction from Dummett."

"Brought the thumbscrew then, have you?" Alex Lyons laughed. "I'd like to see you have a go."

Grantham was not amused. "Alex," he said, "this is a serious matter. Your time is as valuable as mine."

"And the paper's paying, don't forget," Alex Lyons said. "They don't put out easily, you know. A return ticket from London to Sydney on Concorde has to be earned."

"You'll get your story, Alex." Grantham sounded more confident than he was.

Twelve hours later they landed in Sydney. Marchmain's man, a rugged, sun-burnt individual aptly named Jack Cobblestone, was at the airport to meet them.

"We've booked rooms for you at the Wentworth Towers," he said. "You'll have a great view of the harbour." He turned to Alex Lyons. "You'll be glad to hear, Mr Lyons, that Professor Dummett has agreed to give the *Mail* an exclusive interview."

Alex Lyons shot a quick glance in Grantham's direction. Grantham gave him a reassuring nod.

"You're on your way," he said.

"When's the meeting?" Alex Lyons asked.

"The Professor's expecting you around six o'clock this evening. We can take the hydrofoil over to Manly. It's quicker."

Cobblestone came to pick them up at the hotel around five and took them down to Circular Quay, the point of departure for the Manly hydrofoil. He had arranged for a car to meet them the other side.

"We'll drop you off at the Professor's house, Mr Lyons, and I'll send a car to pick you up later, around eight p.m. Will that give you enough time?"

"More than enough," Alex Lyons replied. And then he asked: "How much can I reveal about the results of your investigations? Do you think it's wise to let Dummett know that someone's been through his bank statements, for example? I don't know how you do business out here in Australia. But back in England people tend to get a little stuffy if they think they're being spied on."

Lyons didn't mince his words. When Cobblestone had met them earlier that day, he had passed over a file on Professor Dummett, put together in a hurry by Sydney's top firm of private investigators, which – amongst other things – had revealed very large transfers of funds from abroad in recent months into Professor Dummett's Sydney bank account.

Cobblestone had given Lyons a disarming smile. "I wouldn't want to suggest to a journalist of your standing, Mr Lyons, how best to use the available information. Out here, we tend to play things by ear."

While Grantham and Cobblestone went out to the surf beaches to look at Australia's golden youth, Alex Lyons – as Jack Cobblestone had advised – played it by ear.

He knew the background, no one better. And on the flight over, Grantham had briefed him on the details.

"We're convinced," Grantham had told him, "that Dummett has been suborned. It's a matter of proving it."

That was before Cobblestone passed over the file.

While his wife hovered in the background, eavesdropping without appearing to, Professor Dummett and Alex Lyons, the *Daily Mail*'s star reporter, talked on the veranda. The conversation began with the usual trivialities. Lyons commented on the distant view of Sydney Harbour Bridge and asked what was playing at the Opera. Dummett explained that scientists were busy men, even in retirement, and that neither he nor his wife went to the Opera very often. But the Sydney Harbour Bridge was, he agreed, a fine piece of engineering.

Ten minutes after he arrived, Lyons began to probe – gently at first – into the Channel Tunnel business and the reasons which had led Professor Dummett, at a distance of many thousand miles, to enter the fray so decisively.

"You know, your article has created a terrific stir in Europe," he assured him.

The old man looked ill at ease. "I didn't feel I could be silent any longer," he replied. "Lives might have depended on it."

Lyons led him on slowly. "The line was approved by successive governments, wasn't it? What makes you wish to challenge it now?"

"The evidence, my dear sir," Dummett answered firmly.

"Professor Finzi, the Chunnel Consortium's chief geologist, takes a different view of the evidence."

Dummett scoffed. "I never understood why they appointed Finzi. What does a Roman know about the undersea geology of the Channel tunnel?"

Lyons wanted to comment that Rome was a great deal nearer Calais than Sydney, but he refrained. There was no point in aggravating the Professor unnecessarily.

They had been talking for over an hour before Lyons asked Dummett about his sources of income. He had gone on to suggest, bluntly, that Professor Dummett's authorship of the notorious article in *Nature* might be not unconnected with some very considerable payments from abroad which the Professor had recently received.

Later on that evening, Lyons told Cobblestone and Grantham:

"I expected to be shown the door at this point. And of course I was. I'm glad you two were waiting for me."

Cobblestone had taken them out to a fancy restaurant in Rocks, the colonial slum which had now been upgraded to a fashionable district not unlike, say, Georgetown in Washington, DC. They sat at a table overlooking the water. Half a mile away the spectacular architecture of the Sydney Opera House, illuminated by floodlight, dominated the scene.

Lyons flipped a packet of photographs on to the table.

"We got on quite well at the beginning of our conversation," he said. "We were talking about holidays. Dummett said he never had time to take one. This struck me as odd since you told me he went to Greece last year. He had to go out of the room to answer a call of nature . . ."

"We call it 'pointing Percy at the porcelain!'" Jack Cobblestone intervened, laughing.

"You would! Anyway," Lyons continued, "I looked around while he was out of the room, as any well-trained reporter should, and just happened to find a packet of photographs lying on top of the piano. Dummet features in one or two of the shots."

While they ate, they studied the photographs with care. Some of the pictures showed a quayside scene in what was obviously the main town of some small Greek island. Others showed a more panoramic view of the island, including – in the middle distance – the mountain peaks of another island looming across the water.

"It shouldn't be too difficult to work out where he went from these," Grantham said. "It's not Mykonos, I know that. It's not Rhodes or Crete. One of the Cyclades, I'd say."

Then, as he flipped through the photographs, he said with a tone of conviction in his voice, "Paros, for sure."

"Why do you say that?" Jack Cobblestone asked.

Grantham pointed to a dark, attractive young woman in one of the photographs. She was standing on the terrace of a white house, apparently built of marble, with the blue Aegean as a spectacular backdrop.

"That's Iona Karapolitis. I've seen her picture before and I'd recognize her anywhere. She has a house on Paros."

The next photograph in the pile was a kind of group picture. It showed Dummett standing next to Iona Karapolitis; next to him was Brian Staples, formerly of Channel Ferries, and at the end of the row came a fair-haired, suntanned young man who Grantham immediately recognized.

"Good God!" he exclaimed. "That's the *chasseur alpin*!"

"What do you mean?" Lyons asked.

Pushing the photographs to one side for the moment, Grantham told them.

*

Later that night from his room at the Wentworth Towers Hotel, Alex Lyons telephoned Professor Dummett. He followed a time-honoured journalistic practice, warning the subject of an article of what was about to appear.

"Shall I read you the precise text, Professor?" Lyons asked. At the end of the day, he was a professional and a hard man.

Dummett said nothing, so Lyons went ahead anyway. When he had finished, the journalist asked: "Do you have any comment, Professor?"

There was a long pause at the other end of the line. Finally, Dummett said:

"I never talked to journalists before. I'm sorry I talked to you today. I would be grateful if you could return the photographs which you had no right to remove."

Grantham and Lyons flew out the next evening. Before they left the hotel for the airport, the TV bulletins carried the news that Sydney Harbour Bridge had just claimed its 2000th victim. The television reporters had done some devilling before putting the story out.

"Professor Dummett who leapt to his death from the bridge earlier today," the newscaster said, "was a geologist of international renown and former president of Britain's prestigious Royal Society. The motives behind the tragedy are not immediately apparent. Earlier this year Professor Dummett is thought to have incurred large financial losses through property speculation in the Manly area."

They joined the stream of traffic heading for the airport.

"They'll do an update in London," Lyons said. "It'll make the later editions." He sighed. "That's the way it always is. I've seen it so often in my journalistic life. There's always a money problem there somewhere."

"How did you handle the Karapolitis angle?" Grantham asked. "They could hit the paper for libel, even if it's true. You know what the courts are nowadays."

"I left Karapolitis out of it," Alex Lyons replied. "The Dummett story stood on its own. I pushed him, you know, on the *Nature* piece. I did my homework. I even mentioned the fossils. That threw him, I can tell you. As a journalist, you get to sense these things. I could tell that he didn't believe in the article he'd written and that was enough for me. That's all the story you need. The suicide helps, of course. Gives it a ring of authenticity."

They didn't speak again until they were approaching the airport building. Then Grantham said:

"I'm sorry for Dummett's widow."

Alex Lyons looked at him in surprise. "You're human after all, are you?"

Grantham got through to New York fifteen minutes before Concorde was due to leave. He found the banker in his office.

"I'm glad I got you, Ed," Grantham said. "I thought you might be back in Alaska."

The other man laughed. "That's for next month. Where are you calling from?"

Grantham explained that he was calling from Sydney, Australia and that they were holding the plane for him. He spoke for five minutes, outlining the situation and, at the end of his little speech, made a specific requst.

"We're going to turn this thing around," Grantham said. "We have to. It's moving already. You'll see the papers tomorrow. I'd like you and Morgan Stanley to come in."

"How much for?"

"How much are you good for?"

"Aw, hell, we could pick up a quarter of a billion if we had to."

As Grantham slipped into his seat beside Lyons, the *Daily Mail* man asked him, "What kept you so long?"

Grantham made no attempt to conceal his pleasure.

"The Americans are coming in to the tune of a quarter of a billion. It's not all we need but, by God, it's a start. If the Americans come in, and they're the other side of the Atlantic, how can the Europeans hold back?"

The stewardess arrived and poured the pre-take-off champagne. Alex Lyons lifted his glass. Echoing Grantham's words, he said: "If winter comes, can spring be far behind?"

The two men talked intermittently throughout the long flight. Somewhere over Sri Lanka, Grantham said:

"I never realized, when I took this job on, just how much travelling I would have to do. I certainly never expected to have to go to Australia in the line of duty."

"I don't expect the opposition thought you would go to Australia either. Whoever thought of getting Dummett to write that article showed a good deal of imagination."

Grantham nodded. The incident on the ski-lift, if nothing else, had taught him to take the opposition seriously.

They made a brief refuelling stop in Bombay, then flew up – still at a speed approaching Mach 2 – over the Arabian desert towards the Mediterranean.

The captain came on the air to announce that they were about to overfly Marseilles and would be continuing on to London across France. For the rest of the journey they would, therefore, be flying subsonically.

"I'm going to be in Marseilles next week," Lyons said. "I'm attending the Socialist Party Congress there. I'm rather looking forward to it. It's a long time since I had a bouillabaisse on the Canebière." Then he added, "What do you think of Pierre Leroux? He seems to have the nomination sewn up."

The plane was already beginning its long descent towards Heathrow. Grantham chose his words carefully. He knew Alex Lyons well enough by now to realize that the journalist would not need more than the faintest whiff of a scent.

"The history of the last forty years or so since the last war," Grantham said, "is the history of the decline of the Communist Party in France. The communists have seen their influence drop steadily. The years when they were in the political desert – the years of de Gaulle, Pompidou and Giscard – have been succeeded by an almost equally barren period under Mitterrand. Of course you have had the so-called Common Programme. You have had a few ministers, communist ministers, in the Government. But the reality is that the Socialist Party in France is now the overwhelmingly dominant party of the left and that the communists have withered on the vine."

"So?" Alex Lyons didn't yet see what Grantham was driving at.

"My own view," Grantham continued, "is that the Soviet Union, having failed to influence the evolution of events in France through one means, namely the French Communist Party, is now seeking to do so by another route, that is to say through the presidency of France itself."

Alex Lyons, as instructed by the warning signs, extinguished his cigarette prior to landing. He did not doubt for a moment that Oliver Grantham, with his background in the military, had access to sources which were certainly closed to a mere journalist. But, like any good journalist, he wanted to be sure that he was dealing with fact not speculation.

"Is that, as it were, from the horse's mouth?"

Grantham nodded. "You didn't hear it from me, Alex. But the answer is: yes."

The long, elegant nose of the Concorde dropped before landing. The two men gathered their things together.

"If you do go to Marseilles, keep me posted, won't you?" Grantham requested.

"I'll do my best."

The Rolls was waiting at terminal three. Grantham offered Lyons a lift into town.

Alex Lyons laughed. "The paper will be pleased I saved them the cost of the taxi, anyway!"

As they drove towards Hammersmith, Grantham said apropos their earlier conversation,

"You know it's difficult for us Anglo-Saxons to appreciate the role the French army plays, or can play, in domestic political life in France. Think about the involvement of the army in the Dreyfus case or the Algerian business which led to the return of General de Gaulle. The French Army has always been much more ready than the British Army to involve itself in politics. Beginning with Napoleon!" Then, almost casually, Grantham asked, "Have you ever met Maximilien Miguet?"

Lyons nodded. "Yes, years ago, when NATO was still in Paris and France was still in NATO. He graduated top of the class at St-Cyr, didn't he?"

"Yes. And the youngest officer ever to reach the rank of colonel." And then Grantham continued in a flat, matter-of-fact voice: "People whose judgement I respect tell me Miguet is one of the most brilliant leaders of his generation. I had a talk with him in Paris not long ago and he struck me that way."

Alex Lyons waited for Grantham to say more, but Grantham turned, somewhat abruptly, to the newspapers which James the chauffeur had thoughtfully provided.

26

"I'm glad the boys had a good time anyway."

There was an unmistakable coolness in Lily Grantham's words. She resented the fact that, at least so far as appearances were concerned, Grantham had gone from strength to strength since the break-up of their marriage. If Grantham sensed the rebuke, he ignored it.

"Yes, they did have a good time," he agreed. "I've always liked Méribel. Unfortunately, I had to cut short the holiday. A financial crisis over the Chunnel project. Thank God, that's behind us now."

"Seems as though your time was full of incident." The asperity was still in Lily's voice. "I hear someone shot at you."

Grantham wondered whether one of the boys had told her about Ingrid Lubbeke. He felt certain they would have done. He steered the conversation away from their skiing holiday.

"Thank you for dropping in, Lily. We haven't talked for a long time. I thought we should."

It was the first time that Lily Grantham had visited her husband in his new place. Grantham had offered to come down to Fleet, or to meet on neutral ground. But Lily, with a woman's natural curiosity, had wanted to see how Grantham had fared over the months since she had left him. Or had she, in fact, left him? Who had left whom? These things, she reflected, were never very clear.

She sat on the sofa in Grantham's large first-floor drawing room overlooking Chester Square. Her practised eye took in the contents of the room, the carpets, the curtains, the ornaments, the pictures. Someone, somewhere, had obviously advised Grantham well. Equally obviously, he had been able to spent a great deal of money.

"You must be a rich man, now, Oliver," she commented dryly.

Grantham did not reply to this. There was no point in talking about money. Only the lawyers could handle that side of things. That's what they were paid for.

"It was the boys I wanted to talk about," he said.

It took her a good deal of effort to say: "Can we talk about us too?"

Grantham looked at the woman with whom he had spent more than a quarter of a century. He knew that not a day passed but he thought of her. He smiled. "Tell me about the garden. Are the rhododendrons out yet?"

They talked for most of the afternoon. There were things she had wanted to say to him for years which she had never found words for. And he discovered, to his surprise, that he knew how to listen.

"In a nutshell," she had explained somewhere towards the end, "I want and need more contact, more communication. Life is about relationships, human relationships."

Grantham wasn't sure that he agreed. Deep down he suspected that life was about doing things or getting things done. Relationships tended to get in the way.

"I'm not sure I'm really the right man for that," he parried. "You'll have to give me time. It takes time to work things out. That goes for me as well as you."

They left it at that, both of them aware that possibly some small steps had been taken on the long journey back; but both of them still undecided as to whether that journey was truly worth the effort.

As she prepared to leave, Lily Grantham's eye fell on a drawing which hung beside the fireplace.

"Where did you get that?" she asked.

"Sotheby's. It's by Wallis, a sketch for his painting 'The Death of Chatterton'."

Lily studied the drawing, a crumpled figure lying on the bed, the shaft of light coming in through the window.

" 'I thought of Chatterton, the marvellous boy,' " she quoted, " 'the sleepless soul that perished in his pride.' " She turned to him. "It reminds me of Tommy, Oliver. Tommy Plowright was very close to you, wasn't he?"

Grantham nodded. "That's why I bought it. Poor Jane, she never really recovered from his death."

He showed her a framed photograph the other side of the mantelpiece.

"I found this in a trunk and decided to put it up. That's my older sister Jane and Eddie Plowright in Monte Carlo. There's Tommy, on the left. It must have been a year or two before the end."

Lily Grantham studied the dark, handsome face of Tommy Plowright in his early twenties. As she did so she remembered that dreadful morning when they had heard the news of his death.

"It's good to see that photograph of Tommy there," Lily said. "He admired you so much. The nature of his illness made it so much more poignant."

Grantham held her coat for her. She gave him a brief, businesslike peck on the cheek.

"I'm glad you're looking after yourself, Oliver."

She turned and was gone.

Later, when loneliness had settled in with the night, Grantham found himself wondering whether he was making such a good job of looking after himself after all.

27

When Alex Lyons had told Oliver Grantham that it was a long time since he had had bouillabaisse on the Canebière, he had meant exactly what he said. At least a decade had elapsed since he had last been in Marseilles. Though he recalled, from the visit, the distinctly Arab flavour of the place, he was surprised by the extent to which over the intervening years "l'Afrique du Nord" seemed to have implanted itself in this Mediterranean city.

Lyons had arrived by train from Paris around six o'clock in the evening. The TGV had covered the 862 kilometres in well under four hours. On arrival, he had planned to walk from the station to the Vieux-Port, along the length of the Canebière. But when he had walked down the great flight of steps from the station to street level and realized that his was almost the only white face in sight, he had decided against it. Better not to be provocative. He had taken a cab to his hotel on the Quai des Belges where, happily, he had run into several journalist colleagues and they had set off together in search of a meal.

Charlie Shawcross of *The Times* and George Wheldon of the *Telegraph* had been pleasant enough eating companions. Lyons had returned to his hotel at around 11.00 p.m. that evening in an agreeable frame of mind. After his long and somewhat exhausting trip to Australia, he had needed a little relaxation. A beaker full of the warm South, as Keats had put it. Not that Australia had in any way been a futile trip. On the contrary, the *Mail* had scooped the pool. Even so, thought Lyons, it had been hard work. Marseilles should be different. He was looking forward to hearing Leroux's acceptance speech.

The Conference Centre had been built, at a time when Gaston Deferre was still Mayor of Marseilles, on the left hand side of the Old Port in the shadow of the ramparts and battlements of Fort St Nicolas. As was often the case in Marseilles, scandal had attached to the construction. The city of Marseilles itself had contracted for the Conference Centre and was rumoured to have paid considerably over the odds for it. Marseilles' new mayor, Claude Genet, had promised an investigation when he took office. But so far nothing much had come of it.

Lyons took his seat in the hall next morning a good half hour before Leroux was due to address the delegates. He had time to study the audience. On the whole French political conventions were sober affairs. They tended to spend their time debating wordy motions and splitting intellectual hairs. That was particularly true of Socialist conventions, where an effort had to be made to bring together the many different strands and different personalities in the party. There were the old-fashioned delegates who still owed their allegiance to the SFIO – the Section Française de l'Internationale Ouvrière – the old Workers' International; there was the smarter younger members of CERES – the Centre d'Etudes, de Recherches et d'Education Socialiste; they were the trade unionists with that maze of initials which Lyons never managed to sort out – CFDT, CFTC, CTG and so on.

But this particular convention, Lyons noted, had an unusual element of razzmatazz. Shawcross, who specialized for *The Times* in France and things French, had explained it at their dinner the previous evening:

"Leroux thinks of himself as being in the Kennedy mould. He'll try to turn this into a nominating convention along American lines. I'm told that he's done deals with all the major groupings in the party, so he'll probably succeed."

When, finally, Leroux strode onto the platform and took his seat to enthusiastic applause, Lyons saw what Shawcross had meant. The word was desperately overworked, but no other word would do: Leroux had charisma. It was more Bobby Kennedy's charisma than Jack's. But the quality was there all the same. As the applause continued, Leroux rose to his feet, spread out his arms as though he were embracing the audience, then raised them in a victory salute. Lyons saw the audience react; felt the charge go through the hall, the current of empathy between leader and led. This man has what it takes, he thought. A few minutes later, he was listening to Leroux's acceptance speech. Already Presidential in tone and content, it was pitched at exactly the right level.

"I am not the representative of a party," Leroux said, standing up without notes to address the faithful, "I am not the representative of a coalition of parties. I am the candidate of all the Left, the warm-hearted Left, the fraternal Left, which before me and after me has been and will be the expression of our people's worth. Let me give you what are perhaps old words but for me, for all of us, men and women of the Left, women and men of progress, they have kept all their value. These words are Justice, Progress, Freedom, Peace . . ."

When Leroux had finished, the applause in the hall continued for ten minutes while Leroux stood there, receiving homage, with the cameras of the world on him.

Knowing what he knew, knowing what Grantham had told him, Alex Lyons felt a quick shudder of fear.

That evening he again had dinner with Shawcross, who promised to show him a little restaurant on the waterfront where true *bouillabaisse marseillaise* could be found.

"A genuine working-class fish soup," Shawcross had explained. "No lobster or crab in it. That's for the luxury restaurants. Red mullet, whiting, bass, John Dory, perch, haddock – it doesn't matter what fish you use as long as you boil it hard during cooking so that the olive oil emulsifies and thickens the broth."

Alex Lyons knew an expert when he heard one. The two of them sat together for over two hours in the little smoke-filled restaurant facing the harbour. As far as Alex Lyons was concerned, it was one of the best meals he had had in his life.

Towards the end of it, when the cheeses had come and gone and the plates had been cleared away, Lyons put the question which he had been wanting to ask most of the day.

"You said that Leroux had done deals with the major groupings in the Socialist Party. What kind of deals?"

Shawcross was a wily old bird. He might be the *doyen d'âge* of *Times* reporters, but his senses were still as acute as ever. However good the meal, you didn't pass over your best stories to a rival newspaper.

"You're fishing, Alex," he said. "And I'm not biting." Then he relented, just a little.

"Take a closer look at Leroux's relationship with Guillaume Mauplan, for example. There's something odd there. Two weeks ago Mauplan was still lining up behind Rocard. Then he went off to the Alps to stay with old Louis Baudin and he changed his mind. You could see him on the platform with Baudin today, thick as thieves the pair of them. That's what I mean by deals."

Alex Lyons nodded thoughtfully. "Mauplan comes from the North, doesn't he?"

"That's right. He's a Calais man, but he speaks for the whole of that area outside of Lille, which of course has its own organization."

When he got back to his hotel, Alex Lyons called his office to tell them that he planned to delay his return to London.

"Thanks for the piece on Leroux," the news editor said laconically. "We've used it."

Lyons was pleased. He got paid the same anyway but, even so, he liked to see his name in the lights.

"That's an ongoing situation," he said. "I'm going to do a little digging into the sources of Leroux's support, particularly up North."

"Just get home before Christmas," the news editor said and hung up.

Twenty-four hours later Alex Lyons was standing in front of Calais' town hall, dominated by its massive Flemish-style belfry, at the end of the Boulevard Jacquard. In the park, across the road, he could see the old German bunker which they had turned into a museum depicting the grimness of life under the Nazis. And a stone's throw away he could see the church of Notre Dame, still looking much as it did when the occupying English built it in the fourteenth century.

The Boulevard Jacquard, thought Lyons, was a good place to start. If you were an investigative reporter, it was always good to start in the main street. You could explore the dead-ends later. He spent the morning talking to people. Ordinary people. Shopkeepers, tradesmen, café-owners. He told them the truth, namely that he was a journalist writing for an English newspaper.

When he had seen enough of the administrative and shopping quarters of Calais, he walked on across the George V Bridge into the old Ville Maritime, the original nucleus of the town, where the fishermen lived and where the ferry-boats came in. He talked to another fifteen or twenty people, in passable though not fluent French.

One of the themes he returned to again and again, without apology, was the way these good people, the burghers of Calais, saw their future now that the Channel Tunnel was approaching completion. Would it make a difference to their way of life, to their prosperity?

Of course, he didn't always get the same answer. People didn't always see things the same way. But by the end of the day Lyons was able to propound a neat little paradox: building the Channel Tunnel was a great idea as far as the people of Calais and the neighbouring towns were concerned. In a depressed region of France, the massive work of construction had brought jobs and prosperity. But actually *having* the Channel Tunnel in operation was, he concluded, going to be a different proposition altogether. So much of the trade in Calais and Boulogne and Dieppe and Dunkirk depended on the ferries, on people who arrived by car or on foot on the cross-Channel boats and then spent time and money in the region. Talking to people, as he had, Lyons had been able to detect a growing awareness that the benefits of construction might soon be outweighed by the loss of custom, as tourists who might otherwise have paused on the coast were rushed on through by high-speed trains to their destinations in other parts of France.

A man behind the bar put it best, Lyons thought. Lucidly, succinctly and – from that good burgher's point of view, wholly logically. "*Il faut le construire; et puis il faut le fermer!*" Build the tunnel, then close it!

"Does anyone take that seriously, as an option?" Lyons had asked.

The barman had given one of those classic Gallic shrugs. Political leaders, he had replied, had to take this kind of thing seriously; otherwise they wouldn't stay leaders for very long. Not in the Pas-de-Calais anyway.

"*Et Monsieur Mauplan, il comprend tout ça?*" asked Lyon.

By way of reply, the man had made a circle with the thumb and forefinger of his left hand indicating that Monsieur Mauplan's comprehension of these and other matters was as near perfect as could be desired.

Alex Lyons had returned to London later that evening convinced beyond a peradventure that, if there had been some secret deal between Mauplan and Leroux, that deal somehow, somewhere had involved the Channel tunnel. This was something, he decided, that Oliver Grantham ought to know about, even if it was the merest speculation.

28

For the benefit of Brian Staples and Hans Kruger, whose Greek wasn't up to par, Georgios Karapolitis spoke in English. Staccato, heavily accented English. The anger broke through like a rough sea against a reef.

He paused momentarily in his tirade, to gaze out of his office window at the shipping in the harbour. But the sight of a score of tankers lying idle off Piraeus served only to enrage him further. It was his fleet, his tankers. The last thing he needed to be reminded about, at this particular juncture, was the way the slump in world shipping was affecting Karapolitis interests.

He swung back to face the little group.

"Nothing has gone right, has it?" he snapped. "You try to blackmail Grantham and it misfires. You try a financial ploy, buying up shares in a defunct company – it sounds clever enough – but you get out-manoeuvred. You think up a scheme, again a clever scheme, I admit, to discredit the whole operation just as they go public with their share offer, but that one goes wrong too. Time is running out, my friends."

He strode over to his desk, picked up a sheet of paper and waved it at them.

"These are the figures for the advance bookings for Channel Ferries during the first six months of next year. Of course, advance bookings aren't everything. But I can tell you, these figures look awful. Who's going to book ahead of time on a boat, when they know that the Chunnel will be finished? What do you say to that, Mr Staples?"

In the event, Brian Staples had very little to say. That Georgios Karapolitis's criticisms were justified, he knew only too well. The counter-attack, as he thought of it, had been botched and amateurish.

"I'm sorry," he said sheepishly. "Nothing seems to have gone right."

Staples couldn't resist a quick jab at the German: "I'm afraid Kruger couldn't even shoot straight. If he had done his job properly, we'd be home and dry. But old Hans has to go and stand under an avalanche when he pulls the trigger, doesn't he?" Staples sneered.

The fair-haired German began to protest but Georgios Karapolitis cut him short. "This is no time for bickering. We have a job to do."

He turned to Iona, who so far had been silent throughout most of the meeting. "You're in charge, Iona. You wanted me to let you have the responsibility. What's the next move?"

She looked her father straight in the eye. "Don't bully me, father," she said. There was a steely note in her voice. "I'm still running this operation. I know what to do next."

She turned to Brian Staples. "Tell them, Brian. Tell them what we're planning."

Brian Staples seemed to have aged over the last year. The black hair, still slicked back from his forehead, had begun to grey about the temples. Working with the Greeks had obviously been more of a strain than he had anticipated. But, since the alternative had been bankruptcy, a few grey hairs were – from Staples's point of view – a price worth paying. He stubbed his cigarette out, marshalled his thoughts and began:

"Let me tell you a story first, Georgios. I think it makes the point. Back in 1971, a Peruvian freighter struck a Panamanian tanker in the Channel. The freighter was in the wrong lane. She was northbound so she should have been on the French side and she wasn't. As I say, she collided with the tanker and the tanker exploded and went down off Folkestone with nine lives lost. The British authorities marked the wreck with lights but next day a German freighter, outbound, hit the wreck and also went down, this time with a score of casualties. The British put on a light ship and five buoys with lights, in addition to the lights they already had on the wreck, but that didn't stop another freighter, a Greek one, hitting the collection of wrecks a few days later. So they put on a second light ship, nine more buoys and then a few days after that another supertanker went straight through the middle and only escaped sinking by a miracle."

Staples glanced up at the Greek to see if Karapolitis was following his drift. The gleam of understanding which had begun to appear in the shipping tycoon's eye told him that all was well.

"The point I'm trying to make with this little story," Staples continued, "is that if, after taking all the precautions in the world, you still can't stop supertankers colliding with wrecks in the Channel, how much more difficult it would be to stop them colliding, by accident of course, with, say, one of those construction platforms, Marchprods I believe they call them, which are out there in the Channel at the narrowest point."

Georgios Karapolitis let out a crude wolfish whistle, then roared with laughter. He strode over and clapped Staples on the back.

"My boy, you're learning fast. That's the best idea I've heard in a long time."

Iona Karapolitis, anxious to claim co-authorship of the scheme, added her own footnote to what Staples had already said.

"No reason, father, why the tanker should be traceable to us. We'll have it registered in Panama, with a Monaco address on the papers, a Swedish captain and Goanese crew. The tanker will be heavily insured, for its full replacement value, even though everyone knows you can't *give* them away at the moment."

Georgios Karapolitis loved every word of it.

"And it will be full, of course, when it goes down, won't it?" He rubbed his hands in anticipation of the event. "Two hundred thousand tons deadweight full of cut-price oil *en route* for Rotterdam. Do you know," he turned to Staples, "that you can pick up oil for fifteen dollars a barrel now in the Arab Emirates? That's one of the results of the breakdown of OPEC. Buy it for fifteen dollars a barrel but insure it for thirty dollars a barrel!" Again he rubbed his hands. "Get rid of an unwanted tanker, sink the Chunnel project and make a quick killing at the same time! My friends, I congratulate you all!"

Georgios Karapolitis gave his daughter a huge kiss on the cheek. She blushed with pleasure. It was not every day that her father showed his approval with such enthusiasm.

Staples had one word of caution.

"If the tanker's full when it goes down after hitting the Marchprod, you could have a major pollution incident. That could affect a lot of people along the coast in Britain and France, not to speak of the ecology. Don't forget I'm MP for a coastal constituency."

But Georgios Karapolitis was not to be deterred by such considerations.

"Don't you understand?" he said. "The bigger the catastrophe, the angrier people will be. You don't think that the Chunnel Consortium will be able to replace a rig which has been the cause of a major oil spill, do you?"

Staples subsided. He could see that Georgios Karapolitis had a point.

From where he stood on the bridge of the supertanker *Olive Star*, Captain Sven Thorsson couldn't even see the lights on the bow nearly a quarter of a mile away, the fog was that thick. He couldn't help wishing that the owners or charterers of *Olive Star* – not that he really knew who either of these were – had stuck to the original plan. He had never been too happy about taking VLCC's – Very Large Crude Carriers, as the giant tankers were known – up through the Channel which was, after all, the busiest waterway in the world. Gantry Bay, off the west coast of Ireland, which was his original destination, was a much safer haven to reach than Rotterdam.

He picked up his binoculars and stared into the fog. Visibility, he estimated, was two hundred yards and falling. Thank God they'd given him a pilot for the run up the Channel. A strange little man, Thorsson thought, and he'd seen a fair number of pilots in his time. This one had, quite literally, dropped in out of the sky. *Olive Star* had been off the Lizard when a helicopter had appeared overhead to land amidships with a small berry-like fellow, who introduced himself as Jock Kitson and indicated that he had received instructions to offer the captain of the *Olive Star* all possible assistance during the final hazardous leg of his journey.

At the time, Thorsson had thought it somewhat odd. He had made no request for a pilot. But, in view of the fog warnings further up the Channel, he had acquiesced readily enough. One other thing had struck him as odd and that was that Jock Kitson had insisted on keeping to the English side of the Channel whereas, as Sven Thorsson knew very well, the rules stated very clearly that northbound traffic should hug the French coast. When he had put this point to the pilot, the man had been indignant.

"Either I do a job, Mr Thorsson, or I don't. I can get the helicopter to take me off again if you like."

For a few moments as he stood there on the bridge, Captain Sven Thorsson, his face leathery with a thousand voyages and his beard rimed with white, observed the other man. Jock Kitson seemed to know what he was doing. From time to time he called out his commands and they were repeated by the Goanese General Purpose Rating First Class, Haroon Gunaratne, who had charge of the ship's wheel. Ranged beside the wheel was the array of consoles and screens on which control of the ship depended.

Hunching himself against the fog, Thorsson walked out of the bridge house to the wings. The ends of the promenades hung out over the water – if you were trying to manoeuvre one of these supertankers in or out of port you had to be able to look out over the side. Thorsson went right to the edge of the port promenade. He peered into the mist. Somewhere over there, he knew, was Dover. At the moment they were bucking the traffic. Not for the first time, he wondered whether Kitson knew what he was doing in taking the English side.

Suddenly, he made up his mind. Was he captain, or wasn't he? The captain could always overrule the pilot. He decided to go back and tell Kitson in no uncertain terms that either he brought the *Olive Star* into its proper station or he could get off the bridge.

As Thorsson opened the door to go back into the bridge-house, he heard the first officer, another Goanese, drawing the pilot's attention to a blip which had appeared on the radar dead ahead. Sensing danger, Thorsson hastened across the bridge. He took one look at the radar screen and cursed out loud.

"What the fuck are you playing at, Kitson!" he shouted. But by then it was too late.

Thorsson knew as well as anyone that a supertanker cannot respond to split-second timing. It took at least three miles and twenty-two minutes to stop a 250,000-tonner doing sixteen knots. Drop anchor and you would tear the deck away. You couldn't even steer the brute.

But Thorsson tried to steer it, anyway. As the blower sounded the emergency call "Stations fore and aft", Thorsson shouted:

"Twenty degrees starboard!"

"Starboard twenty!" Haroon Gunaratne replied.

Four hundred and twenty yards ahead of them, the bows of the great tanker smashed into the buoyant platform, severing – as a doctor might sever an umbilical cord – the articulated column which linked the platform with the complex on the sea-bed.

The momentum of the ship, its sheer deadweight in the water, carried it forward relentlessly.

Almost immediately after the impact, the ship began to list to port.

Michael Prestwick was dozing in bed in his cabin on the rig when the tanker struck. Candida Coulton was still down there in the module working on some electronic problem; she hadn't known how long she would be delayed. Prestwick was hoping that she would return to the rig – and his bed – before sleep finally overtook him.

When the prow of the *Olive Star* ploughed into the platform, all hell broke lose. At the first splintering shock, there flashed through Michael Prestwick's mind the image which he had had, not so many months earlier, of a cross-Channel ferry, laden with passengers, missing them by a whisker.

"Oh, my God!" he shouted, jumping up from the bed.

To his credit, Prestwick's first thoughts were not so much for his own safety but for innocent passengers who had suddenly run up against the unexpected obstacle. Though the whole room seemed to be tilted at an angle, he managed to get to the window and realized at once that, whatever had struck them, it wasn't a cross-Channel ferry. The fog had cleared a little and, less than a hundred yards away, he could see the huge bulk of the tanker and the damage to her bow resulting from the impact.

"Jesus!" said Prestwick. It was more of an invocation than anything.

Then the alarm bells on the rig began to ring.

Two hundred and fifty feet below the rig, in the command module situated on the sea-bed itself, the alarm bells also began to ring and the emergency lights flashed on the panels to indicate that the umbilical cord connecting the module to the surface had been severed.

The module's own life-support systems came instantly into action. The self-sealing device, which had been built into the unit against precisely such an eventuality as this, worked perfectly. Though all contact with the outside world had been lost for the time being, and though no one of the twenty or so people in the module had the faintest idea of precisely what had caused their isolation, from a strictly functional point of view the module had passed through its first major emergency with flying colours.

Later on, some of them would recall having felt a sudden jarring shock at more or less the same time as the alarm bells started ringing.

29

For the world's press, which rapidly assembled in and around the straits of Dover, the collision of the Panama-registered super-tanker *Olive Star* with a floating platform being used in the digging of the Channel tunnel was a story of epic proportions. The initial loss of life had been small. The tanker's captain, Sven Thorsson, wisely decided not to go down with his ship. Captain and crew had taken to the boats to be picked up, less than an hour later, by a passing freighter. Two Goanese seamen remained unaccounted for; but that was hardly headline news. On the rig itself, there were no casualties, though the structure was severely damaged with the access column leading down to the sea-bed being totally destroyed.

Nor did the prospect of a major oil slick fouling the English and French coasts dominate the news, though the matter was clearly of concern to the localities liable to be affected. Well-tried emergency procedures were put into action; booms were prepared; spraying vessels made ready; teams of naturalists and conservation volunteers brought together overnight to mitigate the effects of the disaster. As far as the press and television was concerned, they had seen oil-spills before. There had been the *Torrey Canyon*. There had been the *Amoco Cadiz*. There had been the blow-outs in the Santa Barbara channel off the coast of California and in the Ecofisk field in the Norwegian sector of the North Sea.

What made the *Olive Star* episode so stunning and so spectacular, ensuring that it dominated the headlines day after day, was the sheer human drama of the situation. Scientists involved in the space programme had been forced to confront the possibility that for one reason or another orbiting astronauts might be unable to return to earth. The retro rockets, for example, might fail to fire, with the result that the space capsule would be unable to re-enter the earth's atmosphere and the astronauts would, in the most literal sense, be "marooned in space". Up till now, that situation had never occurred but the possibility was always there.

Less familiar to people, and therefore even more heart-stopping when it actually happened, was the idea of men and women being lost not in outer space, but in "inner" space. Ten hours after the accident occurred, it was abundantly plain to men like Michael Prestwick and his fellow-technicians that a full-blown crisis had arisen. Though the command module on the sea-bed was equipped with a one-atmosphere buoyant ascent capsule for escape and rescue purposes, the first indications were that the rescue sphere had been jammed in position after being struck by a heavy object, possibly one of the large cylinders containing liquid gas which was stored on the deck and which had been dislodged in the collision.

It had not been easy in those first chaotic hours to re-establish communications between the rig and the command module. The lines of communication which passed through the access shaft had, of course, been destroyed with the shaft itself. Alternative radio links had to be organized – fortunately the module had a back-up system. And, as a first priority, the hull of the sea-bed structure had to be inspected with a view to determining what damage had been sustained. Only then would it be possible to say when and how the rescue could be carried out.

Grantham, accompanied by David Blakely and Donald Coulton, had arrived on the rig within four hours of the accident. Half an hour later Monique Delacourt flew in from the French side. The platform was still afloat and they decided that, unless conditions deteriorated, it would make a serviceable base from which to conduct the rescue operations.

Michael Prestwick briefed them.

"We've re-established contact with the module," he said. "Divers will be going down about an hour from now and they'll make a visual inspection."

Donald Coulton thought of his daughter trapped below.

"What if the rescue sphere is jammed?"

"We've got time," Prestwick replied. "They've got ten days' life support down there. We'll get them out before then."

Like Donald Coulton, Michael Prestwick was thinking of Candida – but he was also thinking of all the other people down there in the sea-bed structure. People he had known and worked with over the last few months. People whom he had come to trust and who had come to trust him.

Later that day, when the divers returned to the surface, they brought the bad news. Prestwick would have liked to have kept it quiet, but he couldn't. By early afternoon, the rig had been surrounded by vessels of one kind or another chartered by the media. Helicopters, carrying camera crews, circled overhead. In the interests of safety, Prestwick insisted on limiting the number of reporters on the rig. But there was no way he could exclude them entirely.

He held a press conference in the cinema. Speaking in sombre tones and using diagrams, he explained:

"The sphere is positively buoyant due to its own displacement and pressure-proof foam buoyancy arranged in the outer hull, which surrounds the upper section of the sphere." He pointed to the diagram to indicate precisely what he meant. "In theory, once the sphere is released, it ascends to the surface under its own buoyancy and will float there with sufficient stability and freeboard to allow the hatch to be opened. The problem is unfortunately that, according to our divers' report, the outer hull of the module has been damaged to such an extent that the probability of the sphere being free to ascend is very small indeed. There is a lot of débris down there coming from the rig, some of it lying on the hull of the module. Even if the sphere could be freed, that débris would need to be cleared away in any case before rescue could commence. Our evaluation at the present time," Prestwick concluded, "is that alternative rescue systems are called for."

"What kind of alternative systems?"

Alex Lyons, who had followed the Channel tunnel story from the outset, had been one of the first journalists to reach the scene and he put the first question.

Prestwick knew Lyons and liked him. He knew the man would write an honest story. There was no point trying to pull the wool over his eyes, or over anyone's eyes, for that matter.

"The only feasible alternative," Prestwick said, "is the use of submersibles. We are currently exploring those possibilities." And he had gone on to reassure them. "We have at least ten days, ladies and gentlemen. Ten days is a lot of time in this business."

After the press conference, Prestwick met with Grantham, Blakely and Coulton in the same room. Some of the confidence had gone. He looked tenser, more vulnerable than he had been earlier on in the day before the divers reported.

"In spite of what I said at the press conference," Prestwick told them, "we don't have much time. If we're going to use a submersible, as I believe we'll have to, we have to move very rapidly indeed. It may require a government-to-government approach."

"What do you mean?" Grantham asked.

Prestwick looked at him. "I don't want to go into the details. We haven't time for that. Take it from me, because I've studied these things, that there only three submersibles capable of doing the job we have in mind and one of them, the submarine rescue vehicle – the URF – which was designed and constructed for the Royal Swedish Navy by Kockums of Sweden, is – I happen to know – out of action at the present time."

"What about the others?" Grantham asked.

Like everyone else in the room, he was thinking entirely of the immediate situation. What the *Olive Star* incident might have done to the prospects of the Channel Tunnel operation as a whole was not something that at that moment he cared to think about.

Prestwick explained: "There are two DSRVs – Deep Sea Rescue Vehicles – the Avalon and the Mystic, which were built for the US Navy's Submarine Development Group One by Lockheed Missiles and Space Company. Either one of those DSRVs is capable of mating with a 'downed' submarine. The DSRV has a crew of three and can carry twenty-four passengers – or survivors, if you like. The question is: can we got hold of one in time? The last time I checked they were both of them working off the West Coast of the United States. I ought to add that the DSRV crew and supporting equipment can be transported world-wide aboard four C-141A or two C-5A jet transporters. In fact you may remember in 1979 during a test exercise the Avalon and equipment were flown from the West Coast of the United States to Scotland where it made transfers from one submarine, HMS *Odeon*, to another submarine – which acted as the 'mother' – HMS *Repulse*. The mother submarine was ready to leave the dock thirty-three hours after the operation started and it took four hours for the DSRV to mate with the distressed submarine after arriving at the disaster site."

Prestwick saw that he had their total attention.

"Of course, that was an exercise. Things may not always go so smoothly in real life. But in theory, provided the DSRV isn't being used somewhere else and provided the US Government agrees, we ought to be ready to roll long before they start running out of air or food down there."

Donald Coulton stood up. It was as though he had been thrown a lifeline.

"Where's the telephone?" he asked. "I'm going to get that DSRV over here even if I have to charter the plane myself." For the first time that day, Donald Coulton permitted himself to smile, and the others smiled with him.

Seconds later, the mood of optimism had evaporated. The telephone had rung in the conference room and Michael Prestwick had picked it up. He listened for a moment; then he said, quietly: "Hell and damnation!"

He turned to the members of the Chunnel Consortium board who sat with him in the emergency meeting.

"We've got another problem on our hands," he said grimly. "Apparently there are still some people underground!"

Grantham leapt from his chair. "What?" he shouted. "Why the hell didn't we know this before?"

Prestwick looked totally shaken. "Communications with the module are difficult; we've only just established a proper radio link as you know and even that's inadequate. The TBM wasn't driving at the time the tanker struck. Underground personnel had already returned either to the module or to the rig. It turns out there was still a team down there, three people in all, and they never came back up in time. The people in the module thought they'd gone straight up to the surface. Up here, we thought those three were still in the module."

"And the access shaft is sealed now, of course?" Grantham asked.

"Of course," Prestwick replied. "The moment the buoyant column was severed, the emergency systems were activated and the entrance to the shaft was sealed. That's standard procedure."

"So they're on their own down there, are they?" Blakely asked.

It was the first time he had spoken. His normally urbane face looked haggard. He was watching a dream collapse.

Monique Delacourt, who managed somehow to look neat and well dressed even under those horrendous circumstances, answered Sir David's question.

"Yes, they're on their own. They'll have torches, but not much else."

"How do we propose to get them out?" Grantham asked. "The underground chamber is cut off. There's no power down there now the lines are cut. Those men can't climb back up the shaft. And even if they did it wouldn't help them, since the shaft is sealed."

There was a long silence in the room. Outside the window the sea, which had been calm most of the day, was beginning to acquire a choppy look. The damaged platform lurched with the motion of the waves. From where they sat, they could see the oil clearly visible in the water.

The silence lengthened. Then the door to the conference room opened and John Elliot, a tall gangling young man with spectacles and fair hair who served as Michael Prestwick's deputy, came in. He passed Prestwick a piece of paper.

"We've got the names of the people still down there, now," Elliot said.

Prestwick took the paper and looked at it. For a moment his face went white. Then he spoke in a quiet voice, addressing himself in particular to Lord Coulton:

"It turns out that there are four people underground, not three. And one of them is your daughter, sir."

Alex Lyons caught up with Grantham just as he was about to board the helicopter. The news that there were still people trapped underground had got out fast.

For once, Grantham gave a terse "no comment".

Lyons, sensing that his friend was tense to the point of snapping, didn't press it. He dropped back as Grantham ducked under the whirling rotor-blades of the helicopter.

On an impulse, Grantham relented and beckoned the journalist aboard. He knew that if ever he needed the support of the media, he needed it now.

As they lifted off from the pad and swept out to sea, both men could see the immense slick spreading away from them towards the coast. An armada of boats was already in position, dealing with the worst pollution problem of a decade.

"Jesus!" Lyons said over the roar of the helicopter's engines. "Just look at that!"

They flew low over the surface of the water. There was no sign of the tanker but marker buoys were already being towed into position.

"Do you know who owned the *Olive Star*?" Lyons asked.

Grantham shook his head. "The only thing we've got at the moment is a post-box address in Monaco. And that's probably phony!"

Alex Lyons looked at him sharply. "Are you suggesting that the tanker hit the rig on purpose? There was thick fog in the Channel last night."

"That tanker was coming up the Channel on the wrong side," Grantham said. "With a pilot on board. Why don't you look into that, Alex?" He shook his head. For the first time in a long time Grantham seemed depressed. "Not that you'll ever prove anything."

Alex Lyons whistled. "They don't give up, do they?"

The pilot called back to them: "We should be in Gosport in half an hour."

"Gosport?" Alex Lyons didn't understand. "I thought we were heading for Dover."

"I've got to see a man about a submarine," Grantham replied tersely.

*

Buffy Watson was waiting on the pad at HMS *Dolphin*, the Navy's shore-based establishment for submarine training. He greeted Grantham warmly.

"Barely seen you since the Khyber."

Then he looked enquiringly in Alex Lyons' direction. The journalist had pricked up his ears at the reference to the Khyber. But neither Grantham nor Watson elucidated. Grantham introduced his friend.

"Do you know Alex Lyons of the *Daily Mail*? Alex is a good pal of mine, Buffy, and he's got the inside track on this one."

Watson, whose links with the SBS – Special Boat Squadron – went back a score of years to the time when the SAS and the SBS had been part of the same unit – led the way from the helicopter pad to the boat.

"You were lucky, Oliver," he said, as they walked down the catwalk. "*Repulse* has just finished a refit. She was due back on station in a week. You'll find her with her reactor warm and ready to go."

"I know we've been lucky," Grantham answered. "Sometimes you need a bit of luck."

Lieutenant-Commander Bob Perkins was waiting for them in the wardroom of Britain's latest nuclear-powered submarine. He had already set up a briefing.

"The DSRV will be arriving around six a.m. tomorrow morning at RAF Lyneham on the C-5A jet transporters. It will take four or five hours for the submersible to be brought here by road, under police escort, of course." He looked at Grantham. "I know you wouldn't want a lorry to crash into the submersible by accident on the M27. I imagine you've had enough accidents to be getting along with. What was that tanker doing there anyway?"

Grantham made no comment. For the time being he was interested in cures not causes.

"How soon can you leave?" he asked.

"The water in the Solent can be a bit tricky sometimes," Perkins replied. "But we should be away by midnight anyway. Docking may take us a while. The *Repulse* has all the right equipment but this will be the first time we've actually used it. I'll give you a run-through, if you like . . ."

Two hours after it had landed at Gosport, the Marchmain helicopter took off again. As they left the submarine base, Grantham pointed out the tall tower which had been built beside the basin.

"That's the diving tank," he explained. "It's three hundred feet high, or thereabouts. They put men in the bottom of the tank, tell them to hold their breath and wait to see if they come out at the top. The Navy lost a couple of divers that way last year."

Alex Lyons shuddered. There were plenty of hazards in a journalist's life; but – apart from once being beaten up in Khomeini's Iran – he had managed to avoid the extremes of physical discomfort.

They flew out into the Solent, then curled left over Portsmouth harbour.

"I came back here after the Falklands campaign," Grantham told him. "The crowds were lining the quayside."

Lyons looked down. They were passing over the dockyard itself. He could see Henry VIII's salvaged flagship, the *Mary Rose*, lying next to the *Victory*.

"I remember the day they dragged the *Mary Rose* up from the bottom," he told Grantham. "I was out in the Solent on the Trinity House vessel. Prince Charles came and gave us a pep talk while we waited. They had a kind of cradle and a giant floating crane."

"I wish we could get that module up with a giant floating crane," Grantham replied.

They crossed low over Porchester Down, then swung north and east over the rolling Hampshire countryside. The pilot picked up the M3 and followed it.

"We ought to arrive at Heathrow at about the same time as Leeming," Grantham said.

The M3 joined the M25; they were over the Staines reservoir and holding for landing clearance.

"You never cease to amaze me, Oliver," Alex Lyons said. "The accident happened last night and you've already got a submarine standing by for rescue operations, with a submersible being flown in from California. And you've got Leeming coming over too. How do you do it?"

" 'You are old, father William, the young man said . . .' " Grantham smiled. "Prestwick thought he had worked it all out. And in a way, of course, he did. I just took precautions last night, as soon as I heard about the accident. I didn't know until now that we were going to need a submersible, but I thought we might. I didn't know until now that people might still be trapped underground; but I realized it was a possibility."

"So you took the appropriate action?"

"Put it this way," said Grantham: "I made a couple of telephone calls to friends. Like Buffy Watson and Howard Leeming."

Alex Lyons remembered the time he had met Grantham in the

United States. He remembered what Grantham had told him about his visit to the Fairmont Tool Company in Tucson, Arizona. He remembered that Grantham had been quite taken with Howard Leeming and had obviously kept in touch since. Otherwise Grantham would not have described Leeming as a 'friend'.

The helicopter plopped down neatly in front of the Concorde which, itself, had just flown in from Dallas. The ramps had been wheeled up and the passengers were disembarking.

Grantham, still sitting in his seat in the helicopter, caught sight of a tall, sunburned figure striding towards them. He immediately clambered out and moved quickly to meet the Arizonan.

"Howard, I'm so glad you could come."

Leeming put out his hand. "Good to see you again, Oliver. I hope I can be of help."

Grantham turned to Alex Lyons, who was standing behind him.

"Alex, do you remember back in the 'sixties, when oil rigs were sprouting all around the globe, there was a Texan called Red Adair who used to fly around putting out oil-fires? Well, Howard Leeming's got an even bigger job on his hands."

Leeming's face creased into a smile. "Sure," he drawled, "but then Arizonans are even tougher than Texans, aren't they?"

30

The DSRV proceeded on the last leg of its journey, down the narrow road from Fareham to Gosport, at a snail's pace. Mounted on a wide low-loader, it had an escort of police vehicles fore and aft. The inhabitants of Gosport were used to the Navy. Besides the submarine base at HMS *Dolphin*, the Gosport peninsula – that slip of land west of Portsmouth harbour – contained HMS *Mercury* and HMS *Collingwood*, important shore-based establishments involved in training and research. But, in spite of this familiarity with things nautical, the arrival of the DSRV caused a minor stir in the town. By the time the convoy had reached the basin itself, where the *Repulse* was moored, a fair-sized crowd had gathered.

The local journalists had, of course, been tipped off by Alex Lyons' exclusive in that morning's *Daily Mail*. The television networks had sent their camera teams, who had obviously done some smooth talking because several units had been allowed into the base itself and onto the submarine to watch the docking procedure.

Rex Hartley, who usually acted as anchorman for TV South's nightly news programme, had left his desk in Southampton, belted up the motorway towards Portsmouth and was now holding forth, live, to the late afternoon audience. He had the strong features and craggy face of a potential Bosanquet, a hero of Hartley's youth. Viewers loved him.

"Once again," (Hartley stood on deck with floodlights on him as they lowered the DSRV into position) "it's a question of 'the Navy to the rescue'. The ships steamed out of here on their way to the Falklands. Now HMS *Repulse* is heading off on a similar mission. The eyes of the whole nation are tonight riveted on the fate of a score of men and women who are literally trapped on the sea-bed. The built-in escape systems of the sea-bed module have failed to function. The only hope now is a rescue by submarine."

The camera panned from Hartley to the DSRV in the background. Then Hartley walked towards it.

"This is a DSRV. A Deep Sea Rescue Vehicle. It is the only one of its kind in the world."

Actually, Hartley knew that this was not quite true since the *Avalon* had a sister-ship, but it was the kind of thing his audience liked to hear.

"In an exercise which has involved government-to-government contact at the highest level, the DSRV has been flown eight thousand miles overnight, from the coast of California to an airforce base in the South of England – I am not at liberty to say which one – and then it has been brought down here overland to Gosport. The DSRV will be carried by the submarine in piggy-back fashion out to sea. The *Repulse* has been built with the necessary equipment in terms of air-chambers, pressure-seals and so on, to enable it to serve as the mother-ship for the DSRV during rescue operations. It is likely that the *Repulse* will, when the moment comes, itself descend to the sea-bed and will either sit on the sea-floor or hover, as it were, in the vicinity of the marooned module."

Rex Hartley went off-camera for a moment and, in his place, the television screens showed various diagrams depicting the manner of rescue. Hartley, in voice-over, continued his explanation:

"At this point the DSRV will act as a shuttle between the *Repulse* and the module. It may take more than one trip to bring off the trapped personnel, but time should not be too much of a problem. One of the advantages of using a mother-ship which can itself sit on the bottom is that you neutralize the weather factor."

Hartley came back on screen. Viewers could see that his hair was being ruffled by a strong wind as he stood on the deck of the *Repulse*.

"Here in Gosport tonight, the weather is deteriorating rather rapidly. The meteorological people are forecasting storms in the Channel. But once this little team," he pointed to the submarine with the DSRV now firmly locked in position behind the conning-tower, "goes to sea and ducks its head beneath the waves, the storms won't make any difference. Down there, three hundred feet below the surface of the waves, it will be calm water. That is one thing at least which we can be grateful for tonight."

Before the transmission ended, Rex Hartley did a two-minute interview with the captain of the *Repulse*, Lieutenant-Commander Bob Perkins.

"I'm told the Americans have sent a crew along with their submersible, Commander. Do you anticipate any problems in working with the Americans?"

"None at all," Bob Perkins replied crisply. "They have the equipment. We don't. They know how to operate it; we still have to learn."

Perkins looked straight at camera. "Let this be a lesson to all of us," he said. "This time we were lucky. There was a DSRV available. Next time we may not be so lucky. Surely it is time for the Navy, the British Navy, to build its own submersibles."

Like any smart operator, and he was certainly that, Bob Perkins knew that the name of the game nowadays was appealing to the public direct. And the Navy, above all, was adept at making its case, no matter what the Treasury said. That was why Perkins had allowed the cameras on board.

Shortly before midnight, as Perkins had predicted, the *Repulse* left the submarine base at HMS *Dolphin* and headed out to sea.

They held a council of war on the crippled rig first thing the next morning. Grantham took the chair.

"The submarine will be with us by noon and rescue operations will commence as soon as possible thereafter. In the meantime, I want Howard Leeming to explain the plan for reaching the three men and one woman who are trapped underground. Mr Leeming, as you all will recall, is the President of Fairmont Tool, from Tucson, Arizona."

The tall American came straight to the point.

"Miss Delacourt, gentlemen," he began, "we have two options and they are mutually exclusive. The first option is to abandon drilling on the second Marchprod unit, off the French coast; to bring that unit over here and re-establish the articulated column so as to gain access once more to the underground works. This option is technically feasible. It would take maybe twelve or fifteen days to move the rig and some time after that to re-establish contact. But it could be done. The price to be paid, of course," Howard Leeming looked around the small gathering, "is that you would effectively be losing, let's say, a month's drilling by the second Marchprod unit at a time when continued progress on the Channel Tunnel is all the more important because your first unit is out of action. I'm assuming that no problems arise in sealing the access shaft over there and re-opening it when the rig gets back into position." Again he paused. "What I'm saying is that there will be a considerable financial and technical penalty if you take the first option."

Grantham was well aware that the tanker accident had already inflicted a major, though not necessarily mortal, blow to the prospects of a rapid successful conclusion of the boring operations. He wanted to know what else Leeming had to propose.

"What's the second option?" he asked.

The hint of a smile played around Leeming's mouth.

"We've got two, perhaps two-and-a-half weeks to play with, haven't we? Life's going to be uncomfortable down there in that tunnel, but it's not going to be impossible. My alternative proposition would be that you don't move the second rig at all. You leave it where it is. Over there you're using the Fairmont C series tunnelling machines, just as you are everywhere else on this project. One of those machines is already heading in this direction. How many miles have you already covered?"

Monique Delacourt's daily diet was tunnelling statistics. Ever since the accident happened, she had been tense to the point of tears. Even so, she managed a little joke now.

"The French side has been making better progress than the English side, as you would expect!" There was a small appreciative laugh. Even the most anti-feminist engineers on the project had come to appreciate Monique Delacourt's sheer technical competence. "In fact," Monique continued, "TBM number four, which is heading in this direction from the second platform, has been progressing at the rate of over two hundred yards a day. The Lower Chalk does indeed seem like 'Stilton to the mouse'."

"I thought Stilton was an English cheese," Leeming teased her. Then he added, more seriously: "And what is the gap now still to be covered?"

Monique Delacourt shook her head. "I can see what you're driving at, Mr Leeming. But I'm afraid it won't work. There's still two miles to go at least before the two segments of the tunnel join up. Much too far under the present circumstances."

Leeming had taken out a little pocket calculator. "Let's make it simple," he said. "Assume that you've still got four thousand yards to cover. If the machine can do two hundred yards a day, it will take you twenty days. But if we could double the rate of digging, you could cover the ground in ten days. And since, anyway, two miles is less than four thousand yards, even if you couldn't double the rate of digging, you could still be within the margin of safety."

They were all listening to him intently now. He seemed to be offering them the best of both worlds and they could hardly believe what they were hearing.

"I haven't worked thirty years at Fairmont Tool for nothing," Howard Leeming continued. "I know the product. We write in the design specifications for normal operating circumstances. You don't spend several million dollars on a high precision tool and burn it up on the first run. When you've finished one job, you want to be able to use your TBM on another. But today we are not talking about normal circumstances. We're talking about the need to cover, say, two miles in under ten days. It's never been done before, I grant you that. No tunnelling machine in the world has ever bored two miles in ten days."

Howard Leeming was growing visibly animated as he talked. He banged the clenched fist of his right into the open palm of his left.

"But I believe this Fairmont machine could do it if it had to. And I'll tell you something else, gentlemen, I've got Fairmont engineers flying over right now. They'll be alongside that machine day and night. They built it; they ought to know how to operate it!"

He carried them along with his enthusiasm. The option he proposed seemed desperately attractive.

"I see what you meant when you said that the options were mutually exclusive," Grantham commented. "If we keep tunnelling, as you suggest, the rig has to stay where it is. It can't be brought here. But if we do bring it over here, then we can't keep tunnelling."

"Got it in one," Leeming replied.

The meeting lapsed into silence. Grantham made up his mind. They had another full hour before the submarine would arrive with the submersible.

"I'm going to go round the table and ask the opinion of each person present," Grantham said. "We have to weigh up the factors on both sides." He spoke in grave, sombre tones, like a judge addressing a jury before the verdict was to be given. "I want you to know, before you speak, that in the view of the president of this project – I refer to myself – the saving of human life must be the paramount consideration."

"I believe what I propose *is* the surest way of saving human life," Howard Leeming interjected.

Grantham cut him short. "People must make up their own minds," he said firmly.

Michael Prestwick spoke first. The strain of the last twenty-four hours was beginning to show. His face was grey beneath his beard. There had been no contact of any kind with the party trapped in the tunnel since the accident happened. Communications had been severed and it had not been possible to restore them. That one of the persons trapped below should be Candida only added to his anguish. As the captain of the rig, he blamed himself – in part at least – for the accident.

In view of the thick fog that night, he could have turned all the floodlights on the rig, and he hadn't done so. The macabre speculation which Grantham had voiced to Lyons concerning the "accident" had not occurred to him.

"I vote for option one," he said.

Grantham went around the table.

"Lord Coulton?"

Donald Coulton, like Michael Prestwick, had felt the impact of the *Olive Star* incident in the most personal way. He hesitated. As a businessman, as an entrepreneur, as a person who for most of his life had believed that the best way to deal with problems was to forge relentlessly ahead, Donald Coulton found himself deeply attracted by Howard Leeming's bold proposal. It was a high-risk strategy; but the pay-off would be great.

But then he thought of Candida, and the others, down there in the dark. What right had he to hazard their lives further?

"I vote for option one," Donald Coulton said.

Monique Delacourt came out in favour of Leeming's idea. "I know those machines," she said. "Not as well as Mr Leeming knows them, I admit. But well enough. *Ils sont des animaux extraordinaires*. I vote for option two."

David Blakely followed the Frenchwoman and agreed with her. The last thing he wanted was a half-dug tunnel on his hands.

That brought the decision back to Grantham, fairly and squarely.

"I'm sorry the others aren't here. I would've liked to have consulted them. As it is, we shall have to make up our own minds."

As he spoke, Grantham was wondering whether in fact he really was sorry that the others weren't there. Tom Anders, the Dutchman, was a cautious man at heart and Bill Prendergast from Marchmain would probably have followed Coulton's lead, since Coulton was Marchmain's chairman. Prudent men didn't vote against their chairmen – not in public at least.

"It looks as though I have the casting vote," Grantham said. He turned to Howard Leeming. "Howard, this is going to be a case of the New World once again coming to the rescue of the Old. I vote for option two. I say: let's tunnel our way through. The helicopter is standing by to take you over to the other rig. If you need anything, just ask."

The tall Arizonan stood up. He held out his hand to Grantham.

"If we burn up the machine, we'll replace it. Fairmont owes you that at the very least."

Grantham nodded. He thought of Dolores Garcia lying crumpled in the desert.

"That's big of you," he said acidly.

31

The submarine *Repulse* reached the crippled rig an hour earlier than anticipated. It hove to alongside carrying the submersible, as a horse might carry a rider, just aft of the conning-tower.

The helicopter brought Grantham across for a last-minute consultation. The submarine's commander, Bob Perkins, told him that in spite of the rapidity with which the *Repulse* had reached the rig, they had still had time – en route – to try out the "mating" procedures. With the buoyancy capsule blocked, the last thing anyone wanted was a breakdown in the alternative escape system.

With the wind freshening and the pressure of time mounting, Perkins was anxious to get going.

"We shall drop down to the bottom and park about fifty yards from the module," he told Grantham. "The submersible will be launched from there. We'll try and get them all off in one go if we can."

"Do that." Grantham was insistent. If the escape capsule had been damaged, maybe the pressure hull itself had been damaged as well. It could spring a leak at any time.

In the circumstances, Perkins refused to take any reporters or TV cameramen. He was adamant about that.

"I've got some SBS men on board," he told Grantham, "and I'm quite happy to turn them loose if I have to."

"Your decision," Grantham replied.

His relief at the idea of having a momentary break in media coverage was short-lived. Grantham had no sooner returned to the rig than he observed a strange craft bob up alongside the *Repulse*. He recognized it immediately. Television viewers all over the world knew of Professor Auguste Lombard and his famous mini-submarine, the *Lombardie*. Lombard, a bouncy boisterous Frenchman now in his middle fifties, had made an international name for himself as a marine scientist. The

Lombardie had cruised in the Mediterranean and the Red Sea. Lombard and his wife had photographed the coral reefs of the Pacific. Now, by great good chance, the Professor had been cruising in the North Sea when the *Olive Star* struck the rig. Britain's newest and most enterprising television station, TV-NOW, had somehow managed to get in touch with him.

Turning on the television in the wardroom, Grantham heard the indestructible David Frost say: "Hello, and good morning. Standing next to me is France's famous Professor Auguste Lombard. I'm sure you will want to say hello to our viewers, Professor."

Professor Lombard gave a broad smile: " 'Allo, everyone," he said. "*Bonjour.*"

"Thank you, Professor." Frost returned to a waiting nation. "In a few minutes, the *Lombardie* will be following the *Repulse* down to the sea-bed. Professor Lombard's team has been specializing in live underwater photography for years. With his help, TV-NOW will be showing you the rescue operation step by step as it takes place." The cameras showed the *Lombardie* beginning to submerge. Moments later, Frost – this time safely installed in the *Lombardie*'s panoramic viewing lounge – came back on the air.

"We shall be following the *Repulse* all the way down," he said. "Obviously we shall take care not to interfere with the rescue operations in any way. In the meantime, enjoy this message."

Grantham continued to watch the television screen as David Frost was succeeded by a commercial advertisement for cornflakes. He felt strangely helpless. Here he was, in theory in charge of the whole Chunnel operation, and he had been upstaged by a rank entertainer.

He walked back onto the deck of the rig and was immediately surrounded by a posse of reporters and cameramen.

"Are you happy with the way things are going, Mr Grantham?" One of the journalists shouted. "Are you still in touch with the people down in the module?"

Grantham gave a broad, confident smile.

"I'm happy the Navy's here," he said. "And, yes, we're still in touch with the people down below. They know that help is on its way. That's all I can say at the moment."

Instinctively, he moved back to the television set in the ward room. Most of the journalists followed him.

The docking of the DSRV with the command module on the sea-bed took well over an hour. Though the module had been fitted with a second escape hatch in addition to the one contained in the now damaged buoyancy capsule system, the actual manoeuvring of the submersible into the mating position was a delicate operation. Only when the submersible's captain, Jim Matthews – a tall, gaunt American who like the submersible had flown overnight from California – was absolutely confident that the seals were fast, did Commander Perkins give the order for the transfer to begin. And it was a further hour altogether before the submersible was able to slip away from the module and back to the mother-ship.

The fact that all twenty-two of the persons trapped in the module had been brought off without loss of life and given safe haven aboard a submarine of Her Majesty's Navy was a matter for rejoicing not only for those aboard the rig Marchprod One; not only for television and radio audiences throughout Britain; it was, in its way, an event which moved people all around the globe. All the elements of drama were there – the tanker accident itself; the crippling of the rig; the isolation of the module; the logistical feat of flying the submersible halfway around the world in a dozen hours; the cool technical proficiency of the personnel involved in manning both the submersible and the submarine; above all, the happy ending.

Alex Lyons, watching television with Grantham in the wardroom, could scarcely keep back the tears as he saw the submarine, once more joined to the submersible, lift off from the sea-bed to head back to the surface. He put his arm around Grantham's shoulder.

"It's been a long twelve hours, hasn't it? Hadn't you better get out there and welcome them back?"

Grantham stared stonily ahead. "You go, Alex," he said. "It can be your last dateline from Marchprod One."

"Are you evacuating the rig?"

"We have to," Grantham replied. "We're adrift and a hazard to shipping. Heaven knows, without the stabilizing column, the platform could slip over in a storm. Everyone's going to be off here by tonight."

"And you?" Alex Lyons looked at his friend with concern. He thought Grantham seemed tired, more tired than he had ever seen him before.

"I've got work to do, Alex; you ought to know that by now."

"What do you mean?"

Grantham turned to face him. "What you saw this afternoon was just the beginning," he said wearily. "We've brought twenty-two people off the sea-bed, but there are still four people down there, you know. No, not in the module," Grantham went on to explain when he saw Alex Lyons' look of bewilderment, "I mean, down there in the tunnel itself, two hundred and fifty feet *below* the sea-bed. I'm not sure we're ever going to be able to get them out. One of them is Candida Coulton."

"Good Heavens!" exclaimed Alex Lyons. And, for once in his life, he spoke as a human being first, and as a journalist second.

Inevitably, the Press and public saw it in terms of a French TBM racing to the rescue of stranded English colleagues. It was an exaggeration which contained a grain of truth. When the focus of activity shifted to Marchprod Two, located as it was on the French side of the Channel and manned by a largely French crew, it was inevitable that French engineers and French technicians should make the running. Monique Delacourt took control of the rescue operation. While the final decision on all matters of importance was hers, those decisions – as she would have been the first to admit – were almost always based on the advice and judgement of Howard Leeming.

The first crucial decision concerned the rate of advance.

"The limiting factor", Leeming had explained after his first visit underground, "is not going to be the capacity of the tunnelling machine itself. That I can assure you. We're not talking about hard-rock tunnelling; we're talking about soft chalk. You've got twelve two-hundred horse-power electric motors turning the cutter-head; it's a knife-through-butter situation. No reason, technically speaking, why that machine can't move forward two or even three metres an hour. If it was hard rock, you'd have to be stopping to change the cutter-heads. You've got far fewer problems with the chalk. My advice is, drive on as fast as you can, cut the corners on maintenance, you'll have time for that later when the drive is over. As I say," Leeming had continued, "I'm not bothered about the capacity of the TBM. It's the back-up I'm concerned about. You're going to be shifting a lot of chalk very fast. You've got to be able to dispose of it satisfactorily otherwise you'll jam up the whole works."

Monique Delacourt took the point. "We'll look after that side of things. It's a matter of keeping the conveyer belts going and the ships lined up to carry off the spoil from the diggings. If you can keep the TBM going, we can do the rest."

In the event, it had been a spectacularly successful partnership. At the end of the first week, the Fairmont C series tunnel boring machine model B46-101 had broken every tunnelling record in the book. It had broken the best shift record, the best day record, and the best week record. In fact, unbelievably, it had almost broken the best month record too. In seven days of virtually continuous boring, the Fairmont machine had covered two thirds of a mile or more than a third of the required distance.

During that first week of the rescue operation, Grantham spent most of his time either on the rig, Marchprod Two, dealing with the Press or else back in his office in London somewhat desperately trying to keep the Channel Tunnel project going after this major catastrophe. The City had to be reassured; the investors convinced that their money was still safe. And, while he was about it, he took steps to ensure that legal proceedings were started against the owners and/or operators of the *Olive Star*, whoever or wherever they might be, though Grantham was under no illusions that this course of action would produce any swift or positive results.

On the twelfth day following the *Olive Star* Incident, Grantham went underground. He wanted to see for himself what progress was being made. He had been telling the Press that the rescue operation was continuing at full speed and that the breakthrough would be achieved on schedule. He wanted to be sure that his confidence was justified.

Monique Delacourt was waiting for him at the bottom of the access shaft. An underground chamber had been created, considerably wider than the normal dimensions of the tunnel. This was where the TBM had been assembled and where the lining material and other equipment was now stored.

As he shook hands with her, Grantham thought that the Frenchwoman looked tired. He was not surprised. Tunnelling day and night without intermission was enough to tire anyone. And in this particular case, Monique Delacourt was working with the certain knowledge that a failure of any kind, whether human or mechanical, would jeopardize the lives of those still trapped underground.

"*C'est dur, hein?*" Grantham limited himself to one sympathetic comment.

Monique nodded. She was glad he understood. "*Oui, c'est un peu dur.*"

When Grantham had put on his helmet and overalls, they rode the tractor along the track into the tunnel.

"It's all electric down here," Monique explained. "This is a battery-operated vehicle. In some environments, of course, it's simply not safe to use internal combustion engines – when you're working in a coal mine for example. There, any kind of spark can set off an explosion. Here our problem isn't gases, it's ventilation. It's difficult enough keeping the air clean without having exhaust gases to deal with."

"How *do* you keep the air clean?" Grantham asked as they rode on down the track.

Monique pointed to a large duct on the roof of the tunnel.

"It's pumped in up there all the way to the face. The new, clean air arriving at the face drives the old dirty air back. We have a filter system in the chamber. Ventilation is crucial. This is a highly automated business, but you still have to have men up at the face. When the TBM is working, it's generating both heat and dust."

Monique looked at her watch. "You've come at a good moment. They'll be breaking in ten minutes. As you can imagine, we've kept maintenance to the minimum under the circumstances. But I want to have a look at the cutters today, to see how they're wearing. You can come with me if you like."

"I'd like to," Grantham replied.

They reached the face after half a mile. The drive was still in progress. Grantham and Monique Delacourt got out of the tractor, walked a few yards along the track and climbed up a steel ladder to the operator's cabin, which was set on the left-hand side of the machine.

"As I said," Monique explained, "this is a fully automated operation. The machine is being controlled from the sea-bed module, just as it was on your side of the Channel." She pointed to a red light in front of them. "That's a laser spot. If you look behind, you can see where the light's coming from."

Grantham looked back and saw what she meant. About four hundred yards behind them a thin beam of intense red light was being projected down the tunnel.

"That spot of light", Monique continued, "controls the boring direction. You change direction by shifting the rear of the machine up, down, or to one side. The movement causes a slight shift of the cutting head in the opposite direction, which results in a gentle curve and the establishment of a new heading."

"All automatic?"

"Yes. Steering is accomplished with the gripper shoes fully gripped on the tunnel wall."

She pointed to one side. Grantham saw that the grippers were hard against the tunnel wall, and that the thrust cylinders had been energized so that the machine was pushing forward off the wall.

"The cutter-head and conveyor are both running now." Monique raised her voice to be heard over the noise. "When the stroke is completed, the rear support legs are lowered, the thrust cylinders are retracted as well as the gripper assembly, and you're ready for a new boring stroke."

Grantham watched as the process Monique Delacourt had just described was carried out. He saw the grippers being eased off the wall, the hydraulic cylinders retracting and a new position being taken up. The machine operator, sitting in his cabin in front of them, checked the dials.

"It's a safety precaution." Monique pointed to the rows of green, red and yellow buttons. "Though we have the TV monitors and remote control systems for day-to-day running, it's better to have a man here in the cabin. Sometimes you can sense when things are going wrong even if you can't immediately see *why* they're going wrong."

They watched one more drive being completed and then the engines were turned off.

"We start the motors two at a time," Monique explained, "and we stop them two at a time as well. As soon as they've pulled the machine back a bit, we can go forward to the face. I'm afraid you'll have to go on all fours."

Grantham fixed the lamp to his helmet, like a miner, and followed her down to the space between the cutter-head and the motor ring. The head had been stopped so that the door, no more than two foot six high and two foot wide, which permitted access to the face, was at ground level. Monique Delacourt crawled through the opening and Grantham followed her.

The heat was intense and the air was still full of dust from the newly completed drive. Monique held her torch in her hand and allowed the beam to play on the cutter-head.

"We have sixty cutters altogether on this head," she said. "I'm not bothered about the cutters in the middle. They don't travel so far as the ones on the outside, so they don't wear so much. It's the outside cutters we have to look at."

They spent twenty minutes together in that tall narrow chamber between the cutter-head on the giant machine and the face of the tunnel. When they had finished inspecting the cutter rings, Monique shone her torch onto the chalk wall itself.

"See those smooth concentric circles," she said. "Every line is clear and sharp. That means the machine is working in a balanced way and that all the cutters are functioning."

Grantham looked at the wall as she spoke. It was a strange experience. It was as though some giant tree had been sliced to show its annual growth rings.

The dust was beginning to settle. He put his hand out and fingered the chalk. It was warm and dry.

"No water problem here," he said.

"No," replied Monique. "That's good. We're driving at such a rate that it is all we can do to get the spoil away, let alone put the linings up. Thank God we're going towards England at the moment, rather than towards France."

"Why?" There was something in her tone of voice that Grantham didn't quite like.

Monique Delacourt hesitated. Then she said, "The other TBM operating from Marchprod Two, the one driving in the direction of Calais, is running into some water problems at the moment. We're having to go fairly carefully, probing ahead as we go. Don't worry," she added as she saw Grantham's look of concern, "we're not going to make any mistakes. We can probe fifty yards ahead if we have to."

Grantham was relieved. They had enough problems at the moment without having to contemplate others.

As Monique Delacourt delayed to make a further inspection of the state of the cutters, Grantham glanced uneasily at his watch. He had a sudden sensation of claustrophobia. More than a hundred tons of steel separated them from the outside world.

"They're not going to start another driving cycle, are they?" he asked. He made it sound like a joke.

Monique Delacourt laughed. "*Nous avons encore cinq minutes.*"

"Jesus! only five minutes!" Grantham exclaimed. "I don't want to be here when they start the motors!" Without waiting for her, he ducked down and began to scramble back on all fours through the door in the cutter-head. This was one occasion when Grantham was prepared to sacrifice dignity for speed.

Amused, Monique followed him. They climbed back up to the operator's cabin. Monique handed the driver the key and he put it back in the lock on the console.

"All clear now," she said. Then she turned to Grantham, smiling: "I should have told you. One of the rules is that anyone who goes through to the face takes the key with him. It's a fail-safe system. The clutch of the TBM can't be engaged unless the key is in position."

Grantham smiled in turn. "You had me worried back there."

Howard Leeming was waiting for them in the chamber.

"Did you have a good visit?" he asked. "That's some machine, isn't it? How are the cutters standing up? Do you know we've been running day and night for twelve days now and we've only had to change half a dozen cutters? Mind you, that chalk is a tunneller's dream."

Grantham looked at the tall American. He realized that Leeming was enjoying the challenge that had been thrust on him.

"You're breaking all the records, I understand, Howard," he said. "How much further have you got to go?"

"Give me five more days," Leeming replied, "and we'll get a probe through to them."

Grantham made a rapid mental calculation. They'd spent twelve days already. Another five would bring it to seventeen. Seventeen days. It seemed impossibly long.

"Once the probe is through, can you pass supplies through the hole?" he asked.

"Of course," Howard Leeming replied. "Not a lot, but enough."

"Let me know when you make contact," said Grantham. "I want to be there."

Jean-Yves Lamonte was exhausted. He seemed to have been working, almost continuously, for over two weeks. Never in his life had he dug so far so fast. Never had he needed to dig so far so fast. He knew as well as anyone that unless they broke through within the next few days, it would be too late. The scientists, the medical men were all agreed on one thing, that after a period of about two and a half weeks, depending of course on body weights and other metabolic factors, the chances of finding anyone alive would be very slim indeed.

Tomorrow they would run the probe out to its maximum extent. If it encountered the hardened steel of the TBM, they would know just how much further they had to go. He prayed they would be successful. There were men down there, men he had worked with over the years. And there was the girl, too. He had grown to know and admire Candida Coulton. There had been a certain camaraderie on the rigs and she had been a part of it. He hoped very much that he would see Candida again – alive.

Technically speaking, Jean-Yves was off duty. The TBM had been running day and night but now, with the goal in sight, Monique Delacourt – on Leeming's advice – had ordered a short pause. At least a dozen cutter-heads had worn so badly that they would have to be replaced. There was simply nothing else for it. It would be a long and tedious business. Each cutter weighed over two hundred pounds. The bolts would have to be undone. They would have to be lowered by pulley and taken back to have the rings cut off with oxyacetylene cutters and new ones put on. Meanwhile discs would have to be brought up and put in place. At the very least, they had calculated, there would have to be a ten-hour delay.

It had been an agonizing decision for them all. They seemed so close to home. Finally both Monique Delacourt and Howard Leeming had agreed that a delay was inevitable. They would cease operations at ten p.m., then work through the night to replace the damaged cutters with the hope of resuming the drive by six o'clock the following morning.

At eight o'clock that evening, with two hours still to go before the suspension of operations, Jean-Yves, the crew-cut, bull-necked Frenchman who had been as reluctant as anyone to contemplate a break in the rhythm of the work, told the operator in the cabin that he was going forward to the face to have one last look at the cutter-head and the state of the cutters.

"I've got an idea," he said. "We may be able to switch some of the cutters round; put the inside ones on the outside and vice-versa, if you see what I mean. The inside ones are hardly worn. That way, we could save some time. We wouldn't have to bring up new cutters."

The operator, who had had a long day, waved him on. "*Allez-y*," he said. As far as he was concerned, he was going off duty anyway. Another operator would be taking over for the last two-hour shift.

Jean-Yves scrambled down the ladder, then dropped on all fours to crawl through the hole towards the cutting face. The operator had pulled the TBM back a foot or so from the face, so that Jean-Yves would have room to inspect. But it was still a narrow squeeze. The Frenchman straightened as he came through the hole, took out his torch and began his inspection.

At precisely ten minutes past eight, the operator left his seat, climbed down the ladder and began to walk back along the tunnel towards the tractor, without noticing that the fail-safe key was still in its place on the console.

He had to wait a minute or two for the tractor to arrive with his replacement. The two men exchanged brief greetings.

"Jean-Yves is at the face," the first man told the second man.

The second man looked at his watch. "Has he got the key?" he asked.

"Of course." The first man replied. "Do you think that Jean-Yves would make a mistake like that?" he laughed.

As planned, the last drive began at precisely eight p.m. The automatic control sequence took over. The two-hundred horse-power electric motors were started, pair by pair, till all twelve were functioning.

Seconds later the clutch was engaged and the cutting-head began to turn. As it turned, the hydraulic jacks thrust the giant machine forward against the chalk face.

Jean-Yves heard the electric motors start. Instinctively, he patted his pocket to verify that he still had with him the fail-safe key which meant that the clutch between the motors and the cutter-head could not be engaged. It took him a split-second to realize that, for once in a lifetime, and probably because of the overwhelming tiredness which had assailed him after a fortnight of non-stop activity, he had failed to take the elementary precaution of removing the key from the console.

Jean-Yves dived for the hole at the base of the cutter-head, but it was already too late. The head had begun to turn, slowly at first, and the hole was not where Jean-Yves thought it was. Screaming now with fear, he tried to scramble up the turning cutter-head, following the hole as it rose.

Thirty feet from the face, the hydraulic jacks pushed the cutter-head forward with a thrust of almost two million pounds. Jean-Yves' scream died almost as soon as it was born. As the cutter-head reached its maximum rotating speed, his blood and bones mingled with the chalk.

Candida Coulton knew she was going to die. Like the others, she had been seventeen days without food – except for a bar of chocolate which someone had shared out right at the beginning. For the last week they had been without lights as, one after another, the batteries on their miners' helmets had failed. And now they were virtually without water as well. The supply of distilled water which they had found in the chamber (to be used for the batteries of the electric-drive tractor which went up and down the rails between the chamber and the face) was almost exhausted. There was maybe a pint or two left to share between the four of them. The worst thing of all had been the lack of any communication with the outside world. That there had been some major accident, resulting in the interruption of all power supplies and all other lines of contact between the sea-bed module and the underground workings, was evident. But what kind of an accident, none of them knew. As the days passed, and the access shaft remained totally sealed, they began to lose hope.

The four of them spent their time huddled together in the chamber beneath the shaft. If they were to be rescued, that was the obvious place to wait. Two of them were young Frenchmen, TBM operators who were changing shift when the accident happened. The third was a Scot, an engineer who had been on duty in the chamber supervising the evacuation of waste as the conveyor belt which brought the rubble back from the face automatically tipped it into buckets to be carried up through the shaft to the surface.

During the first days of their entombment, they had talked a good deal, as much to keep up their spirits as anything else. Latterly, they had grown increasingly silent. There seemed to be nothing more to say. Nothing to do except wait for the end. The two Frenchmen spent much of their time lying on their backs, apparently asleep. The Scotsman managed to mark out a solitaire board on the tunnel floor, collected a supply of pebbles and small pieces of rock and played endless games. Even when the light failed, he continued to play, feeling for the pieces with his hands.

Candida Coulton was probably the best equipped of all them to deal with the situation. She was a mathematician by training and, as such, was able to fill her mind with abstruse theorems and problems which she had previously been unable to solve.

On the morning of the seventeenth day, speaking slowly and faintly, she said to the Scotsman:

"Do you think they've given up on us, Ken?"

"Dinna fear, lass," the man replied. "We can last a wee while yet."

Candida sat there in the darkness thinking about Michael Prestwick. She had grown close to him over these last few months. Was he still on the rig? she wondered. For the thousandth time she found herself speculating about the reasons for their present predicament.

An idea occurred to her. She touched her companion's arm urgently.

"Ken, do you think they could possibly be trying to reach us from the other side?"

"What d'ya mean, lass?"

"I mean, could they possibly be using one of the TBMs *from the other rig* to bore in our direction? Maybe they're trying to break through to us that way?" For the first time in several days Candida Coulton felt a faint flicker of hope.

In the darkness, the Scotsman shook his head. "They'd never reach us in time."

Candida was not to be deterred. She stood up.

"I'm going to go down to the end to have a look."

They didn't try to stop her. Captain Scott had not tried to stop Oates when he walked out into the blizzard.

When she started to walk, Candida Coulton realized how weak she was. Once or twice, her legs buckled and she had to steady herself against the wall. She kept her direction by running her fingers along the concrete lining, knowing that when the lining gave out she would be near the face. Though the distance to be covered was not more than two and a half miles, it took her over three hours to reach the end. Sometimes, as she persevered in the darkness, she thought of going back but then she asked herself, going back to what? When she reached the end of the lined section, she knew she was not more than thirty yards behind the TBM. She walked even more carefully now. She had no wish to collide with the back of the machine. When, a minute or two later, she felt the huge bulk of the TBM in front of her, she squeezed tight up against he left-hand wall of the tunnel, so as to keep between the machine and the wall. Another fifty yards and she was at the head of the machine, standing behind the electric-drive motors.

She stood there, exhausted by the effort. She was feeling faint and there was a buzzing sound in her ears. She shook her head to clear the noise, but it persisted. Because her faculties were dimmed with hunger, it took Candida Coulton several minutes to realize that the buzzing came from an external not an internal source.

She broke down and cried when she realized that it was the sound of a drill. Her tears were tears of joy.

Candida Coulton got down on her hands and knees and crawled through the opening towards the cutter-face. As far as she remembered, the French engineers had told her that the TBM had just completed a drive when the power supply failed. That meant the cutter-head would be jammed right up against the chalk. If the drill broke through, it would run on to the hard surface of the TBM and the people who were guiding the drill from the other side would know what to conclude. Alternatively, there was a chance, a slim chance, that the drill would actually hit the little opening which permitted the engineers to crawl through from the rear to the front of the machine.

She had kept back a torch to be used in just such a case as this. She knew it only had a few minutes of life left in its battery, which was the reason she had not turned it on during the long walk up the tunnel. But she did so now.

The noise of the drilling increased. Candida Coulton crouched behind the doorway, keeping her body well to one side, in case the drill suddenly lunged through.

When, finally, the slim probe slipped through the opening in front of her, she was crying so much that she could hardly see what was happening.

As soon as it had pierced the wall, the drill stopped turning. Candida shone the torch. She pulled a small metal spanner from her pocket and tapped the end of the probe. Three shorts followed by three longs, followed by three shorts. S.O.S. Then she put her ear to the metal and listened. The response came immediately.

Seconds later, the probe was withdrawn. Candida Coulton sat waiting. Silence had once more descended on the tunnel. If it had not been for the pile of chalk on the floor in front of her, where the drill had broken through, she might have dreamt it all.

She waited ten minutes, twenty minutes in a daze. Nothing happened. She sat in darkness now. There was no point in wasting what was left of the battery. After thirty minutes, her elation was beginning to turn into despair. Perhaps they had not heard her signal. Perhaps she had imagined the response.

Then she heard another noise, not a drill this time, but a noise of something being pushed through the hole which the drill had left. She flicked on the torch and put out her hand to feel the edge of a long metal cannister extruding from the hole. She guided it out, unscrewed the top, removed the contents as a child might empty a Christmas stocking. There was a torch, there was a radio, there was food in the form of chocolate, there was a bottle of glucose. Wrapped round the bottle was a note which said: "Just press the button on the radio to transmit. You're already tuned to the right frequency."

With trembling hands, Candida Coulton picked up the radio and pressed the transmit button.

"This is Candida Coulton," she said. "Can anyone hear me?"

Fifty yards away, Donald Coulton who normally thought of himself as a strong, silent man, and was so considered by others, burst into tears as he heard his daughter's voice. He wanted to say something but he couldn't. He was too overwhelmed.

It was Howard Leeming who spoke for them all.

"Just hang in there, Candida," he said. "We'll be right there."

Over the RT, Candida Coulton told them that she was going back down the tunnel – with food and light for her colleagues. They did not try to dissuade her.

She kept in touch with them as she walked back down the tunnel faster this time. Nothing, she thought, was more debilitating than despair; nothing more energizing than hope.

At one point, she asked if Michael Prestwick was there. He was. He came on the air.

"I'm sorry it took so long, Candida," he said. "Your father's here, you know."

"I love you both," Candida replied. "Tell him."

Michael Prestwick didn't need to convey the message to Lord Coulton. They had all heard it – Grantham, Monique Delacourt, Donald Coulton, as well as the drill operators.

Grantham turned to Coulton, wiping his eyes with the back of his hand.

"That's some daughter you've got there, Donald," he said. "I'm not surprised she beat me at tennis."

Donald Coulton laughed. Or at least he meant to laugh. But the sound that finally emerged from his throat sounded more like a croak of joy and relief.

32

"I cannot tell you how sorry I am, madame. You must believe me." Grantham spread his hands wide. "It was an accident which no one could have foreseen, a piece of monstrous bad luck. Your husband forgot to take the fail-safe key with him and just at the moment that he was inspecting the cutter-heads, there was a change of operators. Otherwise there would have been a man in the cabin who would have prevented the tragedy." He put out his hand and touched the woman on the shoulder. "He was a brave man, was Jean-Yves, you should know that. One of the bravest I have met."

During his long career as a soldier, Grantham had learned that he who bears bad tidings must also be prepared to play the part of comforter. On at least half a dozen occasions, he had had personally to bring news of a man's death to his next of kin. It was a task he hated.

But at least in wartime, the conventions were already established. He, as a commanding officer, knew what to say; they, the bereaved, knew what to expect. Today it was different. There was, first of all, the barrier of language. Grantham's French was serviceable, but it was not capable of conveying the nuances of sorrow. Then, there were the actual circumstances of Jean-Yves' death. Mercifully, Madame Lamonte didn't ask him for details about what had happened to the body. She seemed content with Grantham's prevarications on that score. It was almost as if she knew, without having to be told, that her husband had been ground to pieces against the chalk.

Grantham stayed a good hour in the woman's apartment in the suburbs of Paris near Neuilly. He told her, as gently as he could, that though nothing could of course replace the tough bull-necked Frenchman whom she had leant on for the last eighteen years, nevertheless – in strictly financial terms – she would be well taken care of.

What made the interview even more poignant, from Grantham's point of view, was that – apart from the tragedy of Jean-Yves' death – all was well that had ended well. Six hours after the probe had first pierced through the chalk into the half-built tunnel where Candida Coulton and her colleagues were trapped, the giant tunnel-boring machine had blasted its way through, breaking all its own records as it did so. The two giant machines had come face to face at virtually the mid-point of the Channel. After that, it had been plain sailing. While medical teams stood by, the trapped party had crawled out to be treated like heroes. That Jean-Yves, who had done so much to make it possible, should not have been on hand to participate in the welcome seemed ironic in the extreme.

Finally, when he had said all that there was to say, Grantham stood up to leave. This was the moment, he knew, for relatives and friends to take over, for grief to be shared. The woman, who showed no sign of bitterness, showed him to the door. Even at this low point in her life, she was able to muster a certain rugged courtesy.

"*Merci, monsieur. Mon mari a beaucoup parlé de vous.*"

Grantham climbed back down the stairs and into the street wondering whether Jean-Yves had spoken well or ill.

He made a detour on his way back into the centre of Paris. It was only a short detour. Consulting his map, Grantham realized that Thomé de Gamond's house, now a museum, in Neuilly was only a mile or so from the flat where Madame Lamonte lived.

He pulled up outside the building and rang the bell. A curtain moved behind the window but no one came to the door. Grantham rang again. After about two minutes, he heard slow, shuffling footsteps on the other side of the door; then the bolt was drawn back. The concierge frowned at him. Grantham was his most charming self.

"I'm just passing by. I'm most interested in Thomé de Gamond. Do you think I could visit the museum, if it's not too much trouble?"

The old lady wanted to be able to say that it was already five o'clock and the museum was shut for the day. But it wasn't five o'clock and Grantham was insistent, as well as charming; so, grumbling, she let him in.

The concierge stayed with him as he walked round the little stuffy overheated room which housed Thomé de Gamond's collection of fossils. She watched him carefully as he moved from case to case.

"Don't worry about me," Grantham called out cheerfully. "I'm not going to steal anything. I'll let you know when I come down."

But the old lady stayed obstinately where she was.

"The last time I let visitors stay by themselves in the room," she complained, "they stole some of my best pieces. Look." She pointed to a glass case which, unlike the others, was virtually empty of specimens. "Do you see what I mean?"

Grantham walked over and examined the case. The labels were still there, where the fossils had been, carefully stuck to the green baize cloth on which the fossils had been displayed.

"They must have opened the door of the case and taken the fossils away with them," the old lady continued querulously. "I wonder why they wanted those specimens and not the others."

Grantham, who had been listening with only half an ear, was suddenly alert to what the old lady was saying. "Do you remember what they were like, these people?" he asked.

The concierge nodded vigorously. "Of course I do. They were foreigners." She spat out the word in disgust. "One of them came first, early in the morning. A small, elderly man with white hair, if I remember correctly."

Grantham tried to keep calm. After all, there could still be some simple explanation. He went back to the case and studied the labels more carefully. One label, larger than the rest, gave a general description of the contents of the case. It read: "Foraminiferida found two miles west of Sangatte. The individual labels give more precise locations for each particular find."

Still trying to keep calm, Grantham interrogated the old lady.

"Probably you've forgotten by now," he began, "but can you possibly remember what they looked like, these fossils which are no longer here? What shape did they have?"

Not for nothing had the old concierge tended Thomé de Gamond's collection of fossils lovingly for the last forty years. They were her children, those rough stones and rocks. She knew them as well as she knew the pots and pans in her kitchen.

"Of course I remember," she said with scorn. "They all had circular shapes of one kind or another, interlocking circles, like this."

With the gnarled forefinger of one hand, she drew a pattern in the thick dust which covered the top of a bookcase.

"Sometimes, you know, I used to act as a guide myself," the concierge said. "That was before my feet started to give me trouble."

She seemed to be dragging up from the distant recesses of her memory something which she had once learned parrot-fashion.

"Thomé de Gamond believed that fossils were an accurate indicator of different geological periods of time. In the case of the sea-bed under the Channel – la Manche – he used fossil evidence to distinguish three different geological layers – one clay layer and two chalk layers."

The old woman paused. It was a long time since she had given this particular lecture. Over the years, interest in Thomé de Gamond had dwindled and now only a trickle of people passed through the museum. With an effort, the woman dredged up the facts she was looking for. She pointed to a nearby glass case, still full of specimens.

"These are fossils from the clay," she said. "Most of Thomé de Gamond's collection was like this. See." She pointed to the tiny pieces of rock on the shelves.

Grantham looked at the long spindly shapes, with a few conical forms thrown in. He nodded.

"The clay is nearest the surface," the concierge said. "Thomé de Gamond was diving and picking up what he could find on the sea-bed. You would expect most of the fossils to come from the clay."

The concierge moved on the next case. "But some of his fossils came also from the Middle Chalk. Not so many, of course."

Again Grantham nodded. It made sense. There were certainly places on the sea-bed where the Middle Chalk came near the surface. That was something they had always known.

Finally, she came to the now empty case. "*Ah, oui. Je me souviens maintenant.* I remember now. This was a very special collection. Thomé de Gamond was diving quite near the French coast, just a mile or two north-west of Sangatte, bringing up samples. All the samples in that case, all the samples which have been stolen, *hélas*, came from the *Lower* Chalk."

"Are you quite sure?" Grantham asked. For the first time since he had started work on the tunnel project, he had a sense that things were about to go wrong, totally and irretrievably wrong.

The concierge looked at him in surprise. "*Oui, monsieur*, of course I am sure. That is my job."

Grantham pressed a two-hundred franc note in her hand and ran for the door.

Outside, he gunned the motor of his Citroen DS into life and pulled out into the evening stream of traffic. As he drove, weaving in and out, he cursed Professor Finzi under his breath. What was the man playing at? How could he conceal evidence like that? Was it pride or stubbornness or a mixture of both? If Finzi had discovered the flaw, the place where the Lower Chalk poked through to the surface, why had he said nothing? Had Dummett been right after all?

He pulled on to the *périphérique* heading north. He reckoned he could be in Calais in just over two hours. Perhaps there would still be time.

The *périphérique* was lined with huge posters of the Presidential candidates. Pierre Leroux, who had come through the first round with a commanding lead, smiled down smugly on his inheritance. The Socialist Party posters were well-positioned and clearly illuminated. By contrast, Jacques Chirac's campaign seemed to have slipped into the doldrums. One Chirac billboard had partially come off its mounting, so that the Gaullist's head engaged the passing motorist at a crazy angle.

That Leroux was going to coast through to victory on the second round, Grantham did not doubt. Incredibly, the French still had a love affair with socialism. They might complain about the nationalization of the banks, about the rate of inflation, about the restrictions on foreign travel, about the burgeoning of the welfare services; but they were not yet prepared to face up to the truth. Leroux had campaigned skilfully, and with great charm. He had traded on his charisma, on his Kennedy-type image. And he had got away with it. Grantham doubted whether, even if the French public had known what he knew about Leroux, it would have made that much difference. In some strange way, Leroux had mesmerized the electorate. Anyone who promoted the idea that Leroux was, in reality, nothing more than a Russian agent, would have been laughed out of court. His story would have been accounted a deliberate attempt at misrepresentation, a fabrication, a direct smear. Leroux would probably have emerged the stronger for it.

Swinging off the *périphérique* and heading north, Grantham tried to raise Professor Giuseppe Finzi on the radio-telephone in the car. Twice he found that the lines to Italy were busy; but on the third attempt he got through.

With controlled fury, he asked the Professor: "Why did you take the specimens away, Finzi?"

"What specimens?" For a moment, Professor Finzi, still bleary-eyed from his afternoon siesta, tried to bluster his way out.

"Don't prevaricate!" Grantham snapped. "I've been to the museum! I know."

As best he could, Professor Finzi tried to explain.

"I knew I was right, you see," he told Grantham. "The fossils Thomé de Gamond found meant nothing. They could simply have been a geological freak. To my mind, they certainly didn't prove that our line was faulty."

"Then why did you remove them?"

"Because the doubting Thomases might have used them to justify delay; they might have demanded that we rethink our route. But I *knew* our route was correct. So I acted responsibly. By removing the fossils, I removed the danger that someone might challenge us later on."

Grantham felt some of his fury subside. The needle of the speedometer was hovering around the 160 kmh mark. He eased the speed back a little.

"By God, Professor," he said, "I hope you're right."

Monique Delacourt had decided to christen all the TBMs. TBM number five, which was the machine driving from Marchprod Two in the direction of Calais, she had called Alphonse. It was a name which seemed to suit that particular TBM's personality.

As Grantham was speeding from Paris to Calais, Alphonse was heading on a very slight uphill trajectory towards the French coast. Only a mile, just one mile, remained before Alphonse would join up with Louise, TBM number six, driving seaward from Sangatte. Now that the disaster of the *Olive Star* was behind them, there was a sense of elation in the air. The tunnel had been dug in record time. No other civil engineering project of comparable magnitude, if indeed there *was* a project of comparable magnitude, had been completed with such dispatch. What they had achieved, Monique Delacourt sometimes told her colleagues, was like the Egyptians building the Pyramids in a couple of weeks.

The sense of elation was not only felt on the rig itself; it was sensed underground as well. The engineers, the technicians, the computer men and women, were all of them waiting for the moment of breakthrough.

They knew they were cutting corners the last couple of days. They knew, for example, that they were driving ahead, anxious to cover the short distance that remained, while allowing the lining operation to fall behind. In fact, some twenty yards of unlined tunnel had opened up behind the TBM. It was a logistical problem, as much as anything else. Alphonse was driving ahead so fast on his final burst, that the concrete segments which made up the lining simply were not being put into place in time.

Monique Delacourt, visiting the underground operation at the beginning of the evening shift, saw what was happening and immediately gave the order for the drive to be halted while the lining was completed. At the same time she exploded in a rage at her deputies who had allowed the situation to develop.

"How can I be in six places at once?" she railed.

It was a classic error, the kind of mistake tunnelling text books were full of. That the error could *au fond* be ascribed to enthusiasm, to an eagerness to complete the job, did not make it any the more excusable. They had left themselves in an "uncovered" position, like a foolhardy foreign exchange dealer on a weekend when anything could happen in the market.

With Alphonse silenced, Monique embarked on a detailed inspection of the tunnel roof and walls. She was standing there, shining her torch at the ceiling high above her, when the weight of the water which had accumulated in a pocket in the chalk caused the rock to give.

The water, half a ton of it, hit her full in the face, drenching her from head to foot and knocking her to the ground.

The automatic alarm system was instantaneously activated. The warning hooters sounded.

As the water kept coming, Monique Delacourt called for pumps. Pumps and more pumps. In her bones, she feared the worst. Somehow, they had come too close to the top of the layer of Lower Chalk, instead of keeping in the middle of it. Up above was the greensand. And no one in his right mind would try to drive a tunnel through the greensand.

By the time Grantham arrived underground, too late to prevent the cave-in but in time to help mitigate its effects, an element of order had been restored. The water was still pouring from the roof of the tunnel at a steady rate but the pumps were more or less keeping pace with it.

All tunnelling had, of course, stopped. The giant TBM was silent. The conveyor belt carrying the chalk back to the chamber and thence to the surface had ceased running.

Monique Delacourt greeted Grantham with a look of despair on her face.

"It's bad news, Oliver. The worst news we could have. We're running into the greensand. The Lower Chalk layer is thinning out. We don't have the margin of safety we need."

Monique told him that she had ordered tunnelling to cease on this section of the tunnel.

"We can't tell at the moment how far the problem lasts. In a way, we were lucky we had the water-burst here to warn us. If the TBM had gone driving ahead into the greensand, the whole tunnel could have collapsed and that might have been the end of it. I've seen tunnels before in my time which have had to be abandoned."

"Jesus!" Grantham whistled under his breath.

Then he told her about Finzi. "I've told him he's fired as of now," Grantham said. "I don't understand what he was playing at."

"I do," Monique Delacourt said, after she had taken it all in.

"Professional pride. I've seen it a hundred times. Finzi didn't want to believe he *could* be wrong. He probably thought that if the board knew what he knew, they'd have second thoughts about the route and then the whole project would be delayed. He didn't think that was justified. Perhaps he was right."

"What do you mean?" Grantham asked.

"The greensand is not a problem *once the tunnel is dug*," Monique Delacourt said. "It's digging it that's difficult. Once you've got the tunnel in place, and properly lined, it can withstand any water pressure. After all, one of the schemes was simply to lay a submerged tube on the sea-bed, you remember."

Grantham nodded. "What can you do?" he asked.

Monique Delacourt stared up towards the roof of the tunnel where the water was still streaming through.

"Basically, we've got two options. One is compressed air working. You tunnel under pressure and the pressure holds the walls in shape until you can get the linings in. It's a pretty uncomfortable system for anyone who has to be at the face, but it works. You grout as you go. By that, I mean you treat the ground with injections of cement or chemicals to reduce the permeability."

"What is the other option?"

"Freezing," Monique replied. "They used freezing techniques for difficult parts of the underground system in London, as well as in Leningrad, Tokyo and Helsinki. They also used it for sewer tunnelling in New York City and for railway tunnels in Italy. The effectiveness of freezing depends, of course, on the presence of water to create ice." She gave a short ironic laugh. "We seem to have enough water anyway."

"What would you use for freezing?"

"Liquid nitrogen," Monique Delacourt replied without hesitation. "You discharge the nitrogen directly through tubes driven into the ground being treated. It's much quicker than other methods and the effect will last for about three weeks, which should be enough for us. Of course, it's complicated technically. You've got ventilation problems and getting the pipes in ahead of the face can be a difficult business. You've got to freeze and drive alternately and that can make progress slow. And, of course, the consequences of failing to maintain the freeze until the permanent lining is complete can be very serious."

Grantham realized that from a technical point of view he was getting out of his depth.

He interrupted her, held her eyes with his, pressed her for a simple answer. "The question I really want to know, Monique, is can we do it, or can't we?"

She paused before replying. She seemed suddenly defeated. There were tears in her eyes. They had come so far, so fast. And now this had to happen.

"Of course, it can be done," she replied at last, "if we're lucky. If we've only a mile to go, we can manage that. The real problem, Oliver, won't be technical."

"What will it be?"

"Money," Monique Delacourt replied. "Getting out of here could cost an extra two hundred million pounds. The question is: do we have that kind of money?"

Monique Delacourt's words stunned Grantham. If anyone knew the books, he knew them. He knew how finely their finances had been run, how little the contingency reserve was. In fact, there wasn't a contingency reserve. It was as simple as that.

"No," he replied quietly. He shook his head. "I'm afraid we don't have that kind of money."

33

It was the first time he had seen her in person. He had never realized how lovely she was.

He had given the chauffeur the day off and had gone to meet her at the airport. She had been reserved at first, sitting stiffly in the front seat of the Rolls and staring straight ahead. It was only when Grantham told her that he would take her to Ascot if she could stay until Saturday, that Iona Karapolitis began to relax and enjoy herself.

"I'd love that," she said. "It's years since I've been to Ascot."

And then, suddenly, she started talking about her life in London.

"I was at school in England, you know," she said.

"I know," Grantham replied. "You were at St Paul's, weren't you? Do you want to see the old place?"

He turned off at the Hammersmith roundabout, drove a few hundred yards in the direction of Shepherd's Bush and then swung right into Brook Green.

He brought the car to a halt outside the school gates and switched the engine off. The girls were just leaving school for the day. They streamed out of the school gates in groups of twos and threes, heading for home.

Iona sat there watching. She seemed sunk in thought. Grantham himself remained silent. He didn't want to interrupt. He had planned this little détour long ago and he didn't want to spoil its effect by an ill-considered remark.

After a while, Iona turned to him and said in a quiet, subdued voice: "Can we go now?"

They went to the office in Victoria Street. Sandra Furlong was still there holding the fort. She seemed to be dazzled by the Greek girl's beauty, helped her off with her coat, fussed about asking her whether she wanted anything after her journey. She brought them both cups of tea while they talked.

Grantham was amused. He had expected a different reaction altogether. He had imagined that Sandra might resent his sudden capitulation.

He came straight to the point. "I asked you to come here," he began, "because I think it's time we called a truce. I don't consider that I started this particular war but, in any event, I'd like to see it over."

Iona Karapolitis smiled sweetly at him. "Oh, but you did start it, you know! Building the Tunnel is an act of war at least as far as the ferry-operators are concerned."

Grantham laughed. "I suppose it all depends on your point of view! Let me put it another way. Since this project began you and your team have tried to blackmail me; you have tried to gain control of the old Channel Tunnel Company and thereby prevent the operation from going ahead; you've been responsible for a direct attack on my own life; finally, I am perfectly sure that the incident with the tanker in the Channel which almost resulted in a massive disaster was by no means an accident."

Iona looked at him even more sweetly than she had before, if that were possible.

"And now, I suppose, we are responsible for your latest problems as well. Professor Dummett was right, after all, wasn't he?"

"Ah, yes!" said Grantham, "you were behind the Dummett business too. I didn't mention that."

"Pehaps you should have taken Dummett seriously; then you wouldn't be in such trouble now!"

Grantham realized that the interview was not going exactly to plan.

"That's all past history," he said sharply. "I'm prepared to let bygones be bygones. I'm ready to drop all proceedings, stop the law suit, call off the dogs. But only on one condition."

"And what is that?"

Grantham took his time before replying. It was important to get the presentation right. Iona Karapolitis might guess that the Consortium was in trouble, but she must never know how desperate the situation was. Whatever the reality might be, he knew that he had to give the impression that he was bargaining from strength – offering something, rather than asking or begging for it. The fact that she had decided to come to London at all, in response to his telephone call, was already an indication that he had pitched it about right. But it was important not to spoil things now. Grantham looked at the young woman who sat opposite him. She held his gaze with hers.

"And what is your condition?" she repeated.

"That we join forces – that is my condition. I am proposing that Channel Ferries merge with Chunnel Consortium, that we stop this crazy competition and realize that there is more than enough room for all forms of transport provided we don't spend our time trying to cut each other's throats rather than developing the business the way it should be developed."

He could see that he had her full attention. He was not talking sentiment; he was talking business. And business was something that Iona Karapolitis could understand.

"The demand is there," Grantham continued. "It just needs to be exploited in an intelligent way. We will get the Tunnel built, be sure of that. We will get it built on time. And then what will happen? We will start undercutting the Channel Ferry operation. We will destroy your market, that's what you always feared, wasn't it?"

Iona nodded. "But we would fight back," she said. "We know how to cut fares too."

"Exactly," Grantham agreed. "That is precisely what would happen. Fares would spiral downwards as we each tried to undercut the other. And in the end one or both of us would go bankrupt, which would be to nobody's advantage, least of all the travelling public's. At least if we join forces, we can plan a sound strategy using each mode of transport to the best effect. There will always be people who want to go by boat; there will be people who want to go by train. We could call our merged companies Channel Transport or something like that, and cater for everyone. What do you think?"

It was Iona's turn for reflection. She knew that what Grantham said made sense. She knew that she and her father, egged on by Staples, had been fighting a crazy battle. It was time to bring it to an end. But she also knew that this was too big a decision for her to take all alone. She would have to have time to consult her father. And he in turn would have to get the lawyers to look at it.

"I shall need some time," she said. "Can you give me till this evening?" And then she added, hitting the nail right on the head, "I take it any merger will involve an immediate injection of cash?"

Grantham couldn't help admiring her astuteness. He gave a light shrug of his shoulders as though cash, readily bankable, was the least of his problems.

"I think we could settle for, say, two hundred million pounds as a first down payment in exchange for the initial package of shares. Of course our people would have to sit down and work out the details. It's the principle I'm concerned about now. Could we find some acceptable way of merging our interests?"

Grantham knew it was important not to push too hard too quickly. Like deflowering a virgin.

"Take your time," he advised her. "We've booked you in for the week at Claridge's anyway." Then, tongue in cheek, he added, "we asked them to give you the same room."

Iona didn't rise to the bait. "Same room as what?"

"The same room as you had last time."

"I was never there last time, Mr Grantham."

There was just the faintest trace of a smile on Iona Karapolitis's lips as she spoke.

He sent the car for her before dinner.

"James will pick you up around seven at the hotel," he had told her. "Perhaps we could have a drink at my place before we go out."

Of course she was late. It was past eight o'clock before the door bell rang. Grantham opened it himself and took her upstairs to the first floor sitting-room. Iona Karapolitis looked about appreciatively.

"I used to love London," she said. "It has style."

"Parts of it do," Grantham agreed. "This is one of them."

She was wearing a soft black dress which subtly set off the colour of her skin. Around her neck hung one simple string of diamonds, simple – Grantham thought – if half a million dollars worth of jewels could be called simple.

She smiled at him. "Is the war over? Or is this merely a truce?"

Grantham smiled back. He had only one more card to play and he played it.

He led her deliberately towards the drinks table which he had set up to one side of the fireplace. There was no way she could avoid seeing the photograph. He had been counting on that.

As he turned to ask her what she would have to drink, he saw that she had gone white beneath her habitual tan and looked as though she was about to faint.

"Yes," Grantham said softly. "It *is* Tommy. I thought you ought to know. He often spoke about you. Tommy was my favourite nephew."

She sat down on the sofa and passed her hand across her brow. She seemed bewildered, lost. It was as though the carapace had been suddenly removed, revealing the vulnerable, timid girl behind it.

"It's been such a long time," she said. "Hardly a day passes but I think of him. Of course, I knew about his uncle Oliver, his famous uncle, the military man whom Tommy so much admired. I never knew it was you."

Grantham sat down next to her.

"Perhaps I should have made contact with you before, after Tommy died. But I was abroad at the time, as you know. And then, when I came out of the army, I went straight into this job and there you were working for the opposition, if I may put it like that."

"Why did he do it?" she asked simply. "Did you ever find out? They would never tell me anything at school. I suppose they thought I was too young. And then my parents came and whisked me back to Greece. Was it drugs?"

Grantham took her hand. "No, of course it wasn't drugs. Tommy wasn't that kind of man. He loved sport, he loved travel, he loved life – I suppose you could say. Six months before his death, he learned he had leukaemia. His mother told me. He decided to deal with it in his own way."

She burst into tears then, clutched at him for support.

"I loved him so much," she sobbed. "I've never loved anyone since. Not properly."

Grantham let her cry. If the tears did not come now, they never would.

When she had pulled herself together, she said: "I think I'd better go now. Can we talk in the morning?"

Grantham came back with her to the hotel. He passed her over gently, almost possessively, into the care of the doorman.

"Call me in the morning as soon as you feel like it."

"I will."

To his surprise, she kissed him quickly on the mouth.

She rang bright and early the following morning.

"I want to see you, Oliver," she said.

It was the first time she had called him Oliver. Grantham considered it a favourable omen.

He went round to Claridge's and they had coffee in the lounge.

"After I left you," she said. "I was on the telephone most of the evening. We're going to agree to your offer. The money is on its way."

Grantham heaved a sigh of relief. If the merger idea had been rejected, he would not have known where else to turn. Out there, under the sea, they were holding their own against the water. But without additional funds, the project could never have been completed. It was as tight as that.

Grantham laughed. "The lawyers are going to have a field day with this one. Am I still to be president? What about Brian Staples?"

"Staples is out," Iona replied firmly. "We think it's time Sir David Blakely retired too. He's got too many other interests to give his full attention to our operation. We need a chairman who's prepared to turn this joint enterprise into the biggest transport activity in history."

"Who are you thinking of?" Grantham asked, puzzled.

Iona Karapolitis put her coffee cup down. "You're the only man who can do it," she said, looking straight at him. "We want you to be chairman and managing director of the whole thing. In fact, it's one of the conditions we're going to make in accepting the merger."

"Just because I was Tommy's favourite uncle?" Grantham asked quietly.

She hesitated before answering, lowering her eyes.

"Yes, I admit that had something to do with it. We Greeks have a way of paying our debts." Then she brought her gaze level with his. "But, quite apart from that, you are the best man for the job. The only man."

Grantham was overwhelmed.

"I don't think you will have any trouble with the Chunnel Consortium board," he said at last.

"Do they have any choice?" Iona asked. She spoke with an air of sweet innocence.

The rest of the week passed in a flourish of activity. An emergency meeting of the Chunnel Consortium board was held at which the merger terms were agreed. Sir David Blakely, recognizing the inevitable, bowed gracefully out. He didn't show how much it hurt.

Grantham looked at his old friend. He and Blakely had known each other man and boy. He thought back to the time they had played cricket together at Lords in the Eton and Harrow match. A good captain knew when to declare. Blakely had always been a good captain.

"Thanks, David. You know how much I owe to you, don't you?"

"My dear fellow, it is I who should be grateful to you. Lydia is always pressing me to spend more time in Tuscany. Now I shall be able to." Sir David Blakely had held out his hand to his successor and then, looking a trifle old and stooped, had walked from the room.

During the course of that busy week, Grantham had visited the diggings twice. He had been pleased to see that the massive operation of freezing the underground strata through the injection of liquid nitrogen was well under way. Monique Delacourt and her team of engineers from Falaise were on permanent shift underground and there was no need for him to intervene.

"Give us a month," Monique Delacourt had told him, "and we will have broken the back of this problem."

Barely half a mile separated the two giant machines. The moment of breakthrough, the moment all tunnellers waited for, could not be long delayed.

The weather that week in London was brilliantly clear and warm. Iona Karapolitis, ensconced in her suite at Claridge's, felt at home from home. This was the London she knew and loved. The London of deckchairs in St James's Park, of boating on the Serpentine, of girls in summer dresses walking down Bond Street on their way to lunch.

She felt happy and she knew that one of the reasons she felt happy was Grantham. He was over twenty years older than she was. He was Tommy's uncle. But none of that mattered. When she thought about it, Iona realized that she had been ready for a long time to fall in love with Oliver Grantham. As an adolescent, a school girl at St Paul's, she had heard so much about Uncle Oliver. He had been a kind of mythological figure in Tommy's background. Now the myth had become the reality and it was more potent than ever.

Iona was a direct, straightforward girl. That was one of the reasons she had gone as far as she had. She knew what she wanted and she went after it.

She went after Grantham. When he came back to London after his visit to the tunnel, she gave him dinner at her hotel.

"It's my turn," she said.

"It's nobody's turn," Grantham had replied laughingly. "The chief executives of the newly formed Channel Transport Company are having dinner together, that's all."

Half-way through dinner, she had told him what she felt.

"I can't do anything about it," she said. "I know what I feel. It's the way it is."

She had taken his hand as she sat across the table from him.

"I've fallen in love with you," she said simply. "*Un coup de foudre* as the French would say."

Grantham tried to laugh it off. "I'm old enough to be your father."

That made her cross.

"So what? I've slept with plenty of older men. You look younger and fitter than most people half your age."

Grantham sighed. He didn't want to go down this road. Not at all.

She took him upstairs after dinner. The champagne was already waiting in a silver ice-bucket. She rang for a man to come and open it. There was no point in staying in Claridge's if you couldn't ring for people.

When the man had gone, Iona raised her glass. "You look like him, you know."

Grantham knew that he deserved everything he got. He had after all, in a deliberately cynical way, played the 'Tommy' card in the hope of sweetening the merger prospect in Iona's eyes. And it had worked. But he didn't want her to identify him too much with his nephew. That wouldn't be fair on any of them.

"I'm not dead yet, Iona," he said gently.

She took the point. "I'm sorry."

The tears streamed down her face and Grantham took her in his arms. What else was a man to do when a girl was crying?

She clung to him, pressed her body against his. He was taller than she was. He held her against his chest, one hand cupped behind her head. Her hair smelt as sweet as new-mown hay in a mountain pasture.

"Is this wise?" he began to murmur.

But she silenced him by reaching up on tip-toe and thrusting her tongue into his mouth.

The kiss seemed to go on forever. When at last they drew apart, she said:

"I haven't done that for years. Not like that I mean."

"I haven't either."

She didn't ring for anyone to come and turn back the bed. She simply took him by the elbow, protectively as though he needed looking after, and steered him in the right direction.

Am I going to fall in love at my age? Grantham found himself wondering. Or was this just a mirage, a flash in the pan? Would she kick him out of bed the next morning and ever after pretend that nothing had happened? Women were strange. If he'd learnt one thing in his life, it was that basically he knew nothing about them. On the whole, he just wasn't on the right wavelength.

"What I like about you, among all that I like about you, is that you don't pretend to understand women." Iona Karapolitis wearing precisely nothing climbed into bed next to him.

"I try, but I don't succeed," Grantham said.

He kissed her breasts as she lay next to him. They were small and dark. Her skin was olive-gold, full of the warmth of the south. He ran his lips lightly over her body. He was not a poetic man, but a line of poetry came to mind. "How do I love thee, let me count the ways!"

She arched her back, pushed her elbows into the bed, pulled his head down onto her slim belly.

"Make love to me, Oliver."

He reached out and turned down the light, then pulled her to him – roughly. She was crying and laughing at once. He felt the pain as she dug her finger nails into his shoulders.

"Don't stop," she cried, "please don't stop." Then she shuddered, turned her face weeping to the pillow.

"Oh, my God," she said. "That hasn't happened for so long. Not for so very long."

Grantham leaned over and kissed her eyelids, tasting the salt of her tears.

"Ascot is the only English racecourse that belongs to the Crown," Grantham told her as they drove through Windsor Great Park. "The meeting was founded at the request of Queen Anne. She was out here one day from Windsor and decided that Ascot Common would make the ideal site for racing."

"I'm glad I stayed," Iona said. "It has been a wonderful week."

Grantham glanced sideways at her as he drove. It was Royal Ascot and Gold Cup day to boot. She had dressed for the occasion. A wide-brimmed hat accentuated her profile. To go with it she wore a patterned silk dress by Courrèges which hung lightly on her, showing off the slim girlish figure to its best advantage.

Grantham himself was in full morning dress. His grey top hat, meticulously brushed, almost touched the roof of the Rolls as he drove.

"I'm sorry about the formality," Grantham apologized. "Donald Coulton is rather particular when it comes to racing. The lunches he gives on Gold Cup day are very good value but you have to stick to the rules, particularly if the Queen's there."

"And will she be there?" Iona asked.

"She may drop in on Coulton's lunch-party," Grantham replied. "Coulton's rather a friend of hers. They share the same trainer: Rex Withers. And this is a rather special day for Coulton. Marchjoy is running in the Gold Cup with a good chance of winning."

Lord Coulton's lunch-party was in full swing by the time Grantham and Iona arrived. Coulton had been delighted to see them.

"Ah, my dear Oliver, I'm so glad you were able to get away." He looked inquiringly at Iona. "May I have the honour of being presented?"

When Grantham introduced his companion, Donald Coulton's aristocratic eyebrows lifted fractionally.

"I'm delighted to meet you, my dear." He bowed over her outstretched hand. He took Iona by the arm and steered her away. "I want you to meet my daughter, Candida," Coulton said.

He took her over to meet Candida Coulton and her fiancé, Michael Prestwick. Grantham noted that the bearded young man was looking distinctly uncomfortable in his Ascot finery. He waved a greeting across the floor of the tent; Prestwick waved wryly back and rolled his eyes as if to indicate that he would much prefer to be at work but sometimes you had to make concessions in the interests of good relations.

Donald Coulton had time for a few individual words with Grantham. He put his arm round Grantham's shoulder and eased him to one side.

"I haven't congratulated you in person, Oliver, on your new appointment. Let me do so now." He raised the tall, slim champagne glass. "I can't think of any man who more deserves his promotion. I always thought that cut-throat competition on the Channel routes was crazy. With the merger, you have managed to avoid that."

He handed Grantham a plate of smoked salmon.

"Blakely was getting tired, you know," Coulton said. "He did a wonderful job getting things started, but it was time for him to go."

Grantham said nothing. He wondered whether Donald Coulton would talk about him in the same, staccato way when he had outlived his usefulness.

Donald Coulton was about to continue when one of the stewards warned him that the royal party was about to arrive. He hastily excused himself and went to stand by the door of the tent as the Queen entered.

For the next ten minutes Her Majesty circulated among Lord Coulton's luncheon guests. She moved gracefully, with a small retinue, from one group of people to another.

Grantham walked over to join Iona, who was deep in conversation with Candida Coulton and Michael Prestwick. He arrived at the same time as the Queen.

The Queen smiled as Donald Coulton, who was doing the introductions, presented his guests.

"Of course, I've met Mr Grantham before. Twice, I believe, am I not right?"

"Yes, ma'am," Grantham replied.

The Queen turned to Candida. "And that last time *we* met was on the sea bed, wasn't it, just before that terrible accident?"

Candida Coulton smiled. "It wasn't very nice being stuck underground, I must admit."

The Queen spent several minutes talking with them. As she turned to go she said to Grantham:

"I have the date in my diary for the opening of the tunnel. Are you still going to be on time with all the problems you've been having? We're planning on September 25th, aren't we?"

"I'm quite sure we shall complete the tunnel on time, ma'am," Grantham replied. "The Royal Train will be running through it on that day. And the President of France will be waiting to greet you on the other side. Of course, we may still be doing some work, for example on the service tunnel, but the basic structures will be ready by then."

"I shall look forward to the occasion very much." The Queen smiled and moved on.

After lunch, Grantham and Iona Karapolitis walked around the Royal Enclosure before taking their seats in the stands.

"The Gold Cup is run over two and a half miles," Grantham explained. He pointed out the terrain to her. "Ascot is a right-handed course with a straight mile and a round mile starting from a chute at Swinley Bottom. The home straight is relatively short. You must be well in touch with the leaders at the home turn if you're going to stand any chance of winning."

They watched the first race and then made their way down to the enclosure to see the runners in the Gold Cup being saddled.

"The green and yellow check is Coulton's colours," Grantham explained. "Will Smith's riding for him today. He's one of the top jockeys."

They noted a small, tough-looking little man swing himself up into the saddle. He acknowledged the applause of bystanders by touching his whip to his cap.

"This could be Marchjoy's race," Grantham said. "The bookies were offering evens before lunch and, I'm told, the odds are shortening."

"Have you put anything on yourself?"

"A modest flutter," Grantham replied.

They stood by the rail for a few minutes surveying the traditional scene. Donald Coulton, along with several other owners, had entered the enclosure to have a final word with the trainer and jockey.

Grantham looked at his watch. "We had better get back to our seats. They'll be going down to the start soon."

It was a perfect day. The sun still streamed down from a cloudless sky. Grantham raised his hat once or twice to acknowledge passing friends.

Iona slipped her arm through his. "I'm so glad to be here, Oliver."

Eighteen minutes later, with a smile on his face as broad as a church door, Donald Coulton led in the winner. As he waved his top hat to acknowledge the cheers of the crowd, the afternoon sun caught the bronzed dome of his head. Candida Coulton, standing to one side, ran forward and hugged him.

Grantham cheered with the rest.

"He's been trying to win at Ascot for years," he told Iona. "This is a good day for him."

He took out his binoculars to observe the scene below in greater detail. He watched for a few seconds, then handed the glasses over to Iona.

"The Queen's just going up to talk to Coulton now," he told her.

Iona held the glasses to her eyes. She noted the evident warmth in the royal congratulations. She lowered the glasses.

"Is Lord Coulton a close friend of the Queen?" she asked.

"About as close as you can be outside of the family circle," Grantham replied. "Of course, Coulton doesn't talk much about it. He's not that kind of man."

As they made their way down to the enclosure to join in the celebrations, Grantham reflected that much might depend on Coulton's personal rapport with the Queen of England.

In the evening, by way of celebration, they went to the opera at Covent Garden. Grantham had taken tickets for a gala performance of *Tosca* with Kiri Te Kanawa in the title role. They arrived a few minutes before the performance began to take their seats in a box.

The splendour of the setting, the beauty of the music and the company she kept had an exhilarating effect on Iona. From time to time she closed her eyes and let the waves of sound roll over her. She thought of the days when Maria Callas, another Greek girl, had stood on the stage at Covent Garden and carried the whole of London before her.

At one point, she took his hand and squeezed. "I'm so happy," she said.

At the first interval, an usher came in with a message to the effect that the Prime Minister would be giving a few friends drinks in a private room during the interval and would be delighted if Mr Oliver Grantham and his guest could join her.

When Grantham and Iona arrived at the suite, they found the PM entertaining the American ambassador and his wife, a couple of cabinet ministers, and several luminaries from London's cultural and artistic world.

The PM seemed to be genuinely delighted to see them.

"Of course, I've heard about the merger. Who hasn't?"

"This *is* the merger," Grantham replied smiling. He presented Iona Karapolitis to the Prime Minister.

The PM took Iona's hand. There was a hint of irony in her voice as she said: "Not all Greeks bearing gifts are to be feared, then?"

Iona laughed.

During the interval, the Prime Minister took Grantham to one side.

"There was no way we could have bailed you out, Mr Grantham," she said. "You know that, don't you? It was clear right from the start that the tunnel had to be built without guarantees of any kind, technical as well as political. If you had pressed us, it could have been very tricky. I'm glad you didn't."

"I'm glad we didn't either," Grantham agreed. "Just don't take me to the Monopolies Commission!"

The Prime Minister laughed. "No problem there. After all, you're not a *total* monopoly, are you? There are still the airlines. You don't own the airlines, do you?"

Grantham laughed in turn. "We're working on it."

They talked for a few minutes more, then the three-minute bell rang. Grantham and Iona said goodbye to the Prime Minister and her guests and made their way back to the box.

As they walked through the lobby, a photographer was taking pictures. Grantham couldn't resist saying: "He'll probably send them to me in a brown envelope postmarked Paddington."

Iona Karapolitis had the grace to blush.

Grantham visited the Royal Aeronautic Establishment at Farnborough the week after Ascot. Having lived in nearby Fleet for over twenty years, he knew the town of Farnborough well. And the RAE was familiar territory. Though it would not have been fair to say that the military in Hampshire lived each other's pockets, there was a definite interchange – both social and professional – between the different branches and the different establishments of the armed services.

Once again, the old boy network stood him in good stead. The RAE's Chief Scientist, Dr Simon Carruthers, was one of Grantham's Sunday-morning golfing colleagues from way back.

"Of course, we can get you in to look at the wind-tunnels," he had told Grantham over the telephone. "We'll leave a pass for you at the gate."

In the event, Grantham spent the whole afternoon at the RAE. He looked at open-circuit – or Eiffel – wind-tunnels. He looked at return-flow – or Prandtl – wind-tunnels. He was particularly interested in the full-scale tunnel which the RAE had recently constructed and which was capable of testing actual aeroplanes under near-flight conditions.

Carruthers himself showed Grantham round.

"In practice, full-scale testing is not usually necessary. Provided the model is correctly constructed and *all* variables – not just some of them – are taken into account, there is no reason why a model should not give you aerodynamically accurate results. And, of course, model-testing is a great deal cheaper than the real thing. It can also be a great deal safer! It was wind-tunnel testing which showed, way back in the 1930s, that Sir John Cobb's racing-car – the one which subsequently set the world landspeed record of almost four hundred miles per hour – had an allowable nose-rise of only twelve inches! That was why they chose the extraordinarily level salt flats at Daytona."

By the end of a long afternoon, Grantham had absorbed as much of the theory and practice of wind-tunnels as he felt himself capable of absorbing. Some of the more complicated mathematics escaped him entirely. But the basic principles involved seemed clear enough. One principle, in particular, seemed to be highly relevant. As Carruthers put it:

"In low-speed aerodynamic work – and by low-speed I'm talking of speeds up to 0.5 Mach, or half the speed of sound – *air is an incompressible fluid.*"

In the end, Grantham realized that one visit would not be sufficient for his purposes. He would probably have to return. He could not, in the nature of things, take Carruthers wholly into his confidence. But he was able nevertheless to enlist his co-operation and that of certain RAE scientists.

"So much depends on this," Grantham explained. "I can give you the basic parameters – dimensions, speeds and so forth. But I need to be *absolutely* sure. We can't afford mistakes."

Carruthers hadn't pressed him. He had known Grantham long enough to realize that the plea for help would not be a frivolous one.

34

Grantham hadn't seen the Newham librarian for some time. Somehow the public relations side of the Chunnel operation had sunk into the background. His life had been full of the day-to-day emergencies. Now that the worst was over, he had more time to look ahead.

He looked rather fondly at the precise, tidy man who sat across the desk from him. How much he owed to Arthur Jones's timely warning! Making him a consultant to the Chunnel Consortium with the job of looking after odd public relations angles as and when these might crop up was the very least he could have done for him in the circumstances.

"How are things going, Arthur? Any snags? You know we're planning on September 25th for the Inaugural run. Both the Queen and the new President of the French Republic, Pierre Leroux, are lined up for that day. We don't want any last-minute hitches."

Arthur Jones smiled. "I think the public's on our side. We had to do a bit of lobbying down in Kent. They were worried about the loading loops and their impact on the environment. But we pointed out that putting the goods on trains rather than on heavy lorries was the best possible strategy from the environmental point of view." Jones paused. "There is one thing that *is* bothering me a bit."

"What's that?"

"Rabies." He pronounced the word slowly and clearly.

"What the hell do you mean?" Grantham exploded. "What's the Channel Tunnel got to do with rabies?"

By way of reply, Jones pulled from his pocket a white government-issued pamphlet on which the word RABIES was printed in red letters. Under that was the subtitle: THE RISK TO GREAT BRITAIN.

Jones read out the opening paragraph:

" 'There has not been a case of rabies in animals in the British Isles since 1970 but there is a constant threat of its introduction by animals imported from the many countries where rabies is endemic. Perhaps the greatest threat, however, is from the Continent of Europe through the vast interchange of holiday makers and the high volume of traffic across the Channel. Rabies exists in France, as in Germany, Austria, Denmark, Northern Italy, Switzerland, and Eastern Europe. Rabies is widespread particularly in wildlife. Whilst there has been no significant advance towards the French coast in recent years several cases occurred in 1980 and 1981 in the Seine Maritime Department – the hinterland to Dieppe.' "

Grantham listened intently. "When was that pamphlet written?" he asked.

"April 1983," Jones replied. "There've been some developments since then. I'll come to those in a minute. I'd like to read a bit more."

"Go ahead."

Arthur Jones continued: " 'There is no room for complacency. A reservoir of rabies in wildlife makes control very difficult despite restriction of the movements of dogs and cats. There is a direct menace to human life from animals with rabies. The English Channel fortunately provides an effective natural barrier against rabies reaching the British Isles.' "

Again Jones paused in his reading. "Now listen to this, Mr Grantham. This is what the Government itself is saying, or at least the Ministry of Agriculture, Fisheries and Food. '*Any decision to build a Channel Tunnel would need to take account of the rabies factor and stringent safeguards would be necessary*.' "

Jones put the pamphlet down. "As I say, that was all written back in 1983. Since then, we've built the Channel Tunnel. It's been a brilliant, historic achievement. But I'm beginning to get rumbles on the rabies question. At the moment, it's just a letter here or there in the local press from some animal-lover. I keep my ear to the ground as you asked me to. What worries me is that the odd rumble here or there could quite rapidly swell into a roar of protest. You know how people are. If you get enough people thinking the same thing at the same time and writing to the newspapers about it and going on their local radio station, then suddenly you have a problem on your hands."

Grantham took the point immediately. "What do you suggest?" He had listened to what Arthur Jones had to say once before and it had stood him in good stead. There was no reason why he should not listen again.

"Can you spare the time to come down to Horsham?" Jones asked.

"Horsham?"

"The headquarters of the RSPCA. They have a Wildlife division there. Dr Duncan Wilson who is the head of it probably knows more about rabies and how to control it than anyone else in this country. I've talked to him already and he says he's willing to help."

Grantham stood up. "Why are we waiting?" he asked.

Dr Duncan Wilson was a man of medium height in his late thirties. He had a tough wiry build and the soft-spoken manner of one who is used to spending his time with animals. They sat in his office in the RSPCA's Sussex headquarters while he explained in clear scientific terms the nature of the rabies threat.

"Rabies has occurred periodically in waves throughout history. Europe is currently undergoing such a wave. The present epizootic began south of Gdansk in Poland in 1939, since when it has spread over 1000 miles across North-West Europe. The disease crossed the Elbe in 1950 and the Rhine in 1960, and entered France in 1968, when sixty-three cases of animal rabies were confirmed."

He stood up to pull down a wall chart behind him.

"This shows the spread of rabies across France since 1968. By 1970, six departments were infected – Moselle, Ardennes, Meuse, Meurthe-et-Moselle, Bas-Rhin and Marne. The annual number of cases increased quite dramatically from sixty-three during 1968 to 1027 in 1972 and nearly three thousand in 1976. By 1983, which is the last year for which we have complete statistics, the annual number of cases had increased to well over 4000. with over 80 per cent of the infections occurring in foxes. In fact vulpine rabies, the presence of rabies amongst the fox population, seems to be the principal cause for the spread of rabies across France and the main reason why, in spite of vaccination campaigns, the epizootic front has been advancing steadily."

He pointed once again to the map. "The Centre National d'Etudes sur la Rage – that's France's national rabies centre – records the location of every reported case of animal rabies. It is quite clear from the figures that the epizootic front has now reached the Channel departments. There is a relatively high frequency of infection now in the whole Pas-de-Calais region."

He turned round to face them once more.

"Up till now the English Channel has acted as an effective barrier to the spread of rabies into this country. As you know, we operate stringent regulations to prevent the import of pets, dogs and cats, who might be carrying the disease. If these animals are imported under licence they must be detained in quarantine for six months at the owner's expense.

Dogs and cats in quarantine must be vaccinated against rabies, but we do not operate a general vaccination policy in Britain because we have regarded our existing precautions as being sufficient."

"How does the construction of the Channel Tunnel change the situation?" Grantham asked. "Surely you can still control the entry of dogs and cats into Britain?"

"Of course you can," Dr Wilson agreed. "You can search a train just as you can search a ship. That's not the problem. Or, at least, not the major problem."

"So what is the major problem then?" Grantham asked.

"Foxes," Wilson replied succinctly. "There is a school of thought which believes that a rabid fox might cross from France into England via the tunnel, thus precipitating an outbreak of rabies over here."

Grantham leaned back in his seat incredulously. "You're not suggesting that a fox, particularly a rabid fox, would run almost thirty miles through a tunnel?"

Duncan Wilson smiled wryly. "It's not what I suggest, Mr Grantham. It's what people are prepared to believe. Of course foxes have been known to travel long distances. I've been involved for some years in the radio-tracking of foxes. Basically you attach a miniaturized radio-transmitter to the neck of an animal which emits a pulsed radio signal. This signal can be detected at several miles' distance by a receiver operated by the biologist. A directionally sensitive aerial gives a maximum signal when the axis of the aerial is pointing at the fox, so it is possible to plot the position of the animal from a distance. One of the things we've discovered in studying fox movements over the last several years is that itinerant foxes are in the habit of travelling over much larger distances than resident foxes. Movements of ten or twenty miles a night are by no means uncommon. Technically, it's entirely feasible that an itinerant fox could cover the distance between France and England in far less than twenty-four hours. Personally, I think it's unlikely. But the possibility exists. We know so little about what causes foxes to disperse. And, in the very nature of things, a rabid fox will not be behaving normally."

"Isn't there a technical solution?" Grantham asked. "A fox-trap at the entrance to the tunnel, for example?"

Dr Wilson laughed. "Tunnels have been built all over the world," he said. "There's no way you can stop wildlife entering them."

They talked around the problem for the next half hour. There didn't seem to be any easy solution.

"I suppose all we can hope for," said Grantham, "is to be able to reassure people that the customary precautions will be adequate to meet any new threat which could be posed by the construction of the tunnel."

"Yes, that's about it." Duncan Wilson saw them to the door.

He had one last word of caution. "Remember, rabies is a very nasty thing indeed. That's why people are worried. They have reason to be worried. I saw a man die of rabies once. It was the most horrid sight I have ever witnessed. The spasms of terror were so severe that his whole body arched backwards. He retched so violently as to rip the junction between the oesophagus and the stomach. His cries were distorted through inflammation of the vocal cords so that his voice sounded more like a dog's bark. And remember, too, that once the symptoms of rabies appear, it's too late to do anything about it. Any human patient who develops the symptoms of rabies faces the prospect of certain death. There is only one recorded recovery in medical literature."

Grantham shuddered. "Don't go on," he said. "If enough people start talking like you, they'll close the tunnel down before it's even open!"

35

When the little girl put out her hand, the puppy snapped at it, drawing blood, before scurrying off into the bushes.

"Look, mummy, he bit me!" the little girl cried.

Her mother examined the wound. "It's only a scratch, Mary-Lou. You should be more careful."

"It was such a nice little puppy." The little girl was genuinely upset, as though her faith in the natural goodness of puppies had been severely shaken.

Half an hour later, the family party, on a day outing from London to the White Cliffs of Dover packed up their picnic and made for the car. The little girl, reassured by her parents, seemed quite to have forgotten the incident with the dog.

Dr Graham Bartlett, the elderly gentle-mannered Professor of Exotic Diseases at University College Hospital, London, addressed his pupils in grave and sombre tones:

"The disease rabies," he told them, "is caused by a bullet-shaped virus measuring only 140 × 100 nanometres – a nanometre is 1/millionth of a millimetre. About forty would stretch across a red blood corpuscle. Research has shown that the core of the rabies virus consists of two components, an internal helical structure of nucleic acid surrounded by a layer of protein. This core is in turn surrounded by a membranous envelope which is covered by small spikes. These spikes consist chemically of a glycoprotein and are thought to be important in the attachment of the virus to susceptible cells."

Bartlett's assistant projected some slides to illustrate the lecture. The students scribbled notes.

"The rabies virus travels to the brain via the peripheral nerves,"

Bartlett continued. "Thus when rabies virus is present in the saliva of an infected animal which then bites the victim, the virus is injected into the animal's muscle. The virus makes its way into the axone cylinder and thereafter migrates through the system to the spinal cord and ultimately to the brain. Once in the brain the virus multiplies and then moves out along the nerves again to the peripheral organs. Since nerves lead to almost every part of the body they serve as routes which ensure that the rabies virus ultimately reaches almost every tissue of its victim's body."

The professor paused and looked at the rows of students who confronted him in the lecture theatre. His voice, already sepulchral, dropped another tone.

"I regret to say," he told them, "that this morning, in this hospital, a six-year-old girl, known as Mary-Lou Edwards, died of rabies. This is the first confirmed death from rabies to take place in Britain for four years. Enquiries are still being made as to the possible source of the infection. Mary-Lou's parents have confirmed that five days ago, when the family was on a day-trip to Dover, Mary-Lou was bitten by a dog. The dog has not yet been traced. Nor is it known how the dog, if indeed it was the cause of the infection, itself came to be carrying rabies. As you may imagine, this is a situation of some gravity."

Professor Barlett gave a small, deprecating smile in the direction of his students.

"I would much prefer," he told them, "to have kept my presentation at a purely theoretical level. The hearts of all of us must go out this morning to the Edwards family."

The Professor bowed his head in silence for a moment or two before the gong sounded the end of the lecture.

The Prime Minister found time in the course of a busy morning for half an hour's discussion with the Department of the Environment's chief ecologist.

"The child was bitten by a dog. Could that dog have been infected by a fox?"

Dr Raymond Sandgate, a tall thin man with dark bushy eyebrows, believed in answering questions precisely. In his view, that was what science was all about. Precision.

He looked beyond the Prime Minister's shoulder towards the trees in St James's Park. There was a slightly greenish tinge to the lower part of the windows in the Prime Minister's study. Bullet-proof glass, the scientist assumed.

"Yes, Prime Minister," Sandgate replied in thin, clipped tones. "The dog could have been bitten by a rabid fox. But we would still need to establish how the fox itself became infected."

The Prime Minister stood with her back to the fireplace.

"There's a growing body of opinion, Dr Sandgate, that the disease could somehow have been transmitted by wildlife. As I understand it, the moment the two ends of the tunnel were joined up, animals, such as foxes, could pass through. Is that correct?"

The chief ecologist shook his head. "Theoretically possible, Prime Minister. However, colleagues who specialize in vulpine behaviour tell me it's unlikely that transmission of rabies into the reservoir of wildlife in Britain would happen in this way."

The Prime Minister pressed him.

"Let's just assume for once your colleagues are wrong, and the great British public is right. What happens if rabies has got into the fox population of this country?"

Dr Raymond Sandgate had no doubt about the answer to that one.

"Then we're in trouble. Real trouble. Don't forget that nowadays the fox is an urban animal. That means that the source of infection could be right in the heart of our great cities."

The Prime Minister, who had walked over to the window, swung round to face her visitor.

'What do you mean – an urban animal? Most of my supporters hunt foxes in the Shires, don't they?"

Dr Sandgate permitted himself a flicker of a smile.

"I mean the fox, the twentieth-century fox, is *also* an urban animal." He explained. "The fox population of London, for example, is probably over two thousand. They are particularly numerous, it seems, south of the Thames. Observers like all-night shift workers, railway-commuters, housewives, suburban motorists and so on, report foxes almost anywhere you have garbage. Vixens are known to nurse their cubs in shops and garages and it's clear that the animal makes great use of railway tracks for moving from one district to another."

The Prime Minister shuddered. "You mean if foxes in the Dover area are infected, it's simply a matter of time before they infect their brethren in the capital? They just run up the line?"

Dr Sandgate was not going to be pushed into a corner.

"I don't think we can conclude as yet, Prime Minister, that there *is* a reservoir of rabies in the wildlife populations around Dover, or anywhere else for that matter."

The Prime Minister sighed. She was amazed sometimes at how little political acumen scientists, even eminent scientists, showed.

"Tell that to the House," she said.

When Sandgate had left, the PM conferred with her advisors. Philip Maitland, the Treasury man who served as her principal private secretary, warned the Prime Minister that the first question down at Prime Minister's questions that day was whether the PM would list her engagements.

"There's bound to be a supplementary about whether you have any plans to visit Dover."

"Not on your Nelly!" the PM replied. She broke into a laugh. "I wouldn't go within a hundred miles of the place under the circumstances!"

"You're less than a hundred miles away from Dover as it is, Prime Minister," Philip Maitland admonished her. "And in any case, I think you'll find that the House is not in any mood to tolerate frivolity."

The Prime Minister looked at her aide sharply. "You're being a bit stuffy today, aren't you, Philip?" Then she added, almost reluctantly, "I had better make a statement, hadn't I?"

Philip Maitland was not the Prime Minister's principal private secretary for nothing. He pulled the draft out of his pocket.

When the Prime Minister rose for questions at 2.30 that afternoon, the house was more than usually full. The Whips had done their work. The word had been put around that the PM was going to say something about Mary-Lou Edwards. And the Government wanted to be sure that whatever that something was, it was well received by the House.

Grantham had been warned less than half an hour before the Prime Minister was due to speak. He got to the House in time to take his seat in the Strangers' Gallery just as the Prime Minister rose from her place on the Government front bench. Looking down onto the packed benches, he heard the Prime Minister intone in those clear, well-mannered tones which had over the past five years or so become so familiar to the House and to the nation:

"Honourable Members will wish to know what steps the Government is taking. I can assure the House that scientific enquiries are being pursued with the utmost vigour. We do not yet know whether or not rabies is present, as some honourable Members seem to fear, in the reservoir of wildlife in the Dover region. The Government is prepared to recognize, however, that there is at least some possibility that infection may have reached these shores through the newly constructed

Channel Tunnel. I stress the word 'possibility', since this is a hypothesis which still needs to be verified. In the circumstances, the Government believe it is right that the tunnel should be hermetically sealed until further notice and the Royal Engineers have been instructed to proceed forthwith to effect the necessary measures."

The Prime Minister held up her hand to stay the incipient uproar.

"I am aware," she continued, "that there may be some honourable Members who will consider these precautions to be on the draconian side. Let me simply remind them that it has been the policy of successive Governments, of whatever complexion, to treat the menace of rabies as one of the most serious threats that could ever attack our country. *My* Government proposes to be every bit as serious and as stringent in this matter as its predecessors have been. It goes without saying, of course, that these are temporary measures. In the event that our scientists are able to show that the regrettable death of Mary-Lou Edwards did *not* result from the rabies virus being transmitted through wildlife and that the Channel Tunnel has played no part in the affair, the measures I have announced today in the interest of public health and safety will, of course, be rescinded."

Up in the Strangers' Gallery, Oliver Grantham leaned forward and buried his head in his hands. He could hardly believe what he was hearing. Two weeks to go to the day before the official Inauguration. Two weeks to test out the tracks, iron out any wrinkles, get the bugs out of the system. And then this had to happen!

As the Prime Minister sat down to allow a back-bencher on the Government side to put another carefully planted supplementary, Grantham saw her glance in the direction of the gallery. Without meaning to, he caught the Prime Minister's eye. The PM spread her hands as though to indicate that the situation was not of her making.

Later that afternoon, Grantham sat at his desk in his office with the evening *Standard*, spread out in front of him. The headlines screamed: TUNNEL SEALED OFF! Underneath was a picture of a giant crane lowering what looked like a huge ball of plasticine into the mouth of the tunnel. It reminded Grantham of the stone being rolled into the mouth of the tomb of Christ. Would there be a resurrection this time, he wondered?

Sandra Furlong had left for the day. He picked up the phone and dialled through to Athens direct.

He was lucky to find Iona at home. Grantham quickly explained the nature of the problem.

"We're in real trouble," he told her. "They want us to prove that the wildlife population is free of rabies. But you can't do that. You can't prove a negative. Once the animal lobby gets truly worked up and starts thinking about their pet dogs and cats, or the hunting community thinks the foxes may be slaughtered, we may never get that tunnel open again!"

She instantly grasped the gravity of the situation. "What about the dog? Have they traced the dog yet?"

"No," Grantham replied. It was a question which he had asked himself. "There's been no sign of the dog. It disappeared. There have been no other reported bites, though that doesn't mean there haven't been any."

They talked for a few more minutes.

"Shall I stick to schedule?" Iona asked finally. "At the moment I'm booked to fly into London the day before the Inauguration."

Grantham laughed bitterly. "At this rate there may not be an Inauguration."

Grantham caught up with the couple as they walked away from the tatty little church in Canning Town in London's East End. It had been impossible to hold a proper funeral of course. You couldn't hold a funeral without a body. And in this case there was no body. The remains of poor Mary-Lou Edwards had been taken from the hospital and disposed of in accordance with instructions laid down by the authorities. Basically, that meant ultra-high temperature incineration designed to ensure the total elimination of all viral elements.

The couple turned round as they heard Grantham approach.

"Mr and Mrs Edwards? I just wanted to say how sorry I am about your daughter."

Grantham walked along the pavement with them. The woman was crying.

"Such a terrible death," she sobbed.

There was nothing Grantham could do to comfort her. He felt wretchedly uncomfortable about having to intrude on their grief. But he had no alternative.

"I'm so sorry to bother you at a time like this," he began, falling into step beside them. "But there's something I need to know . . ."

*

They reached the picnic site around noon the next day. Grantham had had to use all his powers of persuasion. At first neither Mr nor Mrs Edwards had shown any inclination to return to the scene of the tragedy. But Grantham had won them round in the end.

"I need to know exactly where you were sitting," he had explained. "I need to know where the dog was last seen. You're the only people who can tell me that. It could make a difference."

He didn't tell them precisely why it could make a difference. He didn't feel that it was necessary to explain his involvement with the Channel Tunnel project. It was better if they believed he was a public health official of some kind. And in a sense, he reflected, that was exactly what he was.

"We'll go down by helicopter," he had offered.

The idea struck an immediate response in both Mr and Mrs Edwards.

"Ooh!" exclaimed Mrs Edwards. "Harry and I have never been in a helicopter before."

Grantham had smiled reassuringly at the couple.

"You'll enjoy the trip. And, besides, you need something to take your minds off your loss."

Grantham had sent the car ahead to meet them on the cliff-top. It would be taking Mr and Mrs Edwards back. He suspected that he might need to keep the helicopter for himself. It was better to be prepared.

"This is where we were sitting," Mrs Edwards explained, as they got out. "Mary-Lou was over here when the dog bit her. It ran off towards the bushes."

They searched for half an hour and found nothing. Grantham could see that the couple were becoming uneasy. He ushered them towards the car.

"I'm so grateful to you for all your trouble. I'm going to stay here for a while and keep looking."

James, the chauffeur, held the door of the Rolls open for them.

Before Mr and Mrs Edwards entered the vehicle, Grantham proffered an envelope.

"I hope you will accept this as a token of my appreciation for all your help," he said. "There's a cheque for £5000 in this envelope. I know nothing can compensate you for what you have suffered. But I'd like you to have it anyway."

When the couple, stunned into silence, had driven off, Grantham got back into the helicopter.

"I want to have a close look at the cliff-face," he told the pilot. "Perhaps the dog ran over the edge."

"I'll do my best," the pilot replied.

The helicopter lifted off, rotors whirring; swung out over the sea, then dropped below the edge of the cliff.

Grantham took out his binoculars. If you were going to look for something, you had to look systematically. While the helicopter hovered two rotor-blades away from the cliff, Grantham searched every ledge and every crack, looking for the body of a dog. It seemed to him to be quite plausible that a puppy, disoriented by disease, might have strayed over the cliff top where a healthy animal would have done no such thing.

He found what he was looking for after twenty minutes. The puppy was lying on a ledge, where it had fallen, forty feet down from the cliff's edge. Grantham would have liked to have gone in closer but they dared not risk it. Even though it was a fine, calm day, sudden currents could have caused the helicopter to swing against the cliff.

They called in the Kent police over the radio.

"Let a man down on a rope if you can," Grantham instructed. "We've got another two hours' fuel. We can stay and mark the place, if you like. Better take breathing apparatus. The specimen could be rabid."

Half an hour later a collection of vehicles congregated on the top of the cliff. There were three police cars, two fire engines, and a safe-disposal unit from the County Health Authority.

When the team was ready, Grantham took off again in the helicopter and, using the radio link, guided the rescue unit down to the ledge on which the dog lay.

Grantham watched the fireman pick up the body of the animal with long-handled tongs and examine it. He heard him say: "I'm putting the specimen in the bag now. Specimen is wearing a collar. Collar has a name on it. Dog appears to belong to a Mr and Mrs R. George of 24, Lubbock Gardens, Dover."

Grantham watched first the bag, then the man being hauled back up the cliff. Then he said to the pilot:

"How well do you know Dover? Do you know Lubbock Gardens, for example?"

"Can't say I do," the pilot replied. "But I've got a street map, if that's any help."

Ten minutes later, Mrs Richard George was considerably surprised to see a helicopter land on her front lawn. She put down the secateurs with which she had been pruning her roses and stepped hesitantly forward to greet Grantham as he disembarked from the machine.

"Mrs George?" Grantham held out his hand in a welcoming fashion.

As he greeted the woman, Grantham's practised eye took in the details of her surroundings. He noted the general air of affluence and the twenty-foot motor boat parked in the driveway. Easy enough to pop across the Channel in that, he thought.

"I just came to tell you we found the puppy, Mrs George," he said. He smiled at her in the friendliest possible way. "Do you mind if I just offer you a word of advice? When the police come, don't try to deny anything. It will only make things more difficult."

The woman put her hands to her head.

"Oh my God!" she cried. "It wasn't our dog, was it? We thought he'd run away."

Late that night Grantham talked once again to Iona Karapolitis in Athens.

"They took their puppy with them on their boat and it followed them off onto the quayside at Calais," he told her. "Just for a few minutes, the woman said. She hadn't even thought about it until I asked her specifically. She was absolutely shocked. The police arrived while I was still there. The George family and anyone who has been in contact with them have all been given preventive vaccinations. You can prevent rabies; but you can't cure it."

"So all's well that ends well, is it? I can keep my booking after all, can I?"

"I think you can," Grantham replied. "That had to be the last hiccup."

"Some hiccup!" Iona's musical laugh sounded over a distance of fifteen hundred miles. Then she added: "I'm coming anyway, Oliver, whether the Inauguration goes ahead as planned or not. It's been ages since I saw you."

Grantham smiled in the broad direction of the Mediterranean.

"I'm looking forward to it. I've missed you."

He realized, as he replaced the receiver, that he probably meant what he had said.

Grantham went to bed that night with a deep sense of relief. He had spoken to the Prime Minister in person and received her assurance that the tunnel would be unsealed within days. The only condition the PM had made, on the advice of Government scientists, was that vaccine bait should be used in a sixty-mile semi-circular buffer zone around the entrance to the tunnel. Whether or not this measure was justified in strictly ecological terms, the Prime Minister wasn't sure. She was sure, however, that it was entirely justified in terms of the reassuring effect it would have on public opinion.

What was more, the Prime Minister had magnanimously indicated that the Government would be prepared to bear the cost of the vaccine-bait programme.

As he fell asleep, Grantham was grateful for small mercies.

36

The Gare du Nord had been totally refurbished for the occasion. The *clochards* had been moved on; the platforms had been swept; inside, the station had been decorated with bunting and outside a red carpet had been laid where the President of the French Republic would arrive.

While waiting, the television cameras showed pictures of the crowds, of the departure board, which indicated that the Presidential Train would be leaving at eleven a.m. from platform 1, and of the train itself.

Roger Daudy, covering the occasion for Antenne 1, had been given permission by the authorities to walk down the length of the train, and to describe the scene for television viewers before the Presidential party came on board.

"I'm standing now," he said, "right at the head of the train. As you can see, the SNCF decided right from the start that this route from Paris to London beneath the Channel should be served by high-speed trains. So what we have here is the classic TGV locomotive – the engine which has made possible the concept of the *Train à Grande Vitesse.*"

As he spoke, the camera caressed the sleek lines of the engine. Viewers could see the tapered nose with twin headlights set either side of the grille and the emblem SNCF beneath. They could see the driver's cabin, and behind that, the bulky compartment where the giant motors were placed.

"We're talking about more than five thousand horsepower here," Daudy told them. "A maximum speed of over three hundred kilometres per hour. Of course," he added, "on this Inaugural run the train will not be reaching those speeds."

He went on to explain, as he walked back down the platform towards the station, that the Presidential train would not in fact be passing that day through the Channel tunnel.

"The President and his party will be proceeding as far as Calais," he explained. "Those of us who remember history will recall how François I, King of France, in 1520 met Henry VIII, King of England, outside Calais. They called the place the Field of the Cloth of Gold. Well, today we are going to see another such encounter, perhaps no less historic. The Presidential train will leave here at 10.15 precisely. It will reach Calais at precisely 12.15. Two minutes later, the Royal train bearing the Queen of England and her party will arrive, having passed through the tunnel. The Royal train will pull up at Calais station the other side of the platform from the Presidential train. The two Heads of State will step down simultaneously from their carriages to meet in the middle. Later, the Queen will board the Presidential train itself and will proceed on that train back through the tunnel in company of the President of France. There will of course be a reception on the French side and a ceremonial lunch. And later this afternoon when the train reaches Dover there will be similar festivities on the English side. It has all been most carefully, and most symmetrically, planned."

As he was speaking, Roger Daudy walked slowly back down the train.

"Immediately behind the engine," he told the public, "is the Express-Grill wagon. As viewers may know, Express-Grill is a private company which has contracted with SNCF to provide restaurant services on the high-speed trains. There are at least a dozen Express-Grill units which, like the locomotives themselves, can be moved around to join up with the appropriate TGV. The Express-Grill units are, of course, totally streamlined like the rest of the train and staffed by professional chefs and waiters of the highest quality. Lunch today will not be served until the party reaches Calais, where it will be the reponsibility of the Mayor, Monsieur Emile Vapeur. But I'm quite sure that the staff of the Express-Grill wagon will be providing drinks and light refreshments to anyone who wants these during the course of the journey to the coast."

Roger Daudy realized it was getting near the time when the President would be arriving outside the Gare du Nord. He quickened his pace.

"After the Express-Grill wagon comes the President's own compartment. Here President Leroux will sit with his ministers and invited guests. Next comes another compartment for guests, then the press compartment. Forty journalists will be aboard the train, as I shall myself on behalf of Antenne 1."

Roger Daudy smiled broadly at the camera. He knew he had only a minute left.

"There is one last compartment at the very end of the train where, as you can see, all the blinds are drawn and the windows are wreathed in black. I must explain that this compartment contains the coffin and mortal remains of the great Leo d'Erlanger, the French visionary who foresaw and worked for the construction of the Channel tunnel over one hundred years ago. In tribute to his memory and in fulfilment of his own express wishes, the organizers of the project have today added this special car to the Presidential train."

As he spoke, viewers saw a photograph of Leò d'Erlanger, which researchers at Antenne 1 had dug out of the files, while Daudy continued in voice-over:

"D'Erlanger insisted that his remains be carried through the tunnel the first day it was opened. Today it has been possible to respect the wishes of the dead – " Roger Daudy interrupted himself, as he received a message through his earpiece. "The Presidential party is, apparently, just arriving outside the Gare du Nord so we shall be moving now to the front of the station to cover this historic moment!!"

The line of bullet-proof limousines swung into the cleared area in front of the Gare du Nord. As President Leroux got out, the band struck up the Marseillaise.

The President walked forward into the station to be greeted by various dignitaries. As he did so, sharp-shooters guarded the roofs of the surrounding buildings and policemen, uniformed and otherwise, scrutinized the crowds.

Monique Delacourt walked about thirty paces behind the President. It had always been envisaged that she and other officials from the companies involved in Chunnel Consortium would participate in the ceremonies of the opening day. But Monique Delacourt had not been able to suppress her pleasure at receiving, two days earlier, a personal invitation from the President to join his party on board the train.

On the back of the invitation, Leroux had written in his own handwriting: "I'm sorry it's been so long since we met. As you can imagine, many things have intervened!"

Monique Delacourt had the card with her still, in her handbag. She wondered what it signified. Did Leroux plan to resume their relationship, now that he had settled in? Was she ready for it?

The band was still playing as Monique Delacourt boarded the train with the rest of the Presidential party.

At precisely the same moment as the Presidential train pulled out of the Gare du Nord, the Royal train left Victoria station in London. Ceremonies similar to those which had been enacted in Paris took place at the English terminus. The Queen and her party had been seen safely on board by the Lord Lieutenant of the County of Middlesex. Ladies and gentlemen-in-waiting had taken up their assigned positions. The party of notables including the Prime Minister, members of her Cabinet, and representatives of the financial and industrial world most deeply involved in the project – such as Lord Coulton, Sir David and Lady Blakely (both tanned and fit after an extended holiday in Italy), George Browning and, of course, Oliver Grantham and Iona Karapolitis – had taken their places in the compartment next to the one occupied by the royal party. The band of the Irish Guards had played rousing music reminiscent of those times when great enterprises, and great expeditions, had begun at railway stations.

The press, already seated in a special compartment linked by telex and radio-telephone with their offices, had begun to churn out purple prose by the yard before the train had even passed Clapham Junction.

For Alex Lyons, it was the end of a long story. A story which he had followed on and off, right from the beginning. There had been times when he doubted whether the project would ever be completed. Times when even Grantham's extraordinary courage and perseverance seemed to have been swamped by events.

He began to type his story directly into the telex machine which linked him with Fleet Street . . .

The royal train had covered about half the distance between London and Dover when Grantham was invited to go forward into the royal compartment. The Queen invited him to sit down opposite her.

"You've had an eventful time, haven't you, Mr Grantham? I've been reading about it in the newspapers." The Queen smiled encouragingly at him.

"We've had some little local difficulties," Grantham replied. "I'm glad to say that's all behind us now."

The Queen glanced at her watch. "I understand we will be entering the tunnel in twenty minutes, is that correct?"

Grantham nodded. "Exactly, ma'am. And twenty minutes after that we will be in Calais."

The Queen seemed genuinely delighted. "I must say I find this all very exciting. Thank you, Mr Grantham, for all your efforts."

Five minutes later, having taken leave of his Sovereign, Grantham walked forward towards the driver's cabin.

They were passing the loading loops at Cheriton. Work, Grantham noted, was still in progress on some of the facilities. But the terminal was already operating. Another small miracle, Grantham thought, given the deadline.

The two men in the cabin acknowledged his entry. Grantham had made his number with them before the train left Victoria.

"Everything going all right?" Grantham asked.

"Yes, sir," the elder of the two men replied. He turned up the knob on the squawk box which was mounted on the console. "We've got a direct radio link with the President's train," the driver explained. "They'll be reaching Calais any minute now."

As they entered the portal of the tunnel, Grantham noted that their speed was sixty-eight miles an hour. Over the radio link, he heard a French voice say: "*Nous nous approchons à Calais. On commence le ralentissement.*"

The second man in the cabin, sprucer and possibly brighter than his colleague, commented: "They're slowing down for Calais, then."

Once they were inside the tunnel, the radio reception began to fade. Even so, all three of them in the cabin of the Royal train heard the shots ring out. Two of them close together, followed by a third about half a second later.

They heard the beginnings of a strangled cry and then there was silence as the signals ceased.

"What the hell! . . ." the driver exclaimed.

Grantham spoke quietly but the note of command was unmistakable: "Bring the train to a halt as rapidly as you can," he instructed.

Suddenly, the lights in the cabin went out, as well as the lights which illuminated the tunnel.

"Someone's thrown the switch," the driver said. "There's no power coming through!"

"Use the emergency braking system then."

Grantham braced himself as the train began to decelerate.

The Mayor of Calais and the dignitaries who waited with him on the platform for the arrival of the Presidential train, had a brief glimpse of two people in tall white chef's hats standing in the cabin of the locomotive as it rushed at 150 kilometres per hour through the station without stopping and on in the direction of the entrance to the tunnel.

President Pierre Leroux saw the sign CALAIS flash by.

"*Qu'est-ce qui se passe?*" he asked sharply.

It took ten seconds, ten long seconds, for the people in the Calais control-box to realize that the Presidential train hadn't merely overshot the platform; it just wasn't going to stop at all.

The supervisor reached for the override switch to cut off the power from the lines.

"*Merde!*" he said, as he pulled the lever.

In the compartment at the rear of the Presidential train, the compartment which had shrouded windows and contained the Erlanger coffin, the four SAS men made their final preparations. Speed and surprise would be the essence of the operation, as of so many operations.

The Presidential train entered the tunnel in total darkness. The downhill gradient compensated for the fact that power had been cut off from the engines. The slackening in the train's speed was barely perceptible.

"Okay, let's go," the leader of the team said. He unbolted the door which separated the shrouded compartment from the rest of the train, and began to slide it back.

Alex Lyons found himself cut off in mid-sentence. He looked up in surprise to see the blank black walls of the tunnel rushing past.

Her Majesty the Queen grasped the side of her seat to steady herself as the train began to slow down. If she was surprised by this unexpected turn of events, she gave no outward sign. Imperturbability on this, as on all occasions, was her watch-word.

David Dimbleby, 'anchoring' this royal occasion, as he had anchored so many other royal occasions, was one of the first to realize the danger. Able to monitor through television screens banked up in front of him the progress of events at half a dozen points along the route from London to Dover and from Paris to Calais, he understood the full horrendous implications of what was happening as soon as the French train careered past the crowds waiting at Calais station.

"The Royal train has now entered the tunnel," he told an eager world. "Unfortunately it appears that, owing to some technical hitch on the French side, the train carrying the President of France has not in fact stopped, as it should have stopped, at the station in Calais. Our last information is that the French Presidential train entered the tunnel two minutes ago at a speed of approximately 150 kilometres per hour. I am getting word that two people wearing chef's hats were seen in the driver's cabin of the Presidential locomotive as it flashed through Calais station. *It is possible*" – David Dimbleby's face looked even graver than it had been looking a few seconds before – "*that two trains, one carrying the Queen of England the other carrying the President of France, are now approaching each other from opposite directions in the underground tunnel along a single-track line at a combined speed which may be in excess of 200 or 250 kilometres per hour.*"

He looked at his watch.

"We're going to stay with this situation, as events develop." He consulted a piece of paper which had just been passed to him. "My people tell me that, assuming the distance to be covered is 38 kilometres, and assuming speeds in the region of those which I just described, a collision between the two trains could – and I stress the word '*could*' – occur within ten to twelve minutes!"

Dimbleby was receiving information through his earpiece as he talked. Now he was able to tell viewers the news that all electric power in the tunnel had been cut off and that the royal train was rapidly decelerating.

"This seems to be good news," Dimbleby said. "However, even the loss of power will not impede the continued forward motion of the Presidential train. The momentum of that train had already built up before it entered the tunnel and now, of course, it will be on a downhill gradient until at least it reaches the mid-point of the Channel."

David Dimbleby wiped a hand across his brow. The tension was beginning to get to him.

Grantham walked back into the royal compartment. He stood by the door holding a torch in his hand.

"Your Majesty, ladies and gentlemen, there is nothing to be alarmed about. We are running into some technical problems. Could I ask you all to stay seated, preferably with your backs to the engine and with your heads buried in your knees? There may be a slight impact and it would be as well to be prepared for it."

Grantham stepped back into the driver's cabin. He looked at the speedometer, which was still working, and saw that the speed had dropped to 30 miles an hour and was still falling.

"As soon as the train comes to a halt, release the brakes, do you understand? Release the brakes! Then get out of the cabin as fast as you can!"

The two men needed no encouraging. As the train shuddered to a halt, they turned and ran.

Grantham looked at his watch. Sixty seconds left. There was nothing to do now but wait.

The four SAS men wearing balaclava-type masks and rubber-soled boots ran swiftly and silently through the darkened train. Inside the Presidential compartment, confusion reigned. The SAS men concentrated on their first objective.

The young man in the driver's cabin of the Presidential train seemed utterly calm and collected. Ignoring the corpses, he turned to the twenty-six-year old girl who stood next to him and said:

"We've got about two minutes left, Greta. Let's fuck. It's as good a way to go as any, isn't it?"

The young man spoke in German and the girl replied in the same language: "Of course it is, Heinz."

Greta Gottlieb threw the chef's hat onto the floor, stripped off her tunic and thrust her body onto his. He leaned back against the console, while she straddled him. He had a gun in his hand, pointed at the door.

"I want it to be our way, not anyone else's," he told her.

She moaned as he entered her, closing her eyes and suddenly thinking about her life now that it was over. What a long way she had come since she left that hotel in the Black Forest and joined the Greens in her homeland of Bavaria!

The German took her as the Englishman had taken her that morning in the Hetzel Hotel, high up above the lake.

"My God! We're going backwards!" Alex Lyons exclaimed. He was sitting, as Grantham had instructed, with his back to the engine and his face tucked into his knees. As a result his words were indistinct, though intelligible. He sounded frightened.

"I'd jump out now if I thought it would do me any good."

Grantham laid a hand on the other man's arm. "Don't. You're safest here."

*

The SAS men blew in the door of the Express-Grill wagon with a limpet grenade and ran forward firing. They timed their entry for the precise moment of impact. As the engine drawing the TGV ran into the backward-moving royal train with an effective collision speed of 15 miles an hour, the SAS men "took out" the two Germans they found in the wagon and then moved forward towards the engine.

For Heinz Seeler and Greta Gottlieb, it was the best way to go. They climaxed together before being throw violently across the cab. One and possibly both of them were already unconscious when the parcel bomb tossed by the SAS team blew the cabin apart.

Five seconds after the impact Grantham opened a carriage door and jumped down onto the track. He still had a torch in his hand. He moved quickly towards the tangle forty yards in front of him, where the two trains had run into each other. He flashed the torch three times to show that he was ready.

Ten seconds after impact, confusion still prevailed in the Presidential train. The party of notables, who should by rights already have been tucking into a sumptuous meal at Calais, endured the crash and heard the gunfire and bombs in a state of shock. Policemen and security guards drew their guns and fired wildly. Bullets whistled in all directions.

Thirty seconds after impact, Grantham saw the answering flash of the torch. Four quick bursts of light, followed by two longer signals, indicated that all was well. It was the moment he had been waiting for.

Grantham pulled the directional transmitter out of his pocket. The message was already pre-coded into a micro-second burst. There was no danger that any unauthorized party would pick it up. He pressed the button to transmit.

Their mission accomplished, the four SAS men ran swiftly on down the track. Altogether, some hundred and ten seconds had elapsed between the moment of impact and the time they reached the special compartment that had been set aside at the end of the royal train. The two security guards – also SAS men of course, who had joined in London – had the door open and helped their colleagues on board. A minute later, the four SAS men removed their balaclava masks and all other traces of their recent successful intervention to change the course of history.

One of the team permitted himself a joke: "Some wild firing by the *gendarmes* there, my friends, *n'est-ce pas*?"

The others smiled. It was the only reference any of them would ever make, for the rest of their natural lives, to the events which had just taken place.

37

General Maximilien Miguet unbuckled the girth on the sweating bay, removed the saddle, patted the horse on its neck and handed it over to the groom.

"Rub him down well, Gaston, won't you? He's a bit hot. We had a good gallop in the Forêt."

The General walked away from the stables towards his ancestral home with a sense of well-being. De Gaulle had waited for the call at Colombey-les-Deux-Eglises. For Maximilien Miguet, the seventeenth-century château just outside the Royal Forest of Marly – Marly-le-roi – half an hour's drive from Paris, had served a similar purpose. Over the years, men of power and influence had come to visit him there. Some had gone riding with him. Many had stayed to lunch. Konrad von Rilke and Count Otto von Rimsdorf had signed the visitors' book; so had military colleagues like Grantham and Peabody. His own countrymen, too, had not been reluctant to make their little pilgrimage to the home of the most distinguished soldier of his generation.

Still in his riding boots, Miguet walked up the splendid staircase to his dressing-room. As he changed into his uniform, he looked out onto the splendid vista of the forest. How often he had hunted among those trees, he reflected. Even now, the sound of the horn came to him, sad and haunting. "*Dieu! Que le son du cor est triste au fond des bois.*" Alfred de Vigny had caught it, hadn't he?

Over there, beyond the forest where Louis Quatorze had ridden with his court, was Paris. Today, after so many years of waiting, he would take up the reins of power.

The car was waiting for him outside the château's grand entrance by the time he had finished dressing. They left immediately. Half-way to Paris, Miguet took a call on the car's radio-telephone. He listened for a moment and then spoke briefly into the receiver: "*Oui. Bien. J'arrive.*"

They drove down the Avenue de Neuilly and entered Paris at the Porte Maillot, then swept on along the Avenue de la Grande Armée at a steady eighty kilometres per hour. Ahead of them, at the end of the wide tree-lined road, loomed the Arc de Triomphe. Miguet kept his eye fixed firmly on that objective.

When they reached the Place Charles de Gaulle – or the Etoile, as most Parisians continued to call the area surrounding the Arc de Triomphe – motor-cycle outriders took up their positions fore and aft. The General sat up straighter in his seat. As they swung right-handed round the great soaring monument and passed in front of the Tomb of the Unknown Soldier, he raised a gloved hand in salute. The time was twelve noon precisely.

The small procession continued, at high-speed now, down the Champs-Elysées.

Miguet leaned forward and instructed his driver to turn on the car radio.

"Let us hear the midday news," he said. The announcer read out the bulletin in grave and sombre tones.

"News is just coming in," he said, "that the train carrying the President of the Republic has been hijacked and that a collision has taken place in the Channel tunnel between that train and another train, coming from England, carrying the Queen of England and her party. It is not yet known who is responsible for the hijacking but international left-wing extremist or ecologist groups based in Paris are suspected. It is reported that the President of the Republic, Pierre Leroux, has been accidentally killed in a shoot-out between French security officers on board the train and the hijackers. In the present situation of uncertainty and confusion, the Chiefs of the Armed Forces have thought it right to intervene for the protection of the Republic. They have asked General Maximilien Miguet to assume power on an interim basis . . ."

"You can turn it off now," Miguet instructed.

"*Oui, monsieur le Président.*"

Three-quarters of the way down the Champs-Elysées, they took the Avenue de Marigny, skirting the west wall of the Elysée Palace. As they turned right at the end of the avenue into the Rue du Faubourg Saint-Honoré, the guards who were stationed in front of the Ministry of the Interior – an elegant building which was once the home of the Prince de Beauvau – caught sight of Miguet's car and saluted.

Seconds later, the tall narrow wrought-iron gates – or *grille* – of the Elysée Palace itself were swung open by the guards on duty and General Maximilien Miguet was driven through into the inner courtyard.

Miguet took his time. All his life had been but a preparation for this hour. There was no point in hurrying things now. He got out of the car as a *huissier* held the door back for him. He walked stiffly, head held high, up the short flight of steps to the entrance. As he did so, the cars carrying the heads of France's Armed Forces – Army, Navy and Air Force – turned into the courtyard of the Elysée.

Miguet waited at the top of the steps for his brother officers to arrive. He shook hands, solemnly, with each of them in turn. Then he led the way into the building.

General Maximilien Miguet's broadcast to the nation that evening was a masterpiece of theatre. He sat behind General de Gaulle's great desk in the Salon Doré, that magnificent room overlooking the Tuileries, still wearing the uniform of a five-star general of the French army and looked straight at the cameras. The medals glittered on his chest. The campaign ribbons bespoke his unique military record. The Second World War, Indo-China, Congo, Lebanon – there had hardly been a campaign in which French troops had been involved without Miguet's presence, in the forefront of the hottest battle.

But the broadcast had also been a masterpiece of tact and diplomacy. Without directly attacking his predecessor whose "unfortunate demise" had led to the present state of affairs, Miguet managed to suggest that the time had come to repair the ravages of Socialism. It was a broadcast which at the same time said nothing and said everything.

Miguet ended his short speech by making a specific pledge to bring France back into full participation in NATO, while placing France's independent nuclear deterrent at the service of Europe.

"We must take our rightful place among the leaders of the Western Alliance," he proclaimed as the television lights shone in the Salon Doré and the cameras rolled.

His final gesture was reminiscent of le Grand Charles himself. He raised both hands over his head in a victory salute.

"Vive la République!" Miguet exclaimed. "Vive la France!".

Epilogue

Sandra Furlong came into Grantham's office to announce that he had a visitor.

"Mr Lyons is here to see you, Sir Oliver."

It had taken Sandra Furlong some time to get used to the idea of calling her employer by his new title, conferred on him by the Queen "for services rendered to international transport". But, eventually, she had decided that Grantham's elevation to a knighthood rather suited the man. "Sir Oliver" had a mellifluous sound about it which accorded rather nicely with Grantham's new status as a major figure in Europe's industrial-commercial establishment.

"Thank you, Sandra. Show him in please," Grantham said.

Alex Lyons looked around with interest as he entered the room. The new offices of Channel Transport occupied six floors of a gleaming skyscraper just off London's Haymarket. Grantham's own suite of rooms was to be found at the very top of the building with a spectacular panoramic view over much of the city.

"Still growing?" Alex Lyons smiled as he took Grantham's outstretched hand.

Grantham looked ruefully at his waist line. "In more senses than one, I'm afraid."

"Don't you get to the gym any longer? I thought you were a fitness fanatic."

"I try to. It's hard to find the time."

Grantham stood up from his desk and escorted Alex Lyons over to a long leather sofa which occupied most of one wall. He himself drew up an armchair.

"It's been too long, Alex. I meant to call you a long time ago. Did you see our annual results?"

"I did," Alex Lyons replied. "Congratulations. Apparently your profits from the tunnel's first year of operation exceeded all expectations."

"They did indeed. We've worked out the rate of return on our investment as being over forty per cent! What's more, the ferry business is booming too. We've been able to sell combined tickets – go over by train, come back by boat. People seem to love it."

"What's your next move, Oliver?" Lyons asked.

Grantham looked out of the window. In the distance, high above St Paul's, he could see a plane banking over the heart of London as it prepared to land at Heathrow.

"In strictest confidence?"

"Of course," Lyons replied. He held up his right hand with his three fingers together. "Scout's honour."

"British Airways is being sold off as the Tories promised. We're going to make a bid for it. Not the whole thing. Just the Continental side. We think it makes sense. That way we're going to be able to operate all the modes of travel together, not just two of them."

Alex Lyons whistled. "Aren't you going to run into trouble with the Monopolies Commission?"

Grantham smiled. "I don't see why we should. We've still got competition. Air France, Sabena, Lufthansa. Mind you, we'll give them a run for their money."

Lyons shook his head in admiration. "I don't doubt it. What can I write?"

Grantham laughed. "Talk about positive forward-looking thinking at Channel Transport and buy a few thousand shares tomorrow if you can, or better still today." He looked at his old friend affectionately. "I'm quite serious, Alex. I owe you a lot. You were there most of the time as a kind of Greek chorus. Only it wasn't, in the end, a tragedy."

"There were moments," said Lyons, "when I feared it might turn out that way!"

The two of them reminisced, as men do, about the events of that epic year when the tunnel was being built.

"What I don't understand," Lyons said at one point, "is how that team of terrorists (or ecologists or whatever you want to call them) knew so much about the detailed planning for the Inauguration of the tunnel. They were able to get hold of the Express-Grill wagon which had been allocated to the Presidential train, kill the assigned crew – that was something we only found out about later – and insinuate themselves into the key position just behind the locomotive. Okay, this was a kamikaze effort to create the maximum attention and publicity. What better occasion to choose than the first run through the tunnel? Their hope was, I suppose, that in addition to writing off both trains and their occupants – including the President of France and the Queen of England – the impact of several hundred tons of metal crashing into each other at high speed in a confined space would effectively block the tunnel for ever. No scenario could have been better chosen for extremists of whatever kind to make a political statement. But I still don't understand how they *knew* so much about it all. How, for example, were they aware that, if they hijacked the Presidential train before Calais and drove it on at high speed through the tunnel, they would meet the royal train coming in the other direction? Was all this information public? The schedules? The timing? You know, Oliver, I'm doing a bit of digging myself. I may write a book. There are one or two other things which are odd, very odd."

Oliver Grantham looked at the journalist sharply. "What other things?"

Alex Lyons paused, marshalling his thoughts.

"Well, for example, the mystery of Leo d'Erlanger's body. There was a whole compartment set aside on the Presidential train for the Erlanger cataphalque. But I was in Paris not long ago and I happened to visit the cemetery at Montmartre where Leo d'Erlanger is buried. I spoke to the caretaker there and asked him whether Erlanger's body had been returned to its mausoleum and he looked very surprised and said that as far as he knew the body had never been moved from its resting-place. So what was that compartment on the train used for? That's something else I'm going to look into."

Grantham sighed. "What else is bothering you?"

"The way *you personally* knew what was happening," Lyons replied in a matter-of-fact tone of voice. "*You were waiting for the crash.*"

"I heard the shots on the radio when I went forward to the driver's cab." Grantham sounded defensive.

"Why did you go forward to the cab *at precisely that moment*?"

"Is this an interrogation?"

"In a manner of speaking, yes."

Grantham sighed again. "Look, Alex," he said, "you can speculate as much as you like, but you'll never be able to prove anything. You can't expect me to help you out. Far too much hangs on this. Far too many people are involved. It's dynamite."

"If you don't help me, I shall print what I know, or what I think I know anyway."

Grantham stood up and walked over to the window. His hands were thrust deep into his pockets, his head was bowed. He seemed lost in thought. At last, he turned round and faced the journalist.

"Can we do a deal?"

"What kind of deal?"

Grantham returned to his chair.

"I'll tell you everything I know. But you're not to use it. I'll speak to you because you're a friend, because you've been in on this business from the beginning. And because I know, finally, that once you've heard my story, you'll understand just how important it is that none of this should ever come out. Will you accept?"

Alex Lyons thought about it. All his instincts as a journalist told him that he should never permit himself to be gagged in advance. That was intolerable. It was the very negation of his trade. And yet, on the other side of the coin, he was consumed by an overpowering curiosity to find out just what lay behind that whole extraordinary episode which had taken place almost a year earlier.

"All right," he said at last, "I agree."

Grantham settled back in his chair to begin what would turn out to be a very long story. He started by describing how he had felt when he left the army.

"You know, Alex, it seemed to me that I had spent the best years of my life in the army, fought hard for Queen and Country, only to find that, in the real world outside, it all counted for nothing. Or precious little. Of course, the Falklands campaign gave us all a temporary glow but the truth of the matter is that a fifty-year old soldier, no matter how glamorous his war record might be – and mine I dare say, was reasonable enough – is only a stone's throw from the scrap heap.

"By itself, that wasn't necessarily very significant. What I found more disturbing, when I left the army, was the sense that though Britain and Germany under Thatcher and Kohl seemed set on the right course, other governments, particularly in France under its socialist régime, were throwing away the gains which had been won at such cost. And just one rotten apple can spoil the barrel. When David Blakely asked me, out of the blue, to take on the management of the Channel Tunnel project, I found that I had in my hands a weapon which I was able to use not just for a technical and financial end, that is to say getting the tunnel built, but also for a political end as well. I didn't realize all this at the beginning. The idea came into focus gradually."

"What idea?"

Grantham did not mince his words. "The idea of using the Tunnel project as a means of intervening directly in France's internal affairs," he replied.

As Grantham continued his story, a note of anger, almost of self-justification crept into his voice.

"I learned from American intelligence, through Peabody to be precise, that Leroux was a Soviet 'sleeper'. That was in the days when Leroux's candidacy for the Presidency of France was just beginning to get off the ground. You may say, why didn't we or the Americans arrange to have him removed or somehow exposed, before he got to a position of power? My answer to that is: we were already looking ahead. We all knew that General Maximilien Miguet was waiting in the wings. It was only a matter of finding the right occasion."

"What do you mean by 'we'?"

"By 'we' I mean men like Konrad von Rilke and Count von Rimsdorf, in Germany or like General Peabody in America. In England, there was myself and Donald Coulton. It was a kind of freemasonry. A military-industrial freemasonry, if I may paraphase General Eisenhower."

Alex Lyons was beginning to grasp the point.

"You mean that you decided that it was better to deal with Leroux *after* he had come to power in France, not before?"

"Exactly. We needed an excuse for a coup d'état involving the French armed forces. There had to be a moment of great drama, great tension. A moment where Miguet could plausibly intervene in order to save the soul of the nation. The Inauguration of the Channel Tunnel was exactly the setting we needed. And, of course, it worked like a dream."

Lyons looked doubtful. He shook his head. "I don't buy it," he said.

"What don't you buy?" Grantham challenged him. "You think our action was evil, immoral? How much more evil or immoral would it have been to let Leroux continue in office, knowing what we knew? In any case, from a strictly professional viewpoint, Leroux, as you know – in fact it was you who first suggested to me – was pledged to close the tunnel down within weeks of its opening. Could we have allowed that to happen? We would have had no redress, no compensation. The Chunnel project was given the go-ahead on the strict understanding that there were to be no political guarantees of any kind."

Alex Lyons continued to shake his head.

"You've still not persuaded me," he said. "Are you telling me that the German terrorists were working for you too?"

"They weren't working for me. They were working for Ingrid Lubbeke. You remember Ingrid?"

"Jesus! you're a hard man, Grantham. You mean you just used Ingrid for your own ends?"

Grantham shrugged. "What choice did I have? She was there, she was available, she was a conduit for the flow of information in both directions. That's how the Germans knew about the detailed planning, because I made sure that Ingrid knew and she passed it on to them. Right from the start, from the very first time I met her, I knew of Ingrid's links with the Greens. And I knew that the Greens in turn were associated with all kinds of terrorist units. What I didn't know, I was able to find out."

"Did Ingrid know you were using her?"

"No," Grantham replied. "She thought *she* was using *me*. She stayed with me as long as she did not because I was good in bed – I'm getting a bit old for that now – but because she knew that if any man was well-versed in the details of that whole Inaugural scene, I was."

"So she thought she was setting you up, whereas in reality you were setting her up?"

"That's about it," Grantham replied.

"What's Ingrid Lubbeke doing now?"

"I don't know. After the débâcle, the German team – or those of them who survived – went to ground. Ingrid hasn't been heard of for a year. No doubt she'll surface somewhere some day."

Alex Lyons fell silent, absorbing the implications of what he had just heard. Then he said:

"I still don't understand how you could take the *risk*. It wasn't just Leroux. There were hundreds of people involved. On our side, the Queen herself was involved. She might have been hurt. I might have been hurt, dammit! We all might have been hurt!"

Grantham smiled at the journalist patronizingly.

"My dear Alex, don't you know that Lord Coulton and the Queen share the same trainer? What do you imagine people say to each other in the Royal Enclosure on Gold Cup day? Surely, Alex, you can see that in the widest sense our plan was in everyone's interest. Britain's constitutional monarch is as concerned with the defence of freedom in the West as much as you and I are. More so."

"But the *risks*!" Lyons persisted. "What if the trains had collided at full speed?"

Again Grantham shook his head in that patronizing way.

"Number one," he said: "there was no question of the trains colliding at full speed. The drivers in the Royal train braked the moment they realized that the Presidential train was being hijacked."

"On your instructions."

"Yes, on my instructions," Grantham agreed. "But they braked anyway. Number two: I knew the power would be cut off the moment the Presidential train passed through Calais station. That was bound to happen."

"And you knew that the air pressure in the tunnel would have a slowing-down effect?"

Grantham nodded. "It was a physical and mathematical certainty. That was one thing I was absolutely sure of. We modelled the whole sequence, you know."

"What do you mean?"

Grantham explained. "Don't forget I used to live at Fleet in Hampshire. The Royal Aeronautical Establishment at Farnborough is just next door. I've got loads of friends there. Farnborough probably has the best wind tunnel facilities in the world. They can model Mach 2 air speeds there if they have to. And, of course, they can do subsonic testing as well. It took them weeks to analyse the problem. We checked and double-checked. This was one time when we had to be sure that the calculations were right. It was a question of determining the rate at which the air would escape round the sides of the train as compared with the rate at which the air cushion built up in front. At one point, we had to go back to square one because the French brought in a new design for their TGV locomotive. They trimmed back the nose on their high speed model – which threw the sums out. In the end, we built a scale-replica of the two trains and ran them through the tunnel towards each other at given speeds to see whether the theoretical predictions were borne out in the event."

"And were they?"

"They were," Grantham replied. "So we had a double handle on the situation. You talk of risk. There *was* no risk."

Their conversation was interrupted as Sandra Furlong poked her head around the door.

"I'm going now," she said. "You remember I'm taking Friday off, don't you? I'm going down to Somerset for the weekend."

Grantham smiled. "The Royal Oak, Winsford?"

Sandra smiled back. "You guessed it."

She laughed in her cheerful carefree way. Ever since she had visited Exmoor on Grantham's behalf over two years earlier, her weekend life had been transformed. Her relationship with the large, jovial landlord of the Royal Oak had flourished. She liked being known as "Bertie's girl".

"If you see Mrs Potter, give her my best," Grantham said. "We'll be having a board meeting soon. Tell her, I hope she'll be able to come to it."

"I'll do that."

When Sandra Furlong had gone, the two men picked up where they had left off.

"What actually happened in the tunnel that day?" asked Lyons. "We are told that the security guards on the train despatched the terrorists at or shortly after the moment of impact. Unfortunately, in the commotion, a stray bullet hit and killed the French President. Is that the whole story? What about the compartment at the end of the train? What about the coffin which was meant to contain the body of Leo d'Erlanger, but didn't?"

Grantham admired his friend's astuteness.

"You're right about the coffin. I let the old Baron down rather, didn't I, by not bringing him along," he laughed. "But I knew he would have been in for a rough ride that day. The coffin-compartment – the cataphalque-carriage as I called it – was the ideal hiding place for the team of SAS men on board the train. There were four of them altogether on the French side. Some of Buffy Watson's finest men. They did a superb job. They moved through the train after the hi-jack like a dose of salts. Mind you, they're trained for it. We modelled that situation too. This time, though, we used real-life trains. Up there in Herefordshire in the SAS compound. We knew exactly how long the men had between the time of the hi-jack and the moment of impact."

"And did you know exactly where on the train Pierre Leroux would be sitting so your SAS men could blow his head off as they passed through the carriage?"

Grantham looked at Lyons reprovingly. "Now, now, Alex. You're letting your imagination run away with you. The official enquiry proved conclusively that the French President was killed by a bullet fired from a gendarme's gun. The gendarme himself was unfortunately also killed in the cross-fire."

Lyons nodded gravely. "Ah, I see. Of course. What would an SAS man be doing with a French *gendarme*'s pistol? That's much too ingenious, isn't it?"

Grantham agreed fervently. "Much too ingenious." Then he added: "It was a very helpful enquiry altogether. Rather like the Warren enquiry after the death of President Kennedy. There were all sorts of questions which were never asked. No one, for example, ever suggested that there *had* been any SAS men on board the President's train. No one suggested that they had, in fact, shot the President. No one suggested that, after the assassination, they had run along the track and boarded a specially prepared compartment on the Royal train, and, of course, no one, in the course of the official enquiry, thought to ask why General Maximilien Miguet was ready and waiting for the call when the call came." Grantham smiled. "Thank heavens they know how to organize these official enquiries in France. It's all so much easier over there, isn't it?"

The two men talked for another hour. Before he left, Alex Lyons asked: "What about Iona?"

"Gone back to Athens. We still work closely together though. She's taken over the whole business from her father."

Alex Lyons could detect the note of real affection in Grantham's voice as he spoke.

"You were quite close to her, weren't you?"

"For a time, yes," Grantham replied. "She wanted to stay, but I told her I was too old for her. I told her I was sure there was some Greek Dionysos waiting for her. In the end, she took my advice."

"And Monique Delacourt? What happened to her?" Lyons asked.

For half a second Grantham seemed to show some signs of chagrin. Though the liaison between Monique Delacourt and Pierre Leroux had virtually ended by the time of Leroux's death, nevertheless it was clear that the relationship had at the time meant something to both of them.

"She went off to Japan," he replied. "Leroux's death hit her hard. When the Japanese decided to press ahead with their second Seikan tunnel using the Fairmont C Series machines and the same techniques that we had developed, namely the Marchprod units and multi-segment approach, Monique Delacourt decided to go off to Asia and run the project for them."

"No questions asked?"

"No questions needed to be asked," Grantham replied firmly. "Leroux was killed by an erratic *gendarme*. Always remember that."

Alex Lyons stood up.

"It's time I was going," he said. "Shall I see you at Candida Coulton's wedding?"

"Of course you will," Grantham replied. "Don't forget, I was responsible for bringing the happy couple together. I introduced them, in a manner of speaking."

Grantham remembered that extraordinary scene when they had been sitting round the conference table on board the rig and had learned that Candida Coulton was still trapped underground. That was the moment, it seemed, when Michael Prestwick had decided to marry Candida – provided she escaped alive.

"By the way, Candida is working at Farnborough now," Grantham said. "She worked out the mathematics for us when we were running the model tests. That's one of the reasons I knew I could trust the results; she doesn't make mistakes."

With his hand on the door, ready to leave, Alex Lyons looked at Grantham. There was a note of concern, almost of pity in his voice.

"You know, Oliver, I followed you through on this one. I'm not sure I agree with everything you've done. But I appreciate your reasons for doing it. I'm not sure I like the way you treat people, but I understand that is the way you are. For the last two years, you've been surrounded by beautiful women of one kind or another. Ingrid Lubbeke. Iona Karapolitis. Candida Coulton. Monique Delacourt. You've probably slept with all of them."

"Only some of them . . ." Grantham began to protest.

But Lyons silenced him. "No, listen to me for once, Oliver. You're a rich man. You've got Picassos and Chagalls on your walls" – he waved a hand in the direction of the paintings which lined the room – "You're a famous man too. More famous than Jimmy Goldsmith. At least you've actually built something. Done something, as opposed to merely shunting money around. But are you a happy man, Oliver? Answer me that!"

"Jesus!" Grantham protested. "Who knows if he's happy? I just like to get through from one day to the next."

For a moment Grantham was angered by his friend's intrusion into his own private life. He believed in arm's-length relationships. Intimacy never got you anywhere.

"Are you trying to write a book about me, Alex?" he asked querulously.

"Not now," Alex Lyons replied. "Not yet. Just wait for my story of the Channel Tunnel project!"

Grantham laughed. "You swore on Scout's honour!" he said.

"I'm a journalist, not a Scout." Alex Lyons smiled and was gone.

Sir Oliver Grantham stayed late in the office that night. When at last he left, having heard from George Browning (still his banker) that the takeover of British Airways was going to plan, he felt tired and depressed. What, finally, was it all about anyway?

He had sent the chauffeur home for the day, so he took the Rolls out of the garage himself. The commissionaire was still on duty and saluted smartly.

Alex Lyons's words niggled at Grantham as he drove round Trafalgar Square and down Whitehall towards the Embankment. With an effort, he tried to see himself as others, like Lyons, might see him. Was he really so rich? Objectively speaking, he supposed he was. Certainly, he had a few million pounds in the bank with a prospect of a few million more. Was he really so famous? Perhaps he was. He had, after all, masterminded the largest civil engineering project of its time, comparable to building the Pyramids. He found it hard to recognize that the name Grantham would take its place among the galaxy of engineering stars like De Lesseps and Isambard Kingdom Brunel. But that, he supposed, could well be the reality of the situation.

And was he, as Lyons had seemed to suggest, a failure as far as his own personal happiness was concerned?

He realized, as he drove, that he had no idea where he was heading. He had assumed, when he left the office, that he was going home. If he was going home, he asked himself, why was he driving along the Embankment? The way to Belgravia from the Haymarket did not lie along the Embankment.

Then where was he going?

He crossed the river at Chelsea bridge and drove on through Putney onto the M3 motorway. He looked at the clock on the dashboard. If he hurried, he might still be in time.

Lily Grantham was in the kitchen of the house in Fleet when the car scrunched on the gravel outside. She heard the door of the car close and footsteps walk round the side of the house towards the kitchen. She stayed where she was, facing the stove, with her back to the door.

Grantham opened it.

"Hello," he said. "I'm back. What's for supper?"

Lily Grantham turned to face him. There were tears in her eyes.

"Oh, God," she said.

He took her in his arms. It had been a long time.